THE RANGE FINDER

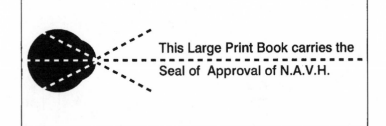

THE RANGE FINDER

A Western Trio

MAX BRAND ®

Thorndike Press • Waterville, Maine

Published in 2005 by arrangement with
Golden West Literary Agency.

Thorndike Press® Large Print Western.

The tree indicium is a trademark of Thorndike Press.

The text of this Large Print edition is unabridged.
Other aspects of the book may vary from the original edition.

Set in 16 pt. Plantin by Liana M. Walker.

Printed in the United States on permanent paper.

Library of Congress Cataloging-in-Publication Data

Brand, Max, 1892–1944.
    The range finder : a western trio / by Max Brand.
        p. cm. — (Thorndike Press large print western)
    ISBN 0-7862-7790-4 (lg. print : hc : alk. paper)
    1. Large type books. I. Title. II. Thorndike Press
large print Western series.
PS3511.A87A6 2005
813'.52—dc22   2005009965

THE
RANGE
FINDER

As the Founder/CEO of NAVH, the only national health agency solely devoted to those who, although not totally blind, have an eye disease which could lead to serious visual impairment, I am pleased to recognize Thorndike Press* as one of the leading publishers in the large print field.

Founded in 1954 in San Francisco to prepare large print textbooks for partially seeing children, NAVH became the pioneer and standard setting agency in the preparation of large type.

Today, those publishers who meet our standards carry the prestigious "Seal of Approval" indicating high quality large print. We are delighted that Thorndike Press is one of the publishers whose titles meet these standards. We are also pleased to recognize the significant contribution Thorndike Press is making in this important and growing field.

Lorraine H. Marchi, L.H.D.
Founder/CEO
NAVH

* Thorndike Press encompasses the following imprints: Thorndike, Wheeler, Walker and Large Print Press.

TABLE OF CONTENTS

The Whisperer

"The Whisperer" made its appearance early in Frederick Faust's writing career, just as a few of his stories were beginning to appear in Street & Smith's *Western Story Magazine*. It was published in the August 21, 1920, issue of *Argosy/All-Story Weekly*, where, that year, five of his seven short stories and five of his six serials appeared. This story of revenge relies on concealed identity — Who is the Whisperer? — one of Faust's favorite plot devices. What is unusual about the story is Faust's use of a woman, Patricia Lauriston, as his point-of-view character at the story's opening. Its inclusion in this collection marks its first appearance since its original publication.

The Whisperer

I

"PATRICIA FINDS WORK"

Unquestionably the average man considers that woman's God-given vocation is the rearing of children. One may even go so far as to say that the average woman concurs in this judgment.

Which prepared the stage for the entrance of Patricia Lauriston, who was not average. Although she admitted that fate and the ways of the world condemned the majority of her sex to marriage, this admission only made her stamp along in shoes a little broader of toe and a little lower of heel. Not that she wished to be mannish. She was not. All she desired escape from was that femininity which bounds its world with children on the one side and a husband on the other.

Neither should it be understood that Patricia disliked men. On the contrary, she frankly preferred them to her own sex. Her whole struggle, in fact, was to be accepted by men as a friend, and it cut her to the heart to watch the antics of fellows who had courage enough to woo her. She noted that men among men were frank, open of hand and heart and eye, generous, brave, good-humored; she noted that the same men among women became simpering, smirking fantastic fools. A man among men tried to be himself; a man among women dreaded nothing so much as the exposure of his own innate simplicity and manhood. All this Patricia had discovered by long and patient experiment.

There was the case of Steven Worth, for instance. Steve was the best friend of her brother Hal Lauriston, and Steve was almost another member of the family. Until, on a day, Patricia came home from school in long skirts. Instead of picking her up by the elbows and throwing her ceiling-ward, as had been his custom in the past, Steve shook hands, blushed, and suggested a walk in the garden. Patricia was only sixteen at the time, but she knew what was coming; a girl of sixteen is at least equal to a man of twenty-six, plus certain instinctive knowledge that has never left the

12

blood of woman since that sunshiny day in the garden when Eve ate the apple and whispered with the serpent.

Therefore Patricia knew exactly what was coming, but she allowed the disease to develop and take hold on Steven Worth. She let him hold her hand; she let him look into her eyes and smile in a peculiarly asinine manner interspersed with occasional glances toward the stars. Three days and nights of this, and then Steve fell on his knees and asked her to be his wife. It didn't thrill Patricia. It merely disgusted her and made her feel very lonely. She told Steve just how she felt and went back into the house.

The next morning Hal Lauriston came to her room and swore that she had broken the heart of his dearest friend and that she was a devilish little cat; the next noon Steven Worth, she learned, had purchased a ticket for South America. Patricia went to Steve and told him — well, she told him many things, and in the end Steve Worth declared that she was the "bulliest little scout in the world" and that he was "no end of an ass." Patricia concurred silently in the last remark. The end of it was that Steve did not go to South America to die of swamp fever, but both he and Patricia knew that they could never be friends again.

The point of all this is that Patricia did not, certainly, miss Steve as a husband, but she regretted him mightily as a friend. She went abroad among the world of men, thereafter, and tried to make other friends to take the place of Steve, but she discovered that after friendship had progressed to a certain point the finest of men began to grow silent and thoughtful and a certain hungry look came in their eyes. The bitter truth came home to Patricia that she was too beautiful to have a single friend; many a time she bowed her head before her mirror and wept because her eyes were of a certain blackness and her hair of a certain dark and silken length. This sounds like fiction, but to Patricia it was a grim and heart-breaking truth.

Now, an average woman of this temperament, at a certain point in her life, would have taken up woman suffrage or prohibition — or Greek. Patricia, however, was not average. She refused to believe that all men are weak-kneed sentimentalists; she looked abroad, like Alexander, to a new world, and new battles.

It followed, quite naturally, that Patricia should go West. For she had heard sundry tales of a breed of men who inhabit the mountain desert, men stronger than adversity and hard of hand and of heart, men too bitterly trained in the battle of existence to pay any heed to the silken side of life. She hoped to find among them at least some few who would look first for a human being, and afterward for a sex.

This would have been enough to send Patricia to the mountain desert. There was another reason sufficiently unfeminine to interest her. One year before Mortimer Lauriston, a second cousin who bore her family name, had been shot in the town of Eagles in the mountain desert by a man named Vincent St. Gore. St. Gore had been tried, but the jury had always disagreed. Patricia Lauriston decided that it would be her work to tear the blindfold from the eyes of justice and bring an overdue fate upon this Vincent St. Gore. She could live not exactly in the town of Eagles, but at the ranch formerly owned by Mortimer Lauriston, and now operated by another cousin, Joseph Gregory. Having made up her mind, Patricia packed her trunk, kissed her mother good bye, and from the train sent back postcards of farewell to her more intimate friends.

Which brings us to Eagles, a white-hot day in May, the hills spotted with mesquite, and below the hills the illimitable plains, the stopping of the stage with its six dripping horses, and the entrance of Patricia into the mountain desert.

She was not disappointed. She liked everything she saw — the fierce heat of the day — the unshaven men — the buckboard of Joseph Gregory waiting to meet her. Even Joseph himself was not displeasing to her, although in a population where none was overly attractive Joseph was commonly called Ugly Joe. His forehead was so low and slanting that his dirty-white sombrero had to be pulled literally over his eyebrows — otherwise it would have blown off. His eyes were small and a very pale blue. His nose was both diminutive and sprawling, as if it had been battered out of shape in fistic battles. Below the nose his face ceased and his mustache began. It was the pride of Ugly Joe. The stiff hairs descended like a host of scimitar-shaped bristles far past his lower lip and at either side the mustache jagged down in points that swept far below his chin. If he had shaved, not even his wife would have known him. Patricia, however, was undismayed. She advanced with her suitcase and claimed relationship.

Ugly Joe parted his mustache, spat over

the forward wheel of the buckboard, considered her a silent moment, and then touched the brim of his sombrero by way of salutation.

" 'Evening," said Ugly Joe, "throw up your grip and climb in."

"But I have a trunk," said Patricia. "Isn't there room for that behind?"

"Sure! Is that your trunk?"

He pointed to a wardrobe trunk that was being rolled onto the "hotel" verandah. She nodded and offered to get help for the handling of the trunk, for she remembered how two expressmen had sweated and grunted over that trunk, but Cousin Joe shook his head and climbed down from the buckboard. He was a short man, bent from riding horseback, and he walked with the shuffling hobble of the old cattleman, putting his weight on his toes. He was short, but exceedingly broad, and, when a couple of men had helped him to shoulder the trunk, he came back, hobbling along with it and showing no apparent discomfort. He dumped it in the back of the buckboard, which heaved and groaned under the burden.

"Might I ask," said Ugly Joe, as they climbed up to the front seat, "if them are all clothes you got in that trunk?"

"Mostly," answered Patricia.

"*Hmm!*" remarked Cousin Joe, and started his ponies over the homeward path.

For half an hour they jolted along in silence over what might have been a road.

"Maybe," said Ugly Joe at length, "you figure on starting a store with that many clothes?"

Now Patricia had prided herself on traveling light into the wilderness. There were only a few negligees, some house dresses, morning gowns, and several riding and walking outfits, as well as one or two tailored suits. She had not brought a single evening dress! Accordingly she stared at Ugly Joe in some surprise, but, before she could reply, he went on: "You're considerable well fixed for clothes and a name, eh? What's your name again?"

"Patricia," she answered.

"Patricia? And what do folks call you for short?"

"Nothing else. Personally I don't believe in nicknames."

"D'you mean to say," said Ugly Joe, much moved, "that, when your ma or your pa speaks to you, they always take that much tongue-trouble and spend that much air? Patricia!" He did not repeat it scoffingly, but rather with much wonder.

Patricia decided that being in Rome she must adapt herself to the customs of the country. "I suppose," she said, "that it could be shortened."

"Between you and me," confided Ugly Joe, "it'll *have* to be shortened. Long names ain't popular much around here. Look at them hosses. S'pose I give them fancy names, how'd I ever handle 'em? S'pose I wanted 'em to stop and I had to say . . . 'Whoa, Elizabeth Virginia, the first, and Johnny Payne, the third.' Nope, you can see for yourself that wouldn't do. A long name is as much in the way as a long barrel on a shotgun when you want to shoot quick."

"What do you call your horses?" asked Patricia.

"The nigh one is Spit and the off one is Fire. I just say . . . 'Giddap, Spit-Fire!' . . . and we're off. See?"

"Oh" — Patricia smiled — "and what will you call me?"

"I'll leave off the fancy part. Pat is a good enough name. What say?"

"That," said Patricia, "will be fine."

"Sure. I'll call you Pat and you call me Joe. Simple, easy to remember, saves lots of wind and talking. Talking ain't popular none with me."

And he proved it by maintaining a resolute silence for the next fifteen minutes. As for Patricia, she was too busy sweeping the plains with a critical eye to wish for talk. Moreover, the silence was pleasing. That was a way men had with each other. She began to feel, also, that she had at last reached a country where a pretty face was not a passport to all hearts; she would have to prove herself before she would be accepted.

II

"THE KILLING OF LAURISTON"

Not that this was in the least discouraging to Patricia. She was, indeed, rather excited and stimulated by the prospect, as an athlete feels himself keyed to the highest point of efficiency by a contest with a rival of unquestioned prowess. She swept the country with a critical eye; she glimpsed the massive, rounded shoulders of Ugly Joe with a side glance; the mesquite-dotted hills, the white-hot plains, the man who lived in them — all were good in the eye of Patricia. She would have accepted the silence of her companion and persisted in it, but she came to this place for a purpose and talk was necessary before she could accomplish it.

"I suppose," said Patricia, "that everyone wonders why I've come out here?"

Ugly Joe had caught the reins between

his knees while he rolled a cigarette. Now he finished licking the paper smooth and bent a meditative eye upon Patricia while he lighted his cigarette and inhaled the first puff. "Don't know that I've heard any remarks," he responded at length. "Giddap, Spit-Fire!"

They jolted over a particularly uneven stretch of the trail. When Patricia had caught her breath, again she said: "Nevertheless, I'll tell you, Cousin Joe. I've come out here to run down the murderer of Mortimer Lauriston."

She waited for this verbal bull's-eye to take effect, but Ugly Joe seemed not a whit interested.

"That ain't hard," he answered. "You can pick him up mostly any day in Eagles."

"I," said Patricia, "am going to have him tried . . . and hung."

"Hmm!" grunted Ugly Joe. "Where you going to get a jury to convict him?"

"Is it hard to do that?"

"I'll say it's hard!"

"Does he bribe the jurors?"

"Nope, not exactly."

"Is this murderer too popular to be convicted?"

"Him?" Ugly Joe grinned for the first time. "Nope, it'd be a hard job to find a feller less popular than this Goggles."

"Goggles? I thought his name is Vincent Saint Gore?"

"Maybe it is, but who can remember a word as long as that? We call him Goggles because of the funny glasses he wears . . . big ones with black rims. Makes him look like a frog. Goggles popular? Not around here, Pat. Nope, he's just a plain, damned dude, that's what he is. Out here for a couple of years for his health. Little, skinny feller who goes around in fancy, shined-up riding boots and trousers baggy above the knees. Lives over to Widow Morgan's house, where he got a piano moved in and he just sits around and tickles the keys, or mosies out and rides a fine, foreign, high-steppin' hoss around. Never talks much to anybody. He forgets everybody as quick as he's introduced to 'em. Popular? Hell, no! Excuse me."

The description was a distant shock to Patricia. She had pictured, quite naturally, a tall, gaunt, swarthy rider of the mountain desert, black-browed, black-eyed, fierce, silent. Instead, here was a man who fitted his name — Vincent St. Gore — possibly some disinherited second son, the black sheep of some honorable family.

"But if he doesn't bribe the jurors, and if

he isn't popular," she queried, "how in the world does he manage to escape scotfree? Is it because Mortimer Lauriston was disliked . . . because the people of Eagles were glad to get rid of him?"

"Nope, everybody liked old Mort. He never did no harm, except when he was full of red-eye."

"Then," Patricia said desperately, "was it because Saint Gore . . . your man Goggles . . . killed Mortimer in self-defense?"

"Pat," said Ugly Joe, grinning again, "the more I hear you talk, the more I see that you are the cousin of my wife Martha. She does just the same way. Get her talking about anything and she hangs on like a bulldog till she's got out of me all I know. I can see you're the same way, and I'll be savin' myself if I tell you the whole yarn right here and now."

"Good," said Patricia, unabashed.

"It was in Langley's saloon," said Ugly Joe. " 'S a matter of fact most of these hell-raisin's begin with red-eye and end with guns. Well, it was along about the middle of the afternoon. I was in there, so was about twenty more. And there was Goggles standin' at one end of the bar, sipping whiskey mixed up with seltzer water out of a high glass. He never would drink whiskey straight like a regular honest man. There he stood, staring straight in front of him that way he has and never seeming to see nothing that happened near him.

"About that time in come Mort Lauriston. He was lit to the eyes, was old Mort, and, when he got drunk, he was some noisy. Which everybody knew he didn't mean nothing and they let him go along pounding 'em on the back. He ordered up drinks for the crowd, and everybody accepted but Goggles. Nobody ever included him in anything. He was just part of the landscape, like one of them hills over there. He was there, but he didn't mean nothing . . . but Mort seen him and he got mad. He goes up and says . . . 'Partner, whiskey wasn't never meant to be spoiled by mixing with water.' Then he grabs Goggles's high glass and spills the mixture out on the floor.

" 'Hey, Pete,' he says to the bartender, 'give this feller Goggles a man-size drink of man-size booze.'

"Everybody laughed. They was all tickled at the thought of Goggles drinking straight red-eye. Pete put up a whiskey glass filled to the brim.

"Goggles was standing there pretty

quiet. He just fixed the glasses different on his nose and stands there staring at Mort. The whiskey has splashed pretty liberal across them fine riding boots of his, but he didn't make an ugly move.

"He says . . . 'Mister Lauriston, I'm sure that you have carried your little game far enough. You certainly don't intend to make me drink that glass of vile bar whiskey.'

" 'Don't I?' says Mort, and the rest of us laughed. 'Bud, you're going to drink every drop of it!'

"Goggles takes off his glasses and wipes them careful on his handkerchief, puts them back, and studies Mort like a rock hound looking at a new kind of ore. He says in that soft, low voice of his . . . 'You are apparently very drunk, Mister Lauriston. What if I refuse to drink this liquor?'

"Out comes Mort with two big gats. He shoves them under the nose of Goggles. 'Drink, you damned foreign English dude!' he says.

" 'Sir,' says Goggles, 'I'm going to drink this under compulsion, not because I fear you, but because I don't want to harm a drunken man. But the next time we meet, Mister Lauriston, I'm going to kill you.'

With that he picks up the glass of booze careful, without spilling a drop, and says . . . 'Here is to our early meeting, sir.' And he drinks the glass down without batting an eye, bows to Mort, and walks out of the saloon.

" 'Well, I'll be damned,' says Mort. 'What d'you think of that?'

"Herb Fisher speaks up and says . . . 'I dunno how you figure it, Mort, but, if I was you, I'd keep my guns ready for a fast draw the next time I seen Goggles. He don't look none too dangerous, but looks is deceiving.'

"Mort, he took that to heart. He left town pretty hurried, and it was about ten days before he come back. At least, he started back, and afterward they found his body on the road near Eagles. He'd been shot fair and square between the eyes and his guns was lying near him with a bullet fired out of each of them, showing that he'd had a chance to fight for his life. He wasn't shot down from no ambush.

"Of course, they arrested Goggles. The sheriff took half a dozen deputies along to help out in case of a muss, but Goggles didn't turn a hair. He walked right into the jail, give a big bond, and never made a move to get away before the trial.

"At the trial he didn't have a chance, it looked like. Everybody knew that Mort was a harmless, noisy sort of gent. Maybe he done wrong in making Goggles drink, but there wasn't no call for any gun play. That was what the district attorney kept pumping into the jury all through the trial and they were all set to hang Goggles. Everybody knew that. But when the last day of the trial came along, right when the district attorney was making his last big spiel, a little piece of paper come fluttering like a white bird through the window right behind Goggles, and over his shoulder, and into the lap of one of the gents in the jury box."

III

"THE PASSING OF KENNEDY"

"He unfolded it sort of absent-minded and read what was on it, and then he stood up slow, like he was being pulled up by the hair of the head. And he says . . . 'God!' . . . just once, soft and easy, but it cut off the speech of the district attorney like a hot knife going through a piece of cheese.

" 'What's there?' said the district attorney.

"But the gent that got the paper, he just passed it on to the gent next to him, and that one turned sort of green and sick-looking and moved it on to the next. And so it went all through the jury box.

"The district attorney finished up, the jury went out and came back in five minutes, saying . . . 'Not guilty!' Yep, it was a unanimous verdict, and afterward everyone on that jury went around telling the boys in a loud voice that he had voted to acquit Goggles, and that he'd like to have the word passed on."

"It was the paper?" asked Patricia.

"It sure was. There was writ on it . . . 'Boys, I've got all your names. If you hang Goggles, you'll have to tell me why later on.'

"And underneath, the paper was signed . . . 'The Whisperer'. Now you know why Goggles ain't been touched by the law and why it ain't possible to get a jury in these parts to convict him. Here's the paper. I got a hold on it, and I've always kept it with me."

He drew it from a vest pocket and handed it to Patricia — a little scrap torn roughly from a larger sheet, and the words on it were scrawled clumsily in backhand, like the writing of a child of seven.

"The Whisperer!" Patricia frowned. "Who is he?"

"Don't you even know that?" Ugly Joe asked in disgust. "Well, you'll hear a pile about him before you been in these parts long. He's a lone rider who hangs out somewhere in them hills. Nobody knows just where . . . about umpteen posses have hunted for him and never got on his trail.

They lay a lot of things to the Whisperer . . . some of them may be lies, but a pile of them ain't. I *know!* He's a sort of a ghost, the Whisperer is. He rides a white horse that can go like the wind, and he wears light-gray clothes, and a white handkerchief all over his face like a mask. Nobody has ever seen his face, but when he shows up, he's known by his voice. It ain't any common voice. It's a sort of a husky hissing, like something had gone wrong with his throat. It takes the heart out of a man just to hear that voice."

"Yes," murmured Patricia, "it's ghostly . . . it's horrible. But are you sure that it was really the Whisperer who threw that paper through the window?"

"That's what a lot of people wanted to know, and particularly Lew Lauriston . . . you know him . . . old Mort's brother. He didn't think the Whisperer had anything to do with the case. So he got Porky Kennedy, the two-gun man, to go on the trail of Goggles and put him under the sod. There wasn't much of a secret about it. Everybody in Eagles knew that it was about time for Goggles to move on his way, because Porky Kennedy had a long line of killings to his credit already.

"Porky went to Eagles, but Goggles

31

didn't show no special hurry about leaving. Finally Porky went to Widow Morgan's house for supper one night. Everybody sat around the table scared stiff, because they knew that as soon as Goggles came in there'd be a killing and one foreign English dude less in the world. But Goggles didn't come in. They began to think that the fool dude finally had got some sense behind them glasses of his and left for parts unknown. But about the middle of the meal, while Porky was telling a long story, the door opened and the wind blew the flame jumping up and down in the chimney of the lamp.

"And from the door there was a whisper . . . 'Kennedy!' And when they looked up, there stood the Whisperer with his white mask and his gray clothes and his voiceless voice. Kennedy pulled his gun, but his hand was shaking so that the gun fell out of his hand and rattled onto the floor, and Kennedy dropped on his knees against the wall and covered up his face in his arms, moaning like a sick kid.

"But the Whisperer hadn't come for a killing. He just vanished out the door. Pretty soon in comes Goggles and cocks an eye over to Kennedy as calm as you please. But Kennedy wasn't interested in any killing just then. He ups from his chair and climbed through the door in about two steps. He hasn't been around these parts since. That's one of the good things about the Whisperer. No robber but himself does much flourishing while he's around. There's some say the only ones he picks on is the other crooks. Others say different. I don't know. Well, a couple of days later Lew Lauriston does a fade away. He didn't even stop to tell us whether the Whisperer had paid him a visit or not, but we just took it for granted.

"So, if you want to try your hand, Pat, why, it ain't hard to find Eagles, and in Eagles it ain't hard to find Goggles."

But the arrows of his sarcasm flew harmlessly over the head of Patricia, for she had fallen into a brown study. Certainly it is not easy to understand Patricia, for I suppose that she never really understood herself. I have never known two people, of all who knew her intimately, who could agree about the main points in her character, and I have always attributed the misunderstanding to the fact that she was so unfemininely serious-minded. Really there was nothing masculine about her except a desire to prove herself of some significance in the world, and, because she was so pretty, she was confronted with an endless struggle to make the world accept her as something more than a mere ornament. Sometimes the very desperation of her efforts to do strong things in a strong way made her as stern and hard as any man, and for this reason quite a few misjudged her — in fact, she misjudged herself. To me there was always something plaintive in the quest of Patricia for herself. At the moment when Ugly Joe ceased speaking, for instance, Patricia was really not thinking of the avenging of Mortimer Lauriston's death. She was merely working out a way in which she could prove to Ugly Joe that there was in her a profound difference from that of his talkative wife. Surely here was a man-size problem — the apprehension and bringing to justice of a murderer who even the rough-handed dwellers in the mountain desert dared not touch.

She said at length: "Has it ever occurred to you, Cousin Joe, that the killer of Mortimer Lauriston was really not your man Goggles at all, but the Whisperer?"

Ugly Joe chuckled. "Has it taken you all this thinking to get that far? Sure, it's occurred to me, and to everybody else. If you ever seen Goggles, you'd be sure of it. I've seen him handle a gun in a shooting gallery. Say, Pat, he couldn't hit the side of a barn with a rock. And there ain't enough heart in that skinny body of his to hurt a swallow. We all seen that as soon as the Whisperer got mixed up in the case. Mort was fast with his guns and he shot straight. It must've took a man about as good as the Whisperer to beat him on the draw and drill him as clean as that after he'd had a chance to work his shooting irons."

"The real criminal, then," mused Patricia, "is the Whisperer." She shivered a little, but went on: "The other man, this Goggles, is evidently just a harmless little cur. I suppose the Whisperer uses him to collect information, and then robs the people Goggles points out to him."

"I s'pose so." Ugly Joe, who was fast losing interest in the conversation, nodded.

"And yet you allow Goggles to wander about at liberty! I can't understand you people, Cousin Joe."

"You would, Pat, if you'd ever had any dealings with the Whisperer. Maybe he's using Goggles and maybe he isn't. We've never had any proof of that. All we know is that he's Goggles's friend, and as long as that's the case there ain't anybody around here with the courage to mix up with Goggles. You can lay to that."

"I know," Patricia said, in the same musing voice, "this Whisperer is a dangerous fellow, but he has his weak point. And I'm going to *get* him through that weakness."

"What weakness?" asked Ugly Joe, wakening to a new interest in the case.

"Goggles! The Whisperer may be an outlaw, but he's a man. This Goggles is merely a cowardly little sneak who hides in the terror of the name of the Whisperer. That's why he had the courage to face Mortimer Lauriston. He knew that he could send his man-killer after my cousin. But I'm going to set a trap for the Whisperer, bait it with Goggles, and catch your man for you."

"Going to do which?" gasped Ugly Joe.

"Wait," Patricia murmured, and smiled into the contented distance.

IV

"A PLAN FOR TRAPPING"

She said after a while: "Cousin Joe, I want you to hire me the four best fighters and straightest shooters you can get. I want four honest men who will. . . ."

"Wait a minute, Pat," answered the other, "I can find you four first-class gunmen, and I can find you, maybe, four first-class honest men, but I'll be . . . excuse me . . . if I can get four honest gunmen. They don't come that way. That ain't their brand. It's this way, Patty. Lots of men can shoot straight at anything but another man. It takes something more than a marksman to shoot down a man . . . it takes a natural killer, and a natural killer ain't often honest."

Patricia sat stiffly erect in her place, but she said firmly: "Then if I have to get a gang of cut-throats . . . well, the end justifies the means. Get me the gunmen, Cousin Joe, and I'll ask no questions about their honesty. Can you get me four men who won't be afraid to fight with the Whisperer?"

Ugly Joe meditated. Finally he said: "I see there ain't any use trying to persuade you, Pat. Just like Martha. I can get you four gunmen who'd do any murder for a price. There's Chic Wood. He climbed a tree with a shotgun over at Tomanac and shot a man for fifty dollars. But he'd maybe want fifty thousand for killing the Whisperer. I could get some more like Chic. D'you want to work with men like him, Pat?"

"The end," said Patricia, "justifies the means. Yes, I want any four men . . . as long as they are dangerous."

"Then I guess I can get 'em. None of the crooks has any special liking for the Whisperer. He's run most of them out of range of Eagles. All you'll have to do is to pay the price. Can you do that?"

"Anything you think they're worth."

"And after you get 'em," said Ugly Joe, "I s'pose you're going to ride through the hills with your posse hunting for the Whisperer?"

"Not at all. I'm going to stay right at your house, Cousin Joe, and wait for the Whisperer to come to me."

"Pat," said Joe solemnly, "if you was a man, I'd say you'd been drinking. Wait for the Whisperer to come to *you?*"

"He will," Patricia answered. "Will you have the four men at the house to-morrow?"

Ugly Joe made no reply, but sighed heavily as he rolled another cigarette. He had heard about this type of Eastern woman, as aggressive as a man, but he hardly knew what to make of her now that she sat at his side. A Westerner is singularly helpless in the presence of a woman. He is accustomed to making his way through a purely physical prowess. Against the peculiar strength of a woman, which is fleshly and yet not of the flesh, he has nothing to pit.

So Ugly Joe felt very much like a tongue-tied boy, unable to recite his lesson to the pretty schoolma'am. If he resented the calm appropriation of his house as the trap that was to catch the Whisperer, he felt a counterbalancing excitement that more than made up. He had shot mountain lions in his time, but this would be a rarer sport.

They reached the ranch house. It was

formed of great adobe walls from three to four feet in thickness — utterly impervious to the heat of summer or the winds and cold of winter. A one-storied structure, it rambled out in a roomy square around a hexagonal patio in the center. The exterior of that house, dirty-brown with deep-set windows gaping like mouths, was quite in keeping with the exterior of Ugly Joe and with the sweep of rough hills and sordid plain on either side in prospect, but the patio within was the special province of Ugly Joe.

Water, for the internal or external application of which the proprietor had little use, was here lavished upon *flowers*. There were many kinds, and exceedingly bright colors, blended with all the skill with which a Navajo Indian weaves scarlets and yellows into his blanket. About these flowers Martha Gregory wandered with a watering can in one hand and a short-handled hoe in the other. With the one she dealt life to the flowers. With the other she dealt death to the weeds — a faultless justice. She was taller than Ugly Joe, and her face was even homelier, with a cast of the Scandinavian expressed by high cheek bones, small eyes, and a perfectly straight mouth so rigidly set that not the least blood-color showed in the lips.

At sight of Patricia Lauriston, the hostess dropped her watering can and embraced her guest with the liberated arm. There was more strength in that one arm than in any two that Patricia had ever felt, and, when she looked up, somewhat breathless, she surprised a smile on the lips of the Amazon. It was like a warm surprise of sunshine on a cloudy day — there was something generously enveloping about it. And Patricia smiled back. After all, there is only one smile for all women when they are kindly moved and genuine. Patricia and "Mother" Martha cast an arm about each other and wandered into the house, completely forgetful of Ugly Joe.

His wife was called "Mother" throughout 10,000 square miles because she had no children and had to vent her tenderness on flowers and broken-down houses and sick children. They still tell the story of how Mother Martha rode fifty miles in the space of a single night — fifty miles through a sandstorm that whipped her face raw — how her horse dropped — how she went on the last miles on foot — and reached the house of Jim Patrick. She saved three lives that time, for Mrs. Patrick gave birth to twins, and the lives of all three hovered at the brink of death for ten days, and were finally drawn back to life by the strong arm of Mother Martha.

That is only one of the stories they tell about Mother Martha. And if Patricia did not know these tales when she first saw her hostess, she must have guessed something of them. For when she passed through the door with Mother Martha, Patricia was extremely glad that she had taken her trip to the mountain desert, and, as I have said, her arm was about the waist of the Amazon.

That evening Patricia borrowed one of Mother Martha's gingham dresses, which flapped about her more loosely than a Kanaka woman's *holoku,* and went into the kitchen to assist Martha. For the good wife would not keep a cook. No one, it seemed, could cook to please Ugly Joe except herself.

The master of the house had already dispatched four riders in four various directions, and late that night, while Patricia sat at the piano — the pride of the house — playing everything from "Swanee River" to the "Maple Leaf Rag", the four messengers returned, and they brought with them four others. Now the messengers themselves were hardy cowpunchers, not overly gentle in feature or voice or manner, but they were missionary spirits of surpassing sweetness compared with the four accomplished ruffians they brought with them. The heart of a moving-picture director would have swelled almost to bursting if he could have seen them enter, for they were ideal figures for that episode in the third reel where the gang of villains pursues the innocent girl — the same episode, you know, where the gallant United States troopers in turn pursue the villains and arrive just in time — well, that's the sort our four gunmen were.

Chic Woods came first. His face was built like some great transatlantic liner, chiefly towering hull with diminutive deck works. Upon that massive jaw and swelling jowl, the diminutive nose, little pig eyes, and forehead lost under a descending scrag of black hair, were set rather as a suggestion of how the face might be finished off than as a necessary part of the countenance. All that anyone would ever remember of Chic would be that jaw and the fang-like teeth and the bull-neck made for hanging on.

Behind him came his antithesis, Harry Yale. He was, as nearly as possible, a figure in one dimension — length. Both his breadth and his thickness were not worth consideration. He looked like a man who had gone without food for a month. There was the blaze of famine in his eyes, for instance, and his cheeks were so sunken that they pulled back the lips at the corners and made Harry Yale seem to smile. It seemed to Patricia the most unpleasant smile she had ever seen. She was fascinated by the man and could not take her eyes from him when he spoke, for with every utterance the great Adam's apple rolled up and down his throat, as if he were trying to swallow it and could never quite succeed.

As for Bob Riddle, who came third, he was far less repulsive than the other two. He was a half-breed, however, and he carried with him that suggestion of mysterious and inexhaustible malice that even a tenderfoot apprehends in a thoroughly bad Indian. He was quite dignified and very silent, which made him seem more venomous than ever.

Against the ugly background of the other three, Jack Tucker was a perfect Apollo. In fact, his good looks had been the ruin of him. They had made him a spoiled child, and out of a spoiled childhood he grew into a youth and manhood unable to accept the rebuffs of the world. When the world struck him, he struck back, and, having a heavy hand and a demon temper, he struck to kill. He had been a gambler for some years, but his killings grew greater than his winnings and he had to move on to fresh fields and pastures new. He was one of those fallen figures that excite no pity because his strength was still great enough to defy the world.

V

"THE TRAP IS SET"

As these worthies filed in, the messengers who had brought them out of the distance vanished through the open door behind them. The gunfighters exchanged no kindly greetings.

"Well?" growled Chic Woods.

"Well?" snarled Harry Yale.

"Well?" grunted Bob Riddle.

"Well?" drawled Jack Tucker.

"Don't all ask me," Ugly Joe said, affable but a little shaken by this terse battery. "Here's the lady that got you brought here."

The piano was in shadow in a corner of the room and the piano itself cast a night-deep, slanting shade over Patricia. She was only visible when she rose to greet the instruments of her will, and, in rising, the

46

light from the lamp fell softly across her face and plashed a little spot of gold on her throat.

"Hell!" snorted Chic Woods at this sudden apparition, and then instantly dragged the hat from his head. The shaggy hair that sprawled in snaky, black locks made him trebly horrible. " 'Scuse me, lady."

"Certainly," Patricia said, hunting through her mind for the words with which she must explain her purpose to these grim knights of the mountain desert.

Here Jack Tucker, smoothing back his long hair and shifting his orange-colored bandanna, stepped forward, hat in hand, as a spokesman more befitting this occasion.

"Me and these other gents," Tucker said graciously, "come here because Ugly Joe sent for us, and he's showed pretty much man to us. But if you want us, you can buy your chips now and start the game. We'll see that it's on the square. I'll be the guy on the stick myself."

The parlance of the gambling house was unfamiliar to Patricia, but she gathered the general meaning.

"Thank you," she said, "my name is Patricia Lauriston . . . but Cousin Joe

Gregory, there, says that I'll have to be known by a shorter name. He has suggested Pat."

"Which I'll agree is a good name," said Tucker. "I'm sure glad to know you. I'm Jack Tucker. This is Chic Woods, here's Harry Yale, and this is Bob Riddle."

She managed to keep her smile steady and shook hands with them each in turn.

"Now," she said to Ugly Joe, "shall I explain why we sent for them, or will you?"

"Pat," said Ugly Joe, "first, last, and all the time this is your party, and run by yourself."

"Very well," she answered. "I've come from the East with a purpose in which I'll need the help of several men who can shoot straight and have the courage to fight. Cousin Joe suggested you. I want to hire you. It may be hard work so that you can practically name your own prices."

"Seeing it's you," said the gallant Tucker, bowing, "I'm here willing to do any of my little specialties at half rates. What about you, boys?"

Their eyes had held like the bright eyes of four birds upon the deadly fascination of a snake. To men who ride alone in the mountain desert, the very name "woman" is synonymous with purity, beauty, and grace; in the presence of Patricia they stood awed, and their admiration — and their grunt of assent — thrilled her more than any tribute from her cultured friends of the East.

"Wait a minute," Ugly Joe announced, "while I horn in a bit. What she wants is for you to get the Whisperer. I thought that would change you a bit!"

The effect of the name had been magical. Bob Riddle leaped back to the door and peered out into the night. Harry Yale and Jack Tucker jumped back to back and stood crouching a little, as though ready to fight a host of foes, while Chic Woods whipped out two guns and stood with them poised. Patricia shrank back against the wall.

"Steady!" called Ugly Joe, after he had enjoyed the full effect of his announcement for an instant. "I said she wanted you to get the Whisperer. I didn't say he was *here*."

They relaxed, but cautiously. Riddle turned only partly from the door. Chic Woods restored his weapons to their holsters, but kept his right hand still in position for a lightning draw.

What Patricia saw, oddly enough, was not the men before her, but him whose name had produced this panic among man-killers. She envisioned him in one swift flare of sure knowledge — big, silent, neither handsome nor ugly, but simply dangerous!

"As a matter of fact," Patricia said, "I am not even going to ask you to expose yourselves by hunting for the Whisperer through the hills. I simply want you to stay here and be ready to fight when the Whisperer comes. For he *shall* come. Will you stay?"

They stayed, and the next day Patricia rode alone toward Eagles. Behind her the trap was ready, a strong trap with four teeth of steel, and more, because in time of need all the cowpunchers of Cousin Joe Gregory could be summoned. What she needed to make that trap effective was to secure the efficient bait, and already she was tasting the joys of victory. She had no difficulty in finding the house of the Widow Morgan, and there, on the front verandah, sat Goggles. She was at a little distance when she spied him and knew him at once by the description. He wore riding boots so highly polished that from the distance they glittered like mirrors, and his riding trousers were of a mouse-colored whipcord, buttoned snugly below the narrow knees. His loose pongee shirt fluttered with the puff of wind, and he lay easily back in his chair, with his slender hands locked behind his head.

Patricia was irritated, and chiefly by the fact that he seemed so cool. She herself was very hot from the keenness of the sun and labor of the hard ride. She swung from her horse and mounted to the verandah. The nearer view merely proved what she had surmised from the distance. His face was very lean and pale, and behind the great, black-rimmed spectacles, large and pathetic eyes of soft brown stared out at the world. He was finished by a dapper little mustache. It did not extend clear across the upper lip, but was merely a decorative dab in the center. At her approach, he turned his head carelessly, and she noted that his face did not light as the faces of most men did when she came near.

With her whole heart Patricia despised him. If he had been himself a slayer of men, she would almost have admired him — there is a place of esteem for a dangerous man — but at this decorative, smooth, lithe sneak, who lived in the shadow of a great outlaw's protection and like a jackal preyed on the leavings of the lion's meal, her disgust stormed up strongly in her throat. It made her face hard, indeed.

Seeing her pause by him, Goggles arose with just that touch of lingering hesitancy that indicates the courtesy of habit and breeding rather than the attention of natural kindliness. He rose, smiled automatically, and offered his chair. Without the slightest hesitancy Patricia slipped into it and sat calmly, staring up at him.

If she had hoped to irritate him, however, she was totally disappointed. He did not even seem surprised, but leaned against the rail of the verandah, brushing his little mustache with a very slender fingertip and looking for all the world as if he had been merely keeping the chair in trust for her. Patricia was quite sure that the man's blood was no warmer than that of a fish. She pictured him, in one of those quick visions of hers, fawning and cringing in the presence of the Whisperer. Indeed, being the servant of such a grim master gave the fellow a sort of dignity. She had to admit it unwillingly. She could only wonder that a lone rider of the mountain desert could choose so despicable a tool. The man was hardly taller than herself and certainly not a great deal heavier. The only admirable physical characteristic about him was a certain suggestion of lightness for speed. She had seen famous sprinters who had the same delicate, almost perfectly round wrists and ankles, the same marvelously slender hands and feet. His feet, in fact, although they were somewhat longer, were hardly a jot wider than her own. These details Patricia gathered in that first steady, rather insolent stare.

Then she said: "Thank you for the chair, Mister Saint Gore. I've just come in from a long ride . . . very hot, you know, and a little tired."

"Ah!" drawled St. Gore without the slightest meaning in his voice, and then, acting upon sudden inspiration: "By Jove, the Widow Morgan has just made a pitcher of delightfully cool lemonade. May I bring you a glass?"

"Thanks," said Patricia. "No."

"No? It's really very palatable lemonade . . . not made with the wretched extract."

"Indeed?" said Patricia.

"Quite so," babbled Goggles, "and the pitcher is so cold . . . well, there's frost on it, you know."

The description sent a burning pang of thirst down Patricia's throat and plunging hotly into her vitals, but now that she had first refused she could not well change her mind. Unquestionably she hated the fellow with her whole soul.

"My name," she broke in, "is Patricia Lauriston."

She waited for the name to take effect — waited for the guilty start — the flush — the pallor of the coward. Instead, he merely stared curiously — a faint curiosity — toward her, and then past her, as if he were lost at the instant in the drifting of a pale, far-off cloud.

"Really," murmured Goggles, "I'm so happy to know you, Miss Lauriston."

Patricia leaned forward to give the first sharp home stroke.

VI

"BAIT FOR THE TRAP"

"I am the cousin," she said, "of that Lauriston whose murder you accomplished through the Whisperer."

At this he started. Not sharply, it was merely a sudden and rather hurt glance down at her face, studying her as if he wondered what manner of creature she might be.

"Oh, dear," Goggles sighed at last. "*You* are not going to bring up that hideous old affair?"

"I have come several thousand miles for that exact purpose," Patricia advised, and the rage that she had been controlling took her by the throat like a gripping hand, so that her voice trembled and went small. For her whole soul revolted at the thought of that stalwart cousin of hers done to death through this paltry cur. She concluded: "And having come so far, I'm certainly going to do my best to bring matters to a crisis."

Goggles sank back against the rail and trailed slender fingers across that broad, pale forehead. "Everyone," he complained drearily, "has been simply wretched to me since the death of that vulgar fellow, and now you come. Well, I'm very glad that you know it was the Whisperer, and not I, who committed the murder."

"No," said Patricia with a fine disdain, "all your part was to call on the bloodhound and set him on the trail of a man you did not have the heart to face by yourself."

"Oh!" Goggles said, and shrank a little away from her. "You don't seem to like me, do you?"

She could not help laughing. The inanity of the fellow was both disgusting and comic. Her laugh jarred to an abrupt stop. "Do you think it strange, Mister Saint Gore?"

"Really, you know," said St. Gore, "I've tried most awfully not to offend you. If my manners have been bad, I know you will excuse me. You see I'm a little troubled with absent-mindedness."

"*Hmm,*" grumbled Patricia, and she seemed very masculine and formidable as she frowned thoughtfully down at him. "The more I see of you, Mister Saint Gore, I wish that I could do to you what I am going to do to the Whisperer."

He was frankly, guilelessly interested at once. "Oh, are you going to do something to the Whisperer?"

"I am going to see him captured," Patricia stated smoothly, "and either shot down or else hanged from the highest cottonwood tree on the ranch."

"Dear me!" cried Goggles, distressed, "you're such a violent person, aren't you?"

"And I'm almost sorry to have it done," went on Patricia, "because something in me admires the man in spite of his crimes. At least he has strength and courage and power of action. I wish . . . I wish that someone of your nature were to be in his place."

"Like me!" poor Goggles gasped, and he edged farther away along the rail.

"Stand where you are!" Patricia cried sternly.

He stopped with a jerk, and his eyes widened.

"But I can't do that," she went on, and paused to meditate.

"I wonder," began St. Gore timidly, as if he feared that she would snap at him in the middle of his question, "I wonder how you will attack the Whisperer. He has never killed a woman . . . but, I suppose, he would . . . he's such a terrible fellow. Quite uncontrollable, you know."

"Perhaps," said Patricia, "you have heard of Chic Woods, Harry Yale, Jack Tucker, and Bob Riddle?"

"Oh, yes," Goggles murmured, "and I don't think you could have named four rougher men. Really, you know, they are the sort one doesn't mention . . . in certain places."

"I have hired them," Patricia said calmly, "to do the work that the law could not or would not perform." She considered him again, thoughtfully. "And in some way I'm going to use you, Mister Saint Gore, but just how I can't tell."

The man seemed to have a special talent for asinine expression of face — utter emptiness of eye. But now a dawn of intelligence lighted his eyes. "By Jove!" he cried, and, straightening, he clapped his hands together and laughed with soft glee to himself. "I have it!"

"Have what?" asked Patricia.

"You see," explained Goggles eagerly,

"it's been useful now and then, but on the whole an awful nuisance to have the Whisperer trailing me about. I'd give almost anything to have the rude fellow . . . er . . . disappear!"

"You would?"

"So, suppose I go out to your ranch and act . . . well, as a sort of bait for your trap. The Whisperer is sure to follow me. He's like my shadow, in fact."

"Do you mean to say," Patricia said slowly, "that you would actually help to betray him . . . your friend . . . your benefactor . . . no matter what he has been to the rest of the world?"

"Now," Goggles said deprecatingly, "you are thinking hard things of me again, aren't you? But the Whisperer is an awful burden for anyone . . . and I'm quite too nervous to have him always around. It would be a most enormous relief to get rid of him."

She closed her eyes and drew a deep breath. The shameless ingratitude and treachery of the fellow blinded her.

"But how," she said, when she could speak again, "could I be sure that once on the ranch you would not sneak away the first time the Whisperer approached you?"

"That's very simple," Goggles answered brightly. "I'll give you my word not to leave until you say that I may go."

"And you won't ride out and tell the Whisperer all of our plan? Hah! He would wring it out of you through fear."

"Well," Goggles said thoughtfully, "I suppose he might, but that would only make him stay the closer. He doesn't fear anything, you know, and he would laugh at the thought of any four men taking him. Even such men as you have. Did you say Jack Tucker is one of them?"

"He is," Patricia said, and in spite of herself she began to almost admire the catlike cunning of the dapper little Easterner. "I see your plan, and I suppose that a man like the Whisperer would take the challenge of my . . . trap . . . as a sort of sporting proposition. Being your friend, he would try to make me release you . . . try to make me give you your freedom." She straightened, her eyes shining. "And that would bring him at last face to face with me. I don't ask anything more."

"You take my breath . . . you really do," said Goggles, "but, if the plan suits you, suppose I go pack my grip? I'm all ready to start."

"Certainly," Patricia said, and her scornful glance followed him through the door.

He reappeared, carrying a bulky suitcase, tightly wrapped and bulging at the sides. His horse was led around at the same time, and the suitcase strapped behind the saddle securely.

On the way out he had little to say. He seemed more amazed than intimidated, and at this she wondered, until she was able to explain it to herself through the fact that the man trusted all things implicitly to the Whisperer and had grown so accustomed to the infallibility of the outlaw that he did not dream of worrying over any predicament. In fact, there seemed no place for worry in the mindlessness of the fellow. Worry, after all, suggests thought, and that was something, apparently, that never burdened the brain of Mr. St. Gore. Once he brought his horse, a fine animal, to a sharp halt in order that he might gape upon a cloud of singular shape that floated down the western sky. Now and then he broke his silence to speak to his horse in a conversational manner, as one might speak to any rational being.

To Patricia, in fact, looking from the fine, high-held head of the horse to the bespectacled face of the rider, it seemed that the brute was by far the higher type of animal. They were in sight of Ugly Joe's place before the fop directly addressed her.

He said: "I presume that I shall have protection against these . . . er . . . ruffians of yours, Miss Lauriston?"

"I shall personally," she answered, "be your guarantee."

"Will you really?" he queried gratefully. "Awfully thrilling to have your interest, you know!"

She looked at him sharply. In almost any other man the speech would have been a subtle jest, but his face was more blankly serious than she had seen it, as yet. They dismounted at the central entrance, opening on the patio. Here Goggles cried out sharply and ran forward a few steps with his arms out-thrown. He whirled sharply on Patricia, his face ecstatic.

"Miss Lauriston!" he cried. "I've been thinking it rather queer of you to bring me away out here, but now I thank you . . . I positively do! I haven't seen flowers like these since I left. . . ." His arms dropped — his face grew grave and almost drawn.

"I beg your pardon?" Patricia queried lightly.

"I beg yours," answered Vincent St. Gore, and he bowed with something that almost approached a gentleman's quiet dignity. "I shouldn't have commenced a sentence which I may not finish."

To Patricia it was as if a cloth of bright, simple colors were suddenly reversed, and on the other side she saw some marvelously intricate design; so much one touch of gravity did to all her preconceptions of the man, and all her knowledge of him as she had seen him this day.

Ugly Joe, crossing from one side of the patio to the other, stopped short. "Hello!" he called. "You got your bird, eh, Pat?"

"You see him," she answered.

Ugly Joe approached to within reaching distance of Goggles, who adjusted his spectacles and leaned forward to peer at the newcomer.

Ugly Joe grew ugly, indeed. "Listen to me, my hearty," snarled the rancher, who had been at sea in his time and whose walk still oddly suggested, at times, the heaving deck of an imaginary ship. "Listen to me . . . you're out here because the lass wants you here for reasons of her own. Maybe she's told you about them. Now I'll tell you one other thing. Don't be lingering around when you find me alone. I can stand the sight of you, maybe, when there's witnesses nearby, but, when I see you alone, I want to fix my fingers in that skinny windpipe of yours. Understand? You damned sneaking cutthroat!" And Ugly Joe turned on his heel, after a farewell glare, and stalked on toward the nearest door with his wobbly stride, lifting high to meet the imaginary deck.

VII

"GOGGLES TALKS"

"My word!" sighed Goggles. "Who is that person?"

"That," Patricia said coldly, "is my cousin, Joe Gregory."

"Isn't he the rough chap, though?"

"Ah!" she cried with a sudden, overwhelming burst of disgust. "Can you call yourself a man? You would shame a dog . . . a creeping, whining . . . dog." She turned and ran from him. She was shuddering with shame and horror in the thought that such a craven, such a spineless cur, could be a man, could walk and talk and think like a man, and yet at heart be such a travesty on all noble qualities of a man. More sickening, because his admiration of the flowers a moment before had made him almost akin to her — had brought a sudden softening and sympathy into her heart. She despised herself for it now — loathed herself, as though she had touched the face of a leper, and the touch had made her unclean forever.

By contrast she drew the figure of the Whisperer. Perhaps at some time in his career a service had been rendered him by this cravenly scoundrel, St. Gore, and now, to pay the debt, he constituted himself a strong and invisible shield between the craven and the world. More and more details of the Whisperer's character were creeping up strongly in her imagination. He was large, undoubtedly, since so many tales were told of his prowess. And that whispering voice, so horrible to hear, was undoubtedly the result of some incurable affliction. She had heard of men with consumption of the throat, which affected their vocal chords so that their voices became like that ascribed to the Whisperer.

Without doubt the man had come to the Southwest to be cured of his affliction by the purer, drier air. To support himself he had been forced into a life of outlawry. Then this sneaking dapper fiend, St. Gore, tracked the man who he had befriended in some small thing years before, and lived off the earnings of the Whisperer's daredevil depredations. In the meantime, the outlaw was dying slowly of his malady, but would be terrible until the end.

This was the story that grew up of itself in her thoughts, until it seemed to her that she could not bear to face St. Gore again. The temptation to shoot him down — kill him like a snake — would be too great.

It was into this stormy mood of hers that harmonious music ran. In fact, it was so akin to her thoughts of the moment that she hardly noticed it at first, and only gradually it grew out distinctly upon her. It was someone playing on the piano in the distant room, the "Revolutionary" *Étude* by Chopin, and playing it with consummate strength and mastery. Not an easy thing to do, as she knew by experience, but this musician played with easy perfection. The difficult bass, which must roll but not thunder, swept by in a vast rhythm like great ground swells that roll along and toss the ship, and in turn block out either horizon and tower darkly into the heart of the sky. She had seen such waves, and she saw them again in the music. The treble darted across the scheme of harmony like sharp, stabbing bursts of lightning, illuminating the whole scene. The "Revolutionary" *Étude* — a study in conflict, in an ominous and rising danger like the passion that had held her a moment before.

She left her room and wandered toward the place from which the music came, paused at the door, and then went sick with disgusted disappointment. It was Vincent St. Gore who sat at the piano. He turned a blank face upon her, finished his passage faultlessly, and then rose.

"The bass," he said, "is in good shape, but the whole upper register is a shade out of tune . . . flat."

She merely stared helplessly at him. He had passed to an Indian basket suspended from the ceiling near a window and holding a flower pot full of crimson blossoms marked with streaks of jet. The large petals were like velvet. Now he turned the basket so that the sunshine in turn streamed softly over each flower — turned it with a lingering delight, and the expression on his face was such as she had seen when he first saw the flowers in the patio.

"Isn't it strange?" he said, turning to her, "that such a rough creature as your cousin Gregory should keep flowers. Or perhaps it's his wife?"

"I think," Patricia responded dryly, "that they are both capable of appreciating flowers."

"Really?" he said, and as usual, when aroused, he shifted his spectacles and peered through them at her. "Very odd, though, isn't it, that they should have the passion?"

"Why?" she asked. It was a burden even to listen to him, and a trial of patience.

"Because," he answered, "it's out of harmony. They love one beautiful thing, and all the rest is discord."

"Perhaps," said Patricia, "they have other qualities just as important."

"Impossible," said Goggles, and shook his head decisively. "There are no others as important as the love of beauty."

"If you feel that way," Patricia said, "I wonder that you can tolerate these people."

"Quite right," answered Goggles, nodding seriously, "but I don't tolerate them, you see. I see no more of them than I do of individual clouds when all the sky is dark. I don't talk like this to them . . . oh, never!"

"It would be unhealthy for you if you did, perhaps," Patricia stated scornfully.

"Would it?" Goggles mused, and canted his head thoughtfully to one side. "Yes, I suppose these creatures would resent criticism with physical violence." He shrugged his shoulders; it was a shudder of aversion that shook his entire body. "However," he said, "I have never bothered talking with them about these things. It would be like sowing the wind, don't you think?"

"Exactly," said Patricia, "and like reaping the whirlwind afterward, eh?"

"I don't quite follow you there," Goggles said, "unless you mean that they might actually strike me? Dear me! I suppose that is possible. One never knows what to expect. Not in these wilds. However, with you there is some difference."

"Hope for me?" asked Patricia.

He considered her with that thoughtfully canted head. "I should really warn you" — he smiled — "that I've acquired a brutal frankness out here in the mountain desert."

"I'm so glad," Patricia stated. "It's the one. . . ." She stopped, but Goggles finished the sentence smoothly for her.

"The one manly characteristic you've found in me? Quite so! Oh, I don't in the least mind people saying such things to me. I've grown quite used to them." And he smirked at her.

She had to grip her hands to keep from striking him across the thin-lipped mouth. "You were saying," she remarked, "that there may be a hope for me?"

"Did I say that? I didn't mean to. No, a woman rarely develops. She is, on the whole, a fixed quantity, and only varies in vanity. You don't mind, do you? I'm quite impersonal."

"My dear Mister Saint Gore," Patricia replied, sighing, "nothing you can say can possibly offend me. Go on."

"Now isn't that comfortable?" breathed the little man. "I foresee some charming chats with you. You have possibilities, I should say, rather of appreciation than of execution. You would not in the least surprise me, for instance, if I heard you discuss an art with intelligence, but I should be much astounded if you performed anything with distinction. You follow me?"

"Hmm," said Patricia.

"You will attempt to remedy this defect since I have called it to your attention, but after a few years you will see that I am right about it . . . a woman never varies, except in degree. You will abandon the effort to create."

She was beginning to forget what the man looked like. She was hearing only the light, smooth voice. She was drifting away into the sea of the discussion.

"There are other things," Patricia said desperately. "There are other things I can

71

do. There is a world of action."

"A world of action," said the little man serenely. "You can give birth to children, love your husband because he provides the food for yourself and your offspring, and rock a cradle. Within those limits, there is almost nothing to which you may not aspire in the world of action. That must be quite clear to you."

"Hmm," Patricia responded again.

"But, after all," went on Goggles, "what is the world of action? What becomes of it? What do we know of the great financiers and bridge builders and lawmakers and statesmen? You can number on your two hands the few to whom certain poets have deigned to give immortality. No, your practical man, your man of action, rots away into oblivion as rapidly as his name rots away on the headstones of his grave.

"What is left of Egypt? The mind that conceived the Sphinx and the author of the story of 'Cinderella'? What of the heroes of Greece, her captains of industry? They are gone except as some poet names them on a random page. And the poets of Greece? You can run the list into scores. We read them as we read Milton and Shakespeare. Well, to get down to modern days, consider Shakespeare. Now, can you tell me, offhand, who commanded the English fleet against the Armada?"

"No," said Patricia, "I can't."

"It was a certain Lord Howard, I think. But surely in his day he was considered much greater than the obscure fellow who pushed a pen and acted the part of a ghost and finally settled down in a pleasant little village to die like a commonplace farmer. Yes, in those days, no man would have hesitated to choose between the fate of a Lord Howard and that of a Shakespeare. But time is the acid test. Time rusts away all your strong iron and leaves only the good untouched . . . only the gold . . . only the beauty. It is the one thing you cannot resist.

"For instance, I called you out of a distant part of the house with music. Because I play that *étude* in a certain way you despise me, d'you see? After I've gone on, you'll think over what I've said, though you're too proud to ask more questions now."

She slumped into a chair. "I'm not too proud," she said. "I do despise you . . . but I want to listen."

"Well," Goggles said, "I like to talk, for that matter. Almost any audience will do for me when I get started. Even my horse!"

He smiled, and, musing upon this absurdity, he drew out a monogrammed cigarette case and offered it to her. She refused sharply. "Ah," said Goggles, withdrawing the case and selecting and lighting his smoke, "you don't smoke? Now, that's rarely stupid of you. You miss a great opportunity, nothing like smoking to set off hands like yours."

She folded her arms to conceal those hands.

"Now," he said, "you wish to seem angry, but secretly you're a little pleased, aren't you?"

"Yes," said the girl. "I like appreciation, no matter from whom it comes."

"Not so well said," answered the dictator of tastes. "Injudicious appreciation is worse than useless. It clogs the mind with inaccuracies. The common herd, for instance, thought much of both Tennyson and Browning in their day."

"But you dislike them?"

"Dislike them? No. When I was a boy, I rather enjoyed them. Then I discovered that Tennyson had nothing to say and knew exceedingly well how to say it, while Browning had a great deal to say, but was never able to utter a single sustained rhythm. Now, in your remark of a moment ago, you were trying to make a hit at my comment about audiences. You missed my point. One talks *with* a companion . . . one talks *at* an audience."

"You are certainly very clear," said the girl.

"Insultingly so?"

"You could never insult me."

"Only weary you, I suppose. And now?"

"I'm immensely interested. Because you pay some attention to the subject that most fascinates me . . . myself."

The eyes of Goggles flashed with enjoyment. "That's bully." He chuckled. "Simply bully! You *are* interesting, but not in the way men have told you."

"Oh?" said Patricia. He was like a dissector, cutting toward the heart of her being, naming each muscle as he passed it.

"You have," said the merciless critic, "the three most important qualities for a woman, their importance ranking in the order named . . . a sound body . . . apparently . . . a beautiful face, and a receptive mind. You have also, in the order named, the three greatest vices of modern woman . . . ambition, discontent, and respect for your *mind*. You are interesting through the clash of qualities."

"And you are under the impression that

I will become. . . ."

"Either a virtuous wife and the discontented mother of many children, or the mistress of a great man and the discontented mother of barren thoughts."

She sank farther back in her chair, regarding him with awe and aversion. It seemed to Patricia that the book of her future was being read with infallible wisdom.

"Which had you rather be?" Goggles asked, and smiled.

"I had rather die than be either!" cried Patricia.

"Ah," said the little man, and raised a forefinger. "Then there is hope for you."

After that she could not get another word from him.

VIII

"A MESSAGE FROM THE NIGHT"

Oddly enough that interview increased her respect for the Whisperer rather than for St. Gore. She saw another reason now why the outlaw should cling to this dapper little fop and extend over him the dark cloak of his protection. It was because the outlaw had been a man of culture and had been ostracized from the paths of civilized men. All that he saved from the wreckage was the friendship and occasional meetings with this St. Gore, this absurd little dude with his cold, keen mind.

If she did not utterly despise St. Gore now, she looked upon him as men look upon some ingenious mechanism that does the work of a man — and yet is not a man. She felt almost as impersonally as this about St. Gore.

Apparently he had the most complete trust in the protection of the Whisperer. For instance, when he sat opposite the four gunfighters at the table that night, he looked at them rather with curiosity than with fear, and studied them with such an intent look that Patricia wished for the tenth time that he would lay aside those absurd, owl-like spectacles.

Indeed, it was the spectacles that gave most of the folly to the face of Goggles. Without them, it would have been an interesting, intellectually handsome face. With them, it became a mere mask of inanity. However, she had known men with minds, but no bodies — men dead below the brain. A typical product of one phase of the 20th Century.

The gunfighters regarded Goggles with a curiosity fully equal to his own and much more openly expressed. They were like four great hunting dogs surrounding the weak, defenseless cub of the bear, but daring not to touch it for fear of the terrible coming of the dam. They measured Goggles across his broad forehead and his narrow cheeks — they measured him across his slender shoulders and through his thin chest. Once Chic Woods, speaking in an aside like a mutter of thunder to Bob Riddle, stretched out his fingers and then closed them slowly — a suggestive gesture, as if he were crushing some fragile object filled with life. Yet for some time no one directly addressed Goggles; the cloak of his master's awful power fell like an invisible sense of awe about him.

Finally, however, Jack Tucker said: "Maybe you don't know, Goggles, that I've figured out who the Whisperer is?"

"How extremely interesting," Goggles said, and smiled benignly upon the ruffian. "Do you really, though?"

"You're damned right I do . . . 'scuse me, lady," said Tucker, "and there was one beside me that knew . . . old Mort Lauriston."

"Well, well," said Goggles, "you've no idea how impressed the Whisperer will be when I tell him that his identity has been penetrated."

"Whatever that means," growled Tucker, "but you can tell the old bird that he's known, all right. Maybe you'd like to hear the story?"

"Indeed," drawled Goggles with enthusiasm.

"By all means," Patricia echoed.

"It was back a few years when the first

paying ore was struck over by the Muggyon Hills," said Tucker. "I was laying about Eagles when one day old Mort Lauriston came driving up to me and says he'd like to have me slide out into the hills with him to a place where he thought he'd got the right color, but he wanted to get my opinion before he got his claim papers.

"I climbed a hoss and we went out into the hills, and there, right on the place where Mort had been digging, was Pa."

"Pa?" queried Patricia.

"I was coming to that. There was a chap come out to Eagles from the East. Awful green tenderfoot. He said his name was Peter Askworthy Howe, but the initials on his suitcase was P.A.H., so we called him Pa right off the jump.

"Wasn't a bad sort, laying aside the funny way he talked. Anyway, it was Pa who'd come along and seen the marks of Mort's digging. He'd opened up the stuff himself, and, being a rock hound, he seen the first glance that there was plenty of color . . . real stuff. So he staked out a claim. We come down and allowed to him that Mort had the first jump on that spot. He told us to go to . . . well, not just in them words, him being particular polite, always.

"He allowed that he was going into Eagles to get his papers. Well, we knew that he'd beat us on a ride, because he had a pretty nice piece of hossflesh with him. He climbed into the saddle, and then I shot the hoss.

"Sort of peeved this Pa, because he ups and grabs his gun. Which was some foolish move, considering how fast Mort was with his six-gun. He put three chunks of lead into Pa's chest inside a space the size of your palm. Of course, the tenderfoot didn't have no chance. He didn't die for a minute, and, before he kicked out, he rolls himself over on his back . . . he was a big gent . . . and pulls himself up on his hands."

" 'Lauriston,' he says, 'you and Tucker will never enjoy the money you make out of this mine. My brother will track me, and he'll learn who killed me. He'll kill you, my fine fellows, and, if you started riding now, you could never ride far enough away or hide so well that you could get away from him.'

"With that he kicked out. Now, I got a considerable respect for what a dying man says, and I allow that the Whisperer is the brother of old Pa. Yep, his name is Howe and he's filled one part of his bet by getting Mort Lauriston. The other part is to get me. I knew the Whisperer was on my trail, and that's why I've been so scarce around these parts lately. I figured he'd a good chance of bumping me off while I was alone. But now that I've got these three bunkies, I guess he's out of luck. What say, Chic?"

"I'll tell the world he's out of luck!" growled Chic.

"Damn his eyes!" broke in Ugly Joe. "When he finds them, he finds me with 'em. Listen to the wind, lads! Glad we're in port tonight."

For the gale had risen suddenly, and now made the stanch adobe walls quiver time and again, and little drafts set the flames jumping in the lamps. Mrs. Gregory rose to fasten the shades on the western and windward side of the house, and, opening a window to do this, a piece of paper, evidently inserted under the edge of the window for this very purpose, whipped from the sill and came fluttering across the room like a white bird, settling gently on the center of the table.

Jack Tucker, cursing softly, leaned forward and snatched up the paper, unfolded it, and read aloud, slowly, with a grim-set face:

Gents, I've been waiting for you a long time. I never expected to get you all together. Harry Yale, you come first.

The Whisperer

Tucker tossed it down for examination by any who cared to look. Gingerly, like men touching deadly poison, they raised the little paper one by one and examined the clumsy, scrawling handwriting. It was backhand, and the letters were formed with the same crude care that a child of seven uses.

"At least," Patricia said thoughtfully — and she and Goggles were the only calm people in the room, "it proves one thing. The Whisperer is not your man Howe. This is some uneducated man from the mountain desert. Look at his writing! Isn't that a sufficient proof?"

"Ma'am," Chic Woods said hoarsely, "nothing proves anything about the Whisperer. I don't mind a man . . . but a damned ghost. . . ."

His eyes traveled across to Harry Yale. The tall man stood like one transfixed, swallowing hard, so that the great Adam's apple jumped up and down his throat. Through that bronze tan he could not show pallor, but his lips seemed to have grown harder set, and they were pulled toward the hollows of his cheeks by the ghastliest of grins. In the silence that followed, every glance turned finally upon Harry Yale. He stood it for a moment, and then in a sudden fury he pushed back his chair, rose, and smashed his great, bony hand down on the table.

"Am I dead already?" he roared. "I ain't any ghost now, am I? Look somewheres else . . . and to hell with you all!" He strode to the door, hesitated with his hand on the knob, and then jerked it suddenly open, and stood tense, staring into the dark beyond. He closed the door, disappearing into the farther room. Chic Woods raised a shaking hand and mopped his forehead.

IX

"THE SECOND AND THIRD MESSAGES"

Patricia, with her four gunfighters, felt like a general with mighty forces to direct. It was she who planned the campaign for the next day. She schemed in this way: First of all, Goggles was almost certain to use his freedom at once and ride out to meet the Whisperer, who he would supply with accurate information concerning all that went on in the house. Her plan was to trail Goggles when he rode out, using Harry Yale to do that trailing, because Harry had now the most vital reason for wishing to get at the great outlaw. One man could probably trail the inexperienced Goggles very easily, and the other three in turn would follow Yale at a safe distance, scattered out on either side of him. In case Yale were to find the Whisperer, they could gallop in at once to his assistance, enveloping the outlaw.

She disclosed her plan to the four men, and they agreed readily. Any plan was a good plan to them. What they wanted was action, and quick action to get at the common enemy.

She proved a true prophet. Almost immediately after breakfast Goggles sauntered out toward the barn and a few minutes later was riding toward the hills at a brisk gallop. He was not out of sight before Harry Yale, spurring at every stride, raced after him, and behind Harry, at a short interval, came his three companions.

Patricia, from the kitchen door, watched them disappear with a smile of content. The Whisperer, certainly, would expect some dilatoriness in the campaign against him, some waiting for his nearer approach, some elaborately calculated ambuscade. This quick action, nine chances out of ten, would throw him off his guard. And in the presence of four men like Yale and the others, one mistake would be the last. She felt a queer pain, as well, at the thought that through her this wild scourge should be removed from the mountain desert. No matter how terrible he might be, it would be like the shooting of an eagle — a grim thing to see the air robbed of its lord and its tyrant.

By noon the riders had not returned. In the dusk of the evening Woods, Riddle, and Tucker, hot, weary, discomfited, trotted up to the barn and came in silence to the house. In the first wild burst of speed Harry Yale, better mounted than the others and riding without caution, had outstripped the others, and they had lost him in the windings of the hills. All the rest of the day they had stalked him, but could not get his trail again. They told this tale to Ugly Joe. To Patricia they would not speak at all. She had been the general, and she had failed her army in time of need. For her own part, a sense of guilt oppressed her. Somewhere out there in the gathering dark the tall form of Harry Yale must be motionless. Over it the buzzards, perhaps, were already gathering.

In the midst of her despair there was a shout from outside the house, and she ran out to see the form of a horseman rapidly maturing through the dark.

"Hey, Harry!" called the chorus of his bunkies.

But after a moment, a soft, thin voice answered: "Halloo, there."

"Goggles!" groaned Chic Woods.

"Goggles?" Patricia repeated, and she wished him heartily a thousand leagues under the honest earth.

He came, trailing his feet with weariness, having put up his horse in the barn.

"My word," sighed Goggles. "Will you believe that I was lost in those wretched hills? Yes, indeed! I should hardly have found the house if I hadn't seen the lights at last. Think of wandering all night through those hills. I'm going straight to my room." And he went.

The others settled down at the entrance to the patio to visit. They were silent; for an hour the only sound and sigh was the occasional scratch and blue spurt of a match. They were thinking of Harry Yale, and they were thinking of death.

But at the very moment that Ugly Joe finally rose and turned toward the house, they caught the patter of trotting hoofs through the night, hoofs that clapped the earth more loudly, chugging, at last, in the sand directly before the house as the horse came to a halt. They were too excited to challenge the rider.

"Halloo!" called the voice of Harry Yale.

A happy cheer answered him. Woods and Riddle ran toward him.

"Stay where y'are!" barked Harry Yale. "I got an oath not to stop with you."

"You met him?" called Patricia.

"I'm saying nothin' except this thing," answered Harry Yale. "Bob Riddle, you're the next to go. That's straight from the Whisperer."

"Wait!" called Chic Woods. "Yale, y'ain't going to leave us up in the air like this?"

"Chic, if you come near me, I'll start a gun play. I'm under 'n oath higher'n heaven and deeper'n hell. S'long."

The hoofs started again and chugged softly away through the night, fainter, fainter, until the last patter died out. As for the men, none of them stirred, but Patricia fled back into the house and found Mother Martha.

"I want to stay with you tonight," she pleaded. "I'm afraid!"

"Of what, honey?" asked Mother Martha.

"Of ghosts!" said Patricia. "Of ghosts!"

"I'm older'n you, Patty," Martha stated, "and I've seen a pile more of the ways of the mountain desert. You'll never get the Whisperer this way. He'll hunt down men one by one, just the way he did Harry Yale today. Poor Harry Yale. He's done for. To-morrow he'll take water from a Chinaman.

That's the way of the Whisperer. If he don't kill the body of a man, he kills the heart, which is worse, a lot."

"I won't give it up," said Patricia. "I daren't give it up."

"Why not, honey? Who elected you a manhunter?"

"It's the first thing I've tried by myself . . . the first real work. I've got to win! And I *will* win, because he can't beat me until I release Saint Gore from his parole with my own lips."

"Patty," Mother Martha assured, "I've seen stranger things than that happen on the mountain desert."

Not a comforting thought for Patricia to carry away to her bed. She lay awake long, considering it. For how, after all, could the Whisperer force her against her will to retract the parole of St. Gore? Perhaps at the point of his revolver, perhaps by striking down Ugly Joe — and even Mother Martha. Yes, to the Whisperer, neither man nor woman made a difference.

When she finally slept, it was only to dream of a great weight that pressed down on her, an invisible burden that beat against her out of the thin air like the wings of some tremendous, ethereal moth, suffocating her, pressing her, resistlessly, to the ground, killing her in the very sight of her friends.

She woke the next morning with little violet circles painted beneath her eyes, and in her throat a steady burning. The rest of the household was already at the breakfast table, in silence, and, when she entered, everyone looked up, but no one spoke, except Goggles. He was more dapper than ever, and seemed to have perfectly recuperated from the effects of his long ride of the day before. There was even a little touch of pink in his usually colorless cheeks.

He rose blithely at the sight of Patricia, and pulled back her chair. Her loathing of him rose to a physical horror. She could not sit down while the man stood behind the chair.

"Thank you," she said heavily, at last. "Won't you take your chair again?"

"Oh," said Goggles, "of course, if you wish."

She looked across to Ugly Joe and met a scowl in reply. "What is it?" she asked.

No one would speak, at first. Then she noted for the first time that Bob Riddle was not there.

"The Whisperer," she gasped. "Last night?"

There came a peculiar, hysterical laugh from Chic Woods, and his little pig-eyes wandered wildly. He tossed a scrap of paper across to her. "I found that tied on the horn of my saddle this morning. Maybe you can make it out for yourself." She read:

Gents, I'm gone. Nothing this side of hell can bring me back, so don't try. All I can say is: Chic Woods, your turn comes next, and God help you.

Bob Riddle

She read it again, and this time aloud, and, as she finished, Chic Woods sprang up, cursing hideously. He was plainly hysterical with fear.

"I start myself," he cried. "Tucker, if you're wise, you start with me. Any man I'll fight, but this damned ghost. . . ."

He turned and fled through the doorway. He was never seen again, it is said, in the mountain desert. Whether he met the Whisperer and death on his flight, or whether he simply left forever his old haunts will never be known.

X

"THE MESSAGE TO PATRICIA"

As for Jack Tucker, he leaned forward heavily on the table and followed the flight of Chic Woods with haunted eyes.

"For me, there ain't no use in running," he said slowly. "I can see that plain. I can see why the Whisperer didn't shoot up the rest, but just scared 'em off. He didn't want 'em . . . he was wanting only me. He *is* Howe, by God, and first he got Mort and now he'll get me! He's cleared out the rest . . . well, if he gets me, he'll get me in this house . . . d'ye hear? Nobody'll make me leave it. I got two guns that shoot straight and clean, and from now on I eat in my room . . . d'ye hear?"

To his glowering eyes everyone who sat at the table apparently had that moment become an enemy. He pushed back his chair, and backed from the room with his hands dropped to the butts of his guns, and through the rest of the day nothing could induce him to leave his room, until the supper hour. It was Mother Martha who finally brought him down. The day of self-imprisonment had changed him. He came down with a soft and cautious step, like some beast of prey, and he fixed on Ugly Joe, who passed him, a curious stare. Joe said afterward that he thought for an instant that Jack Tucker had lost his mind. At any rate, the gunfighter went down quietly to the dining room and accepted the chair that Mother Martha pulled back for him, and ate the food she placed before him.

No one but Mother Martha is responsible for the story of what followed in the next few minutes, but the word of Mother Martha, hitherto, has been more easily passed than current gold.

She was much worried about Tucker, she said, for when a man shuts himself up with a worry or a fear, he's very apt to lose his mind. It was for that reason that she persuaded him to come down to the dining room. The man was apparently in a panic of wild, soul-consuming fear. Not the sort of fear that makes men run, but the kind that makes them more dangerous than maniacs. She tried to encourage him at first, telling him that he was afraid of nothing. She assured him, finally, that the Whisperer had not a reason to injure him any more than the outlaw had already injured the other three gunmen. For the bullets that killed the man, Howe, had been fired by Mort Lauriston. She had scarcely finished this assurance, when Tucker leaned across the table toward her and said in a ghastly murmur: "You fool! D'you think I'd've told the truth before Goggles, that damned spy of the Whisperer? Nope, this is the way Howe died. He was standing by his claim, and Mort and I rode up, and dismounted. Mort asked him for the makings, and, while Mort was rolling a cigarette, I come behind and stabbed Howe in the back. He dropped, but, being a big man, he died hard. While he was lying there, he told us that he had a brother who'd kill us both . . . a brother we couldn't get away from. Mort laughed at him, pulled out his gun, and shot him three times through the breast. That's how he died! But me . . . I used the knife first . . . and by the knife . . . God knows, but I'm afraid . . . by the knife the Whisperer'll kill me . . . cold steel . . . a sharp edge. . . ."

Then, according to Mother Martha, she heard the most horrible sound of her life, something between a moan and a whisper, like the sound of a wind, far off and yet near. She could not tell where the sound came from — the open door, the window, or the ceiling above them. It took the shape of a voice — a voiceless voice, which said: "Jack Tucker, you come next!"

Tucker jumped up with a scream and fired two shots through the open door and another through the window. Then he turned and damned Mother Martha, saying this wouldn't have happened if he'd stayed in his room. So he ran, cursing and shuddering, to his room.

Mother Martha had Ugly Joe call in four cowpunchers from the bunkhouse, and they searched all the vicinity of the house and particularly the sand outside the dining room window, but not a trace of a man's foot was revealed by their lanterns. It was decided, then, to place a guard over the house throughout the night; the next day they would bring out a posse from Eagles. Four men were posted, one at each corner of the house, and at a distance of about fifty feet, so as to command a full sweep of the surrounding ground. It was a dark night, and for this reason each man had a small fire of mesquite wood. The purpose was not to entrap the Whisperer, but simply to warn him away.

Afterward each of the guards swore that he had remained awake and on the alert, not wishing to fall asleep and have a knife slipped between his ribs by the Whisperer before he awoke. Each of the four was equally vehement in the defense of his individual vigilance. For it was known that all four had worked hard that day, and there were many possibilities that they drowsed beside the fires.

What actually happened, at any rate, was that shortly after midnight the household of Joe Gregory wakened with a scream tingling in their ears. With one accord those inside the house and the guarding cowboys outside, rushed for the room of Jack Tucker. Ugly Joe himself called out a challenge and was the first to enter, a lantern in one hand and a revolver in the other.

Behind him came his wife, Patricia, and then Goggles, his lean, trembling limbs wrapped in a dressing gown of linen, stamped with a pattern of gay Japanese flowers. They found Jack Tucker lying face downward in a rapidly widening pool of blood. As they turned him on his back, they found that he had been stabbed three times in the breast, each wound enough to cause death. His own jackknife was still gripped in his hand, showing that he had died fighting, and not, at least, surprised from behind. There was still a lingering life in him. When he opened his eyes, the first thing that they encountered was the horrified face of Patricia leaning close above him.

His lips writhed, parted, and he said: "You . . . come next . . . he . . . told . . . me."

"Told you that she . . . that the girl . . . comes next?" cried Goggles in horror, and he leaned close to the dying man.

Tucker screamed, struck at the face above him, and died.

XI

"THE FOLLY OF WOMEN"

Patricia, heartsick and weak, did not wait to help care for the body of the dead man, but went back to her room. Ugly Joe stopped at her door a moment later to say that he had placed eight men on guard, instead of four, and that there would be no more trouble that night, at least. The next day he would take her to Eagles.

Nevertheless, she arranged the lamp on the little table at the head of her bed, so that, by striking a match, she could have a light in a second. The wick of the lamp was turned high, and she made sure that the supply of oil was sufficient. After that she lay in the dark, certain that she would stay awake until the dawn. But the very violence of the succession of grim pictures that passed across her mind wearied her.

Her last consciousness was that of shifting the revolver under her pillow so that it would be easier to grasp.

When she woke again, it was with the suffocating consciousness that there was another living, breathing presence in the room. It struck upon her as vividly as a flood of light. She knew that from somewhere in the dark eyes were upon her. She was as conscious of it as a man may be of the sound of his beating heart, although that may be audible to no ear but his own. At length she made it out — not a shape or any suggestion of a form — it was merely a certain lightening of the utter black near the window and toward the corner of the room. It did not move, but she knew.

Then Patricia was glad, very glad, for there was no fear in her. She was perfectly calm, her hand perfectly steady as she drew out the revolver steadily, softly from beneath the pillow. She had never been so happy in her life, for she knew that she was meeting a test from which the strongest of brave men might have shrunk. She was about to meet the Whisperer face to face.

It must be understood, in order to follow what Patricia did next, that the little table rose almost a foot above the level of the bed. When the lamp on it was lighted, therefore, a thick shadow fell directly on the bed, through the rest of the room, and particularly the ceiling was well lighted. First she flattened herself on the bed — next she trained the revolver on the gray shadow of the corner. Finally she took a match, scratched it, lighted the lamp — and then gripped the revolver hard, her finger on the trigger. All that could have been seen of her, indeed, would have been the first flash of the light on her hand and wrist as she lighted the lamp. Instantly afterward she was lost in the black shadow that swam across the bed in waves, because the unsheltered flame from the lampwick tossed up and down.

But what Patricia saw in the corner of the room, leaping suddenly out of the dark, was the figure of a man in gray clothes, wearing a tall, gray sombrero, with a long white mask across his face, and two dark holes where the eyes must be. She saw his hands; there was no weapon in them.

"Stand perfectly still," said Patricia, "I have you covered with a revolver. I shoot well, and at the first move of your hands I'll press the trigger."

Then came the sound that she had heard Mother Martha describe earlier in the evening, but far more terrible than any description — a voiceless voice — something between a whisper and a moan, ghastly, unnerving. At the sound her arm and hand shook — her very brain reeled.

"I have not come to harm you," said the Whisperer, "I have come only to make you give Saint Gore his freedom. You have only to speak a word, and I shall be gone again. Say it."

"You will only leave in the power of the law," said Patricia. "I have you now . . . I have only to press the trigger. . . ."

"But you cannot," said the Whisperer. "You were cool a moment ago, but now your voice shakes . . . you dare not raise it so that others in the house might hear . . . your hand is growing cold. . . ."

"You lie," said Patricia. "Help! Cousin Joe!"

But even as he had warned her, her voice was only a dry whisper. The hysteria of blind fear seized her at the throat. She knew that in another second he would be complete master — she could feel her strength slipping from her.

He raised an arm and advanced a pace. "I am waiting," he said. "Be brave . . . I have not come to harm you . . . you have only to speak and I will disappear. . . ."

Then she fired.

It seemed as if the Whisperer sat down, shoved abruptly toward a chair, and then he collapsed along the floor.

She leaped from the bed. In the distance she heard many voices — shouts — running steps. Over the prostrate figure she leaned, tore away the mask, and looked into the calm, steady eyes of Goggles. She could not conceive it at first; it was like the miracle that surpasses belief. The revolver clicked on the floor, fallen from her nerveless hand.

"You . . . you . . . you!" she could only stammer.

"I," Goggles said faintly, and smiled up at her. "The game's up, but it was jolly while it lasted."

There came a banging at her door — the shout of Ugly Joe. She leaned, picked up the revolver, and ran to the door, which she set a little ajar and peeked out.

"I can't let you in . . . I'm undressed. I was handling the revolver . . . and it went off . . . I'm not in the least hurt."

"Thank God!" groaned Ugly Joe, and voices behind him echoed heavily: "Thank God!"

She closed the door, barred it again, and ran to Goggles. He had struggled to a half sitting posture, and, as she leaned over him, his eyes widened with a sort of fascinated horror.

"You don't understand," he said. "Open the door . . . call them in. I am the Whisperer."

"Hush!" she said. "Little fool, be still."

She leaned and picked him up. He was hardly heavier than she, and she bore his weight without great difficulty. With her strong young arms, she felt the frailty of the outlaw who the whole mountain desert had feared. For an instant his head lay helpless against her bare shoulder; the nervous right hand that had dealt death once that night hung limply down. She felt the quick, shuddering intake of his breath against her throat.

Only an instant, and then she laid him on her bed. There she tore open his shirt.

"The left side," he said. "You meant well, but the bullet must have glanced . . . on the ribs. A fraction of an inch closer in, and. . . ." He set his teeth with a light click and closed his eyes against the pain.

Then she found the wound. It was bleeding profusely, but she saw at a glance that it was not serious. It had glanced, apparently, from a rib, as he suggested, and had furrowed through the flesh along his side — a grisly painful wound, but not mortal. She ran to her suitcase, ripped a linen shirt into narrow strips, ran back, and made the pack and bandage. She had studied a little of first aid, although she had never before had occasion to make use of it.

He helped her as well as he could, rolling from side to side, although the pain sent the sweat out upon his forehead. When she was finished, he leaned heavily back on the pillows. His face was almost as white as the bedding, and the hand that lay across his breast was marvelously fragile, almost transparent.

"In a moment," he said, "I'll be able to go." He opened his eyes. "But you," he said, "I don't understand . . . why. . . ."

"I don't understand, either," she said. "I don't want to understand . . . I don't want to think . . . except to get you safe and well again."

"And you won't turn me in . . . the Whisperer? Think of the name of it? Think of the fame of it. Think of what it would mean to you."

"Do you really expect me to?" she asked.

"I don't know. I thought I knew . . . a good many things . . . about you . . . and other women . . . but I've been a fool, I guess . . . a great fool. Most men are . . . I guess . . . about women."

"And I, too," she answered. "I've been a great fool, but I think I've found myself in time."

For the conclusion of the story we may as well take the version of Ugly Joe Gregory, as he told it many times in the saloons of Eagles, for every stranger had to hear the story of the last appearance of the Whisperer, and Ugly Joe had the only authentic version.

In ending the story, he always said: "No, I never seen him, but my wife heard his whisper. And while I'm spreading on the talk, I might as well tell you something else damn' near as queer as the things the Whisperer done them three days.

"There was a dude out here . . . a no-account damned dude we called Goggles from his funny glasses. Most of the boys around here remember him. He was a sort of go-between for the Whisperer. And he was the one, maybe, that brought all the hell to poor Tucker and the rest of 'em. He was at the house, you know.

"Well, the dude must have been pretty badly shook up by the bad way Tucker died, because the next day he come down with a fever and stayed in bed off and on about three weeks.

"The funny part was that this girl . . . this Pat I been telling you about . . . got a pile interested in the dude when he was sick. You couldn't pry her away from his bed. Women are queer that way, but she was the queerest of the lot. Day and night she stuck by him like she was his sister. Wouldn't even let Mother Martha, who knew a pile more about nursing than she ever did, help her once in a while.

"Martha, she pretended to be pretty wise about something, but it was all Indian to me. But in the end, well, sir, the dude went back to Eagles, and Pat went with him. And right over there in Widow Morgan's boarding house, in the front parlor downstairs, they was married. Can you beat that? You can't. I'll bet you can't!

"I s'pose she got so used to taking care of the poor dude that she couldn't get along without him. That's the way Martha explained it. Martha was that way herself at one time. She took care of a calf that got cut bad in barbed wire, and afterward she wouldn't never let me sell that calf or market him, but just kept him hangin' around, useless, till he got to be a steer and died of old age. Yep, women are sure fools about some things.

"There was one funnier thing, too, that

come out after Pat married that gent. It seemed that Vincent Saint Gore was only part of his name. The whole of his name was Vincent Saint Gore Howe."

Flaming Fortune

The issue of Street & Smith's *Western Story Magazine* dated February 19, 1927, marked the first and only appearance of "Flaming Fortune". George Owen Baxter was the Faust pen-name under which it was published, as were six other short stories and three serials that year. Additionally 1927 saw the publication of two short stories under Faust's John Frederick byline and five serials and three short stories under the Max Brand byline. "Flaming Fortune" is a wonderful tale of love and greed in which an attempt is made to break the spirit of the hard-working, honest protagonist, Henry Ireton.

I

"A FIGHT FOR PROSPERITY"

When Henry Ireton went courting, he called on the father and the mother of his lady. Henry had always been a dutiful child, and he expected to find nothing but duty in others. So he sat in the parlor and talked to Mr. and Mrs. Corbett Lawes. In the meantime, Rosaline Lawes sat under the fig tree in the yard, admiring the black pattern of the leaf shadows on the moon-silver of the ground, and admiring, also, the handsome bold face of her sweetheart, Oliver Christy. Through the open windows, she and Oliver could hear the heavy voice of the youth her parents preferred.

"I paid five hundred and eighty dollars to the bank, today. That clears all the buildings."

There was an exclamation of pleasure

from Mr. Lawes. "How long has it taken you, Henry?"

"Five years, sir."

"A long time . . . the way you've worked."

"Well, I haven't rested none."

"But I'll bet that the bank was pretty surprised, the way you took hold of things."

"Well, the president had me into his office."

"He did! Why didn't you tell us that right away?"

"It would have sounded like boasting, maybe."

"Oh, not a bit!"

"Well, President van Zandt said that he'd been keeping an eye on me ever since I took over the place, when father died. He said that at that time the ranch was mortgaged for a lot more than it was worth. That the ground was wore out, and everything was falling to pieces, and the rolling stock was broken down. And everything was at wrong ends. He wondered how I had made anything come around right."

"He well might wonder," said the thin, sharp voice of Mrs. Lawes. "I hope you told him, Henry dear, that it wasn't owing to no help that you got from him."

"That wouldn't be just," said Henry Ireton. "The bank could have closed down on me any day. But they let me go along and work the thing out my own way. They never pressed me. A couple of times they let the interest run over a whole six weeks."

"Stuff!" Mrs. Lawes said. "Mighty glad they were to see their investment secured. Go on, Henry. You've no idea how interested I am."

"Me, too," said Corbett Lawes. "Doggone me if it ain't like a fairy tale, what you've done with the old place!"

"Well," said Henry Ireton, "I just explained things to Mister van Zandt. That was all."

"Go on and explain the same things to us. I've never really understood just what you've done to make that ranch come to life."

There was a little pause after this.

"Now listen to him blow, will you?" Oliver Christy chuckled.

"Well," said the girl, "it's better to hear him talk about something than it is not to hear him talk at all. He's always been like a wooden Indian, every other time. Just plain dumb."

"Your old man likes him pretty well?"

"Dad says he's a safe man for any girl to

113

marry, and Ma, she agrees."

"In the beginning," said the heavy voice of young Henry Ireton, "everything was pretty much gone to pot, you know."

"Don't I know, though! The fences was all rotten, and the house and the barns and the sheds was all falling down!" Mr. Lawes announced.

"Yes," broke in Mrs. Lawes, "and I had a peep into the kitchen, and such a place I never seen in my life! There was a hole rusted clean through the bottoms of all those kitchen pans, I do declare."

"There was a hole rusted clean through the bottom of the whole place," said young Ireton with a heart-felt warmth. "It was all gone. Three sacks to the acre was about the best wheat crop we'd have in ten years. The barley wouldn't thrive none. Oats would do no good. Every bit of the tools and the rolling stock had been sold to pay the expenses of Dad's funeral."

There was another brief pause.

"It was really pretty bad for Henry to face a thing like that," Rosaline said, in the shadow of the fig tree.

"It's what he was made for . . . buckling down and pulling the plow. Why, he's *built* more like a plow horse than a man! Ever watch him dancing?"

"No," sighed Rosaline, "but I've danced with him, and that's worse than watching him."

The voice within the house resumed: "Well, I had to work the ground. I mortgaged my soul, sold off the cows, and got together enough money to go around and buy implements at sales all over the country. I got the stuff together and brought it back and patched up the plows and the broken-down wagons and the rakes in my blacksmith shop. I even learned how to fix the insides of a mowing machine if it went wrong. Fact is, I think that I could pretty near make a whole mowing machine, folks, just with crude iron, a forge, and a hammer, with fire to help me out." He said it not boastfully, but seriously, soberly, after the fashion of one who is thinking back to the actual facts and stating them without exaggeration.

There was an exclamation, and then Corbett Lawes said: "I've seen you working in your blacksmith shop. I believe that you could make an *adding* machine there, if you set your mind to it."

"Maybe," serious Henry Ireton agreed, "if I had to. But I'm awfully glad that I don't. Anyway, that winter I got the tools together, and I sold off the three good horses on the place, and got eight ratty things in their place. But those eight rats did the work of eight real horses. I used to rub 'em down by hand, curry 'em deep and hard, feed 'em by hand, too, pretty near. And I made them snake the plow along nearly as good as Charley Crosswitch's big eight!"

"Well, you got the work done, and that was the main thing," said Mr. Lawes.

"Then I put in that potato crop that everybody laughed at so much."

"I remember smiling a bit myself, son. It did look queer to see a potato patch on a real ranch, where nothing but grain had ever been raised as far back as people could remember."

"I know that it looked queer. But it was the raising of the grain that had killed the land. And that was why I put in potatoes, and then sowed alfalfa. After I paid for the alfalfa seed, I was clean broke and didn't have a penny for food."

Another pause.

"Why, lad, how in the world did you live? Borrow more from the bank?"

"Borrow more? The bank would have had me arrested if I'd had the nerve to borrow more money. No, I couldn't borrow. But I had a gun. That old Colt that Dad owned. And there was plenty of powder and lead."

"You mean that you hunted for a living? But you never been any hand for a gun or for hunting, Henry!"

"No, I sure wasn't. But I had to, so I did."

"You didn't have the price of cartridges, though."

"I made my own cartridges at home. There was powder and lead. I've told you that. I nearly blew the gun to bits, toward the start. But I'd already learned how to repair things. And I fixed it up so that it would shoot."

"Well, but what could you get?"

"Squirrels and rabbits, all the year 'round."

"Hold on! Hold on! Squirrels and rabbits . . . with a Colt . . . and you not any practiced shot?"

"I'll tell you, Mister Lawes, when you get hungry enough, you *have* to shoot straight. And I learned quick. Before I had pulled up my belt three notches, I could knock over a squirrel nearly every time if I was within a decent distance of it. Anyway, it was a cheap meat market. And when I learned how to find the rabbits, I had them for a change. So I got through the year.

The alfalfa didn't do well. Not the first year, you remember. But the potatoes, they saved my life. I had the crop ready before anything else was on the market, and I got all the real top-hole, fancy prices. It was wonderful the money that I took out of that ground from the potatoes. That carried me through to the second year and gave me seed money and a little extra money after I'd paid off the interest at the bank. But the first year was the worst. After that, I began to make a little progress."

"Don't skip anything, Henry. We want it all, my boy!" called Lawes.

"Well, then, the second year we had the floods. They washed out a lot of the crops, but they made my alfalfa wonderful, and I cut four crops and got nearly six ton to the acre. The potatoes were good, too. But the alfalfa was the best. If I'd been able to seed the whole place, I would have cleaned out every cent of the whole mortgage, that year, y'understand? But I'd only been able to put in a bit. Well, I got more than twenty dollars an acre, and, as for the expenses, there wasn't many, because I done most of the work myself. That crop was my big boost. It let me pay off the interest, that year, and a slice off the mortgage, and fix up some of the fences, and get some better horses, though I still kept the old broken-down string of eight. I worked 'em hard, but I never broke them down, and, after that, I always had two men working on the place for me. Beans and potatoes and alfalfa was the trick for the third year. The alfalfa and the potatoes didn't amount to much, but the beans did amazingly well.

"The next year, I saw that alfalfa was too big a gamble. But those crops had done what I hoped for. They'd refreshed the soil and put the nitrates back into it . . . the nitrates that fifty years of grain farming had taken out. I learned all about them from a smart college man. So I worked along till the fifth year, and now things are really pretty well fixed. And the mortgage is pared down to a reasonable size."

"Oh, you've wiped it almost out, Henry. It's not as big as it was."

"No, it's about a half of what it was. But as the bank said, the place was away over-mortgaged. But in another three years I'll have it wiped out. Because I've got what I need to work with, now."

"Tell me what you've got, Henry," Mr. Lawes said. "Add up the list."

"I'll tell you, then. Every fence post is sound, and the wire is new. All the sheds is better than new, and the house is rebuilt from the cellar to the garret. And the barns are loaded to the gills with good first-class hay. And the stalls are holding three eight-horse teams not second to none in the county. And I have first-rate rolling stock. Plenty of plows and wagons. The house is furnished all through. And best of all, I've got first-rate credit at the bank. They'll trust me. They believe in me. And that's why, Mister Lawes, I've come over special this morning, to ask you if my marriage with Rosaline could be set right soon."

II

"AN EYE OF RED"

In the darkness beneath the fig tree, Rosaline caught the hand of Oliver Christy and stood bolt upright, with a gasp.

Then they heard the voice of Mr. Lawes, strong and exultant: "Lad, there ain't a man in the county that I'd rather have in the family than you. Furthermore, the day that you marry Rosaline, I'm gonna clear off the remainder of that mortgage!"

"Oh, Oliver!" breathed the girl. "What am I going to do?"

Said the voice of Ireton within: "Thanks. But I don't want no help. I've started this job, and I'm going to bulldog it through. I'd rather. It'll take a few years more, but I want the fun all for myself."

"I understand," said Lawes. "Well, let it be that way. You know that my wife and me have always favored you for Rosaline. There's only one thing that we've set our hearts on . . . to have you get yourself clear of the woods."

"I remember," said Ireton. "You said that if I could ever go to the bank and get another five thousand dollar mortgage, then you'd know that I'd succeeded. Well, sir, I milked Mister van Zandt today. All I have to do is to ride in tomorrow and sign the papers."

"Henry, I congratulate you!"

"Thank you, sir. And what about Rosaline? How does she feel?"

"Leave me to handle Rosaline," said the father. "I've raised her right, and she won't dare to disobey me, no matter what ideas she may have."

Mrs. Lawes put in a little timidly: "Only . . . you think that you could make my girl happy, Henry? You think that you could make her love you?"

There was another little pause.

"That clodhopper," murmured Oliver Christy, beneath the fig tree, and he laughed silently and briefly.

"I'll tell you," Henry Ireton declared, "when I first met her, she was in the third grade, and I was out of school. I set my heart on her then. I ain't a flashy fellow, but I'm tolerable sure and steady. I set my heart on having her, and I'll never stop till I do. Is that straight? Or does it sound like bragging? Well, I never bothered trying to make love to her, because the words for that ain't handy to the tip of my tongue, you see?"

"I see, of course. Still. . . ."

"Well, once I have her, I'll start in winning her by showing her that I love her and that I value her. I think that I'll convince her. I've had lots of dogs, Missus Lawes. I never had one that didn't come to love me."

Rosaline clapped her hands over her ears and bolted away from the tree, and Oliver Christy followed her.

"Hey, Rosie. Don't act like that. You ain't married to the dub yet."

She stood wringing her hands, stamping, very pretty in the moonlight, which made the outer fluff of her yellow hair like a pale mist of fire.

"Then stop him, stop him!" she cried. "Oh, Oliver, if you love me, do something!"

"Well, I'll do something. I tell you, I will."

"Oh, can I trust you?"

"Yes. But if I stop him. . . ."

"Yes, then I'll marry you. I don't care

when. I'll . . . I'll even run away and marry you. I won't care what Father says."

"You promise that?"

"I do!"

"Kiss me, Rosaline."

"I . . . no, but after you've stopped Henry. Then I will, and marry you."

"I'm going to do it."

"But how? How?"

"There are ways of doing everything. I've got to think this here out."

"Then go think now . . . quickly, dear Oliver."

When he was on his horse, Oliver Christy could not help wondering why it was that he felt more like a loser than like one who had been victorious. But he rode up the moon-whitened way with increasingly high spirits until he came to the crossroads. Lights gleamed from the Ireton house, just up the fields. The barns and the sheds of the Ireton place loomed vast and dark before him. From the dust there arose nearby a slender, shadowy figure, and a rusty, croaking voice said: "God bless you, Mister Christy."

"Hello!" Christy shouted, reining his horse aside. "Where the devil did you come from?"

"Not from the devil, Mister Christy," said the beggar, his two canes wobbling back and forth under his weight. "Not from the devil. God keeps some of the poor and the afflicted wandering around this world of His so that the best people can have a chance to show their charity, dear Mister Christy."

Mr. Christy was the smoothest of dancers, and the softest of whisperers in the ears of pretty girls. But among men, he could be as stern as the next one. Now he pointed the butt of his quirt like a gun at the head of the beggar. "Cut out that whining," he remarked. "It don't buy you anything from me. I'll tell you what. A beggar is no more to me than a weed. No more than the tarweed in the field, yonder."

For a puff of wind had brought the pungent, half fragrant odor of the tarweed to their nostrils.

"Tarweed leaves a stain," said the beggar in his broken voice, his rusty, untuned voice. "It stains the cuffs of your trousers and it stains your hands."

"What do you mean by that?"

"Why, Mister Christy, charity is the thing that washes the stains away again."

"You're more than half crazy, old man."

"Not crazy. Only, I see the truth. And the truth always looks like madness to those who don't know it. I tell you, charity is the finest cleanser in the world. It launders things cleaner than soap powder ever could. It takes even a black soul, dear Mister Christy, and makes it as fresh and crisp and white as a best Sunday shirt. Would you believe that?"

"I'd believe," Mr. Christy said, "that you're partly brave and partly a plain old fool. Now get out of my way."

"Oh, dear Mr. Christy," said the beggar, "I wouldn't ask you for much. You see, I never ask for much, and that's why I have to ask so often. Twenty-five cents would make me happy for the night and give me a meal."

"Twenty-five cents? Look here. You go to the poorhouse. That's the place for people like you. Keeps you from being a public nuisance. You hear?"

"Well, I hear you. But I hope that I shall forget what you say. I to the poorhouse?" He shook his ancient head.

"What good are you, then? Tell me that . . . what good are you?"

"Well, sir, I'm around and see things. I tell them when the under-proppings of the bridges are getting rotten and unsafe. I tell them when the fences are getting weak. And I tell them a lot of other things. I watch the whole countryside the way that a mother will watch her household, you understand?"

"Who asks for your watching? Who wants your watching? Have the supervisors of the county ever asked you to take on this sort of work for them? No, they haven't, and, what's more, they never will. Now, you get out of my way, and keep out. I'm going to have a talk with the sheriff, and see if he'll let an old vagabond like you go about being a public nuisance the rest of your life."

He turned the head of his horse and galloped up the road that led past the Ireton house. But when he came still closer, he stopped the horse again. He looked back, but in the moonlight there was no sign of old Tom Elky, the beggar. Perhaps he had crawled back under some culvert to sleep there until the sound of hoofs brought him out to stop some other traveler with his whining voice. Christy was glad that the old man was out of sight. Although why he should be glad, he hardly knew.

Glancing across the glistening field of wheat toward the Ireton house, he could not help shaking his head in wonder. He lighted a cigarette and smoked it with a frown. For he felt that the very outline of that house was, in a manner, a reproach to him. He could remember that, in other days, that outline had been no more than a low, broken-backed hulk shouldering at the sky, hardly to be seen on a rainy night. But in the last year it had risen high and spread out its arms like a dead thing come to life.

Yes, and life was certainly here. On this nearest forty acres, long famous for the poverty of its soil and usually used as a pasture only, Henry Ireton had raised his celebrated crops of potatoes at which the whole county had laughed so heartily. Now that field was put out in potatoes no longer, and such a crop of wheat as stood here Christy had never seen before. He judged that it might run twenty-five sacks to the acre, or even more. The straw was long, and it seemed that they had been packed in by hand, and arranged all at one level. And this crop from the old pasture! The broken-down forty acres!

The whole affair seemed to Oliver Christy like a living miracle. In Henry Ireton, he vaguely sensed a prodigious strength that would go on expanding and expanding. Another two or three years, and all his mortgage would be swept away.

He would be married to lovely Rosaline Lawes, and by that act he would cease to be partly ridiculous and partly horrible. For all of the Iretons had been unsocial, undesirable people — big-limbed, dark-faced people, loving fights, drinking much beer, throwing their money away, and totally inefficient and dangerous members of society. Half a dozen of the line had died with pistol bullets through their bodies, and others had been ended by drink and wild ways. Out of that muck the form of Henry Ireton had risen. A brutally powerful body was his, but a face more open, a forehead more expansive than theirs had been. More mind and less beast — and mind and beast-strength together had built the new big Ireton house and put up those vast barns, where now, some thirty draft horses were housed, all with fine new harness, and pullers of brightly painted wagons, so that the teams of Henry Ireton were showpieces, so to speak, admired by the entire county. There were other silhouettes to take the eye of Christy. He threw away his cigarette and scanned the great humpbacked stacks of straw and the higher stacks of hay.

What, after all, had Oliver Christy to show in all his life that would compare with this achievement? He sighed and bit his lip, and that moment, smelling smoke, he looked downward and saw a growing eye of red opening upon the ground.

The cigarette that he had thrown so carelessly into the dead grass of the roadside.

III

"A CROOKED SHADOW"

He swung down from his horse anxiously and snatched his slicker from behind the saddle. Then he saw that two or three blows would easily put out the blaze, and he rested easier. It would be very odd, he thought, if such a fire should suddenly sweep away the five years of labor that young Ireton had invested in the place. What would Ireton do then? Begin over once more like a slave bending at a wheel?

His laugh was short and fierce, and suddenly he looked over his shoulder and down the road. There was no one in sight — not even the bent form of the beggar. And the wind — it was blowing softly but surely straight toward the house of Ireton. Straight toward five years of slavery and misery and accomplishment.

Oliver Christy, with an oath, flung himself back into the saddle. At the same instant, there was a loud crackling and a long arm of yellow tossed twenty feet into the air beside the fence. Christy, frightened and startled, leaped his horse aside and into the deep ditch that ran along the other side of the road. From that point, only his head and shoulders were visible. He could not be seen, but he could very well watch. Taking out his handkerchief, he mopped the cold beads from his forehead and studied this wave of destruction.

It was hardly a thing to be believed. First the flames ran like a creeping serpent, growing broader at the head, across the strip of short stubble that had been cut in the spring to make a way for the harvester that autumn. The head of the serpent of fire reached the standing ranks of grain, thoroughly dried out and seasoned perfectly by the sun of many weeks. Then there was a distinct crash, as though something had fallen. The flames, exploding upward, cast a wide shower of sparks and flaming bits of wheat stalk as far back as the place where Christy sat his saddle. Then, with the growing wind behind, cuffing them along, the flames raced across the field for the Ireton house, exactly as a sprinter leaps from the mark and then set-tles quickly into a driving stride. Throwing out its arms on both sides and rushing for-ward, the fire threw its head a hundred feet in the air. All the ground over which it hurled itself was left black, covered with slender snakes of dying crimson.

Before the blast, a loud shouting rose from the house of Ireton, and Christy saw forms of men, looking ridiculously small and stripped of strength, come out of the house and rush away toward the barn. He had forgotten the barn and the horses in it. And now even the blood of Oliver Christy curdled. But he set his teeth. Better wipe out the whole thing. For give such a fellow as this Henry Ireton his thirty fine draft horses, only, and he would use them as a seed out of which all of his fortunes would be swiftly rebuilt. Like the hundred-headed Hydra, he would quickly be more formidable than ever.

He saw the mass of fire strike the house like so much volleyed musketry. Windows smashed. Every room was flooded with a living river of fire, and a cloud of smoke shot up above the stricken and doomed house of Ireton. Past the house instantly ran the long arms of the flame. At a stride it reached the barns. A freshly made stack of straw became in an instant a bright crimson pyramided against the night sky. And the whole side of the barn smoked the instant it was touched, and in another instant it was tufted and tasseled with flames. The dwelling house, in the meantime, was belching fire and darkness from every window. The sheds were going up with a roar. Then from the barn Christy heard the human-like scream of a tortured horse.

He had steady nerves, had Oliver Christy. Being an only son of a wealthy man, he had spent most of his life thinking about himself and his personal comfort, but now he found that a new idea was foisted into his mind. He shut it away.

"To him that hath, it shall be given; from him that hath not shall be taken away. . . ." That phrase leaped through his mind, and he smiled grimly. Fire on the ranch of Ireton, fire in his sheds, his haystacks, his house, and fire in the soul of Ireton himself. What would come of it?

The entire side of the barn that faced that way was now writhing red with fire, but he could see the southern face of the building, and through that face men began to break, working fiercely with axes, cleaving a pass out from inside the barn. Now a man struggled out, and led behind him a horse. But the wild confusion outside maddened the poor beast. It reared, turned, and, neighing wildly, ran back into the doomed barn. Another horse was led out, but now the stubble around the barn was a living sheet of flame, and the poor beast could not be saved. All the rest were lost, unless, perhaps, a way could be found through another part of the barn to freedom.

No, it was far too late! All around the barn, sheds and shocks of hay and rubbish were aflame, and now the fire had curled around all four walls of the big building where most of the wealth of Henry Ireton was concentrated.

Mr. Christy had seen enough. It was too bad. He told himself that he was very sorry for poor Ireton, but, after all, is not all fair in love? And he, Oliver Christy, a son of the old and honorable Christy family, had chosen lovely Rosaline Lawes for his wife. What right, therefore, had a clodhopper to come between him and his will? So thought Mr. Christy, and, galloping his horse up the big ditch, he was soon away from danger — danger of being spotted in that neighborhood — and so he came on to his home.

He found that the whole neighborhood

had become alarmed by this time. He himself joined the volunteers rushing to the fire, and he arrived there in time to see the smoldering heaps of ruins of barn, and house, and smoking stacks, with now and then a long hand of fire shooting up from a jumble of wreckage. It made an oddly interesting picture. It made him feel that he had looked at a scene of war. He himself had worked this magnificent destruction!

But, most interesting of all, as he was walking along, his father caught his arm very suddenly and checked him. "Not that way, Oliver," he said. "The poor fellow is there. We mustn't bother him."

It was Henry Ireton, standing with folded arms, viewing the red-hot ashes that remained to him out of five years of hard labor and mighty hopes.

"Has he said anything?" asked Oliver Christy of someone nearby.

"It was a funny thing," he who was asked answered. "When Ireton seen what had happened, he walked around as calm as you please. Telling people not to work, because everything was too far gone. I thought sure that he had everything more than covered by insurance, the way that he was acting. But he didn't. Seems that his thrifty nature didn't want to pay out good hard cash for insurance, and the result of it was that he is cleaned out. He ain't even got timber left to make the fence posts."

"And he made no complaints?"

"Only one. 'I wish that they could have saved the gray gelding,' says Ireton. That was his best near leader, you know. The first good horse that he ever bought, and a jim-dandy, you can bet."

Afterward, Oliver Christy rode slowly home with his father.

"I hope that doesn't break the spirit of young Ireton," said the elder Christy. "That fellow has steel in him, but a disaster like this would take the temper out of the best sort of steel, you know."

"He'll go to the devil," Oliver hissed sharply. "I know that fellow. I knew him long ago. Besides, the bad blood has to break out in him some of these days."

"Do you think so? I used to think so, too. But perhaps he used up all the devil in him, fighting his way through poverty and misery. He put his strength into his plow and his blacksmith's hammer. And perhaps you'll see him starting again. For my part, I intend to advance that boy some money. I have faith in him."

"In Ireton?"

"Yes."

"Why, sir, I think that you'd be throwing your money away. I'd never risk a red cent on people of bad blood."

"Well, perhaps you're right . . . I remember seeing old Champ Ireton run amuck with a pick, one day, and nearly kill three men. I've seen other Iretons go wrong. Perhaps this lad would go the same way, sooner or later. But still . . . what a stroke of bad luck."

"I've heard you say, sir, that the right sort of a man compels the right sort of luck to follow him."

"Well, that's true, too. You seem to have a head on your shoulders tonight, my boy. Perhaps you're getting out of your foolish ways. I wonder, Oliver, if you're actually coming into your manhood at last."

Oliver said nothing, but he could have laughed to himself. After all, it was the first really important act of his life, and what quick results it was bringing to him. For he knew that his father had always looked down at him as a sort of weakling — not weak in the fist or slow with the gun, but weak in heart and character. Now the elder Christy was talking to him as to an equal. To an equal! Perhaps, before long, he would be able to see those rare and wonderful qualities that Oliver Christy had always sensed in himself. It was like the dawning of a new and better life.

They rode into the yard of the house, gave the horses to the Negro stableboy, and, as they were sauntering toward the dwelling, a crooked shadow walked out from beneath the chestnut tree.

"God bless you, Mister Christy, father and son. Is there any charity for an old man, tonight?"

It was old Tom, the beggar, leaning upon his two crutches.

"Here's ten cents," said the elder Christy. "Send the old pest away, my boy."

"Get out!" thundered Oliver Christy.

"Oh, Mister Oliver," the beggar said, "ain't you going to let me talk to you a minute . . . alone . . . about something special . . . important?"

"What?"

"Something, Mister Oliver, that I seen this very night."

IV

"A BEGGAR BARGAINS"

Oliver Christy twitched the quirt between his fingers. He was not one of those who allow a foolishly romantic respect for years to influence him in his actions. Rather, he felt that an old fool was infinitely worse than a young fool and should be treated with an according contempt. But now he hesitated. There was a certain amount of meaning in the words and in the attitude of the old vagrant.

"Go ahead, sir," he said to his father. "I'll see what's on the mind of this old scoundrel."

Mr. Christy went on into his house, and his son remained behind.

"I knew you were an obliging gentleman," said the beggar. "I knew that you'd finally stop and talk with me."

"You knew nothing of the kind," said the other. "As a matter of fact, I haven't three words for you. If you can tell me something of real interest, do it at once. Otherwise, you get this quirt right on your infernal shoulders."

Tom Elky swayed back and forth upon his canes, shaking his head. "Well, well," he said, "I suppose that you would hardly take the time to consider that remark of yours . . . you're so hasty, Mister Christy."

"Look here, Tom, I won't waste time on you. Have you anything to say or not?"

The beggar shrugged his shoulders. "No, sir. I haven't a thing to say."

The quirt whirled up in the hand of the youth. "By fury!" he cried. "I've a great mind to thrash you for your impertinence! But I think that you're a little mad."

"No, sir, not a bit. Besides, speech isn't the best thing in the world."

"What do you mean by that?"

"Speech at the best, sir, is only silver. But you know the old saying, that silence is golden?"

Mr. Christy dropped the hand that held the quirt. "Silence is golden?" he repeated with a snarl. "Silence is golden?"

"Exactly, sir. I knew that you'd understand."

The young rancher remained a moment, stiffly attentive. "Come over here away from the house," he said, and he led the way to a bridge that spanned the creek nearby, a foaming, dashing little stream that poured out its hoarse voice continually in the ear of the ranch house.

"Now tell me what you mean . . . silence about what?" asked Christy.

"I don't like to say, sir, even here."

"You don't? Come, you'll have to talk out . . . to me."

"Well, sir, fires don't start from no cause at all."

Oliver Christy bowed his head a little, and waited. Then he controlled himself and said: "I don't understand what you mean by that."

"I'll tell you then," answered the cripple. "I mean the fire that wiped out young Henry Ireton tonight. Just after you passed that way."

The quirt shuddered under the convulsive grip of the youth. "Now I begin to follow you," he said. "You'd accuse me of that?"

"No accusing, Mister Christy."

"Will you stop whining? We're alone here. Say what's in your mind."

"Well, sir, after you passed, the fire began."

"Tell me this, Tom. Do you think that a single soul in the county would believe that I burned out Henry Ireton?"

"Why, sir, the fact is that I think they would."

"Tell me how you make that out?"

"Why, I'm an observer, sir, as I told you earlier in the evening. . . ."

"Confound you and your observations. What have they to do with the case?"

"I mean, sir, that I pick up trifles that other folks don't pay much attention to. So I've come to know that both you and Henry Ireton like the same girl . . . like her a good deal."

Christy recoiled a little and set his teeth. "But how could Ireton, burned out and penniless, marry her?" Oliver Christy cast a glance at the boiling face of the creek. He cast another glance over his shoulder at the house, and then he made a stealthy, long stride forward. "Come closer, Tom," he said, "and we'll talk this over in a friendly fashion. . . ." He reached out his hand to the shoulder of the cripple. He advanced the other hand, and then stopped convulsively, for old Tom had shifted both his canes into one hand, and with the right he now jerked a short-barreled, old-fashioned Derringer from his coat pocket.

"It don't look much, but it shoots straight, sir," Tom said. "I wouldn't take any chances with it, if I were you."

"You'd murder me?" Oliver Christy cried, springing back.

"If I did, sir, the creek would soon roll your body away. And there'd be nobody the wiser, for a long time. When they were wiser, who would ever think of suspecting poor old Tom Elky? Who in the whole country, sir?"

They remained for a moment staring at each other. There was still a bright moonlight from the western part of the sky, and by that moon they studied one another.

At length, Christy said: "I think that we'd better be amicable, Tom."

"There's nothing that I want more, sir. I can't be hostile to Mister Christy's son. I can't afford to be."

"I understand that."

"Thank you, Mister Oliver."

"You want money."

"I haven't any great expenses, sir, but a man needs something to hold body and soul together."

"Well, tell me what you want?"

"You have a rich father, Mister Oliver."

"My father is rich, but I'm not."

"He trusts you, though. He's very fond

of you. What's his is yours, in the long run, I suppose?"

"As a matter of fact, you're wrong. He's tight as the devil with me."

"Too bad! Too bad! I was going to suggest ten thousand dollars. . . ."

"You old scoundrel! Ten thousand dollars?"

Tom Elky hastened to add: "But I'm not grasping, and now that you've explained the way that things are, I'll cut the claim way down. I'll make it only five thousand."

"Five thousand! You might as well ask for diamonds! How can I get you five thousand?"

"Well, sir, I wouldn't press you for the whole thing at once. I'd just take your note. Payable on demand. That's the way to write it out. Say . . . five hundred down, and the rest payable on demand. That would do very nicely."

"Why, you idiot, that's a small fortune!"

"Very small. Very small to a rich man like you, sir. I know that you handle greater sums than that every month."

"Tom," said the other, "if you turned in my check for that amount, I'd simply be disowned. And there would be an end of me, and of your claim, too."

"Well, sir, perhaps you're right. So you

could make out say ten checks, for five hundred apiece. Then I'd turn them in one at a time. Money lasts me for a long while. You wouldn't be rushed any."

"Oh, Tom, I curse the day that I ever saw your ugly face!"

"I'm very sorry, sir. But a body has to pick up a living. What can an old man do except to stay about and observe matters . . . pick up little things, here and there?"

"You hypocrite! You whining old dog!"

"Six thousand, sir, will be about the right amount."

"You're putting your claim up higher? Let me tell you in plain common sense that I'll give you five hundred dollars, and not a penny more. Not a penny! You can make up your mind to that, or to nothing."

"Sorry, sir. Good night, then." He began to back clumsily away.

Oliver Christy followed, in great anxiety, so that his face glistened in the moonlight with cold moisture as though it were covered with grease.

"Wait a minute, Tom."

"Well, sir?"

"We'll split the difference. We'll call it twenty-five hundred. Heaven knows where I'll get it. But we'll put the sum at that, eh? Be a good fellow and see reason, will you?"

"I've stood here and been insulted . . . called a dog and a scoundrel and a hypocrite," said Tom Elky, "and I don't mind having those names thrown at me, except that, after they've been called, they have to be paid for. I only asked you five thousand, but now the price has gone up to six thousand, and there it sticks."

"Tom, Tom, it'll simply ruin me, and be no good to you. For mercy's sake, give me a chance on this."

"I'm giving you your chance. You've got more than six thousand dollars in the bank, in bonds."

"The devil! How did you know that?"

"An old man has got to go around observing the trifles, and remembering what he sees and what he hears. And putting the information away in his mind. I have shelves and shelves filled with information tucked away in my mind, sir. I ruffle up the whole lot and get out the name of Oliver Christy, and you'd be surprised at what I know about you, sir."

"You've surprised me enough, already. I don't want to know any more. But suppose that my father asks to have a look at those bonds . . . as he does every month or so?"

"Why, sir, you'd have to find a new plan,

I suppose. There are ways for a rich young man to get money."

"Tell me how?"

"Why, you could go to old man Sackstein. He lends money."

"Yes, at twenty percent."

"That's only a fifth. He would give you money, I'm sure. He knows that the whole great estate of Mister Christy will come to you someday. Why, he'd be glad to lend you money, I'm sure. So let me have your notes, Mister Christy."

"Oh," groaned Oliver Christy, "this thing is just beginning to take me by the throat."

V

"A MAN OF RUBBER"

The worse the medicine, the sooner it should it be taken. So thought Oliver Christy, and after he had brooded for a few days, he went straight to the office of Israel Sackstein, the money-lender. In the hands of the beggar, Tom Elky, there were twelve notes for five hundred dollars. To be sure, there was a verbal understanding that Tom Elky was not to present those notes for collection before the lapse of a year. That is, they were not to come in faster than once a month. But, in the meantime, who could tell what freak might take the fancy of the old man? Or who might wheedle the notes away from him and suddenly present them?

It would be ruin. The elder Mr. Christy had stood a great deal from the fancies of his boy. Many a thousand he had spent, and he had declared that he had had enough. Thereafter, if Oliver could not demonstrate that he was capable of acting like a sensible grown-up man, he could get out in the world and shift for himself. That prospect Oliver hated. Not that he was too stupid or too weak to work, but he felt that work would degrade him utterly. Work was for slaves and for slavish spirits, not for masters of men like himself.

There was, more than this, a vein of bitter sternness in the soul of the elder Christy, and if the older man were to learn the nature of the hold that Tom Elky possessed over his son, nothing could prevent Mr. Christy from disowning and disinheriting the boy. Of this, Oliver was shrewdly aware, for all of his life he had made a study of his father — a study that was of infinite value to him in teaching him just how far he could go.

He knew that he was now walking along the dizzy edge of the precipice, and one false step would ruin him. The Christy fortune would go entirely into the hands of charity, and Oliver would be left destitute, with a great number of expensive habits and no means of gratifying them.

He was very irritated by this affair, and he cast the blame upon two people —

Rosaline Lawes and big Henry Ireton. He was very fond of the girl, of course, but certainly he had never contemplated such a danger as this for her sake. To crush Ireton with the butt of a cigarette was a pleasant idea. But to be pauperized for the sake of Rosaline was simply ridiculous.

So, as his bosom swelled, he remembered that for the past year and a half he had been watching himself with a scrupulous care, taking heed that his expenditures should not pass a definite mark. He had gained much in this manner. He had made sure of the inheritance, unless some accursed freak of chance should throw him off the track. In the meantime, there had been the growing hope that the elder Christy would die. He was afflicted with a mortal disease. The doctor had thrice told Oliver that the sad day was rapidly approaching. If only what must happen, would happen soon.

Devoutly Oliver Christy turned up his eyes and breathed forth what was almost the first truly ardent prayer of his life. Let the days of his father end. For what good could the man do now? He had labored, lived, loved, been happy. It was high time that he should step aside and permit a gentleman to take the reins of the fortune in hand.

"The generation which makes the money rarely has the slightest idea how it should be handled," Oliver was fond of saying.

At least, no doubt as to how money should be spent troubled the broad bosom of Oliver. So, on this day, he mounted his best horse and swept off down the road for town. He was in somewhat of a hurry, but he did not mind swinging to the side so as to pass the black face of the ruined farm of big Henry Ireton. For one thing, it had become a sort of gathering place for gossip, for people came from far and near to see the wreckage of the brightly promising farm. A score of insurance representatives had come out to take pictures and hear the story told of all that the farm had been. It was just such a tale as brought them business.

Henry Ireton was ruined, beaten into the ground, and his heart broken. Mr. Oliver Christy was very sure of that, and he was not sorry. The wretched business had cost him so much peril and mental discomfort that it would have been a fine state of affairs if Ireton had not, in fact, been utterly destroyed.

On the way, he met none other than Mr. Lawes, and the heartiness of the latter's greeting was a story in itself.

"Why, Oliver, you haven't been to see us for a long time. What keeps you away?"

Very different from the old days, when Oliver was the unwelcome suitor, and Henry Ireton the favored fellow. Christy smiled to himself. He understood very well what the change meant.

"I'm going to see the remains of poor Ireton's place," he told Mr. Lawes.

"Poor lad," Mr. Lawes said a little shortly. "But, after all, when a young man knows too much to take the advice of his elders, and will go ahead on his way in spite of everything that can be said . . . the punishment be on his own head." He added, looking dourly upward: "The punishment be on his own head!"

"I've often thought that there might be something in that very idea," admitted Oliver Christy.

"There is! There is!" Lawes declared, growing more excited. "Fine a fellow as ever lived . . . but would a man want to trust too much to such a headstrong young chap who is always risking everything on one throw of the dice? I hope not!"

Oliver said pointedly: "Does Missus Lawes agree with you, sir?"

"She does," Lawes said, growing a little red. "She absolutely agrees with me, you may be surprised to know. But there's nothing to keep people from changing their minds when the truth is offered to them, is there?"

But even this was not enough for Oliver. He wanted an unconditional surrender. So he said: "I wonder if you exactly mean that the engagement of Rosie has been broken off?"

"I mean exactly that and nothing else!" declared Lawes. "Why, sir, I shudder when I think of what might have happened, if she'd been committed to the hands of a headlong headstrong man such as Ireton. Besides, he's below her! You realize that?"

It was perfectly obvious that he wished to draw on his roadside companion to commit himself still further. But Oliver merely said: "There's no credit left to him, I suppose?"

"Not a cent's worth!" declared Mr. Lawes. "What happened to him in the bank . . . well, I'll repeat it to you in his own words. He told me about it. I must say that the poor boy is honest. He went to Mister van Zandt, and told him what had happened, and that the face of the farm was swept as bare as his hand, and he wanted to know if Van Zandt would advance him money on a fresh mortgage.

What answer did Van Zandt make, do you think?"

"What was it?"

"He simply said . . . 'My boy, Stonewall Jackson was a good man and a religious man, but, when he found an officer who failed, he didn't much care whether the officer was foolish or simply unlucky. He changed the officer for another. Now, I know that you have worked hard for five years, and you're done very well up to this time. I'm glad to see that you don't want to surrender even now. But, from my point of view, I'm no longer interested. You can't force fortune to change her ways. She has her favorites, and she has those that she doesn't care to favor. You understand me? I don't want to put more money into your hands.' "

"That's rather straight talk," Mr. Oliver Christy commented, "but though I'm sorry for Henry, I can't help agreeing with Mister van Zandt."

"He's a sound man, is Van Zandt," said Lawes. "Very sound. Knows business and knows men. I'm sorry for Ireton, too. Very sorry. I want in the worst way to see him succeed. But I'm afraid that he's nothing but a bulldog. A plain bulldog. And bulldogs can't win the greatest prizes. Not in this world of ours, constituted as it is."

"*Humph!*" said Oliver Christy. "I should say not."

"You'd think that the poor boy would give up, though, wouldn't you?"

"What?" young Christy cried. "Hasn't he?"

"Not a bit. Wait till you see."

Oliver was stricken with amazement — and a sort of perverse fury. Was it possible that this fellow could still win out? Then he added: "Well, perhaps he'll pull through, after all."

"Not a chance in the world, unless he can get a loan of money right away. Not a chance in the world. And who'll loan him money?"

"The same people who would try to carry water in a sieve, I suppose."

"Exactly! You have a penetration, Oliver. I'm glad to see that you understand these matters so well."

"Thank you."

They turned into the last lane.

"Look, Oliver. There's a crowd yonder. What's happened?"

They galloped hastily ahead and found some half dozen buggies gathered along the fence, where men and women going to and from town were staring across the fields of Henry Ireton. Where the black heaps of the house lay there was now a little ragged tent standing, and an open-air fireplace just outside. Farther on, there was a hayrack, a broken-down affair, with some remains of hay in it, at which four rattle-boned horses were eating, and a few bales of hay lay upon the ground. A red-rusted gang plow was not far off, and in the distance was what was left of the black-smith shop, and particularly the anvil and the forge, which had remained intact. More than all that, to show that the place was under control, a fence was being run down on one side of the burned wheat field.

"What in the world is it all about?"

"Don't you see, Oliver? The queer man is going to sink in his teeth and not let go. He's worse off than ever . . . well, really not worse off than he was five years ago. People can hardly believe their eyes. And no wonder. There's no heart in that man, otherwise, it would certainly be broken."

They made hurried inquiries, and soon the story was told, and they discovered that by using patches of credit and money owing, here and there about the country-side, Henry Ireton had managed to get to-gether these horses and the rest that was seen. He was plowing a vegetable patch by the creek bottom now. And he was fencing the burned wheat field, because even half-charred wheat has its value. It will fatten pigs handsomely, and Ireton intended to use it for that purpose.

The man was of rubber. The harder he was floored, the more quickly he bounced back to his feet.

VI

"THE MONEY-LENDERS"

"His luck has run out," Mr. Lawes observed, when his companion at last turned away with him. "And it will never turn back to him. He succeeded for a while. But there's a flaw in the Iretons, as other men have found out before me. A big flaw. They can't win out in the finish."

It cheered Oliver Christy to hear this. He had almost felt that his masterstroke, which had involved him in such difficulties, had been struck in vain. It had given him Rosaline, it seemed. He had only to ask for her, and she was his. But she was not enough. He was not even sure that he wanted her at all. But now, it seemed, public opinion sided with him in downing this man. Disaster had struck down Henry Ireton, and the entire countryside enjoyed the spectacle of his fall. They would not let him rise again, no matter how he might struggle to that end.

So thought honest Oliver.

In the meantime, since the Lawes' place was on the way toward town, he turned in to visit Rosaline. He stayed on the front porch long enough to bask in the bright, welcoming smile of Mrs. Lawes. Then he went off to find Rosaline.

He saw her coming down from the dairy, carrying a bucket, her sleeves rolled up to her elbows. The moment he saw the sun sparkling in her hair and glistening along her round throat, he knew that he wanted her, indeed. Wanted her with all his heart! He hastened to take the bucket of grain and scraps.

"What in the world are you doing, Rosaline?"

"I'm going out to feed the chickens."

"Why, you silly dear, isn't there a hired man to do that for your father?"

"There's a hired man to help my father. There may not always be a hired man to help me."

"What? Am *I* to turn pauper? And have you changed your mind about marrying me?"

"I told a man this morning," Rosaline said, eying him steadily, "that I wouldn't be in a hurry to marry you."

"The deuce you did! Who did you tell, Rosie dear?"

"Henry."

"Henry who? Camden?"

"No. Henry Ireton."

"What the devil? Has that fellow been showing up here to beg for sympathy after he was burned out?"

Rosaline looked deeply into the eye of Christy. "Don't talk like that, Oliver," she said. "I tell you, I've never seen such a man as Henry Ireton was this morning. You would have wondered at him. You would have stopped hating him."

"I don't hate him. I despise the poor clod, and that's all."

"He's not a clod."

"I've heard you call him worse than that a thousand times."

She said illogically: "Father and Mother haven't the least use for him now that he's been broken. At least, now that they think he's broken."

"By my word, Rosie, you've fallen in love with him!"

"No. I don't think so." She became a little pensive, and then went on: "I wish that you'd seen him coming down the path there, Oliver. His tattered old clothes, all baggy at the knees, and his hollow eyes."

"And his grimy whiskers," added Oliver with a sneer.

"He was clean as a whistle," said the girl a little hotly. "You mustn't talk about him like that. He's a man."

Sharp, hot words rose to the tongue of Mr. Christy. But this girl seemed so crystal clear and lovely in his eyes this morning that he could not take chances by opposing her. He listened to what she had to say further.

"He came to talk to me," she went on. "I didn't want to see him. Mother didn't want me to. She met Henry at the gate and told him he mustn't have any more hopes of me. I couldn't afford to wait another five years. That was so brutal! I came out and met him. I told him that I was glad to see him. I wish that you could have heard him talk, Oliver . . . so gently and, yet, so steadily. He said that he was afraid that it was only pity that was working in me. And he said that he would get on without the pity, but that he realized that he had made a great fool of himself in working directly for dollars and thinking that a wife would come on the side, so to speak. And he wanted to know if I could possibly give him a few months, or even a few days to work some sort of a miracle, and come to me again. He wanted to try to work the miracle, and try to make me love him, you see."

"What's so fine about that, Rosaline?"

"You don't think so? Well, I thought so."

"What did you say?"

"That I had never cared about him. That I liked him better that minute better than I'd ever liked him before. And that if I loved him, I'd marry him in five seconds. No matter whether he had five cents or not."

"You didn't mean that!"

"Didn't I? You just bet that I did."

"Rosie, I think that the scoundrel turned your head."

"I don't know. I do know that from that minute I began to think seriously. I always thought that I wanted an easy life. Now I don't know. All at once I knew that I would have to be at least *prepared* for anything. Prepared to marry a pauper."

"But what about me? Have you forgotten your promise to me? If anything stopped your marriage with him?"

"No matter what I promised you, I wouldn't marry you if I didn't love you, dear Oliver. You can always know that, because it's the plain truth. Oh, I wouldn't dream of marrying the best man in the world, no matter how well I had sworn to do it, if I found the day before the marriage that I didn't love him."

"And you definitely don't care a whit for me?"

"No. I didn't say that. I'll tell you, Oliver, that you've always been so handsome, and so much desired at the dances, that I've just taken it for granted that I loved you . . . because all of the other girls mostly did. Don't simper like that and look so silly, Oliver. I'm not saying it to flatter you. I'm just telling you what's been in my mind. If I let you hold my hand, yes . . . and kiss me a few times . . . I don't know whether it was because I cared a lot for you, or just because I thought that it was really the thing to do."

"Tell me one definite thing?"

"If I can."

"Are you engaged to me or not?"

"Most decidedly not. I wouldn't trample on Henry's soul like that. I told him that he could have some time, you know."

Oliver Christy remained staring at the ground and biting his lip. And then he flashed a quick glance up at her. "You're really a great girl, Rosaline. I don't blame you for not wanting to grind him into the dirt. I don't want you to, not for a minute. Let that go. Give me time, Rosie. Will you do that?"

"I will. And . . . I wish that you'd give poor Henry a hand. If he'll let you."

"If he'll let me?" Oliver laughed hollowly and bitterly. "That *is* a bit of a joke, old dear!"

"Well, you go and try it. Tell him that you want your father to arrange a five thousand dollar credit for him. And then see what happens. Because you'll be . . . oh, so terribly surprised, I think. I don't think that he'd take a penny from you. You go and try. Oh, that would be a fine thing for you to try, Oliver dear!"

Her shining face dismissed him. He went off and took his horse and went slowly down the road. He had permitted himself to say one sharp thing to Mrs. Lawes: "I don't think that Rosaline has much time for me, Missus Lawes. She's too busy with the chickens, you know."

That would bring Rosaline a talking-to from her mother who looked a sensible person, to say the least. It might even inspire the authoritative hand of Mr. Lawes, and Oliver grinned a little at the thought.

But, between them, they should be able to bring the silly creature to her senses. Ah! — to be able to listen in at that talk.

He went straight on toward town. Rosaline — and Ireton — and the Lawes — and the destroyed farm became of less and less import to him. He began to think more and more of the greater climax that lay before him. He was to try to get money — lots of money — six thousand dollars in cash. And he was to try to get it from the formidably famous Sackstein. Just how he would persuade the gloomy Sackstein he did not know. But, at least, he was reasonably sure that even Sackstein would hesitate before refusing anything to the son of Christy, the millionaire. The more he dwelt upon the power of his father, the more secure he felt, and so he went into the town with a better nerve, and straight on to the office of Mr. Sackstein.

It was hardly to be called an office. Over the livery stable there were three or four rooms, and there dwelt Mr. Sackstein. There he conducted his business without a secretary, just as he lived without wife or child or servant. Men said that as much as a $100,000 in cash often was held within the capacious arms of Mr. Sackstein's old-fashioned safe. Half a dozen times clever robbers had raided the premises. There they always learned that Mr. Sackstein possessed other old-fashioned articles, notably old-fashioned Colts of a ridiculous date and pattern. However, from his hand the bullets from these guns flew straight to the mark.

At various times, five men had given up their lifeblood upon the naked floors of Mr. Sackstein. Recently it was beginning to be understood, even by the boldest and the greediest, that he who took the Sackstein fortune would probably have to pay down more than even that fortune was worth.

Sackstein never dreamed of a different address. He was known in his place above the livery table. Men traveled 500 miles to come to him and make him strange proposals — for he had an ear for everybody. He was a court of last resort. He was the goal of desperate missions. It was well known that he would risk $50,000 in a cause from which a bank would shrink instantly. Many were the fortunes that he had lost for these wild ventures, these truly lost causes. But many and vaster fortunes he had made in the same manner.

Young Oliver Christy, looking at the battered, sagging door that gave entrance to the stairway, wondered how many lost souls had entered by this means before. Then he pulled the door open, and climbed safely up the steps, until, at the upper landing, he heard a loud voice, its words muffled a bit by distance and intervening partitions — the voice of none other than big Henry Ireton, who it seemed had come, also, to this court of last resort.

VII

"IF THE DEAD RISE!"

A sneer touched the lips of Oliver Christy, and yet there was complacence in his eye, also. For this was the result of his own handicraft, that had brought Ireton to such a pass. Mounting a step or so higher, he could hear all that passed, for the voice of the moneylender was as piercing as a steel drill, and the loud, rumbling of Ireton echoed all through the building.

Those tones were dying away now, and the last that Christy heard was this: "That's the lay of the land. I've been cleaned out and gutted, but that ground is rich. I've fertilized and rotated crops until I've freshened it up. The fifty years of wear and tear it has received have been made up for. I could put in five wheat crops one after another and always get a good yield.

But I don't intend to do that. I tell you, there's a future before that place. All along the creek, there's soil so rich that it will do for truck farming. And with fifteen hundred dollars, I can run a permanent dam across the little creek and hold enough water there through the year to irrigate that low ground. Think what good fresh vegetables would bring in this city where everybody lives out of tins!"

"I don't know," said the money-lender. "Tinned food is the lazy man's habit, and the lazy woman's habit. You can't say how it will change with 'em. Tell me, how many acres have you altogether?"

"Two hundred and eighty-four."

"That's a round bit of land."

"For the truck gardening, there's about forty-five acres of the low ground. That ground is made up of pure river silt. It's so rich that you wouldn't believe it. I can run in some laborers and farm that ground for every kind of vegetable. I'd go halves with them. I give the ground and tools and such. They give the handwork, which is the most important part of the game. We split the profits fifty-fifty. Now, that may not seem very much to you, but I've worked the thing out. I tell you, if I can sell those vegetables at all, every acre of that ground will show at least a thousand dollars in stuff during the course of a year, with any luck at all. Split that thousand two ways. It gives me more than twenty thousand dollars for my share. Twenty thousand dollars a year from that bit of land."

"Not possible," said Sackstein.

"It doesn't sound possible, because you're like the rest of the people around here. You've got your guns sighted for wheat and cattle and such games. But there's other work worthwhile. Nothing looks possible until it's done and finished."

"Just what, in a word, do you want?"

"I want twenty-five thousand dollars from you."

"Twenty-five thousand! How much land?"

"Two hundred and eighty-four acres."

"What's the sale price of that land?"

"With the barns and the house down, and the whole place burned black, I've had an offer of a hundred and fifty dollars an acre for the farm."

"That would be close to forty-five thousand dollars?"

"Yes."

"And what's the mortgage?"

"The mortgage is for thirty-one thousand dollars."

"Let me see. Thirty-one thousand . . . and twenty-five thousand. You want to hold mortgages for fifty-six thousand dollars on land that won't bring you in forty-five thousand dollars at a quick sale!"

"That's what I want."

"For how long do you want the loan?"

"Five years."

"How will you pay?"

"Not a penny of interest the first year. After that, I'll pay you twelve percent for four years. That will give you about ten percent return on your capital."

"You offer me ten percent in a deal where I'm apt to lose the whole capital sum!"

"Put it higher, then. Name your own item, and I'll see if I can stand it."

"I should say, twenty percent."

"You want to double your money in five years?"

"I take a great risk."

"That rate would bleed me to the core," Ireton said after a pause. "It would mean five years of horror for me. Well, I've had five years of horror already, and I'll undertake five years more. Do I get the money?"

"When could you build your dam?"

"Inside of two weeks."

"And get in a crop next spring?"

"No, the fall is coming on late. I'll get in a quick crop of vegetables the minute the water has raised behind the dam. I'll catch the market with some late things and get fancy prices for them. For that matter, if this town won't take the stuff, I can slap it into fast trains and send it express to the nearest city. That would cut down my profits, but still it would leave me a fine margin. I'll raise four crops a year on that land, Sackstein."

"Wait a minute." A chair scraped back.

Oliver Christy snapped his fingers softly and shrugged his shoulders. If Ireton could get money as easily as this, how simple it would be for him, the son of a rich man who was dying. Yet he was irritated. Ireton had been put down once. He would be better pleased to keep the farmer down.

"You want twenty-five thousand dollars?"

"Yes, Sackstein."

"Count that money."

"This is thirty thousand."

"You keep the extra five thousand so that you can live like a man and not like a dog from now on."

Mr. Christy leaned against the wall of the stairway, hardly able to give credence to his senses.

"And sign this note, Ireton."

"Heavens, man," Henry Ireton cried, "you only ask for forty thousand dollars the end of five years . . . and you extend the time at six percent if I am not able to pay then! What do you mean?"

The snarling harsh voice of Sackstein said: "I ain't interested in these deals, Ireton. I ain't a bit interested. I like chances. I like big chances. Chances on men and weather, and dead mines, say. That's the way that I like to venture my money, and make big or lose big. But this deal of yours, it's too small. It's too safe. It's too sure, and I ain't interested."

"But you risk thirty thousand . . . ," began Ireton.

"I don't risk anything," said the other. "I know you. There ain't anything that you couldn't do. If it came to a pinch, I suppose that you could make yourself good weather and turn the hail away. Well, I've followed you. I know you planted potatoes and worked over 'em and got yourself money and elbowroom that way, while the whole county laughed at you. But I didn't laugh, young man. No . . . I knew. And when your place was gutted by the fire, I knew that you wouldn't quit. There isn't any risk for me. Instead of giving my money to a bank to keep for me until something worthwhile turns up to invest in, I give it to you. Within two years, you'll have enough money to pay me back. But don't bother. Keep plugging away, and, by the very end of five years you'll have your house and barns and all rebuilt, and enough to pay me off, and fifty thousand in cash, besides. In the meantime . . . I think I could let you have a little more money, young man, that is, for just one purpose."

"What purpose?" Henry Ireton asked, his voice quite shaken and off key at this singular speech.

"To marry on," said Sackstein.

"What!" cried Ireton. "Marry, when I've been. . . ."

"Burned out? Young man, marry that girl poor. Marry her rich, and she'll keep you rich. Let her work. She wants to work. She needs to work. I know women. You believe what I say." And he added: "I'm putting in another twenty-five hundred. That gives you plenty. You go get married. Go quick!"

"But," Ireton exclaimed, "she wouldn't have me! Her father and her mother. . . ."

"Her father and her mother ain't her," said Sackstein. "You go and try her. Because I know. You go try her and see what's what. As for her father and mother, just let them know that you've raised thirty thousand dollars. That's all."

Henry Ireton was saying: "I want to say. . . ."

"I don't want to hear you!" barked Sackstein. "I'm pleasing myself, not you. I don't often have a chance to put money on a sure thing. Now go back to work. That's where you want to go. Don't wait for nothing, except to pick up the girl on the way. Good bye. Don't talk back to me. Good bye!"

Oliver Christy slipped softly down the stairs and around the corner from the door; he stepped in the shelter of a little group of poplars.

From that covert, he watched big Henry Ireton stride out from the money-lender's door and go off up the street, leaning eagerly forward, like a man walking into the teeth of a heavy wind. There was a sway to the shoulders of Ireton that reminded Oliver of the walking beam of a big steam engine. He watched Ireton out of sight, and then he turned in at the door of the money-lender, once more, and went slowly up the stairs. For he was filled with anxious thought. Not twenty-four hours ago,

Rosaline Lawes had been a person of no importance — just a grade better than the rest of the pretty girls who could dance well. But now she had stepped far higher, by the operation of the law of supply and demand.

There was only one girl, and two men wanted her. Where he had felt himself invincible with women in the past, he was by no means so sure at the present moment. For this fellow had risen from the ground where he should have remained for the rest of his life. He had found generosity in a man whose heart was supposed to be harder than chilled steel. And if a fellow could work such a miracle as that, might he not, also, work another miracle with Rosaline?

Storm clouds, then, were gathering around the head of Oliver Christy. As he climbed those stairs, he wished fervently that the flames that had scoured the fields of Ireton, bare and black, had also consumed the master.

But as the thing turned out, it seemed that the dead could rise from the grave!

VIII

"BURNING VISIONS"

However, while Oliver Christy, in a black frame of mind, climbed the steps toward the office of the money-lender, the happiest man in that county was big Henry Ireton, striding up the street toward the spot where he had left his horse. He had his hands filled with such tools of power as he had never dreamed of before. Ready money! It meant nothing to him for its own sake, but because, with it, he would transform his farm into a garden, a bit of fairyland, covered with greenness and richness and capable of pouring out a glorious tribute every year.

He had asked for $25,000, in the first place, because he had wanted to be able to cut down the size of his demand if necessary. He had imagined the hands of Sackstein thrown into the air, and an exclamation of protest and rage breaking from his lips. But, instead, a sort of divine madness seemed to come upon the man. There were extra thousands, and many of them, in the hands of Henry Ireton.

Well, he would use every penny of that money and turn it into a shining account. In the meanwhile, he could not help glancing upward, now and again, and noting the drifting of the white, massive clouds across the face of heaven. He was filled with gratitude. On this rare day, thoughts of God swept through his mind like the passage of the great clouds through the heavens. He determined, with this vague swelling of his heart, to make his life better, and more and more fruitful.

He passed by a school. A throng of children had poured out for the recess, and their shouting and their tumult were stilled, while many hands pointed toward him. He was the man who had worked so vastly hard and from whom misfortune had stripped away the fruits of labor. So in a silence, awed and reverent, they watched him go past.

A fire came into the hollow eyes of big Ireton. One day those children would have cause to know him better, and to know him without pity. Yes, one day he would be rich. He felt the sinews of money, of power. All was his — granted a little time for him to bring his wider schemes into execution. Then he would build such a school as the town had not even dreamed of. He would give them the best teachers. And he would build them a fine high school, too, where boys, such as he himself had been, could receive an excellent education.

The fire still burned in the eyes of Ireton as he went down the street, although no trace of a smile appeared on his lips. He reached his horse, mounted, and turned toward the bank, and then he paused. In that pause, a new resolution came to him.

So he hurried straight to the bank, and, as he entered the front door, he saw President van Zandt turn hastily away. He knew the meaning of that haste. Van Zandt did not care to meet face to face with the man to whom he had recently refused money.

Up to the cashier's window went Ireton. "Hello, Ransome," he said. "What's my account?"

"Six hundred and twenty-two dollars and sixty-three cents," replied the cashier after a moment.

"Close the account for me, will you?"

As he stood with broad back turned at

the opposite counter beneath the window, writing his check for that sum, Ireton could hear the murmur go up and down the bank. He was a known man, surely. He could have lived all of a most prosperous life and yet not have sunk into the imaginations of people as deeply as he had through this recent calamity. People looked at him with awe, yes, and with a sort of terror, as though he were a man who had known all of the horrors of hell.

Then a stir, a brisk footfall, and the hand of a man on his shoulder.

It was President van Zandt. "Now, my boy, you're not thinking of closing out your account and carrying on without a banker?"

"D'you think that's foolish?" Ireton asked, controlling himself. But he began, as though automatically, to shuffle in his hands the great sheaf of banknotes that Sackstein had so readily entrusted to him.

That rustling, soft noise caught the attentive ear of the banker. He could not help looking down. A look of startled wonder shot across his eyes. He almost forgot what he was saying. "Yes, yes, my boy. If you ask my advice, I must tell you that I think a man has cut off his right hand when he gives up a bank where he is known!"

"What good is it to be known here?" asked Ireton. He allowed his voice to swell a little. "I'm going to John J. Rix and let him handle my money for me."

"Rix!" Van Zandt laughed with a broad sneer.

"Rix ain't a fool," Ireton declared. "He started with nothing. He's got a tidy bank, now, because he knows how to back men. He's growing every year."

"It's a small amount," said the president. "I do hope that you're not going to trust a little bank like that with any considerable sum!"

"Only thirty thousand dollars," Ireton said.

"Thirty . . . good heavens! Where did you . . . ?"

"From Sackstein."

"What! Have you lost your soul?"

"Look here. Does that look like selling my soul? I get thirty thousand for five years. And at the end of that time, I pay back forty thousand."

Van Zandt clasped a hand against his forehead. He could not speak, for the nonce, and now, from every part of the bank, attention had been focused upon them.

When Ireton spoke, all could hear, for he could not lower his voice. It would swell out loudly in spite of himself. It had a powerful hum, like the sound of whirring machinery. "I'll tell you what, Mister van Zandt, I banked with you for five years and did a lot of business through you. I've paid you fat interest and premiums on thousands of dollars. I've never missed an interest day. And I've never begged off. You know that. A few days ago, when I came in, you said that my credit was ace high. Then along came a fire and wiped me out. When I came again, you couldn't see that I was the same man. There was soot on me. You thought that the fire had burned my heart out. But it hadn't. I'm the same man that made the old farm pay, and I'm going to make it pay bigger. But I'll not work through you. Rix is square, and he knows men. *He* gets my account."

Mr. van Zandt was still blinking, and he could only cry out: "My boy, my boy, such a sum, in such a bank . . . why, it's unheard of! Rix only carries a few hundreds at a time . . . the cowpunchers put their paltry little savings with him. And. . . ."

"That's the kind of a fellow I want," said Ireton. "The sort of a man that wouldn't trim the cowpunchers with their little accounts of ten and twenty dollars. As for his being small, he's growing. But you're shrinking. Five years ago you were bigger than you are now. Five years from today, you'll be shrinking still smaller. And one of these days John J. Rix is going to run you out of the banking business, because he knows how to risk his money on men, and not on acres of ground!"

As he strode through the door, he had a feeling that Van Zandt was curling into a corner, very badly sagged, and that there was something like a cheerful smile sparkling behind the eyes of the clerks. Very plainly they had heard some one speak aloud the things that they had been thinking for many years.

Across the street and into the bank of John J. Rix went Ireton. There were two clerks and Rix himself. That was the entire staff. A burly cowpuncher was telling John Rix how he chased a fine band of wild horses across country but could not get their leader — a matchless pacer.

"Is that band still together, Jerry?"

"Yes."

"You're broke, now, and you want me to fix you up for another run?"

"That's what I'd like."

"Well, this time I'll fix you, but you play

to take the wild mares as you run the leader. We'll hope for the leader. But, at any rate, we'll make money on the mares."

"Will you do that, Rix?"

"I will!"

"Man, but you are a square shooter!"

"No, it's just business to me. Have a talk with Mitchell, there, and get it fixed up in detail with him. Hello, Mister Ireton."

"Hello, John Rix. Can I open an account?"

Not a shadow crossed the stern face of Rix. "I'm glad to have you. Gladder to have you than I am to have your money. And I don't suppose that there is much money?"

"Well, not a lot."

"I want you, just the same. You'll raise money for the bank, and, although my resources aren't very big, as you know, I'm going to scrape together what you need."

"You don't know. . . ."

"I do know. You want cash to turn back into that land."

"Hold on, Rix. How would you lend it?"

"Six and a half percent will do for this bank."

Ireton laughed aloud, so great was his joy. This was a man, indeed. "Sit down and tell me what I can expect from you.

Then I'll go away and think it over. And tomorrow I'll make my deposit."

Hours later he left Rix. Burning visions had unrolled before their eyes. He knew that he had at last found a man thewed and sinewed like himself. What could stop them, now?

In the dusk he started to ride out from town, and heard a hail from the side of the road.

"Hello, Henry Ireton! What are these wonderful things that we hear about you?"

Aye, that was Corbett Lawes.

"It's late, Henry," he said. "You better plan on having supper with us as you go on out. Wait a minute . . . I'll telephone to the wife to have things ready for you!" He ran back from his buckboard into the store that he had been leaving.

Ireton stared down the road, smiling faintly. It was not Lawes that he was seeing with his mind's eye. It was Rosaline as she had stood before him earlier in the day. She had not failed him. Rix had not failed. What did fires and follies matter when one could find, in a single day, one real woman and one real man!

IX

"A FINANCIAL SURGEON"

It was long before this hour, of course, that Oliver Christy climbed the stairs to the office of the money-lender. He was received in the usual fashion of Sackstein. That is to say, after he had knocked at the door at the head of the steps, a sharp, bitter voice called: "Who's there?"

"Oliver Christy," he answered.

There was a moment of pause, and then followed several soft clicks that he knew were caused by the moving of the well-oiled bolts. Then the door opened, and before him was an open doorway. He heard a voice saying: "Come in, Mister Christy!"

He strode into a little, dingy room. On the opposite side of it stood Sackstein, a tall, stooping man. He was so broken by age, or by sickness, that his bent attitude gave one continually an impression that he was lost in contemplation. But he was never lost. His keen wits were perpetually working, as Olive Christy well knew. More than once desperate fellows had gained access to this chamber and had attempted to shoot down the old man while pretending to talk business matters over with him. But not one succeeded. The reason lay on the table before Sackstein in the form of two heavy revolvers, not of the latest model, but of an undoubted accuracy and ready condition. You might say that these were the only friends and protectors that Sackstein had in the world. But there could hardly have been any man who wished for less protection and friendship than he. Twice a week a woman came to the rooms and cleaned them thoroughly under the keen eye of the master of the place, and it was said that his entire stock of information concerning the outside world was gained from these visits. An adroit questioner can learn much from even the humblest source.

But it was certain that nothing could induce Sackstein to leave his chambers. There he remained and watched the world from afar — and never missed a significant detail that might affect his own affairs. Up and down through the mountains men ventured on expeditions in which thousands of his money were committed to the hazard. Still he remained behind in the dingy little rooms, and let fortune take care of her own.

Now he said to Oliver Christy: "I first have to ask every man to close that door."

Oliver closed the door.

"And then to sit here."

Oliver took the chair, but since he was facing rather sharply toward the brightness of the window, he strove to hitch it back into the shadow, but found that it was fastened to the floor. He had to remain where he was, partly blinded by the light, and awkwardly uncomfortable before the keen glance of the money-lender. No doubt that was a contrivance on the part of Sackstein that had been carefully thought out before.

"Now," said Sackstein, "what brings you here?"

"Money," said Oliver Christy. "I've come for money, of course."

He could not help speaking rather sharply — it was such a foolish question. As though anything under heaven, except money, could have dragged him to such a house as this.

"You've come for money," said Sackstein.

"Well, well, well! And yet I suppose that you have a good deal from your father every year?"

"We are not speaking of that," said Oliver. "The point is that I wish to have money from you. Six thousand dollars."

"That is the point, of course," said Sackstein, "but at the same time one wishes to know. There are ways of throwing money away. Money is my lifeblood. You ask me for six thousand drops of it. Then you are angry when I ask you why you should need that blood . . . you who have so much of it! For your father is a rich man. Quite a rich man. Quite a rich man!"

"Yes, a little more than 'quite', I presume," Oliver stated, more irritated than before. "I suppose that he's about the richest man in the county."

"In the county? Ah, no, no!" said Sackstein. "By no means as rich as all that."

"Are you sure?"

"Quite."

"That he's not the very richest man in the county?"

"Quite."

Oliver slumped indignantly back in his chair. "I'd like to know who is, then," he said.

"I wouldn't tell you that," Sackstein said impolitely. "But I would name a few who are richer. There's Samuel H. Chandler. He's richer."

"That old scamp?"

"He has just above a million dollars."

"What? My father is worth five or six times that amount!"

"Your father, young man, is worth a shade over six hundred thousand dollars. That is to say, he's worth that much if some of his present investments turn out fairly well. It's a mistake for elderly men to invest too much. Men who are past a certain age, and who are invalids."

Beads of cold moisture stood out on the forehead of Oliver, and his eyes thrust almost from his head. This was a dreadful shock to him. "You've no way of knowing," he gasped.

"I have, though. I never make mistakes about such things. Money is just hard, dirty stuff to you. To me, it is the air I breathe, the food I eat, the drink I taste. So I know all about the money affairs of our neighborhood."

"If you did," said the boy, "you wouldn't tell what you know to me. Not unless you had some distinct purpose. . . ."

"I tell you," said the other gravely, "because your father has not more than ten days to live."

"Ten days!" Oliver gasped, standing transfixed beside his chair. "Ten days! But the doctor said. . . ."

"The doctor is a kind man. He lied a little. More than a little."

"But why should he lie?"

"You will see, after a while. But now tell me . . . knowing your father is to die within ten days, do you still wish to get money from me?"

Somehow, one could not doubt the exactness of the information that this man claimed to have. He spoke with a resolute certainty. There was a ring of iron knowledge in his tones. He could not be wrong.

But before ten days passed, long before, he would have to reckon with the first of the notes of the beggar. Yes, the entire lot might be presented at the bank, and then what would happen? One glance at them would ruin him with his father — cut him out from the old man's will. There were only ten days to wait. No matter if the size of the estate were so vastly reduced from his great expectations. Still, there was over half a million, and that would take a good deal of spending. What was six thousand, then, to him, who would inherit so much in a day or so?

"Yes, yes," he said aloud. "I need the money. I'll have to take six thousand dollars at once."

"Six thousand dollars is a great deal of money," said the other.

"Come, come! I happen to know that you've just given thirty thousand dollars to that pauper, that burned-out rat of a fellow . . . Henry Ireton!"

Sackstein whistled. "So, so, so," he said. "You don't like poor Henry Ireton?"

"I? I never think about him. It's not a matter of likes."

"Well, he is a great young man," said Sackstein. "But to provide for him, I had to strip myself. It left me very little, and very soon I expect great demands."

"I know that this is the sort of nonsense that most money-lenders talk."

"You have heard others, I suppose?" Sackstein said.

"Well? Will you talk sense to me?"

"I try to talk sense. I try to tell you that a while ago money was cheap, but now there is a premium on it."

"No! You mean to say that a few minutes ago you were willing to give to Ireton. But now you see a chance of trimming a customer, and so you want to hold me up!"

"Tush, tush. You talk very violently, young man."

"Well, be brief. Tell me what I must sign. I want six thousand at once."

"I prepare the paper . . . at once." He took a blank note from the table drawer and scratched a few words of the statement in a hand that accomplished much with little trouble. "There it is," he said.

Mr. Oliver Christy found himself staring down in bewildered lack of understanding. "Man," he said, "do you realize that for six thousand dollars in hand, you demand twenty-five thousand dollars in three months?"

"That is what I have written down," Sackstein agreed, and he met the enraged stare of Christy with an unfaltering eye.

"Twenty-five thousand damnations!" Oliver cried, leaping to his feet. "Do you mean that . . . ?"

"Hush," said the other. "Hush. I hate loud talk."

There was so much iron of determination and contempt commingled in his voice that Christy suddenly saw in amazement that Sackstein meant exactly what he demanded. Four hundred percent for a three months' loan! It was a usury too dreadful to believe.

"Only tell me," Oliver said, trembling with fury, "what has made you ask such outrageous terms?"

"Because I thought I could get them, and I still think so," Sackstein declared. "You have to pay me for the insolence with which you entered this office, the scorn with which you stared at my poor room, with the disgust with which you eyed me . . . and above all, you have to pay for your self-certainty, and for your knowledge of how I treated the burned rat . . . as you called Ireton. You have to pay for most things. But then, you can afford to. What are a few thousands to a rich-blooded fellow like you, with half a million in hand? Besides, the need is very great . . . the need is very great. I am a financial surgeon. I am only called in on rare emergencies. And then I am at liberty to charge a round fee to a rich patient." He added the last words with a sneer, and looked so coldly in the face of Oliver Christy that the latter winced.

"Give me the money," he said, "but if there were any other place where I could get it, I wouldn't be here, Sackstein. Perhaps someday I shall be able to take revenge on you."

X

"BEGGAR'S PHILOSOPHY"

From the office of Sackstein, Oliver Christy came forth in a grim humor. However, once he had paid such enormous price he might as well turn his money to the best advantage. And that was to find Elky and pay off the blackmail as soon as possible. Someone was always sure to know where the old fellow could be met. Now it seemed that he was last observed on the road out of town, wandering toward the old dead town of Sandy Gulch. In that direction, accordingly, rode Oliver Christy, and at a brisk pace.

He was a full three miles from the town when a stumble of his mare brought her down on her knees and sent Christy flying over her head. But he fell without breaking a bone, and, springing up again, he ran back to her and found her well enough.

She had not even skinned her knees, and the cause of the trouble was, apparently, that her off foreshoe had wedged neatly between two rocks. For, when he examined that hoof, he found that the outside of the shoe had snapped squarely off for almost an inch from the point. He mounted and went on again more slowly, thanking heaven that his neck had not been broken in the fall.

His spirits rose, after a time. There had been enough discouraging events within the last few days, but in the sea of troubles there was one spark of encouragement, and that was that his father had not ten days to live. How the old money-lender could know was certainly beyond the comprehension of Oliver, but it did not enter his mind for a moment to doubt the prescience of Sackstein. Such a man as he simply could not afford to make mistakes. A moment later, sighting the wavering form of the cripple before him, he called out in a tone of positive cheerfulness.

Tom Elky turned and regarded the rider with some doubt in his mind. He shifted both his canes into the left hand, leaving the right hand free. What that movement meant, Oliver Christy could not help understanding. He had seen the blunt-nosed weapon produced before. But he had no intention now of attacking the old fellow.

"Tell me, Tom," he said as he came up, "what is the reason a man can forgive another man after he's been wronged by him? Because I feel that I could almost forgive you, Tom."

"Mostly it's that way," said the beggar. "I'll tell you why. The people we hate are the ones that we have wronged. We hate them because we know that they have a right to hate us. They've seen the devil in us, and therefore we loathe them. But if a man harms you, on the other hand, you're apt to respect him. You may be hot against him, but, at the same time, you cannot help feeling his strength. You'd be glad of his friendship."

"You're a philosopher," Oliver announced, smiling in spite of himself. "You're a philosopher as well as a beggar and blackmailer. Is that it?"

Tom Elky merely smiled. "You've got some sort of a message for me, I suppose," he said.

"I've come to make you a proposal."

"Well, sir, I'll listen to it."

"You have notes of mine for six thousand dollars."

"And I'm a sad man that I had to ask for them."

"I know how sorry you are. But tell me . . . will you do a stroke of business for yourself and sell me those notes at a price?"

"What sort of a price, sir? Suppose that I turned those notes in at the bank? They'd be pretty sure to honor them."

"Not a penny of them! I haven't an account big enough to feed a sparrow."

"Well, well," murmured Tom Elky. "But your father . . . what do you propose, sir? And where is that first five hundred that you promised to me?"

"This is not the day that I promised it to you. But today I could show you something better. I'll compromise with you. For three thousand dollars cash, give me those notes."

"What? Fifty percent of the whole thing?" The cripple laughed excitedly.

"Why not? Three thousand dollars is a fortune."

"Not half as big a fortune as six thousand, sir. No, not for three thousand."

"Well, I'll strain myself and make it thirty-five hundred."

"I'll tell you what I'll do," Tom Elky bargained, "and that's this . . . I'll take five thousand dollars cash from you on the spot. And then I'll give you the notes."

"Five thousand!" shouted the youth. "Five thousand dollars?"

"Yes."

"Not a penny more than four thousand."

"You're not talking to me, then, Mister Christy."

"Hold on, Elky. I can barely manage forty-five hundred. How is that?"

"Why, sir, I'll make it a gentleman's agreement at that figure, if you can't afford to live up to the terms of your contract with me. Have you got the money?"

"Have you got the notes?"

"Here, sir."

"Let me see them."

"I'd rather see your money, Mister Christy."

"You old, doubting scoundrel. Here it is, then."

"Thank you, sir. I'm very glad of that. Thank you very kindly, sir."

He took the money and passed over the notes, and young Christy touched a match to them and watched them burn.

Afterward, he regarded the old man with a snarling look of dislike. "That money has cost me something," he said, "and I may as well tell you, Tom, that I had the other fifteen hundred here ready to pay you for the notes, if I'd had to. I'm fifteen hundred in on the deal."

"Maybe the forty-five hundred will last me out my time," Tom Elky said with perfect good nature. "I'm not a man to mind a sharp bargain, because I've had to drive some on my own account in the past . . . as you may remember, sir."

"I remember," Christy assured Elky. "I was a fool that night. But I'll never be such a fool again. And it may very well be, Elky, that one of these days you'll run out of coin and remember the old story and come trying for blackmail once more. I warn you now that you'll be risking your wretched head if you do."

"I know that, sir. No, I've played my hand for what it was worth, I suppose. Now I'll have to rest content. And, after all, you'll have to agree that forty-five hundred dollars for the observations of just one night . . . that's not so very bad, sir?"

"You old devil!"

"No hard names, sir. By the way, I think your horse has a broken shoe, by the marks."

"Never mind that," said Christy. "But see that you remember what I told you about blackmail. You caught me the first night and troubled me a little when I was nervous. But that will never happen again."

"All right, all right," said Elky. "I've forgotten all about the Ireton fire. And I suppose that the rest of the people will, too, before long. They say that he's got big backing, and that he's going to be able to open up in grander style than ever. They say that in the very first five years he'll be able to strike out wider than before."

"Do you believe that, Elky?"

"Why, a man could believe anything about a fine young fellow like Ireton. He's proved what there is in him."

"Bah! I'm sick of the talk about him. Suppose that he slips once more. Could he get backing for a third time?"

"If he slipped once more?" Tom Elky, repeating the words, shuddered a little and shook his head.

"What's the matter?" Christy asked.

"Why, if Ireton slipped once more and lost everything the way that he did in the fire . . . if that happened, why, he would never do another lick of work."

"He'd sit down and mourn, eh? Break the heart of the puppy, would it?"

"Break his heart? No, it would start him breaking the hearts of others. If Henry Ireton is ever put down again . . . why, the gent that puts him down had better have the wings of a bird, because unless Ireton is killed, he'll run amuck. I know his nature. If he's checked again, the world will pay for it."

"You think he would go bad?"

"Let me tell you something," said the cripple. "When his supply of chuck was low, he used to kill squirrels. And you know what he used to kill them with?"

"Well?"

"With an old Colt."

"I've heard that yarn."

"You don't believe it?"

"Not a word."

Tom Elky shuddered with a sort of uncanny pleasure, and then he murmured: "I didn't want to believe, either. But then I saw with my own eyes. Just the heads, Mister Christy, just chipping off their heads. A bullet apiece, very neat, and never anything wasted. He says to me . . . 'If only I had a smaller gun, I could save money. Ammunition for a revolver is too expensive to waste on squirrels, Elky.' That was what he said to me. I remember the day well. And him with three days' whiskers on his face, standing behind his forge and whanging a big bar of iron with his hammer. He has a grand right arm. He could make a fortune in the prize ring, if he missed out farming. But no . . . let him fail once more, and he'll take a short cut to fortune with a gun in his hand."

"You're fairly sure of that, it seems to me."

"Oh, I'm fairly sure, well enough."

"Perhaps he'll have a chance, one of these days. Good bye, Tom."

"Good bye, sir. And remember what I said."

"What's that?"

"We hate the men we've wronged, not those that have wronged us."

Oliver Christy turned in the saddle and regarded the grinning old man for a thoughtful moment. Then he rode on. He was beginning to turn a new series of thoughts through his mind, and they were not unpleasant thoughts — so little unpleasant that, in riding, he could not help whistling a little again.

He took the way toward the house of Lawes, for the day was wearing late, and in that house there was always a welcome waiting for him.

XI

"STAGED BY THE DEVIL"

That the devil had taken charge of the life of young Oliver Christy will be more than apparent before we have proceeded much further in the course of this history. For all that Oliver accomplished can hardly be placed against him too directly. There were other affairs to be taken into consideration. Perhaps he was too sorely tempted to resist. For, as he jogged his horse through the shadow of the trees before the house of Mr. Lawes, he did not have to enter the place in order to see what was happening.

A big lamp cast a broad glow over the porch of the house, and on that porch sat Mr. and Mrs. Lawes, and their daughter Rosaline, and with them was none other than big Henry Ireton. The center of the group was indubitably Henry. He talked, with few gestures, but with an earnest rumbling in his voice that rolled out to the roadway and hummed like the sound of hornets in the distempered ears of Oliver Christy. For Mr. and Mrs. Lawes to hang upon the words of that young man seemed bad enough, but worst of all was Rosaline Lawes in person — a shameless and abandoned baggage!

For she leaned a round arm on the back of Henry's chair, and peered over his shoulder, now and then, at the design that he was sketching on a piece of paper that he held. Not many glances for his sketch. Most of the time her head was raised toward her parents, as though she already knew exactly what Ireton was saying, and all his plans.

Oliver Christy sat his horse in the dusk of the trees that shadowed the road and cursed the sight, and cursed the girl, and, above all, he cursed the man who was the central figure of that scene. The girl, perhaps, could be said merely to err. But Henry Ireton was a manifest villain. In what the villainy of Ireton consisted, Oliver Christy did not pause to seek. The fact was that his heart was so tormented by overwhelming jealousy that there was a mist before his eyes. He knew that he hated

Ireton. He knew that he wanted to rub out the farmer as a boy rubs out a word on a blackboard. Let no trace be left. But, on the other hand, it would be no easy trick to rub out Henry Ireton. There was enough blood and bone in him to make annihilation a difficult job.

So great was the ache in the heart of Oliver Christy, that for a moment he thought of snatching out a Colt and trying a bullet for the head of Ireton, and it was no sudden compunction of conscience that stopped him. Rather, it was a knowledge that all his muscles were twitching and his body shaken so from head to foot that no gun could be fired accurately from his hand at that moment. So he remained staring hungrily. The beauty of the girl fascinated him because of the very indistinctness on account of the distance. She was not herself, but was all that he had ever hoped or dreamed she might be. She was not Rosaline Lawes. She was simply "beauty of woman". Then she laughed, and the sound made him almost cry aloud.

He turned the head of his horse and rode carefully away, praying that his presence so nearby should never be detected. And, as he swung into the long, twisting lane that started toward the house of his father a scant mile from that spot, the devil who was so apparently managing this affair from beginning to end plunged him into a brand new adventure.

There was a clatter of hoofs behind him, and three riders swept up.

"Hello, stranger. Is this here the way to the Christy house?" called the foremost.

"Yes, and I'm Oliver Christy."

"If that's your name, shove up your hands. I want to talk to you." The stranger then added slowly: "And I dunno that you'll need your hands for your answers. You being an educated man, you don't need gestures."

"Good," Oliver Christy said, nodding at them. "I see you fellows know your business. What do you want of me?" He lifted his hands above his head without any sensation of nervousness or of great anger. Rather, this affair was a soothing thing to him. Compared with the vast irritation of his heart, this hold-up was as nothing whatever.

"You've got six thousand dollars with you," said the spokesman, while the other pair circled rapidly behind Oliver. "You've got six thousand. Now let us know where you carry your wallet, and, when we have the coin, we'll turn you loose and ask you no questions."

Oliver Christy merely laughed.

"You won't tell us?" This came in a more threatening tone.

"Three quarters of that six thousand is gone already."

"What are you kidding us about that for? Where could you have spent that money this side of town?"

"Well, there's my wallet in my inside coat pocket . . . no, on the other side. You count what's in that wallet. Then tell me if I lied to you."

The wallet was snatched out, and the leader growled: "Keep a gun on this bird. He ain't as mild as he talks. I know him." He began counting the money that he had found and cursing between the hundreds. "It's an outrage," he said. "There ain't more than enough to wet the throat of the three of us, boys, because he's told the truth."

"Unless there's some more money hiding about him," another of the trio said.

"He ain't that kind of a crook," replied the leader. "No, there's no danger that he's got more stuff around him. Fifteen hundred! And we expected enough to get us to. . . ." He was checked by a warning word from one of the others.

"What do we do with the big boy now?"

"Aye, what do we do with him?" was echoed by the third.

"There's the roar of the creek, not far off," responded the leader.

The blood of Oliver Christy stopped in full current for the moment, but then he saw the leader shake his head violently.

"Killing before, that ain't so bad," said the leader. "It's got to be done, sometimes. But killing afterward . . . why, that's murder. An' I won't be no murderer. No, sir, I'm gonna keep my hands white."

"I wish," said another, "that we could send to the devil the bird that gave us this bum tip."

"It ain't so bad," said the leader. "We've got something to travel on now. And we'll need it. But I wish that we could take a crack at something really big . . . that's my wish, friend. Christy, if we turn you loose, will you not try to trail us?"

"Boys," said Christy, "there are three pretty good men here. And it's a shame that so much nerve has to be wasted."

The leader chuckled softly. "You ain't grieving one half so much as me and the rest," he said, "and if you know of any little jobs around this part of the world that we could fit our hands to. . . ."

"Not so big as that," Oliver stated, his

idea growing fiercely in him.

"How small?"

"Well, there's only one man."

"One? That's neat! How much of a man?"

"He's got an old, rusty Colt. That's the only sign of a gun on his place."

"Aye," said the leader, "this sounds sweet. I take it that there's some gent that you ain't very fond of, Christy?"

"Yes, that's about it."

"What's his name?"

"Never mind his name. You're new to this country?"

"Yes, I'm new to it."

"All of you?"

"Every last one of us."

"Suppose that I take you to thirty thousand dollars in hard cash, my boy?"

"Thirty . . . ten thousand apiece? Why, old son, that would be about man-size for us."

"Hold on," put in a member of the crew, "we don't hold out on a partner, do we?"

"I was talking like a swine," said the leader. "No. We don't hold out. Why you should need money, heaven knows, your old man being as rich as they say he is. But you're due for your quarter of the loot if you put us onto it."

"I don't want the money," said Oliver.

"That's what they all say . . . mostly . . . till they see the coin. And then they change their tune. But where's the lay?"

"The first lane," Christy explained, "there on the right, and then straight onto a main road, where you turn right as far as a broken-backed barn on the left side of the road. . . ."

"Big boy," cut in one of the trio, "showing is better than telling. That's what the teacher used to say when I was a kid. Who is the gent you're sending us after?"

"Never mind his name. You want money, don't you? Or do you want the dope to write a newspaper article about it?" So the leader silenced his too officious follower. "Mister Christy, we'd take it mighty kind if you would show us the way," he went on.

All of this time, Oliver Christy was meditating profoundly. The devil had placed these tools at his service. He would be worse than a fool if he failed to use them.

"Follow me, then," he said.

"Wait a minute, old-timer. You get back the wallet and what was in it, first."

"Thank you."

"And if this deal works, we'll call you the whitest man that we ever met up with."

A white man! Even Christy had to

shudder a little as he listened. But presently he touched his horse with the spurs and set off at a round pace. The three followed, and with a dust cloud whirling up behind them and turning the lower horizon stars dim, they galloped down the lane that he had first pointed out, turned onto the broad main road, and sped on through the night until they saw before them the broken-backed barn.

Now they were close, and Oliver drew rein. "You go on into the field beyond this one," he commenced, "and wait till. . . ."

"Hold on, big boy. That's too thin. We go over there alone, and, while we wait, you round up some other friends . . . no, we don't doubt you none, but still we ain't fools. You see our reason?"

"I see your reason," said Oliver, "and I'll go with you and see the whole thing through. Why not?"

XII

"THREE AGAINST ONE"

There are some who say that to conceive is really the same as to plan, and to plan is, vitally, the same as to act. But the advocates of such an idea should have stepped into the heart of Oliver Christy for a moment as he strode across the fields with two of his new companions.

As for the remaining of the trio, he had been left with the horses, because it was always well, in such affairs, to have the means of retreat well secured. Surely three of them, striking by surprise, should be enough to master a single man. For this reason, as the fourth and youngest member of the party remained behind, the three of them went across the fields. The horses were concealed in the shadows of a dry slough. That left them means of retreat near at hand, and at the same time invisible.

The big body of Oliver Christy fairly trembled with delight as the time for action approached. All the other matters of his life seemed nothing whatever. Yet it seemed to him rather strange that he who had sent that field up in smoke — partly by accident — should now be lying in wait in the blackened stubble of his own making and striving to destroy the owner of the field in a new way.

He said: "I'll tell you this. The man that we're waiting for is not such a giant. Not any larger than I am, as a matter of fact. But he's a regular Hercules. Naturally strong, and he's made himself stronger all his days by hard work. Besides that, he's a very good shot."

"What might you mean by that?" asked one of the three. "Will you tell me what you might mean? Some gents can shoot pretty straight at a target . . . rifle or revolver. Some are only good with a rifle. Some can hit a target, but not game. And I've known lots of bang-up hunters that was no good at all when it came to a flurry with other men. What sort of a shot is this here friend of yours that we're laying for?"

"I only know this," Christy advised,

"that, when he was low in funds, he used to get his fodder by shooting off the heads of squirrels."

"Hello! That's pretty rare! But I've managed it myself, now and then, with a good rifle that I had. Not often, but I got them now and then, the tricky little devils."

"With a rifle, yes," Christy agreed. "But this fellow was using a revolver."

"What?"

"An old-fashioned revolver that most men couldn't work at all."

This statement was followed by silence for a moment, after which the leader said: "You know that this here yarn is the facts?"

"I know it," said Christy. "I never saw him do it. But I've heard him say what he did, and he isn't the kind of a fellow who would lie."

"Look here," said the leader of the crew, "you have been mentioning a gent that has thirty thousand dollars, and that lives here in that tent in the midst of this burned-down house and sheds and haystacks, and all that. Tell me . . . does he own the land?"

"What's that to you?"

"Questions don't do any harm, but what I was chiefly thinking was that you've been telling us about a gent that was a hard worker . . . strong, and steady with a gun . . . and what's wrong with him, I would like to know? Because I never have hankered to get on the wrong side of a decent gent."

"You never have?"

"No."

"Then get out of here," Christy declared savagely. "I'll take on this job by myself, because I think that I could use thirty thousand dollars." He added after an instant: "Don't start whispering with yourselves, and don't try dirty work, my friends. I have a pair of guns with me, as I don't mind telling you. And I know how to use them, and use them fast. Now put that in your pipe and smoke it. You stay here and work with me and stop asking your asinine questions, or else you cut loose from here and leave me alone. I don't care which."

This stern statement reduced the others to a moment's silence, after which the leader said calmly: "You're a rough bird, I see. Well, I don't mind roughness when I'm making a fair share of money out of it. I don't take lip, but I don't think that you mean this for lip. It's just your way of expressing yourself, I suppose. But look here, *amigo*. You get away with this, just now, but don't try that line of talk again. The bigger they are the harder they fall is my motto."

This, in turn, brought no rejoinder from Oliver Christy. He was, in fact, a little ashamed of his outbreak, and yet, in the speaking, never had words been sweeter on the tongue than these. All the violence in them did not offend, but rather delighted him, and, as he spoke them, he had thrilled and filled with a grim determination to be at least as bad as his threat.

"Hush!" said the third man. "Do be steady. There's someone coming."

Down the road passed the beating of hoofs, and then through the gate into the field came a single rider, who dismounted at the little tent. They watched his outline as he tethered his horse.

"Now," said Oliver Christy. For a savage wave of emotion had risen in him, and he wanted to close on his victim that instant.

"Wait!" the chief cautioned. "Wait, man. There'll be a better time in a moment."

But he strove in vain to hold Oliver Christy down. They had tied handkerchiefs over their faces, and now, as they rose, the three white spots were visible for some distance.

Yet that was no advantage to Henry Ireton. He had turned his back in the act of carrying his saddle toward the tent, and the first he knew of danger was the hard-jabbed muzzle of Christy's revolver poked into the small of his back, while the hoarse, shaken voice of Christy bade him put up his hands.

Up went his arms mechanically — and then jerked almost down again as he remembered the vast prize in cash that he was carrying — and his hope for victory in his labors as well.

"Don't do that again, bo," cautioned the leader. "Go soft and easy, kid. Otherwise, I'll blow you to bits. We're playing this game for something more'n pin money."

"Very good," Ireton said. "I understand. You've beaten me. It's in the belt." He spoke so quietly that one might have thought his heart was not breaking.

Christy ripped the belt away from his victim, and opened it. It was fairly jammed, in the money compartment, with bills of large denominations. A faint cry broke from each of the three. For that instant, their interest in the plunder they had received was greater than their interest in the man from whom they had taken it. Their guns were still pointed in his direction, but their attention had wavered, and, in that instant, Henry Ireton struck.

He had not been afraid from the first — not afraid for himself, but for his money. It was more than life to him. Now, as he saw his ghost of a chance, he used the weight of his fists with glorious effect. The left hand smote the assistant to the chief on the side of the head and staggered him terribly, although he blazed away with his revolver and punched a series of bullets at the sky. His right hand, falling with more effect, nearly dropped the leader. Then he leaped for Oliver Christy, who held the money belt. He leaped blindly — and got the barrel of a Colt slammed squarely between his eyes. The gun exploded at the same moment, and Oliver Christy, standing fairly over his victim, fired straight down at his head.

"You've killed him!" said the leader of the crew, creeping nearer.

"What call had he to cross me?" Oliver Christy asked. "He's taken no more than he deserves. I've no regrets. Is he surely dead?"

"I don't feel any heart action. No . . . and there's blood here between the eyes. You've shot him through the brain!"

"Dead men keep tight lips," Christy said with a grunt of satisfaction. "Now let's clear out of here. The noise of these guns may bring someone. But first . . . have we left any sign behind us?"

"Such as what?"

"Such as they could trace us by?"

"Old son, you been reading books."

"Yes, if you want to put it that way."

"You go home and stop worrying. You're fixed. They'll never find us."

"You haven't dropped anything. And there are no fingerprints on the body?" Christy asked.

"No, I guess not. Come over here. Strike a light, Shorty. Hey, here's Sammy, come with the horses . . . like a good kid. He's never off the job. Sammy, come here. Shorty'll strike a light, while the rest of us split up the boodle on the spot. That's the most satisfactory way, eh?"

"A lot the most," said Shorty obediently making the light.

"Now let's have the stuff, big boy," said the leader.

"One moment," Oliver Christy said. "Who suggested and planned this affair? Who brought you here, and then who was it that pushed the deal through, after Ireton had knocked the pair of you down?"

"I wasn't down!" said one.

"You were done for, though, shooting in the air like a drunk."

"Big boy, wait a minute. How much would you claim?"

"Not claim, but take. I'll take just half of this stuff. That leaves five thousand apiece for the rest of you."

"Ye gods, man," said Shorty, "are you gonna throw your life away?"

"You won't let me have it, then?"

"Are we crazy?"

"Boys, hold on!" gasped Sammy. "He ain't dead!"

"Who? Ireton?"

"Yes. There . . . he's moving . . . he's gone!"

"Who?"

"Ireton!"

For the big shadow of the supposedly dead man had jumped from the ground and lunged for the tent.

Three guns blazed instantly after him. But Christy was already sprinting for dear life. He knew that there was apt to be a rifle in that tent, and he did not care to be standing in shooting distance of a rifle opened on them in the hands of Ireton. So catching his horse by the bridle, he threw himself into the saddle and shot away across the field.

XIII

"HONOR AMONG THIEVES"

Although Oliver Christy fled fast and first, he was not such a vast distance in front. The other three were not a fraction of a second in following an example so quick and intelligent. They flung themselves headlong at their horses, but they paid the penalty of an instant of delay. Such penalties are constantly paid, the world over, but in no place so often, or at such a terrible price, as in the Western states.

Lying prone, in front of that huddle of a tent, regardless of the crimson that was spreading over his face, Henry Ireton cuddled the butt of his rifle against his shoulder and took aim. He had only starlight for his shooting; otherwise, not even Oliver Christy, head start though he had, would have escaped.

The rifle spoke, and the horse of the leader pitched high in the air and fell down with a human scream of pain. The outlaw himself had landed on his feet, like a cat, still running in the direction of freedom. The rifle spoke again and Sammy threw wide his arms and pitched headlong for the ground. A third time Ireton fired. But, after that, the riders drove into a thick veil of darkness. For some moments there remained vague shapes before the eyes of Ireton, but he knew that he was shooting by guess, rather than by aim.

The leader had reached the body of Sammy, where it lay crumpled on the ground, and, great as was his fear of the deadly marksman in the dark behind him, he was true to his instinct of leadership and crouched beside the fallen man.

"Sammy! Sammy!" he gasped. "Are you gone?"

"I'm done," groaned Sammy. "That hound is a cat. He can see in the dark. So long. Give Sally. . . ." So he died.

The leader remembered freckled Sally. Give her what? The golden watch, perhaps, that was Sammy's most precious possession. He wrenched it away, and, starting to his feet, still bending low, he raced away again. Fortune favored him for the good heart he had shown. The horse of Sammy had slowed to a dog-trot. That fine gelding the leader caught, and in another instant he was off on the traces of the fugitives, where their vague outlines were rapidly melting into the night before him.

Fast and furiously he rode. Three times fences rose before him, and three times he recklessly put his mount at them, and cleared them, flying. That brought him up with the other two, for the great weight of Christy in the saddle had brought him back to his companions in mischief. As they came into a road beyond the long fields, a white hand went up through the eastern trees, and a pale moon showed them to one another.

"Sammy dropped!" Shorty exclaimed.

The leader answered gravely: "Poor Sam is dead. God rest him. He was a bunkie."

That was the epitaph of Sammy, but, with a sigh, Shorty added: "It comes high, big money does. Always. And now do we get the coin?"

"You get your half," big Oliver Christy announced.

A twitch of a hand, and Christy found the revolver in the hand of the leader pointed toward him.

"Christy," said the outlaw, "I've been

trying to treat you like a man. But I see that there ain't any use. Gimme that belt!"

The hand of Christy had dropped into his coat pocket. "I have you covered from my pocket, man," he said.

"How do I know you have a gun there?" sneered the other.

"You take your chance on it, then, and see what happens."

"Christy," said the outlaw, "they're apt to come swarming around us at any moment now. There's no doubt that, if Ireton was able to shoot that way, he wasn't dead, he was only stunned. He wasn't even badly wounded. Such a man as him will be a hard one to put off the trail."

"You told me he was dead," Christy said bitterly, "and, if I hadn't been sure of that, I would have stopped and finished the hound. But I trusted to your word. Confound him! He'll make trouble for me, until one of us is dead. Tell me one thing before we make the split . . . how did you find out that I had six thousand dollars?"

"Let that rest."

"Sackstein told you," Christy conjectured, "because nobody else could have known. Sackstein told you, and that he would work in company with you to rob me of the money that I had from him. Isn't that a fact?"

"Who is Sackstein?" the leader asked.

A stinging retort almost burst from the lips of Christy, but he controlled himself. "Here's the belt," he said suddenly. "Count the stuff, you. There's ten thousand apiece for us." As he spoke, he flung the belt to Shorty, and the latter greedily opened the money compartment.

"Nobody would accuse you of being in this game for the fun of it," said the leader, as Shorty counted out the money. "But the fact is that I pay the dead men and the living as well. There's no shares lost by going West. Not with my men."

"You mean that you'll pay Sammy a share, too?" Christy asked.

"I mean just that."

"So that you and Shorty can split it up between you as soon as you're out of my sight?"

"Do you think so? You don't know my reputation, if you say that, my friend. Sammy has an old aunt that raised him. She could use seventy-five hundred a lot better than any of the rest of us. And she's going to get it."

"I've got your word for that." Oliver Christy sneered.

"It's good enough authority for you," the leader replied hotly. "Let it go at that, because you won't get any better chance. Now that I've got the drop on you, I've a mind to croak you . . . you've been so keen to beat the rest of us out of our shares."

"Try it," Oliver Christy challenged. "I invite you to step out and try it, old son. You and me could have a fine party, on the strength of that. You and me and Shorty. I don't ask for trouble, but just one of you start to fade away with that money."

After this a moment of pause followed, the horses stamping and tossing their heads impatiently, and the steam going up from them through the moonlight.

"All right," the leader said at last. "Have you made the split, Shorty?"

"Yes."

"Then count out a share to Christy."

It was done, the bills being shuffled rapidly into the ready palm of Mr. Christy. He received seven thousand five hundred dollars, exactly.

"Now," said the leader, "the time has come for us to quit each other, and I got to say that I'm glad to go. I like to be in strong with my partners, I don't mind saying, but I never before seen a man that I could leave so easy as I can this one here.

I'm through with you, Christy. I hope that I never have to lay eyes on you again. For all of the murdering, cold-hearted swine that I ever met, you're the meanest and the worst. Shorty, let's get out of his sight!"

They reined their horses back, whirled them around, and galloped rapidly away.

Behind them, they left Oliver Christy thoughtful and somewhat down-hearted. For he had not yet grown entirely calloused. There was still some room for kindness in him, and still some vanity of gentleness and the desire for the respect of his fellow men. He did not care so much for love. But he wished to be respected. Respected for strength and valor. But even those criminals despised and hated him. And that cut him rather deeply. However, he could not remain foolishly there in the road, waiting to be taken. So he turned the head of his horse and cantered briskly away toward the house of his father.

It was not very late when he arrived in view of the light that shone continually from the lower windows of the front hall. But what amazed him was the glitter behind the windows of his father's bedroom, just above. The elder Christy was in the habit of retiring early, and had been ever since his fatal illness commenced. But here it was nearly eleven, and there were all of these lights. Oliver Christy pushed his horse rapidly ahead, swung down, and strode up the steps. The pale, drawn face of the servant at the front door told him everything.

Up the stairs with a bound, and into the room where there was a hushing of whispers. Figures drew back against the wall. He stood above the white, dead face of his father and wondered at the softness of the dead man's smile that had been so pinched and stern with pain during the last years of his life.

Then he went downstairs again and poured out a drink. He needed to be alone and to meditate and to add up, as it were, his account of the events that had happened on this day. He knew that he had in pocket $9,000. He knew that he had paid off a blackmail debt of $4,500, and the total left him in debt to Sackstein for $25,000. Only $13,500 to show against a deficit of $25,000, and this in spite of the fact that he had used guns, trickery, and the advantage of number, and secret information secured as an eavesdropper. That, too, in spite of the fact that the stain of one man's lifeblood was already upon the money that he held. It began to appear to young Christy that, after all, it might be just as well to avoid sin hereafter. It hardly paid. It was distinctly a losing account.

He finished his drink and extended himself more comfortably in his chair. After all, he had finally spiked the guns of Henry Ireton. He had stamped that man out of his way. Rosaline would become Mrs. Christy. The face of life would smile for Oliver. Yet he could not be sure. He could not be *quite* sure. What was overwhelmingly important was that he had failed to kill Ireton.

The devil had certainly been in that piece of hard luck.

XIV

"SLUMBERING GIANT"

There is no giant so large that he may not be stunned by a blow that is heavy enough. Henry Ireton was stunned. He knew that he had slaved for many years. He knew that he had conquered, and then chance had wiped out his victory in a cloud of fire. It had not entirely destroyed him, however. No, for he learned that his work had won him the confidence of men and women, and, when he started on the upgrade, the first person to meet him with kindness had been Rosaline Lawes. She had given him heart to try his fortune further. The adventure with the money-lender had been in the nature of a miracle. Then there had been the dealing with John Rix. At the very moment when he was reëstablished, the money had been snapped up out of his hands. He had been left empty-handed.

Not quite empty-handed. Yonder in the field lay a dead horse, and near it there was a dead man. He went out and looked at them with vague, regardless eyes, and then he turned sadly back to the tent — no, not so much in sadness as in a daze. There in the tent he sat with fallen head.

The news traveled rapidly up and down the countryside, for when was there a time when the story of tragedy did not leap like lightning?

The sheriff came — big, urbane — a man gentle in speech as he was terrible in action. He touched the shoulder of Henry Ireton.

"Ireton, I'm sorry," he said. "Tell me what's happened?"

Ireton pointed to the field where the dead man lay, and bowed his head.

"But the way it happened . . . I want to know that. And how many of them were there?"

Ireton's head rolled loosely back on his shoulders. "I dunno," he said.

The sheriff looked down for a moment into that blank, stricken face, and then he, too, retired. "Leave that man alone," he ordered. "Wait for a doctor, will you? Leave him alone until a doctor has a chance to get at him."

A doctor was brought. He found a passive patient. The doctor came out from the tent even graver of face than the sheriff had been. "I'll tell you what," he said. "If the poor devil had another house standing here, filled with livestock, I'd advocate putting it on fire at once."

"What do you mean by that?" asked the sheriff.

"I mean that he's in very bad shape. He's fallen into an apathy that may mean any number of things. But for my part, I think that it means a broken heart."

"Broken . . . nonsense," said the sheriff. "That fellow is tough as iron."

"I've had to do with these iron men before," declared the doctor. "These mountains are filled with 'em. They do very well under certain conditions. But usually they're best for work that needs edged tools. Now Ireton is that sort. Give him a mountain to move, and he'll try to move it. But give him a mystery, and he's up in the air."

"I don't follow that drift," the sheriff said, gnawing at the end of a sandy mustache.

"Listen," explained the man of science.

"When this chap received for an inheritance a property mouse-eaten with debts, and worn out by stupid management, it was a concrete objective for him . . . and he started marching straight toward his goal. It took him five years. But he beat the game. The whole county knows what punishment he took in turning the trick. It was a grand thing . . . a miracle, I'd say. Then came the fire. Well, that was chance. A bad blow. A sickening blow that would have stopped most men dead in their tracks. But in seven days this fellow Ireton had started the machinery of credit working and was back on his feet . . . more strongly fixed than ever. But just on the heels of that reëstablishment comes a second attack that wipes him out. He's robbed. And mark what happens, not to his pocketbook, but to his mind. He doesn't mind the money loss. At least he could recover from that. But what destroys his morale is that this blow comes . . . through no fault of his own. It unnerves him. It's a mystery. Why should bad luck pick him out like this and kick him twice? He can't understand, and, being baffled, he's entirely at sea. His will fails him. And inside of two or three weeks . . . we'll bury that iron man, Sheriff."

"Hello! Hello! You haven't been drinking, old man?"

"Not a drop. Except on Saturday nights. Not a drop. When he dies, it'll be a cold, perhaps, that'll turn into pneumonia. Or it'll be from a consumption that will develop and run at a gallop through him. Because, man, he's going to be so weakened by his grief and his bewilderment that the first disease that comes along will kill him as surely and as easily as a bullet planted between his eyes."

"I guess I sort of understand," the sheriff said slowly. "I had an uncle, once . . . by the way, how bad Ireton's face is, eh? Somebody must have fired a gun right into his eyes. He is burned and blackened with the powder burns."

"And yet they missed him," said the other. "Well, and they battered him with some heavy club. I tried to dress the wound between his eyes and clean his face, but he brushed me away. You've no idea of the power of that man's arm, Sheriff."

"I have, though," the sheriff contradicted, smiling grimly. "I remember when young MacMahon ran amuck one day. He'd come down from the lumber camp, filled himself with liquor, and started out to paint the town red. I heard of it and started to get him, but I was ten miles off when the message got to me. When I arrived, I was just in time to see the finish. MacMahon had ridden down the street, a gun in each hand, shooting at the lights on each side, in the homes. Halfway through the town he met Henry Ireton, driving a farm wagon. He shoved his guns into the holsters and roped Ireton with his lariat. Before the noose was pulled tight, Ireton stood up . . . I saw this . . . and jumped for MacMahon like a tiger cat. He reached the horse of the lumberjack. He pulled MacMahon out of the saddle, and they had it out, hand to hand. MacMahon stood half a foot higher than a tall man. He was a giant. But Ireton folded him in his arms and smashed his ribs like chalk. You could hear the bones snapping in the poor devil's body. MacMahon was a fighting devil. But I heard him scream with the pain of it. He crumpled in the dust, and Ireton left him lying, face down, and got on his wagon, and drove off. No, there's no man in this county that would take chances with that fellow with bare hands. Now you tell me that Hercules is going to die of a broken heart?"

"Yes . . . or go crazy. He has to be brought out of the stupor that he's in at present. Has he any very close friends?"

"No, but there's a girl."

"Good! Get her."

They got Rosaline Lawes. Mr. Lawes was by all means against her coming.

"There's been a friendship between her and big Ireton," he told the sheriff. "But you can't expect a girl to throw herself away on a pauper and. . . ."

Rosaline cut in sharply with: "Friendship? I was engaged to marry him. And I'm still engaged! And I'm going to him as straight as I can."

"Rosaline!" her father shouted sternly.

"I'll be on a horse in two minutes," she said to the sheriff. "Will you go with me?"

"Honey," said the sheriff, "I never done nothing more willingly."

In another moment or two they were on the road, and the sheriff explained as well as he could what the doctor had said. He cautioned: "You'll find him looking awful. They bashed him in the face before he ran them off."

"What do I care how his face looks?" cried the girl. "I know what his heart is, and that's what counts with me. But don't you know who did it?"

"No, we can't even identify the dead man."

"Ah, if he'd only killed them all."

So they swept up to the place. There was a score of people wandering around the field, looking at the spot where the dead man had been found, and at the dead horse whose body had not yet been removed. The sheriff and the girl went past these and to the tent where big Ireton still sat in his stupor.

Nearby, old Tom Elky, the beggar, took off his hat and stretched out his hand to them.

"You scoundrel!" snarled the sheriff at him. "I've a mind to take you to jail for this. Turning the misery of an honest working man like Ireton into capital for your own lazy hide!"

"I've been a working man in my day, Sheriff," whined Tom Elky.

"You have? Tell me one good thing you ever accomplished in your whole worthless life?" He pushed past the beggar to the tent, Rosaline in tow.

There the sheriff waited outside. He merely had a glimpse of the girl falling on her knees at the feet of Henry Ireton, and then he turned his back sharply, but still her broken, choked voice came out to him. He shook his head and breathed hard and moved farther off. "Women," he said huskily. "Well, God bless 'em."

"Aye, aye, sir," said the piping voice of Tom Elky.

The sheriff started and looked askance at his unsought companion. "Bah!" he said. "Get off this land!" And he moved a little farther on.

A minute later Rosaline Lawes came out, weeping, terribly shaken. She ran to the sheriff. "Do something! Do something!" she said. "I think he's lost his mind. He just sits there. He didn't seem to know me. When I began to sob, he took my face in his hands and called me little girl, and told me not to cry and to go home to my mother . . . he didn't even know me!"

XV

"THE BEGGAR TAKES A HAND"

"If she didn't turn the trick, no woman could," said the doctor to the sheriff. "Now what can we try?"

"There's John J. Rix getting out of that buggy, just now. Try Rix. He's Ireton's banker now, they say."

They met Rix at the fence. On the way to the tent, he listened to the doctor with an intent frown.

He looked up with a smile and a nod. "I know," Rix said. "He thinks that he's ruined. I've seen men smashed like that before by money loss. Wait till I have five minutes with him. I'll bring him back to life."

Both the sheriff and the doctor were near enough to overhear most of what John J. Rix said to Henry Ireton on that day in the tent, and their report of it did much to bring to Rix the business and the confidence of the entire county later on.

They heard the banker say: "Ireton, you've had two doses of bad luck. That's your share for the rest of your life. But don't think that I'm through with you. I trust you still for a money-maker, old fellow. Keep your head up. I can't finance you to the tune of thirty thousand dollars, but I can do enough to build barns and sheds for you, livestock and tools can be bought with my money, and I'll keep you going with seed and every other necessity. We'll make a campaign of this together, Ireton. Are you agreed? Do you hear me, man? Well, I'll say it over again and. . . ."

And over again he said it. But there was not a ghost of a response from the big farmer. The doctor and the sheriff moved to the road with Rix who was much moved by what he had seen.

"If what you had to say, Rix, couldn't move him," said the doctor, "then nothing could move him. We've tried a man, and we've tried a woman. They've used the two best arguments in the world . . . money and love. And he's still not touched. What can we do?"

"Go deeper still," said the banker,

clenching his fist. "The man in him is dead, I tell you. There's only one brute left. He looked straight through me the way a lion looks through you when you stand in front of the bars of the cage in the lion house. I never had such a chill go down my spine. I tell you, Sheriff, that fellow is breaking his heart because he doesn't know how to get at the fellows who robbed him."

"That may be," said the sheriff. "But one of you suggest something, will you?"

Nothing could be suggested. It was the final opinion of the doctor that the big fellow should be left alone, undisturbed by a crowd, and allowed to rest, if he would, until the following morning. Then if life and activity had not come back to him, he should be removed at once, and cared for in some public institution if there were no friend to take him in. Certainly he was in too strange a situation to be left to roam at large.

So the crowd was driven from the fields of Henry Ireton. The last to go was the old cripple, Tom Elky, hobbling on his canes, and very loath to move, because he had reaped a rich harvest from the people who had come to the place that day.

"Put him in stir, Sheriff!" called a

strong, cheerful voice. "Because I don't think the old rascal deserves a penny of charity. Search his pockets, and I'll bet that you find money enough to keep him the rest of his days."

Elky jerked his head around toward the speaker and saw, sitting on a fine horse, in a gray suit with a black, broad band around the upper arm, none other than young Oliver Christy.

"Who would I get lots of money from?" he croaked back. "From you, Mister Christy? And what would make you give money away? Not charity, I'm thinking."

There was a subdued chuckle from the bystanders, and, in the midst of it, Christy rode off in a rage, for he was not celebrated for his generosity.

"Mind you," called the sheriff as he rode away with the rest of the company, "mind you, Elky, you're to keep away from this place and leave poor Ireton in peace!"

"Aye, aye, sir!" But to himself Tom Elky added: "Me that never done no good in my life, eh?" He paused, leaning upon his canes, close to the fence, and, with a grim frown, he thought back over his years of life. No good deeds? He would raise them to his memory one by one. But the triumphant smile began to fade from the lips of ancient Tom. Year by year and decade by decade slipped in review past his mind's eye. Still the great good deed did not appear. There had been many and many a fine hope, and many and many a noble thought. But deeds are the current coin that passes in this world of ours. And what had Tom Elky done? He looked up with a sudden gasp at the pale blue of the sky. He looked down and shook his head, and at that moment he saw something printed on the ground that made his brows pucker.

Only the print of a horse hoof, but it was enough to make Tom Elky gasp, and then glance sharply over either shoulder. He looked again, and, turning about, he retraced his way across the field, studying a trail, until he came to the side of the tent, where all the trail disappeared in a blur of recent sign. Then he drew himself nearer on his sticks and looked through the open flap of the tent into the blank face of the man within.

"Good day, sir," said Tom Elky.

There was not a shadow of understanding on the face of Ireton.

"Good day, sir!" Tom Elky said again, adding: "I was thinking that I might be able to do something for you, sir. Something in the way of getting your money back for you."

"Aye," said Henry Ireton. "I thank you kindly. Good bye, I thank you. I want to be alone."

"I mean," Tom Elky cried in a sudden passion, "that I want to take you where you'll get the heart's blood of him that robbed you last night!"

As by a miracle, the body of the strong man was filled with life. He rose. He strode forth, and his hand fell on the shoulder of little Tom Elky. The cripple cringed help-lessly away.

"You old snake," Ireton said, "you were lying here in the field, watching, and you saw it all, and recognized 'em in spite of their masks. Aye, and you've kept the knowledge until you knew that they were safely away."

"I wasn't here! I wasn't here!" Tom Elky protested. "But I tell you this . . . Oliver Christy was in this field last night or this morning. He wasn't here this morning be-cause I seen him come and go again. And there you are."

"Wait, wait!" cried Ireton. "Christy's a rich man. And what have I ever done to harm him, tell me?"

"You fool!" snarled Tom Elky. "What's right or wrong to a skunk such as Oliver

Christy? As for a cause . . . aren't you engaged to the girl that he wants to marry? Isn't that enough for him?"

"Rosaline? Rosaline?" whispered Ireton. "I think she was here this morning."

"Crying at your feet. Yes, she was here."

"Never mind her," Ireton hissed coldly. "I want to know something more about the same fellow Christy. I want your proof that he was here last night. Because if he was . . . if he was. . . ."

"I seen the mark of the shoe of his horse."

"How can you tell a horse by its shoe?" Ireton asked.

"Because his horse yesterday was shod with one broken shoe, and this field has prints of a broken horseshoe in it."

"Ha," Ireton murmured. "I think you know what you're talking about. Do you? Do you, Tom Elky?"

"I know! Go prove it with me. Come . . . look out yonder at the sign of a. . . ."

"I don't want any proof. I want Christy! It's he that I want. I'm going now."

"Where?"

"To find him."

"Not in broad day."

"Aye, in broad day!"

"And what'll you do?"

"I'm going to kill him. I'm going to take him in my hands and kill him, Tom Elky. Stop holding to me, or I'll throw you down!"

"You won't, Ireton. You won't. Listen to me. I only wanted to stir you up and do you good. If there is a murder done, the sin of it'll be on the head of Tom Elky."

"Keep your hand off me!"

"Ireton, dear Henry Ireton, kind lad, listen to me. They've got all the other things against me in heaven. I've been a sneak and a coward and an idler and a traitor. But there's no red mark against me. There's no blood, Henry. Don't you put it against me now."

But Henry Ireton jerked himself rudely away, and Tom Elky fell upon the ground.

He gathered himself up and brushed the dirt and the soot of the black stubble from his face. "God forgive Tom Elky," he said. "God . . . don't count it against me." Then he saw the figure of Ireton striding away, and, scrambling to his feet, he started after it, screaming. But that was quite vain. He saw Ireton reach the fence and vault across it into the road, and then he was out of sight around the next bend.

There was nothing to be done, and the terrible silence of the naked countryside settled around the heart of Tom.

XVI

"IN LAWES' DINING ROOM"

That day was one of the great ones, if not the greatest, in the life of Oliver Christy. He had begun in the early morning by discharging on the spot with no extra pay for long service, all of the old retainers who were distasteful to him — and, in the eyes of Oliver, nearly every one who had ever borne a tale to his father about him was an enemy. Then he had given directions to the undertaker to proceed with the arrangements for his father's burial, and he had ridden over himself to arrange at the church for the most magnificent funeral that the town had ever witnessed. By doing such credit to the dead man, he felt that he was very directly doing credit to himself.

When this was done, he had gone here and there, always with a very grave face, collecting little speeches of sympathy, and scoffing at them in his heart. For he felt that any son must rejoice to come into the fortune of a rich father; and he believed that these speeches of confidence were the rankest sort of hypocrisy. That was one of the main charges that Oliver leveled against the world — hypocrisy. He felt that he saw through it and, for his own part, believed that all human actions may be well enough motivated by sheer expediency.

So he came around past the scene of his last night's exploit, and he could not avoid stealing close enough to see Henry Ireton within the tent. It gave him an immense thrill of satisfaction. But then, just as he was riding off, he learned that Rosaline Lawes had come to Ireton that day and attempted to rouse him. It caused a sudden and violent reaction in the heart of young Oliver Christy, and straightway he was flying down the road toward the house of Mr. Lawes. It would be seen what effect the inheritance of a great estate had upon Mr. and Mrs. Lawes, even if a young girl had been so rattle-brained as to lose all sense of proportion.

It was nearing dusk when he reached the house of Lawes, and he was received by Mrs. Lawes at once and with great unction. She was a practical woman, was Mrs. Lawes, and Oliver had recognized that element in her nature long before.

He went straight to the point. "I want Rosaline. I can give her the sort of a home that she should have. Tell me, Missus Lawes, will you back me up with her and with your husband?"

"You'll need precious little backing-up with my husband," said Mrs. Lawes. "He's got an eye in his head, I hope, and can at least tell white from black, poor man. As for Rosaline, she'll come around in time. Just give her a day or two. Let me tell you something, Oliver Christy. All young girls are a little crazy. I know that I was. And when Rosaline had a chance to throw herself away on a bankrupt farmer, it appealed to her romantic self. She wanted to do it terrible bad. You wouldn't believe! However, when she comes to understand that poor Henry Ireton is really quite simple-minded now. . . ."

"He was never much better at any time," Oliver commented coldly.

"Maybe not. Maybe not," Mrs. Lawes responded hastily. "However, he's all broken now."

"I saw him sitting like a great calf," Oliver said. "His spirit is broken."

"Well, Rosaline is in bed. She's cried herself into a fever. But she'll come 'round. There's common sense in her. Now, dear Oliver, you stay here and wait till my husband comes. Well, isn't that his step on the porch now?"

Oliver stayed. He stayed till dinnertime, and the talk was all that he could have wished it to be. There was no question of opposition. All should be as he wished. Only, they must go slowly and softly, for Rosaline was a stubborn girl with the fierceness of a tigress, when she felt that she was in the right.

The telephone began to clamor. But Oliver Christy knew that nothing could come to that house by way of news so important as the things that he had to say to this pair.

"Take the thing off the hook and let it hang," he suggested. "I hate a telephone. I never knew anyone to hear anything of importance over the wire, did you?"

So, when Mr. Lawes could not at once understand the message, he followed that clever suggestion and left the receiver hanging off the hook.

"Couldn't get the name," Mr. Lawes stated. "Anyway, they weren't asking for my name. That's all I was sure of. They must have the wrong number. Listen to it buzz, still, like a hornet."

They finished their coffee. But no sooner was the telephone placed on the hook than it sent a thrilling clangor through the house once more.

"I'll answer it myself," Oliver announced curtly, and he snatched it off the hook. "Hello?"

A hoarse voice shouted dimly back to him: "I want Mister Lawes's house. I want Mister Lawes's house. Is this the right place?"

"Yes," Oliver answered, and he added to his hosts: "Some drunkard on the wire, it seems. I can hardly hear his voice."

"If this is the Lawes' house, then is Mister Christy there?" called the other speaker on the telephone.

"I'm Oliver Christy."

"Thank God!"

"What's wrong?"

"I thought you were a dead man before this. I've been trying to get you. Something wrong with the phone. I sent off fast riders. But I thought that he would beat them. . . ."

"Peters? Is that you?"

"Yes, sir."

"What nonsense are you talking?"

"No nonsense, I'm afraid. He means

deadly murder, sir."

"Murder?"

"Yes."

"Who . . . what under heaven . . . who are you talking about?"

"Henry Ireton. He came here with blood on his face. A dreadful sight. He asked for you. When he couldn't get you here, he said that you were probably at Mister Lawes's house, and he took a horse from your stable and started off at a wild gallop without so much as a saddle blanket beneath him to. . . ."

"Great heavens!" cried Oliver Christy. He dropped the telephone receiver. "Let the door and the windows be closed, Mister Lawes!" he cried. "Send for all your servants! Call in the men from the bunkhouse. Lose no time. Lose no time in heaven's name, or I'm a dead man! Henry Ireton is coming here to murder me!"

Mrs. Lawes started up with a scream. Lawes himself turned deathly pale, and his face grew flushed.

"I'll . . . I'll send word . . . Ireton has waked up!" gasped Lawes. And he began to rise. He had no time to complete the movement, for a heavy step crossed the porch, and the door to the dining room opened. They saw the lamplight flash far away on the green face of a tree in the garden. Then the shadowy bulk of Ireton entered the room — Ireton with the crusted blood still streaking his face — Ireton with his eyes on fire.

Oliver Christy leaped backward with such a shriek as could never come twice from the throat of any human being. He tugged and pulled a revolver from his clothes. He fired.

But Ireton leaped in. A second bullet seemed to be fired at him in vain from the shaking hand of Christy. Then Oliver Christy went down with a crash before the charge of the farmer. Twice they rolled back and forth on the floor. Then Ireton rose to his feet. In his hand he held Christy's gun, gripped by the barrel. On the floor lay Christy, not dead, but senseless.

"Now let them come and hang me," Henry Ireton said quietly.

They did not hang Henry Ireton.

In the first place, it was long before Oliver Christy recovered enough to appear in court against the other man. In the second place, when the sheriff sat down one day with the pale-faced, bandaged convalescent, something snapped in Oliver Christy.

The whole story of his misdeeds burst from his lips. He could not help talking. He confessed it himself. His nerves were gone from the moment when he first saw the dreadful figure of Henry Ireton stalking toward him through the door of the Lawes' dining room.

But there was no legal punishment for Christy. He was allowed to pay for his double crime as far as money could pay for it. But as for pressing a prison sentence, Henry Ireton relented.

Newly married men are too often foolishly forgiving of their foes.

The Range Finder

The year 1925 was a prolific one for Frederick Faust in which he saw published seventeen short stories and eight serials. Under the Peter Henry Morland by-line, "The Range Finder" appeared late in the year in the November 14th issue of Street & Smith's *Western Story Magazine*, in which all but two of the serials appeared that year. A first person narrative, "The Range Finder" tells the story of James Lang, newcomer to the West, and his adventures while guarding a mine and befriending a dog named Barney. This is the first time the story has been reprinted.

I

"A MAINE MAN'S DEFEAT"

My name is James Lang. I am forty-seven years old, but, according to my lights, I've lived only about the last fifteen years. Up to that time I lived in Maine, where my father, my grandfather, great-grandfather, and all the rest back to Sixteen-Fifty something, have always hung out.

I spent those thirty-two years like most of the other folks in that part of the world. I did my share of schooling, playing, fighting, and squawking. After I got big enough, I used to go out in the woods and do lumbering for the paper mills, cutting down the saplings, I mean, and the other scrub wood that goes to the pulp mills. It is amazing to think of the thousands of miles of newspaper articles and headlines I have cut down with my own axe! If I could be paid for it at a cent a word. . . .

However, to get back to Maine. I say that life was not living, and it really wasn't because I formed a taste for something bigger and better, as I think, later on. In the winter lumbering was bitter hard work. You know, of course, that the thermometer up there thinks nothing of hitting thirty degrees below zero. That is easy to write down, but mighty hard to live through. The days are really not so bad, because then a man is dressed for the cold, and he's usually working and keeping his blood humming. But if you sit down to eat, you're chilled through before you get the first sandwich down your gullet, and it takes a swig of smuggled Jamaica to wake you up. The nights are bad, too. You people who have always lived in a warm climate — or a *decent* climate — have no idea how the cold will come fingering under the thickest blankets, prying down your backbone, and settling in the tips of your toes. It's a fair bet that you don't really get an hour of sound sleep out of every ten that you spend with your eyes closed during Maine nights at a lumber camp in winter.

When we came out in the spring, I was a hunter. Perhaps that sounds a good deal better to you. Of course, there *is* sport in it. But just about the time that the Maine woods get comfortable in temperature for people, they get comfortable for midges, black flies, mosquitoes, and a million other things that fly and crawl.

I was a pretty good hunter. I had the natural gift for trailing, and I loved guns. Which is the main reason why this little confession has to be written — hunting and guns.

Trailing in the Maine woods is a job all by itself. To those who have never been there, I'll say that the country is broken all over with little hills and cut across by creeks, rivers, ponds, and lakes. Every inch of the land that is solid enough for the purpose is covered with what the Maine folks call a forest. A Westerner would call it overgrown brushwood. Those Maine trees are just big enough to be irritating and just small enough to give you no lumber.

When you track a deer through ground like this, you have to keep your wits about you. A hundred deer can dodge you in every quarter section that you pass over; you have to move along almost smelling your way, because mere eyes and ears will never turn the trick. I mean this literally. A hunter has to have an extra sense. Of course, it really isn't the sense of smell, but I'd as soon call it that. At any rate, I was equipped with an extra lot of that sense. Ever since I was a little youngster, I was known for it.

My father and even my cousins, when they wanted to kill something extra bad, would always try to snake me along with them, even before I could handle a gun well enough to take part in the shooting. I've said a hundred times to some fellow along with me — "There's a deer on the far side of that hill." Or: "There's a deer in those woods, there." Sometimes I was wrong, I admit. But about five times out of ten I was right. I don't know what to call that extra sense. A lot of people have it, more or less. Mostly they don't talk about it a great deal, because it's hard to put it into words.

I could endure black flies or mosquitoes for the sake of enjoying myself with a gun. I used to think that I was about as good a shot as any man ever needed to be, until one day a young fellow came up hunting from New York. He was making a buckboard do cross-country tricks in most amazing style and covering country where even a mountain sheep would have been afraid to trust itself. He dropped in at a camp where I was with half a dozen other men, all hunters.

He said that his name was Cobden, and sat down to eat lunch with us, passing around high-powered cigarettes afterward — the kind that put a tickle in your nose just to *think* about smoking them. After that, somebody began to talk about the fine shooting that his cousin could do, and then about a friend he had in Carolina — I said that I thought Maine men were about as good hands at shooting as anybody in the country.

This Cobden had sat and listened to this for a long time. Here he began to laugh.

"Why," he said, "you fellows have still-hunted up here for so many generations that you can't hit anything more than fifty yards away. I'll put up a target at seventy-five yards and beat the lot of you . . . this revolver against your rifles."

He had a long, snaky-looking .22-caliber revolver. I found out afterward that it was just a target gun. It shot with an extra easy trigger, being very light and especially well balanced for slow, deliberate shooting. However, the idea that any revolver in the world can beat out rifles made us laugh. In another minute, we had laid some bets with this Cobden, and he had paced off seventy-five yards and blazed a chunk off the face of a tree. The place that he shaved off with that stroke of the axe was not more than four inches square. I waited for him to make it bigger, but he didn't. He just turned around and came back to us.

"Now," he said, "we're going to shoot at that target. Each of you shoot in turn, and, after each of you, I'll put in my shot. We'll shoot like this . . . one of you stand off and count one, aim . . . two, fire. Because, of course, you wouldn't ask me to allow you to take a long bead . . . rifle against revolver."

That was fair enough, as anyone could see, but the more we looked at that little blaze on the face of that tree, the more nervous we got. The reason being that at seventy-five whole paces that white spot looked almost like nothing at all. I had used a rifle all my life, and so had the rest of them, but our shooting had been at game that we had still-hunted until we had it dead to rights.

Well, I'm ashamed to say how that shooting match turned out. Just by luck, I hung my own bullet right in the center of that white blaze; one other Maine man got his inside a corner of the white spot. The rest were nowhere. Two others hit the tree and the rest didn't even land on that. But the New Yorker stuck five of his six .22s right in that blaze, and three of his six shots were grouped as close as anybody could ask in the center of the spot.

We paid our bets, but he wouldn't take the money. He only laughed and said that it would have been robbery, because he had spent too much of his time in the West, where men really *have* to shoot if they want to get game.

Beaten, and with our money refused, we listened pretty respectful and didn't sass him back, although we were all fighting mad. There never was a Maine man that wasn't proud of his state, no matter how much he might have to cuss her in spots. I'm no exception to the rule.

However, this Cobden said: "Out yonder, if you can't draw your bead at three hundred yards and shoot pretty accurately, you had better not go out hunting at all. I've done a lot of mighty pleasant shooting at greater ranges than that. A lot bigger! I'd be ashamed to tell you fellows at what a distance I killed an antelope one day, but, after it dropped, I had to walk an hour to get to the body. Though I admit almost all the way I was climbing down one side of a cañon and up the other side of it. . . . the body having fallen on the far side of a ravine from me. However, I'm nothing extra among those fellows. I do fairly well as a hunter with the average run, but I'd never pretend for an instant to stack up against their *real* hunters. Those men simply have long-distance eyes, and they have a wonderful way of judging distance. I can guess my hundreds pretty well, but I've known men who could say . . . 'That's about five hundred and seventy-five yards!'

"Well, you get at the end of five hundred yards and see how much difference a miserable little twenty-five steps makes one way or the other. Not much to your eye, but all the difference between a dead deer and a missed one, or a merely scratched one that you chase for half a day and lose at the end of your chase. No, those old-timers who really hunt, in the West, are jim-dandies. I wouldn't stack up with them at all. But one of them taught me what little I know, both revolver and rifle."

That was all he said. He was a windy youngster, a good deal too proud of what he could do, particularly with a revolver. At that, he was very neat with it. He stood out at thirty good man-size paces and clipped the edge of a dime. He did other things about as good.

"You ought to go on the stage," said one of my friends, "because there's a lot of people that would pay money to see you."

"There's a lot of people that would pay money to laugh at me, too," said Cobden.

That little day's work changed my life — completely. After Cobden left that camp, I spent two years thinking about what he had said to me — and that is no exaggeration. I had been so humiliated that I couldn't get over it. Of course, thinking about it wasn't a remedy. I practiced, too. I fairly lived with a revolver and a rifle during those two years. In the winter, when it was so cold that you had to shoot in gloves, I kept right at the job, even so.

When I tell you that in those two years I just about used up my wages to find myself in powder and lead, you can gather how much tonnage I poured into targets. It was not all shooting, either. I tell you, I put myself through a terrible course of sprouts.

You see, I was thirty years old when I met Cobden. Every man, when he gets to be thirty, likes to be proud of just one thing that he can do pretty well. In my case it was hunting. Shooting, of course, is at least fifty percent of hunting. So Cobden had given me a shock that lasted. I decided that if I were *not* a good hunter, I had to make myself one at once, or else there would be no excuse for my existence.

II

"WESTWARD HO!"

The biggest part of shooting is to find the target. Granted that a man with good nerves can hold a gun steady, and that a man with a clear eye can hit the mark, the distinction between very good and very bad rifle work, as Cobden had pointed out to us, lies in range finding, of which my still-hunting had never given me the slightest comprehension.

I used to spend hours marking down points around me and making a guess at the yardage, rifle in hand. Then I would go out and pace off the distances. It was devilish work. Some days I would hit off the distances close enough to have made a kill every time. Then there would come a change in atmosphere; the air would get cloudy and I would be thrown clear off in my calculations. Again, there would be a crystal-bright day, and *that* would make a fool of me. Or the glaze from snow, a cold in my head, a headache, almost any little thing would make me fall off — not much in the shorter distances, as I got better and better at that range-finding work. At 300 yards and more I was constantly off.

After I had been working like this for more than a year, I met an Army officer who showed me a lot of practical ways of getting the range, some complicated and some simple, although only the simple ones were of much use to a hunter who has to sight his game, make his guess, and then shoot — all in a second, say.

However, I had my bright moments. I remember calling a tree 590 yards from my post and pacing exactly 589. I was so delighted with myself that I did a war dance on the spot. And the very same afternoon I made a fifty-yard error on the same locality. That is the fortune of the range finder.

Between pacing out distances, wearing out shoe leather, and burning up ammunition, I worked myself thin and got a long-distance squint in my eyes. I'm afraid that I always looked as though I had just lost half my family, and I couldn't sleep well at night.

Then I would see that young Cobden laughing and saying: "You Maine hunters, you can never get the hang of a rifle. You haven't the air for it out here." I always thought that remark was mere mockery, and I couldn't get over it.

Well, I had been working away in this fashion for two years, with rifle and with revolver, getting so improved that I couldn't see any advancement in myself from week to week — but only from month to month I could tell that I was stepping forward. About this time I picked up a paper that advertised excursion rates to the West. It wasn't the rates that interested me. It was the idea of going West. I never had any idea of saving up seventy or a hundred dollars just for the sake of taking a train ride of few thousand miles in length. For the first time the idea of leaving Maine jumped into my brain with a click. That night I lay awake and studied the darkness, asking myself why I should not go to the land of the good hunters.

I drew down the balance of my wages the next day, and with a rifle, a revolver, a lot of poundage in ammunition, a book of practical range finding, and eighteen dollars in cash, I started, vaguely, West.

Three months later I arrived. I had

begged and stolen part of the way. I had worked enough to pay for another section of the ride — but, finally, there I was — in the West. I woke up one morning in an empty boxcar, with my hip and shoulder bones being jolted right through the flesh on the dancing floor of that car. When I edged the door open and looked out, I understood what Cobden meant when he had scoffed at Maine air.

This was different, more different than I could believe. I was swinging up a long grade, with the engine moaning and snorting up ahead of that long line of empties. Off to the north my eye was jumping across twenty miles of hills, maybe fifty miles of open, and huge mountains piled up in browns and purples. Beyond all that were the sky-blue mountains of the horizon.

There had never been a time in Maine when I had been able to see even the firs of these distances with any clearness. This Western air was like a crystal well. Distance simply diminished objects in size — and their outlines remained practically as clear as ever. To me, with my eye muscles trained for focusing quickly through a filtering of mist and wood smoke, this clarity of the air was like a godsend. The only thing that made me squint was to shut out the excess of light, which was more than I needed. I sat there and gaped at the scenery, not noting a single detail of the beauty of color or of form, but only losing myself in dizzy, drunken plunges of the eye.

The next time that train stopped, I did not ask where it was going, or what the country was like in the region. I walked up to the station boss, and said: "Will you tell me what the name of this town is?"

He looked at me, knowing that I was a tramp who had been using a boxcar without paying freight, and his lip curled. Then his eye ran over my rifle and revolver, all strapped on as big as life. He said: "This town is Elmira. Why? Are you going to stay and have a meal with us?"

I laid a hand on his shoulder. He didn't like that much, but I was a good deal too happy to pay any attention to a little thing such as his likes or his dislikes.

"Are you a citizen and a steady liver in this town?" I asked.

He said he was and shrugged my hand off his shoulder. Then he asked why I wanted to know.

"Because this here town looks to me like home, stranger, and I aim to stay here a considerable slice of my life."

"Well," he said, "we welcome all kinds here." Then he turned his back on me.

That was not particularly hospitable, but I was nothing very much as a picture to please the eyes. I am a couple of inches over six feet high. I weigh in speaking distance of 200 pounds. I wear a number twelve shoe, and I've never yet run across a glove that would hold my hand without groaning. My muscles are not big, but I'm stronger than average because, as a smart doctor told me once, my sinews get a good strong leverage on my bones, making a pound of my muscles work just as effectively as *two* pounds of muscles do in another man whose ligaments don't take hold of the bones so far out toward the end. What this means is that on a dead lift, I'm a pretty weak man. I can't carry a load any good at all. But I can hit a hard punch and walk fast, though I'm no good at running.

However, I don't want to give you my idea that I'm a freak. I'm just what even a mother would have to admit was "plain". I have a hinge in the middle of the back of my neck, my nose and my jaw are long and lean, and my mouth was made extra special in width and limberness. Otherwise, my legs are longer than they would have to be, and so are my arms, a good deal.

This ought to give you a pretty good idea of me. I'm ashamed to say that a lot of hundred-and-fifty-pound men could break me in two, if it came to wrestling, but even now — at forty-seven — it takes a licking good young 200-pounder to stand up to me for a single minute with the gloves. Boxing and shooting were the beginning and end of my talents. I had gone through a little schooling. I could read and write and figure, and all that. I didn't have any vice, except plug chewing tobacco and Jamaica rum, and I had never had a real sick day in my life.

So there I was, thirty-two years old, with fifteen cents in my pocket, a fifteen-dollar hole where my stomach should have been, a rifle, a revolver, and a wish to have a few more looks at these mountains and the shootable things that were in them.

That town of Elmira was not much more worth looking at than I was. Like me, it was chiefly bones. I mean it was stretched out on the shore of a lake, with the big rocks sticking up pretty unsightly here and there. There was a sign painter in that town. You could tell that clear from the railroad, because every sign had been made so that it faced the rails. By the look of those signs and what they said about Elmira, I judged it had a boosters club or a chamber of commerce, or maybe both.

Those signs said that Elmira was a boss place for anybody who had weak lungs, bad heart, troublesome kidneys, failing liver, or an ailing stomach. It said that real-estate investors should wake up and look that way for investments; it also invited the rest of the globe to keep its eye fixed on Elmira in the day and also in the night. It said there were excellent hotel accommodations in Elmira, and it allowed that the bathing in the lake was the finest fresh-water swimming that the world could offer. I could guess that it was about the coldest, because my eye made only about two jumps from the summit snows to the blue-white waters of that shivering lake. Everything except the tops of those mountains was burned and brown-looking, saving the patches of trees — maybe a couple of hundred acres of them here and 500 there.

In spite of the signs and all the good things that was mentioned on them, I decided that maybe I could get along with that town pretty well. So I unlimbered my joints and strolled down toward the town, taking in the details of the surrounding 10,000 square miles!

It was a pleasure to breathe that air, in spite of the alkali sting. It was a pleasure to see the brown shadow of the mountain standing deeply in the waters of the lake. I decided that I would go into the store to get more information. So, into that store I stepped — and into one of the worst tangles that any human being ever found in his whole life.

III

"ENTER THE HERO"

It was the rifle and the revolver, of course, and the heavy ammunition belt that made the difference. I looked like a walking arsenal, but I had no idea that was not the ordinary guise of a Westerner. I thought, from the little I had heard and read, that in the West men used guns like friends from whom they never wanted to be parted. When I tramped into that store, I got myself stared at, of course.

There were a couple of cowhands in there just sitting and sunning themselves, as you might say, in the memory of how big they had spent their money that day. Besides that, there were three or four other men — a trapper and several others, all old hands in that part of the country. I suppose that I could not well have fallen in with a less green crowd than these fellows. They were all as hard as nails — real range men. When I saw them flashing side glances at me, it never occurred to me that I looked a bit queer or out of place. As a matter of fact, there wasn't a single man of the lot that had a gun. At least, there was not a single gun that showed — which makes a big difference.

I said "Howdy" to them as I came in, and I went up to the counter to buy some crackers and cheese. It was about the worst cheese that I ever laid hold on in my life, at that. As I sat there in the corner of the room, munching, I said: "This cheese is old enough to talk for itself, storekeeper."

You would think that he would get a little offended at that, but he didn't.

"There is just no way," he said, "to educate that cheese. I agree with you, exactly. That cheese is old enough to walk and talk. But it won't improve itself none. In my father's time and in mine, I've known that cheese for close onto fifteen years, and it don't seem to get sense."

He kept his face very straight, and so did all the rest of them. They just looked at him very sympathetic to have found a cheese as simple as that. I ventured to laugh a little. They all looked quick at me, as if they wondered what it was that I had found to laugh at.

A man of about my own build and looks — tall, broad, and bony — stood up and stretched out his length, saying: "I'll have to be getting along."

"Sit down and rest your feet, Luke," somebody else said. "I ain't had a chance to look at you yet."

Another man remarked: "You being a hunter yourself, Luke, maybe the stranger could tell you some yarns about hunting in his part of the country that would do you good to hear."

As solemn as judges, they all turned, looked me over, and nodded. Luke said: "I see you always keep your guns right with you. That's a single-shot rifle, ain't it?"

I said it was — and a breechloader, of course.

"Well," said Luke, "I suppose that you hardly never have to take more than one shot at a thing?"

I began to guess that he was joking. Still they all kept all their expressions so well in hand, looking at me so admiring, that I lost that suspicion pretty soon. So I replied that I missed now and then, the same as any man. They asked me how I was on long-distance shooting, and I said that I was pretty good at a 150 and 200 yards.

"Well, well," exclaimed Luke, "that is pretty long range work, all right. I suppose that you have downed a pile of deer and bears?"

I said that I had got a good many deer and bears — the little black bears, of course. They seemed just as interested as ever. How was I to know that every man in that party had downed his grizzly, and that there wasn't one of the lot that wouldn't consider 200 yards almost point-blank shooting at almost any kind of game? I couldn't know. But all those devils were sitting around waiting to work me up to a point and so to make a complete fool out of me.

Luke said casually and slowly: "I know a fine hunter down in the Panhandle that used to practice on little birds. Not setting still, but on the wing. He got so that he didn't need no shotgun when he wanted a mess of birds. He just would step out and collect them with his rifle, y'undestand?"

I would have doubted any man in the state of Maine who had said such a thing, but in this new country I was only covered with awe.

"Why," said the storekeeper as quick as a wink, "I don't doubt but the stranger here could do the job pretty good. He has a hunter's real eye."

"I don't know," said Luke, "but I would be willing to bet a dollar against him."

In a minute they seemed to have worked up a bet on my shooting. I said that I didn't feel like trying my hand, because I was out of practice — by that meaning that I hadn't done any shooting for two days, and that was a long dry spell to me in those times when I lived for the sake of my guns. But they wouldn't take no for an answer. They got me out in front of that store. Yonder was a barbed-wire fence, with half a dozen little gray-brown birds hopping on and off again, flitting around very restless.

The storekeeper said: "You count three to let him get ready. Then I'll throw a stone and scare up those birds, and he can have his shot."

They were all so nervous about it that I was afraid not to try the shot, because they seemed to take for granted that a really good rifle shot would be able to do a trick like this. I lay right down on my stomach and steadied that rifle on my hand and prayed that I might have luck. The three was counted, and the stone was thrown.

There were about a dozen of those little

birds, and they did what you've likely seen them do yourself. First they dropped off the top wire and seemed to tumble toward the ground. Then they dissolved themselves into beating wings so's you could hardly see their bodies, and they all picked out different points of the compass and scattered toward them.

In shooting ordinary game, a man gets pretty highly strung, but for trick work like this, you have to have your wits working on ball bearings, I can tell you. I tried to get a bead on that flurry of little nothingnesses. I couldn't. Finally, as I saw them skidding away, I was ashamed of myself and just pulled the trigger blindly.

I lowered my rifle with a foolish grin, not even looking. You should have heard them grunt with pure astonishment. One man, who was too far off to think that I would hear him, said: "Dog-gone me if he *didn't* get one of 'em!"

They stared at me good and hard. I suppose that fool grin of mine must have appeared to them as a mere smile of confidence and satisfaction. For they had seen what I had not seen. One of those little idiotic birds had by chance dropped into the path of my bullet!

The storekeeper was very excited. He

got a hammer and stake and drove the stake down on the spot where that bird had fallen. Then he started to write on a piece of clean white pine. "Shot by . . . what's your name, stranger?"

"James Lang."

"Shot by James Lang at forty-five paces, on the wing; witnessed by . . . just you write down your names, boys. I don't want to be called a liar when I tell about this later on!"

They all lined up, very serious, and wrote down their names.

Of course, I gathered by this time that they had been only stringing me at the first and trying to make a fool out of me. What chiefly surprised me was the very great seriousness with which they took this shooting as soon as it was actually done. I could see that there was a difference between bullets in Maine and bullets in the Southwest. In Maine, shooting was just a plain sport.

Out here men shot for a business — or else for the sake of their lives. What every one of those fellows had registered inside of his heart when he saw that bird drop was a bit of gratitude to the Lord that *he* hadn't been standing up to me at that time.

I was pretty busy and pretty silent, figuring out all of this. I passed a rag through the barrel of my rifle while I was thinking it over, because there's no time like cleaning a rifle so good as the time before the burned powders has dampened and set on the steel.

"It don't mean much to him," muttered somebody in a corner of the room. "Look how matter-of-fact he takes it. Must be an everyday thing with him."

Of course, I was matter-of-fact and not proud. I was only mighty ashamed of myself that I didn't have the nerve to tell those men that hit was pure accident. But they started right in making so much fuss and trouble about the thing that I hardly *dared* to confess to them — if you can understand what I mean by that.

They took my shame for indifference, and that just rounded off the picture for them. What they thought about me was that I was one of those terrible men that you read about everywhere and actually meet — a couple of times in your life — in the West. I mean, the "dead shot". Mostly dead shots are dead liars and no mistake. Here and there you'll come across the real thing — a man who seems unable to miss, who keeps his talent bright and free from rust with a couple of hours of practice every day of his life.

Wild Bill, of course, was the great example. He was hero and killer. There has never been another like him; there never *will* be another, because the conditions that he lived in will never be duplicated on the face of the globe. There were others almost as great as Wild Bill — men who could whirl on the heel and in evening light, at a hundred yards' distance, kill with a snap shot from a revolver.

Well, when those fellows saw the miraculous shooting of that little bird, they were certain that it was the coming of another of these heroes of the West. They got reverent right away. The storekeeper wanted to know at once would I come home and have supper with him, because he had a couple of old rifles that might interest me, one of them having belonged to Billy the Kid. And a couple of others put in and would be glad to have me along.

Luke Ridgeway, the tall man who looked enough my style to be a cousin, said that he would be glad to have a chance to talk over a little business with me — just the sort of business that a man with my love of hunting would be glad of.

Considering that I had spent my last penny on crackers and cheese, that sounded good to me. It was with Ridgeway that I went down to the hotel, and I sat opposite him at supper.

IV

"THE PROPOSITION"

I don't remember all that we talked about, except that he asked me a good deal about Maine and the hunting there. The important part of the conversation sticks in my mind rather than the trimmings.

Before supper was over he proposed that I should go up and hold down his shack in the mountains for a while. He himself was leaving, and he would be gone anywhere between three and six months. In the meantime, he had a little shack on a mining claim on the shoulder of a mountain about five days' packing from Elmira, or about three days' ride. He had a couple of horses up there and a cow that was just fresh. Besides, his cabin was fixed up very comfortable, he said, and he didn't want to leave all of these things without a caretaker. Just now he had an old Mexican up there working for him — a Mexican with a halt in one leg, so that he was pretty sure to be honest for the simple reason that he couldn't very well run away with anything that he stole. Luke Ridgeway proposed that I go up there and camp on that claim of his until he came back, because he had business that took him away. He said he might not be back until six months were gone.

I said: "Suppose that you don't show up even at the end of six months or more?"

He thought for a time before answering: "I'll tell you, Lang. If I'm not back within six full months from today, you can take that cabin and everything in it for your own."

He said that in such a serious, thinking way that I could see at once that he really thought there might be a strong chance that he would not be alive at the end of the six months. That, in turn, made *me* do a little pondering. When a man has a comfortable place and a paying little claim, such as Luke said his mine was, why should he go away for anything from a quarter to a half of a year?

There didn't seem to be much sense in that, especially when he seemed to be running the chance of losing his life while he was away. However, stronger than any doubts that might be floating in the back of my mind were two very tempting facts: that this would be a boss way to get acquainted with this new country — and that I was flat broke. Here was the means of accumulating a small stake. He didn't offer much — only twenty dollars a month. But he pointed out that the cabin was fixed up very comfortable, there was fine shooting all around, and nothing to do except to take care of myself, two horses, and a cow. Altogether, I really couldn't have hit upon a better scheme than that, and I asked him how it chanced that he didn't offer a place like that to some one of his old friends.

"Two reasons," said Luke Ridgeway. "One is that most of the boys wouldn't feel right working for as little as twenty a month. And the other is that, when I saw how you handled a rifle, I just naturally wished that you could have a chance of doing some hunting around that cabin of mine." He looked me straight in the face when he said this. But there was a film over his eye, and I knew that he was lying.

Of course, you say that I immediately quit cold on that job the minute I smelled a rat, but I didn't. No, the danger in that job was simply a greater attraction to me, and all the more because I couldn't guess what it might be. I agreed to travel up into the mountains with him to see the cabin. If everything sized up as well as he said that it did, I would be happy to take up his suggestion. He agreed that was only fair, and he said he was so sure I would like the place that he was willing to invest all the time and trouble of journeying clear back into the mountains to that cabin with me, with the chance that when he got me there his work might be all for nothing.

He loaned me two dollars to pay for a bed and my breakfast at the hotel. I promised to start the next morning.

I spent the evening rousing up as much information as I could about Luke Ridgeway. I figured that anything that I could learn would be worthwhile. It wasn't hard to get people to talk. They had heard about my shooting from the store, and they were glad enough to chat with me. A friendly lot you'll find Westerners to be if you get on the right side of them. The stories about silence west of the Mississippi usually mean that the people are shy and inclined to be suspicious of strangers.

What they told me about my friend Luke Ridgeway was that he had been a prospector for the past ten years. For another ten years before that he had been a cowpuncher. Usually he had been working around that part of the country. He was about thirty-six years old. The time that he hadn't spent around there had been put in south of the Río, for he had made several trips to old Mexico.

As for his living, he struck a fair mine now and then. For the past seven or eight months he had been coming to Elmira occasionally with gold that he took out of an old mine up in the mountains. He paid for plenty of provisions, bought himself a horse and the cow of which he had told me, and all around seemed to be prospering very well. It was suspected that he had struck a very well-paying mine, and that the reason he was making a long trip away from the place was that he might want to show ore specimens and so forth back East in order to get the mine financed on a large scale.

All of the talk sounded fairly reasonable. When I tried to get more particulars about the mine, there seemed to be no difficulty in learning even more than I needed to know. In the old days that mine had been worked by the Indians under Spanish supervision. They had done a lot of tunneling and drifting through the rock. For my part I knew nothing about mines or about mining. I gathered that this was a considerable bit of work in the Spanish days.

Usually where the Indians had mined, they had smelled out every bit of pay dirt. Now and then they overlooked something that was quite good, and this appeared to be one of the cases. Luke Ridgeway, prospecting through the mountains, had taken a look at the old mine about eight months before, after he had been away on a three-years' trip to old Mexico. By chance he had blundered on a vein of pay rock. The result was that he had been churning out money ever since.

When I had heard all of these details about Luke, the mine, and the general history that lay behind the man, I decided that perhaps my first suspicions had been all wrong. Before the next day was over I was sure of it.

Luke Ridgeway was as frank and open as any man I had ever known; he was particularly anxious to have me talk about myself, also keen to see some more of my shooting. I wasn't fool enough to commit myself. On the first evening we went out to see what we could see near our little camp — we were simply riding up — I was on one of Ridgeway's horses — with packs behind our saddles. Before we had gone a quarter of a mile from the place where we had left our horses hobbled, a deer flashed out of some shrubbery just in front of us.

It was a nasty shot — not more than twenty-five or thirty yards away, but there was only one flash at that deer as it got from one covert into the next. However, that was just the sort of work that my Maine shooting had equipped me for. These neat little hand-to-hand shots, as you might call them, are just what a man gets a thousand times while still-hunting through close cover. Fast as that deer ran, the butt of my rifle leaped to my shoulder faster, and I got in a shot. It plunged into the cover while Ridgeway was still barely turning around and unlimbering his rifle.

"A fast try, anyway," he said.

"And a dead deer, too," I said.

He gave me a look that was pretty eloquent, but after what he had seen at the store the day before, he wasn't going to commit himself too far in criticism until he made sure that I was not able to live up to what I had said.

We hurried up to the edge of the covert and we saw at once a streak of red across a bush.

"By gad," muttered Ridgeway, and he was really more impressed this time than he had been before. "Accuracy is one thing, but speed is another! However, I don't think you could have more than scratched. . . ."

Here we stepped into a little clearing in the bush. On the far side of it the deer lay — dead. The bullet had clipped right through him, from side to side.

Ridgeway was tremendously excited, and he declared that he had never seen such shooting. What he did not know was that my attention had been called to a little streak moving through the covert in the first place, so that I was more than two-thirds prepared for a glimpse of the deer as it came into the narrow gap. Ridgeway didn't know this.

"That's neater work with a rifle than I ever saw with a revolver. Why do you carry a Colt?"

I didn't say anything. It's pleasant to be admired even to excess. However, when we saw another deer in the distance, and Ridgeway started for it, I gave the deer an unnecessary glimpse of myself and scared it away without Ridgeway suspecting me, because that one deer was enough. I didn't want to have to show myself up in his eyes by missing with a long-distance shot. And miss I surely should have done, because I had not yet arranged myself in relation to the crystal-clear atmosphere of that country.

We had venison that night and carried the best of the meat with us the next day.

It was a grand ride. We were climbing all through the three days, but not climbing fast. There was just a pleasant diversity of scenery. I was busy drinking in the colors of those brown mountains and those green-black streaks and patches of evergreens growing on them, and I was getting my eye used to range finding in this new air.

My system was simply to measure the walking step of my horse. When I knew that, I could tell myself the distance to any object ahead of me and then count his steps to the spot. I was wonderfully wrong, at first. I would have undershot everything. But very quickly I began to get it right again. That, and listening to the tales of Ridgeway about mining, and dodging his efforts to get me to shoot at every buzzard that flew into the sky, kept me busy until we were in sight of the cabin.

V

"A PERFECT CABIN"

Well, when I saw that cabin, I knew my new friend was not a liar about the place, whatever might have been back in his head besides. That cabin was placed in the finest spot that I've ever seen. It was one of those places where you say: "Why doesn't somebody build a hotel here and make a resort? It'd be famous quick."

Yet there never are hotels in those places. They have to stay close to the railroads, and the people that plan the railroads have a sort of a natural gift for finding the ugliest ways across the mountains.

You see there was a cracking big mountain ripping away up into the sky. On a shoulder of it, a quarter of the way up, there was a comfortable meadow, with that cabin in it, a flash of water streaking down beside it, and green trees scattered around through all of the hollows of that big mountainside. On the top was a cap of snow, and all around those mountain ranges hit the top of the sky. You could stand there beside that cabin and keep busy for hours, with eyes traveling faster than an arrow goes, but seeing new things all of the time.

When we got to the cabin, I noticed that the shoulder was a fine meadow, covered with extra fine grass. That little creek stretched its elbows in a pool, very fine and comfortable. And there was the cow — no wild longhorn, but a sleek-sided Durham with a creamy look to her eyes.

I couldn't help saying to Ridgeway: "Look here, Ridgeway, why should anybody in the world want to be a king when he might come out here and build this cabin, like this, and have this sort of country to look at?"

He agreed, saying he knew that I would be happy there. When I got inside the cabin, it was so fine that I just laughed and went around looking at everything, enjoying myself as much as though I had made them with my own hands. Because, if I were to be there from three to six months, there was a good *reason* why I should want to see everything.

There were three good rooms in that place. It was a regular house rather than a cabin. It was built of logs that were trimmed down and leveled by hands that knew their work, I can tell you. There were no chinks and holes between the logs; they hadn't picked out a single tree with a knothole drilling through the heart of it. It was built so that you could get clearance if you stood up and stretched your arms above your head. That's plenty high for any room, and low enough to give you warmth in the winter. That cabin sat right down on the ground like it meant to stay there for a while, and you could tell by the solid look of it that it was going to be a long liver.

There was a bedroom fixed up with four bunks. The two upper bunks would fold up against the wall; the two lower ones were all fixed up with springs and mattresses and everything. Should you want more blankets for the winter, why — just open a cupboard at the side of the room, and there you would find a fine stack of them all ready for you.

A good strong table made of planks about three or four inches thick, with a pair of hurdles to hold it up, was in the room — the kind of a table it does a man's heart good to see. There was no fancy varnishing surface that makes you afraid to leave a cigarette, and it would hold all the magazines and the books you might chance to heave at it. If, by chance, you were to lean back in your chair and rest your heels on the edge of the table — well, where would the harm be in that? Take it by and large, that was about as good a table as you would find, and the floor, too, wasn't made to be worried over by womenfolk. It was made of big rough planks as strong as stone, pretty near. Nobody would bother to scrub that floor. Just give it a good sweeping out, and that would be plenty. If you were to drop a cigarette there and step on it to put it out — why, that was all right. If there was no ashtray handy, which there usually isn't, you could just knock the dottle out of the pipe onto the floor. Nobody's heart would break.

It is queer what a relief it is to get into a house where it is plain to be seen that there never was a woman and there never will be. Why, a good Maine woman would have broken her heart, scrubbing in that house. It would have taken her about six weeks to get that place what she would call presentable. And when she got all through, she would have taken all the joy out of that house for any man.

The living room-dining room was a fine place, too. Its fireplace was one of the kind that don't need a lot of chopping and splitting of the wood. You just take a sapling and bust it in two, and then you could be sure that there would be a way of fitting it into that fireplace. The hearth was made of stones a foot or so across, and set in not too particular, not smoothed off too much. It was so big that it would take a man-size spark to jump all the way across it.

When I saw that cabin I said to myself: "Home! This is home!"

When we passed from the dining room to the kitchen, I saw that the man who built that cabin was not only a mighty fine fellow, but a genius, too. The kitchen had everything that a man would ever want — from a big sink where you could wash a bucket to a big chopping block where you could break up a whole deer in no time. The stove must have been packed in all the way from Elmira. Five days of packing — over a trail that no wagon in the world could ever have lived on for five miles together. It had four legs, and the legs had pillars of stone that they were built into. You could reach under that stove and clean there, but you couldn't move that stove. Not unless you wanted to

301

take it apart and put it together again on the spot — which would be something like throwing away a year of your life! It was the sort of a stove that the boys could lean on — where it wasn't too hot. It wouldn't shake and think about falling down. I never *saw* such an oven! You could handle a whole winter's supply of meat in a single sitting, with a stove like that. It had big pot-holes in the top and two lids all fitted up with inside rings, so that you could put a small pot next to the fire there. The firebox just made me laugh — I was so happy over it. It had a grate that could be raised or lowered. When it was raised, the box wouldn't hold more than a single, good, big armload of wood. That was enough to cook your meal and heat the water, afterward. When you lowered that grate, you could stack in enough wood to bake bread or cook a deer in that enormous oven. Of course, it wasn't economical. But what difference did that make when you had a whole forest at your back door?

I said that there was a boiler. Yes, sir, the genius who built that cabin hitched a pipe and pump that ran down to the pool. It brought the water up to a tank on the side of the hill above the house. And there was a line running from the kitchen door to the windmill that stood by the tank, to pump up the water, so that you could just stand there and turn it off or turn it on. Did you notice that you never remember about the tank running over until you are warm in bed?

That kitchen would have pleased me if it hadn't had a single thing in it except the stove and hot-water boiler. But that wasn't all. I would be almost ashamed to tell you how many pots and pans there were in that house, all good, honest, unbreakable iron. No tin, no brass, no copper, no aluminum — nothing foolish, but just iron that will blacken up and look more natural and comfortable all of the time. Some folks will never be happy until they have glass things for baking. But I say that a pot of baked beans in a glass dish just looks miserable and suffering. Iron is the boss stuff. And that kitchen was full of it.

If you wanted knives, there was a whole rack stuck full of everything from butcher knives to skinning knives. And are the knives dull? There was a fine pair of grindstones in the corner, one rough enough to work on an axe, and one smooth enough for the honing of a razor.

I put that in for the polishing touch. I just want you to understand that cabin was perfect!

VI

"A MOAN IN THE NIGHT"

When I got through surveying that cabin, I told Ridgeway that it beat anything for comfort that I had ever seen. I added: "If this cabin had a cellar, it would be a regular palace."

Ridgeway laughed and said: "I don't know what you like in the way of cellars, but maybe you would like to see the sort of a dugout that's under this shack?"

He lifted a section of flooring in a corner of the kitchen — a heavy section that hooked onto an iron ring and worked back on hidden hinges, very smooth and heavy, because that flooring was two and a half inches thick. Underneath, there was a flight of steps, and Ridgeway showed the steps to me with a lantern that he carried. We went down into the snuggest little cellar that you ever saw; it was piled around with things that Ridgeway had had packed up from Elmira — all sorts of canned stuff, jars of jelly and jam, together with a regular all-winter supply of ham, bacon, flour, and such things — which interested me a good deal since I had decided that unless I wanted to do a lot of packing to Elmira and back, I would have to live on salt and the meat that I could shoot in the woods.

There was no window in that cellar, and yet the air seemed fresh, and the walls were not damp. I pointed this out to Ridgeway who admitted that it was queer. He simply said: "This is a mighty porous rock that lies under the house. You never can tell how fast winter will sink away through sandstone and gravel."

Then he took me to the mine, asking me if I were interested in mining — in a way as if he wanted me to say no. So I answered that I didn't see why people wasted their lives mucking away underground when they could have mountains like these to look at, and so many tons of game on foot and on wing. That answer seemed to please him a good deal. The mine was very old and big. He showed me some of the old, narrow diggings that the Indians had made. We even found a remnant of one of the baskets in which they had carried ore up the long, long ladders to the mouth of the mine. What leg muscles those Indians must have had, I remember thinking at the time. But hand labor was cheap for the Spaniards in the New World.

He showed me a little drift that he himself had cut off from a shaft near the mouth of the mine and told me that was where he got his gold. I didn't ask any questions, and I didn't look too close, because I could see that the less interest I showed in that section of the mine the better pleased he would be. No wonder! How could a man go off and leave a gold mine for six months in the hands of a stranger whose honesty he didn't know from the honesty of Adam? I supposed that he had showed me the drift he was working at once, because it would keep me from thinking that anything was made a mystery to me; also, it might put me on my honor more, about not working that drift.

To make that point all the stronger, Ridgeway said: "I'll pay you fifty dollars right now. That's full wages for two and a half months. But if you're to run short of provisions, that money would keep you going. And if I'm gone longer than that time, I'll pay you the other part when I come back and find that you've left everything shipshape."

That was evidently his way of saying that, if he came back and found that I had not been messing around with that drift, he would pay me in full. I jotted that idea down in my mind in red writing, as you might say. I didn't intend to raise any blisters on my hands breaking rock for the sake of gold that I might get out of that vein.

What interested me in that mine was just the large size of it and the way they had tunneled here and there. Now and then you would come to a place where a little tunnel you could hardly creep along would open out into a cavern as big as a room, where they had worked out a pocket of pay dirt long ago. Maybe you would find on the floor of that old cave a broken-pointed pick that had been dumped there 400 years ago!

It was a pretty ghostly trip. When we got out of those tunnels into the open air, I reckoned that it would take a month for me to dry the dampness and mold out of my lungs and out of my mind.

Ridgeway could hardly keep from showing how it tickled him when I told him that. I said: "I should think that, if a man ever got into trouble with the law, he could just walk into that mine and disappear, and it would take a thousand men a year to find him there."

Ridgeway gave me a quick side glance — a regular ripper! Then he said: "Now, whatever put that idea into your head? *You're* glad to get out, aren't you?"

I said that I was, and he said that he believed nobody else would like it much better than I did. However, after Ridgeway went off that evening, taking the old Mexican with him, the thing that hung in my mind was the side glance that Ridgeway had shot at me. You'll often do that, you know — just forget all about a man except one expression of his face. If you step back through your list of acquaintances, you'll find that one of them is grinning, the other fellow is laughing, and the old skinny maiden aunt is shaking her gray head and looking sour. Mostly they are in action. Friends, of course, are different, and you'll see them the way that they really are, changing from one thing to another, happy or sad — and you'll see them, somehow, without any face at all, but just as a sort of a feeling, you know.

Well, the way that I saw Luke Ridgeway

was with the devil of suspicion flashing in his eyes as he looked aside at me. It made me mighty uncomfortable; it gave my whole memory of him a very ugly cast.

After he was gone, with the humpback old Mexican, Diego Alvarez, riding along beside him — Diego was the fellow who had been temporarily taking care of the cabin — I sat down to have a pipe and a quiet little think all by myself. Ordinarily you can never think so well as you can when you're alone. I sat out in a rough chair — there were a couple of them under the pines behind the house — and tried to work the problem out.

If Ridgeway could trust that Mexican with the shack for a week, he could trust it to him for six months, it seemed to me. What was there that made me so attractive to Luke as a caretaker? Was it my shooting? Could he pretend that he really cared how much sport I had with a rifle on his place?

Very often a man will take a fancy to you and give you his trust. And you will take a fancy to another fellow and give him your trust, just in a flash. But from that side glance of Luke's I knew that he didn't have any fancy for me; he didn't even trust me. He really didn't like me at all, and he didn't want to have me around. Yet there was a reason that made him mighty, mighty glad to have me in the cabin while he was away!

I decided that I would go over the whole matter in detail, bit by bit, and try to make some head out of it, like a detective. But the first thing I knew, the evening came walking over the mountains, very grand, and here I was letting my pipe go out, just sitting there and admiring the world that I'm privileged to be sitting in.

Have you ever used a microscope and slid the wing of a fly under it? All at once what was just a little film of transparent stuff is now a sort of a miracle, with queer tints of red and blue on it, with wonderful veins running through it, all fashioned as if out of a translucent metal in scales — more beautifully than any human hands could ever work it. That is evening on the mountains — just as though they were put under a microscope, all the stupid, brown monotony and the burned look of too many hot days go away from them. They are magnified into a pure greatness and beauty.

I sat out there for more than an hour, feeling better than a king. Those mountains marched up to me in golden fire and rose, and walked away again in purples and amber and sleepy blue under the stars, until I remembered that I was mighty hungry.

There was only a single spark winking among the ashes of the firebox, but when I shaved a stick of wood into feathers and put it in with a bit of kindling heaped on top, the draft in that stove was so fine and strong that I had a ripping fire cracking there in no time. Taking the lantern down into the cellar, I stood there for a while wondering at the sweetness of the air in that place. However, the food stock interested me more than the condition of the air, just then. I got me a tin of coffee, some bacon, flour, jam, and canned apricots. Then I went upstairs and did some cooking.

To have such good things to work with made me happy. I got the fire to roaring and mixed up some pone for the oven. When that was baking, I decided on a stew. Well, before I got through, I had in that stew dried venison, a bit of the pork, canned tomatoes, celery powder, diced potatoes, onions, and a few green peppers — and dog-gone me if I didn't find even some garlic, which is the most boss thing in the world for making a stew — a stew.

Along about half past seven I started that supper, and about half past nine I started to eat. It was eleven before I had finished my pipe under the stars and gone to bed. I was happy, I can tell you. I was completely happy. That cooking was about the best time that I had ever had that I could remember. Most women should be in heaven, having all the handy tools that they have to make themselves and their kitchens comfortable. But a woman is not that way; she's not meant to be happy, so long as there is a chance for her to be mean and critical and ornery. A woman would scrub her kitchen floor just for the sake of seeing her husband step on it, so that she could rip into him for making a spot.

But there was nothing in the shape of a woman to bother me up here. Not a sound was around, not a breath was stirring — except the wind moaning very faintly farther up the hillside. I listened to it for a while, and then I closed my eyes and was just about sound asleep when a moaning began to come closer to the cabin. It had me out of bed and standing up in my bare feet with a rifle in my hand. There was no wind that ever lived that could have made a moan like that. Only a heart that was suffering could have made it.

I sneaked to the back door to listen. Yes, that noise was right there at the back door, and there was a little scratching sound under the door! I lighted a lantern and looked. Dog-gone me if there wasn't a little streak of crimson leaking in through the crack beneath that door. With my revolver in my hand, I put the lantern where it would throw a shadow on me, then snatched the door open and presented the gun.

There was nothing outside except a wall of blackness that sort of fell in on me. Down there at my feet lay a dog, flattening his head against the doorstep, battening his ears down, and whacking the floor with his tail to say that he would be an extremely good dog, if I would be nice to him. Well, a dog can take a hop, skip, and jump right into my heart about as quick as anything in the world. This here was just a common brown-and-tan cur dog with no more spirit than a mouse. I could see that with half an eye, but I couldn't leave it out there. The chief reason was that it was so pitiful and down-hearted; the other was that it had a bullet drilled right through both of its hams. It had dragged itself down here to the doorway. Perhaps it had known the old

Mexican and that had brought it here for help. Of one thing I was certain: it was not Ridgeway's dog. There is something in the eye of a man that can love a dog. And Ridgeway didn't have that look about his eye.

VII

"TROUBLE AHEAD"

When I picked the puppy up, I reached my hands around him and hit a tender place. He gave a yell and set his teeth on my arm, but not hard. He began licking my coat right away to ask my pardon and show that he had meant no harm.

I spread him out on the kitchen table, set my teeth, and cleaned those wounds. It was the worst thing I ever had to do in my life, but there is nothing much surer than that a dog will get an infection in a cut if there is half a chance. When you hurt a person, you can explain that it is for his own good — but when it comes to a dog or a horse, you just have to do what you think is good for them and hope that they may come to understand, someday. I took a rifle ramrod, soaked some cloth in iodine, and then tied that pup so it wouldn't wriggle while I put the iodine through and through its wounds. The yelling that dog did would have raised an army, but then it got so weak that it just lay on its back and rolled up its eyes and groaned like a dying man.

No doubt it would have been better if I had babied that dog for a while and given it some strength with a bit of meat — because it was two-thirds starved. But a man usually will grit his teeth and want to get the worst of anything over in one gulp. If a doctor tells you that one pill is good, you have an idea that two will be twice as good. So while I was iodizing that dog, I did a mighty good job of it, I can tell you.

Well, his tongue was hanging out of the side of his mouth before I got through with him. But when I gave him a smell of the remnants of that stew that I had cooked for supper, he came two-thirds of the way back to life at a single step. He lit into that stew as if he were inhaling mist, not eating solid food. So I just gave him a couple of gobbles, and then took him into the bedroom with me. I put a dish of water in there, but he wasn't a bit comfortable on the floor and kept jerking and whining. Finally, after I hadn't closed my eyes all night, I got up, gave him a cursing, and put him on the foot of my bed. That fool pup just stretched out, gave a deep sigh, and the next moment he was sound asleep.

I was between laughing and swearing, I was so mad to think of how I had lost a whole night's sleep. Yet I was so glad to think that the dog had forgiven me for torturing him, and had only gone to sleep when he got in touch with me.

Pretty soon, it was broad daylight. As soon as I got up and left the room, that dog started howling for me. I went back, swore, and shook my fist at him. He just lifted up his head and sort of laughed at me, as much as to say: "There you are! And I'm mighty glad to see you!"

I couldn't be mad at him, after that. I carried him outdoors, and then I brought him into the shack, put him on a bed of sacks, and left him there while I cooked his breakfast and mine. He kept his head up, watching me all the time, almost wagging his tail off when he smelled the good food cooking. But he didn't whine or yip once — except when I stepped out of the room. Then he set up a yell that made the mountains ring! Confound that dog, he had me going. Just in the distance I walked down to the lake for a plunge, and back again. I didn't stay to dry myself at the lake, but ran all the way to the house with the clothes in my hands, freezing in that cold mountain air.

He stopped his yelling, when he saw me, and I couldn't beat him when he began to whine with joy. I saw that dog was simply afraid to be left alone. The world had used him so badly that he had to be with humans or else break his heart, grieving. It made my heart squeeze up as small as a crab apple with pain to see the size and the make of a dog like that, equipped with no more spirit than this! He was a good, roomy-built dog. I suppose he would have weighed seventy-five pounds. He had a fine, long snout, and teeth good enough for a bull terrier. He had the legs and the body of a good running hound. His hair was short, but there was a good, heavy outer layer of bristle, like the coat of an Airedale, that promised to see him through snowy winters. I suppose that at least a dozen bloods were mixed into the last few generations of his ancestry. He wasn't bad-looking — but there was no heart in him at all.

There were two openings for me. One was to kill the dog and bury it. Then I would be free to go off hunting. The other thing was to stay right there at home and live on dried meat and canned food until those shot wounds were cured.

I decided to kill him, of course. And, of course, I didn't. For two mortal weeks I took care of that dog, until the fool could walk around again. Yes, sir, and, at the end of two weeks, I took my rifle and started out to hunt, with that mongrel wagging his tail, hobbling behind me, whining now and then with weakness and with pain.

I couldn't scare him into stopping that whining. He wasn't in the least afraid of me. Not in the least. Because I had never had the heart to strike him, I suppose. And the contrast between me and the other men that he knew was so great that he just took me for a different breed. All the fool would do would be to put up his ears and waggle his tail when I scolded him. I couldn't help loving him for it.

He was never a crowding dog. I mean, he never took advantage of me, but always wanted to be helpful. He picked up what he learned around me by signs and not by lessons. After supper, for instance, he always saw me pull off my heavy, walking boots and put on some soft deerskin moccasins that I had found in the shack. Before he could walk well, he would come hobbling over to me with those slippers in his mouth as soon as he saw me pull off my boots.

He learned to do other handy things. Every minute that he was awake, he never took his eyes off my face. No, it was simply impossible for me to teach him with a whip. He learned enough things just out of affection.

The first day we went out walking, we found out that the game had come down to the edge of the meadow, because I had done very little shooting during the past two weeks, of course. Even with a lame dog to cripple me, I got a deer. The dog was prouder of that than I was. He walked around that deer, smelled the blood, growled, and sat down and watched every lick I made in cutting it up. You would have thought that he had killed that animal.

After that, the dog and I hunted every day. I have to admit that it was a treat to have him along with me. He shook the cramps out of his weak hind legs. The wounds had cured wonderfully well; very soon he was running as free as if nothing had ever happened to him.

A month after I got the dog, I found out his origin. I was cutting down a tree for firewood, and the dog was scouting around in the distance when I heard a gunshot and a yell from the pup. He came scooting to me and squatted between my feet with his tail between his legs. His hair was bristling along his back. He was growling and whining all in a breath — a picture of the maddest and most frightened dog you ever saw in your life! I just had time to pick up my rifle and drop my axe, when two men came sauntering along through the trees, one of them with a rifle ready.

He sang out: "Stand clear of that fool dog, stranger! Barney, here's your last day on earth, damn your stupid eyes!" He pulled his rifle to his shoulder.

Barney wanted to run, and he wanted it bad. But when he thought of running, he shivered closer against my leg and then looked up to me to know what he ought to do. I told him to cheer up, and then I said to the stranger: "Look here, if this is your dog, and you want to get rid of him, just leave him with me. I don't mind taking care of him."

He was a mean devil, that stranger. A big, ugly-faced brute, the kind of man you could imagine shooting his own dog.

He said: "Maybe that's kind of you. But I don't want anybody's help. I'll handle that dog myself. I paid my money for him, and I'll have the finishing of him. Won't I, Jerry?"

Jerry grinned and said that he supposed Bill would have his own will.

So Bill told me to stand away from that dog because I was apt to get my shins splintered.

It made me mad. I slung my rifle under my arm and looked Bill in the eye. "Bill," I said, "if you want trouble, I don't mind saying that I'll give you a double handful. Now get out of these woods and get quick. You hear me talk?"

He heard me talk well enough. He made a forward step to show that he couldn't be bluffed.

Jerry read me better. He said: "We ain't so much bent on killing that dog that we want to kill a man along with it."

I was really so worked up that I would have shot — and shot to kill — if Bill had given one wobble to the rifle he carried. He looked me over again and decided that it was foolish to make a great matter out of a dog, so he backed up a little and, from the edge of the trees, said: "I'm not through with you. I'll come back for you, and maybe I'll get the dog, and the man, too!" With that he backed up and got away into the trees.

I couldn't resist the temptation, although it was very wrong. I loosed a bullet through the trees. At the sound and the cracking of the slug through the twigs and branches over their heads, that pair of scalawags let out a couple of yells. I could hear them legging it away as fast as they could run.

But Barney — that was the chief joke. He saw his former boss disappear, and he sneaked out a pace or two toward the trees. Then he gave a growl, and, when the two of them ran away, he tore after them as far as the edge of the trees, as though he intended to run them down and eat them up.

When he got in the shade of the trees, he changed his mind and came back to me, wagging his tail and stepping high. Killing deer and running men were a part of his lifework, to see the way that pup acted. I had to lean on my gun and break out laughing, I was so amused. Yet even while I stood there laughing, I knew that I had the chance of big trouble ahead of me. The brute face of Bill and his sneaking partner, Jerry, promised loads of trouble for me, and I guessed that it would be some time before I should be able to sleep solid through the night.

There was never a guess that panned out closer to a true prophecy.

VIII

"BARNEY GIVES THE SIGNAL"

By this time, I had been over a month in Ridgeway's cabin. I had come to like it better and better, so much that I began to dread the day when I should have to leave the place. Of course, when you begin to worry about leaving, time flies. The month was no more to me than a week, I can tell you, but what convinced me that I had been for a considerable time in the place was my work with the rifle. I had gained the faculty of hitting off distances, long and short range, very well.

I had grown to like the clear air for shooting. The oddest thing was that I could do a good deal better in the early morning before sunup, or in the late evening just before sundown, when the colored light and the land mist gave the air a density something like that of Maine.

Take it all around, it was a grand month I spent — even though I can look back now and see that I was spending it on the brink of a precipice. When I think back to those days and remember that odd bargain that Ridgeway had made with me, when I recall some of his odd expressions, it seems that I was a complete dunderhead not to have guessed at all sorts of terrible trouble long before it came. Well, looking backward, we can all be good second guessers.

That day of the meeting with Bill the Brute and Jerry the Sneak, I got back to the cabin and took the precaution of cooking my supper before it got dark. I was ready to close up shop before twilight came and made it necessary for me to show a light. You can trust me that I had no desire to light a lamp by which that precious pair of scoundrels could shoot me. Murder was just their level, and the safer the murder, the better.

When I had the work done up — because it's a lot better to get all the dishwashing done in the evening, and have a clean deck for the morning — I went around and locked up. Another good thing about that cabin was that it had extra strong locks on the doors and on the windows — big locks that were sunk deeply in the logs.

I closed the front and back door and locked every window. Then I made a round of every window in the house, trying the locks all over again. When I had done that, I went back to the bedroom, opened the window there, and went to bed, because I guessed that Barney would give me the signal if anyone tried to get into the house from *that* angle.

Lying awake just long enough to smoke my good night pipe, I thought over the killing of a deer that I had nabbed that morning. I had stalked him over a range of hills farther down the valley; when I got a chance at him, he was lining out and away across a crest. I just managed to try a snap shot and that shot was a 400-yard guess. I had fresh venison that night for supper. It wasn't altogether luck, either, that shot. So I had something worth dreaming about, and, when I went to sleep, I had just about forgotten Mr. Bill and his friend, Jerry.

I had been asleep a good long while — I found that out later — but it seemed to me that I had barely closed my eyes when I felt a cold, wet nose poked into the palm of my hand. I lifted my head to curse Barney, and then I knew by the shuddering of that cold nose that Barney was scared almost to death, so scared that he didn't dare move or yip. When a dog is as frightened as that, it is time for a man to watch his step.

First of all, I slid the revolver from under my pillow and looked toward the window. That window held a mountain's peak and a half a dozen stars like a little painted picture, but there was no sign of a man's head and shoulders there. Then it came over me that somebody might have climbed through the window and might be crawling toward my bunk across the floor.

That was the most cold idea that ever came to me in my life, I think. I could feel Barney shivering and shaking more and more every minute. That didn't help the state of my nerves any. I pushed myself up on one elbow, inch by inch. One board in the bunk was a little loose, and every time that I moved around in the night, it was apt to slip a little and screech like the devil. Well, this night as I started moving, I cursed my foolishness in not having nailed down that board a long time ago. You know how it is about some things. You always swear that you'll do something, after you get to bed at night, and then you never think about until you're in bed the next time! I prayed that board would make no noise as I sat up in the bunk. Of course, my prayer wasn't granted.

No, the board slipped and gave a groan, just like a man in pain. I freshened my grip on my Colt, and swung myself up to my knees with a jerk, because I knew that this would bring on a crisis of some sort. Nothing rose at me from the shadowy floor of the room, and there was no squeak of a footfall in the doorway. But all at once, Barney let out a cross between a growl and a howl, and started for the door of the room so hard that his claws slipped and scratched on the floor a minute before he could get himself started.

That scared me for Barney. I yelled at him to come back, but right then he was interested in his own ideas a lot more than mine. He headed out through the doorway, into the kitchen, lickety-split. Then I heard a howl from him — sharp and high as a whistle, not the yelp of a dog that gets a kick and runs away, however. It was the yell of a dog that is hurt but hangs on all the harder. I hadn't expected that much spirit from old Barney, of course, and I was proud to hear that sound.

I told myself that I would find the man and the dog fighting in the kitchen, and that I would put an end to him, then and there. When I got to the kitchen, there was no man either lying or standing there. Barney was a dim silhouette, running around the edges of the trap door to the cellar and whining.

What could have been better than that? I could tell in an instant that I had something trapped down there. Of course, I remembered that cellar was dug out of the solid rock and that there was not a sign of any opening to it except through that same trap door. What I earnestly hoped was that Jerry and Bill might both be in that cellar. At any rate, I decided that I would camp in the kitchen the rest of the night.

I put a blind across the kitchen window, so that if one of the pair happened to be on the outside of the house, he couldn't pot me as I lighted the lantern. Then I made myself a light and put a rifle handy, although inside a house there is nothing to beat a Colt that shoots .45-caliber slugs. It knocks you down even if you're not killed instantly. After I had a light, I caught the ring of that cellar door and lifted it just a fraction of an inch, calling down through the cracks: "Bill and Jerry, or whichever one of you may be in the cellar, I want to warn you right now that there is no way out of that place except through this trap door! Now, partners, you can stay in that cellar until you die for the lack of water. Or else you can come up and give yourselves up. If you give yourselves up, just throw your guns up through the trap, here, and then come up, one at a time, and I'll promise that I won't knock you in the head. Does that sound good to you?"

There was no answer out of the cellar, and I sat down to wait for a while, for I figured that they would feel around and light matches until they had convinced themselves that I was right.

Well, I sat there until the morning light began. Still there was no voice up from the cellar, although I opened the trap door twice and urged them not to make things worse for themselves by trying to hold out on me.

After morning came, I opened up the house. The fresh dawn light made me feel a good deal more at ease and more rested. While I was out of the kitchen, Barney didn't leave the trap door for an instant. He sat there, just whining with eagerness. There was only one wonderful thing about that to me — which was that Barney should have shaken off so much fear of his old boss between the afternoon and the night. Barney was so smart that I decided that just one sight of his former master streaking it away on the run must have decided him that the man was a bluff — and so he was.

Well, when I began to feel better, I decided that the best way to wear out the nerves and the patience of any prisoners would be to let them hear me cooking breakfast. With a great rattling I started a fire, singing and carrying on in great style. There wasn't a peep from the cellar. Then I remembered that there was a lot of canned fruit down there that would give them drink enough to last them for a long time — and enough other kinds of food to carry them along for a year. How could I keep those prisoners down there for any length of time?

This was a new angle on the deal and brought a chill down my spine. I decided that I would have to have it out with them in a little confab, then and there. I propped up the trap door with the bottom of a chair, and I called out to them down there — but that instant Barney squeezed through the gap and plunged down the stairs into the terrible blackness of the cellar!

I gave him up for a dead dog that instant. Then I heard him raving and yelling again. There was only one way to interpret that — my men had got away!

However, a man can't stand by and abandon his dog, even if there *is* danger. So I took my courage in my teeth, so to speak and, throwing open that trapdoor, went down, lantern in hand.

The minute that I stood in the cellar room I saw that it was empty of men. There was just the food supply ranged around on the shelves, or boxed up and lying on that wonderful dry cellar floor. Yes, sir, the two men were gone — if there had been two — and here was Barney, like a little fool, scratching away at an edge of the wall.

Most of that cellar was finished off smoothly, but there was one spot where you could see that the tools of the workers had failed them — or their patience had given out — apparently because the hardness of the rock was much greater at this point.

At this point, the wall projected into the cellar a little, presenting a side like that of a vast, rudely made boulder. *This* was the point where that foolish dog was scratching like a mad thing.

"You little idiot," I said to Barney. "Are

you going to tear up a million tons of solid granite to get at them?" Then I had to sit down and hold my head in my hands.

Where *had* my quarry gone? Certainly, if there is any truth in a dog's nose, Barney had heard those men, or that man, retreating in my house after I sat up in my bunk and made the noise. The sound of the retreat had encouraged Barney to trail them into the kitchen. They must have disappeared down the trap — and thence into the cellar. But how could they have faded through the cellar wall? Then I remembered something that had been told to me beside some campfire, about the keen senses some dogs have for spirits. It is said that a dog can tell when a ghost walks near. . . .

When that idea came to me, I stared at the boulder where Barney was still scratching and whining and sniffing with a new feeling. That Barney would have persuaded any man to do something. He ran to me from the place where he was scratching and wearing out his nails on the hard rock. He caught me by the trouser leg.

"All right, Barney," I said. "I'll show you what an awful fool you are."

I went up and got a pick and came back.

While I was gone, Barney went almost mad, but, to my astonishment, he would not leave the cellar.

I got the pick ready, gave it a swing, and whanged away at the spot where Barney was scratching. The pick simply rebounded from the terribly hard face of stone.

"You see?" I cried to Barney.

He merely looked up at me and wagged his tail in great pleasure at the thing I had done. He sniffed the spot where I had struck and stood back, looking so expectant that I could not help breaking into a laugh. Neither could I help striking another half-hearted blow. And that light swing of the pick sank to the wood in the solid stone.

IX

"MORE SURPRISES"

Those of you who have done any boxing know how it feels when, after milling around with the other fellow for a long time, you manage to clip your knuckles against the point of his jaw in just that magic place known as the button. Suddenly the big, strong fellow turns limp, staggering before your eyes. Perhaps he falls flat on his face. Not because you have struck him with any very great force, but because you have nicked him on the right spot. It's a queer experience, but it could never stack up with what I felt when I drove that pick home. I knew at once that something was wrong. I had jammed that pick into a hollow in the rock — not forcing it through the solid stone at all. So I heaved at the haft of the pick, and presently I could feel the point wobbling around on the inside of the big stone. I got very excited at this. I jerked harder than before — and suddenly I saw the whole great boulder in front of me quiver and stir.

I leaped for the stairs and ran halfway up to the kitchen level before my pulse rate began to sink toward normal. I had an idea that I had been prying at some vital spot in the foundations, and that I was on the verge of drawing the whole wall down on top of me. But another idea had come to me, a storybook idea. I went back to that boulder, where Barney was still whining and scratching, and I began to work at it and feel it all over. Finally the whole mass gave and turned a little to one side. There was a little click — and now I knew that this was a part of a complicated blind. The side twist of that heavy mass was simply the first part of the necessary combination for opening it. I pressed in with all my might, but the wall was firm. I tugged toward me — and the wall lunged into my face and knocked me down.

So exquisitely balanced was that mass of hundreds of pounds that a child could have swung it back and forth, and revealed what I saw before me as I sat up from the ground again — the long, slanting mouth of a tunnel sinking rapidly down into the earth. I held the lantern before this gap, half expecting to have a shot fired at it from the depth of the hiding place. But there was no sound of a gun. It occurred to me that it was very queer that Jerry and Bill should have known all the intimate secrets of a place like this. If they knew how to escape through this tunnel, they had doubtless entered by the same place. Long hours ago they had gone away and were now, no doubt, discussing methods of doing for me in a new attempt.

I had enough for the time being. Going back to the kitchen in time to save my bacon from burning, I ate a breakfast that had the chief emphasis laid upon coffee — extra black and lots of it. When I had downed the third cup, my spirits were rising again.

I went back to the cellar and started down that tunnel. I had a lantern on which I had arranged a hood. It enabled me to throw just a single ray of light before me, from time to time, to show me the way. And I had a thick piece of cloth wrapped around each shoe to prevent any noise underfoot.

That tunnel had not gone far — always sinking rapidly toward the bottom of the earth — before I began to realize that there was a good deal of similarity between its dimensions and those of the cuts and tunnels that I had seen in the old mine that Ridgeway had introduced me to. I wasn't sure until I came to a great cross-cut. Two separate drifts joined the one in which I was, and, where they focused on mine, there had apparently been a great chamber store with rich ore. At least 20,000 cubic feet of rock had been removed from this single point! Unquestionably this was a section of the mine. I could realize the true vastness of the work that the Spaniards had extorted from the Indians in the old centuries. I also realized that it was madness for me to attempt to follow the trail down this drift. I might simply lose myself in a maze of the underground works, or perhaps walk right into the muzzles of the guns of Jerry and his friend, Bill. So I went back.

Even Barney, who had been sneaking along ahead of me in a most tigerish fashion up to now, seemed to lose all of his interest in the affair as he came into the big chamber where the great pocket of ore had once been removed. He lay down at my feet and remained panting there until I started back, when he readily walked on ahead of me.

I got to the cellar and closed the rock door, securing it by giving it a strong wrenching twist to the side. Then I went back to my rustic chair under the pines to enjoy a doze in the morning warmth of the sun with the sweetness of that purified air around me. Nothing could warm a corner of my heart, and the foul dampness of the great tunnels remained in my soul, as it were, for long hours. I thought again of the deadly side glance that I had received from the eyes of Ridgeway. How could Ridgeway have known and planned upon my meeting with big Bill and his sneaking companion? Finally I decided that I must go for help. Yet how could I go without most signally betraying the trust that Ridgeway had placed in me?

Finally I was very set on remaining in the cabin — no matter what happened, or how many Bills and Jerrys were in hiding for my scalp. If they came and found the shack deserted, they would be pretty sure to pay their attentions to me by stealing whatever they could remove and putting a match to the rest of it. That shack had a personality for me. I would have cared a great deal more about the destruction of that house than the death of almost any man I knew about.

I got some of the bad taste of that affair out of my mouth with a ripping good lunch that I turned in and cooked, very soon — a lunch so good that I thought that the smell of the stew cooking must have been strong enough to draw the sneaks up out of their hiding places even if they were plotting my death at that instant.

Barney was sleepy after that. I opened the trap door, but he merely yawned at it. That made my own nerves a good deal more steady. I took a nap myself. Then we got up and started on a short hunt. I never had to hunt far, if it were merely venison that I wanted. Although I wasn't in any need of venison, having killed only the morning before, still, who could resist the temptation of walking out with a gun in a country like that?

However, the only deer that I beat up was a huge stag that started in the wrong direction when it winded me and came crashing straight toward me. When it was three steps away, it saw me with my rifle at my shoulder. It stopped so fast that it almost shook its hide off over its head. Well, I followed that fool stag for a long distance with my rifle, and I didn't fire — I hardly know why, except that the fear in the face of that poor, scared thing was most awfully like fear in the face of a man. Anyway, I let it go. As a sort of a reward for holding off, you might say, I had a shot at a coyote not ten minutes later.

It's my opinion that the coyote is the wisest thing that lives on four feet. I'm pretty sure that in a country where there is a good deal of shooting done, the coyotes will soon learn to recognize the scent of a gun and the hunter, and follow them for what they may leave behind. Why not? I have seen so many men cut a few steaks out of a deer's carcass and let the rest go to feed the first thing that comes along.

At any rate, I felt eyes behind me, and, turning sharply around, I got a hard shot at a little gray streak. It hadn't expected me to turn like that, and it jumped sidewise into a bush. But I had it fairly in my sights, and, when it dropped in the bush, it wasn't interested in getting up again. That was a strange rifle shot. When I examined the body, I found that the bullet had cut through its whole body, and come out through the left hip. It didn't leave a large hole where it came out, and that meant that it had remained without spreading, no matter how many bones it had bitten through on its journey. It was a bad pelt, a good deal of the hair off and in a half-mangy condition, so I let the body lie as it was and started rounding back toward the cabin, because I began to feel guilty after even such a short absence as this.

I came back past the mine and looked in at the mouth of it as I went. The shadowy heart of it had a different meaning for me than it had had the day that Luke Ridgeway showed me through the place as far as I wanted to go. I had just stepped back out of the entrance gap in the hillside, and I was taking notice how the mounds of rock — the result of the digging in the mine — that lay around me had been silted over by several centuries of mountain winds, crumbled by the snows and the suns of hundreds of fiercely alternating seasons. Now a skin of soil had gathered, and in this soil the grass had taken root. Here and there, some big boulder thrust its gray knees out into the light of day and would continue to do so for another million years, no matter how thick the dust blew that way in summer.

It does a man good to take note of things like this. The reason is, I suppose, that it makes dying an easier thing by a whole lot. We push our heads above the soil and grow a while, and turn to seed, and drop back into the ground — well, there's nothing so terrible about that. I don't need to be told stories about complicated heavens in order to make me look at death with my eyes opened.

I was still wandering about like that; Barney was chewing a branch of a dead bush that he had taken a fancy to, when all at once he dropped flat on the ground. It didn't take me long to think matters over. I was sort of absent-minded, just then, and that's the best condition to be in to take suggestions quickly, and at the same time take them hard.

I dropped, too, hitting the ground as flat as Barney was himself. Oh, bless that dog and his bad nerves! If he had been a brave pup, he would have stood up and growled. Then the bright idea of dropping for that ground would never had occurred to me. I would have stood up. At the best I would have been able to turn around and get a rifle bullet through my breast, instead of through my back. Yes, sir, for the trigger finger of that murderer was already crooked around the trigger of that gun so hard that he turned the bullet loose even while I was dropping. I heard it bite past me with a whiz. Looking to the side, I saw a man jump behind a tree.

You might say that I *expected* a man.

What beat me was that it was not Bill or his pal, Jerry, that I saw, but an olive-skinned Mexican.

X

"A DISCOVERY"

You have to remember that my rifle was a single-shot affair. I couldn't waste the bullets trying to scare the Mexican from behind the tree where he was taking shelter at that moment. I dropped that rifle and jerked out a Colt. There I lay on my belly, only wiggling around until I was facing the tree behind which the man had dodged. I might have spent an hour there, waiting for a chance at his brown face.

Here the dog began to show signs of life. He started out and wriggled forward on his belly, very scared, as I could see from the way that he was shaking and hugging the ground, but determined to have a look at the man behind the tree. I had to laugh at that dog, and yet I had to admire him, too. It was what you would have called in a man a fine exhibition of moral courage, because Barney was making himself do things that he didn't want to do, at all. He got around beside the tree, and then it was a grand joke to see him sneak along by inches, sticking his head out and then jerking it back again, as if he were afraid of what he expected to see there. Poor Barney! Well, he finally jumped around that tree — and there was no Mexican bad language in answer. So I jumped up and hurriedly ran in.

The ground shelved down sharply on the far side of that tree. All that the Mexican had had to do was to get down low, on hands and knees, and crawl away. It was only wonderful to me that he hadn't gone to take up a new position among the trees and there pot away at me as snugly as you please. However, he had simply made his getaway. That was a little odd, considering the murderous, cunning look on his face.

I leaned against that tree, feeling weak and sagging at the knees. Yonder was Barney, as busy as a bee, running this way and that, wagging his tail, his nose working down on the ground. No matter how afraid I was of what might be waiting for me yonder among the trees, I had to go ahead. As long as that frightened dog would run the trail, I had to run it behind him.

He worked straight ahead among the trees, keeping pretty much in a straight line and working along fairly fast, while I began to admire his intelligence and surmise that there must be foxhound blood in him.

Just then I passed a bit of soft loam. There I found the footmarks of a man walking straight back along the line that Barney was following. Yes, sir, that idiot dog was running the back trail and not the forward trail at all.

It was too late to start over again, even if he had sense enough to try the forward trail. So I let him work away. After all, it was almost as worthwhile to discover the back trail of this would-be murderer, as it was to learn where he had taken himself after missing his shot — through no fault of his own.

We worked steadily through the woods, across a clearing and another stretch of forest, and then came whang straight upon the mouth of the mine, but not into it.

Barney stood there on the edge of the shadow, wagging his tail, as much as to say that he would be glad to go on in — if only I would encourage him a little. *I* needed encouragement to go into a place like that. If the Mexican had come out from the mine, he might very well have gone back into it by a circuitous way around. If he went back there now, it would be a sure way of committing suicide to follow that trail down into the darkness.

I was pretty curious, naturally. Finally I went to the shack, got a lantern, and lighted it. Then I hooded that lantern as well as I could and started back. Barney, for the first time, had failed to keep right at my heels. There must have been some bloodhound in his veins. At any rate, he certainly loved a man trail. I found him sitting down halfway between the house and the mouth of the mine.

He was extremely glad to see me, and we went back to that well mouth of watery blackness. I treated myself to a good, long look at the sunshine world around me. I remember particularly taking notice of a silly blue jay, flashing and floating above the tips of the pine trees and scolding some squirrel at a great rate. A mighty peaceful and bright world for a man to leave, of course. Finally I turned my back on it and forced my steps into the mine.

Using the lantern only once in a while to keep track of where I was going, I pulled aside the hood just enough to loose a single shaft of light. One wink of the light was all that I allowed myself at a time. My head was getting a good bumping on the tops of the tunnels along which we were walking or crawling, for Barney was working at a brisk rate. The ground was damp there in the mine, which made the scent hold clearer. He kept right along, never more than ten steps ahead of me, however. There was not *that* much recklessness in my dog.

Once, I heard the rattle of a rock behind me. It was not imagination; it was exactly the sort of a noise made when a stone stirs under the tread of a man — a grinding, rattling noise all in one, if you can understand what I mean by that. It scared me almost to death. I dropped on my knees and put my shoulders against the damp wall of the drift. Then I called to Barney in a whisper. He didn't need to be called twice. That infernal coward of a dog crouched between my knees, trembling and crowding back against me. Confound a dog like that! A man expects his dog to learn politeness from him, but he reasonably can expect to learn courage from his dog. Any mongrel ought to be foolishly reckless, except when he hears his master's voice. Barney let me keep up heart for both himself and me, which was very hard work.

We waited there for a long time. Just as my nerves began to settle down, and I had decided that there was nothing in the mine, after all, that the noise had been made by a fall of loose rock, Barney would give a start and set my nerves jumping.

Maybe we were there ten or twenty minutes, although it seemed ten times that long before I set my teeth and stood up to get back out of that mine. When I stood up, Barney seemed to think that I meant to go on with the exploration. He started again on that back trail, and shame made me follow him, instead of turning back.

We came presently down to a sharp angling turn of the passage, against the wall of which I thumped myself pretty hard. Then Barney disappeared! I loosed a shaft from the lantern, and I whispered — but Barney was gone. I thought how many stories there are of sudden pits in the middle of a mine — down the abandoned shafts of which a man may drop a hundred feet or more to his death. Perhaps that dog was gone, without a sound.

Then I heard a faint sound just above me as I thought — a sound like a man's breath, suddenly taken as he is about to make a violent effort. I crouched and looked up, raising an arm to shield myself. Then I heard that sound again, but this time, to my great relief, I realized it was the snuff of a scenting dog. I flashed a ray from the lantern, and it struck on the opening where a raise had been sunk in the top of that drift along which we had been working. I climbed up on it, the lantern in one hand and a Colt in the other. The first flare of the lantern light showed me the silhouette of Barney working around on the floor of a little chamber just big enough for a man to work in, keeping on his knees. It showed me the chamber, and a rusty pick on the floor of it, and along the side a streak several inches wide that glittered with a regular embroidery of golden thread.

I know nothing of mining, mining methods or ore, but any child could have told in one glance that this was an enormously rich vein. I knew nothing of the way that veins may pinch out of gold pockets. It seemed to me that the vein there must represent another regular Comstock Lode. I crawled up and unhooded the lantern. Then I sank that pick into the vein and broke off a little chunk of rock. It fairly flamed in my hand, it was so interlarded with the precious stuff. It seemed to me heavier than any rock that I had ever weighed, although perhaps that was just the excitement of the moment. A fever came up in me to tear away at that vein then and there, to pick loose all that I could carry away with me. Afterward, I had a moment of saneness in which I sat down and held Barney by the nape of the neck to keep him from making any noise and disturbing me.

Of course, this was the vein that Luke Ridgeway was working in the mine, and not the sham place that he had showed to me. This was his hidden place that kept him up there among the mountains — not the freedom or the hunting, no matter what he pretended. This was the stuff that he ground up in his little hand mill. No wonder he had been taking out enough to keep himself going. In fact, if he did not have thousands of dollars' worth of that metal hoarded away somewhere near the cabin, I would be very much surprised.

Then there was another difficulty thrown in my way. When he had a treasure like this in his hands, why would he leave the mine and go away? To be sure, he had made certain that I was a greenhorn from a part of the country where gold mining had never been seen; so his secret was fairly safe with me. Yet men do not leave such a thing as that gold vein, unless they have desperate reasons, very desperate — life-and-death reasons.

Another thing popped into my mind, then, with a shock that stunned me. Barney had followed the back trail of the Mexican to this place. That meant that Ridgeway was not the only person who knew about the mine. The Mexican knew, also. That was why he was taking pot shots at me from behind trees. He thought that *I* knew, too. He wanted to remove me from the scene before he went ahead with his operations and began to clean out that vein. That made the whole thing fairly clear to me. Only two points remained to puzzle me. One was that the Mexican had not been able to locate this far-hidden pocket in the old mine, unless he had previous knowledge of it. The other point was that I should have had the coincidence to fall into trouble with the Mexican and Bill and Jerry — one on the heels of the other.

I had the gold fever, sure enough. But I had the will to live just a little bit longer, still. So I pocketed that specimen, and I started back out of that mine, with Barney showing me the way like a regular partner. As I got to the good, honest sunshine again, I didn't pause, I made a way back among the trees and, watching every step of the way, I cut back toward the cabin.

XI

"DANGER"

The whole place was terribly changed for me. Before, there had been nothing but a lazy good time and general fun, hunting, cooking, and pleasing nobody but myself. When I sneaked back toward the shack on this day, I knew that I would have to live like a condemned criminal until I had settled the Mexican, or until he had settled me. There would be no more easy excursions along through the hills.

Only one thing helped me — Barney. He had been a scared dog all his life, and he had formed the habit of keeping his eyes open and looking around to see what was what. That would help me now. Every third glance I sent at Barney to see what he was doing in the way of registering fear. From that minute on, I was mighty glad that dog was a real coward, afraid of everything in the world except me.

When I got to the shack, I sent Barney in first. He nosed around and looked things over. He came back to me and wagged his tail, showing me that there was no danger in the shack. I thanked God for that dog, again. Then I went in to look things over — not things in the shack, but what I was to do to meet this double danger — on the one hand from Jerry and Bill, on the other hand from the greater danger — that Mexican.

The latter was the main trouble. I had bluffed Jerry and Bill away once, and I might be able to bluff them away again. The face of that Mexican was plain bad and mean and dangerous. He was a mighty nasty fellow. A child could have told that in any language. His little, bright, black eyes with the yellow showing where the white should have been, and his broad, Indian-like features, made me know that he would hunt me down exactly as a Indian might have hunted down an enemy in the old days out in this same country.

Altogether, it was a pretty nasty fix.

I thought of one chance that might be a solution, right away — which was to go back to the mine immediately and find the pocket, and stay there beside the gold, knowing pretty well that, if the Mexican had been there once, he would surely come there again. Perhaps that was the best and the quickest way out of the tangle, and I'm ashamed to say that the reason I didn't take that solution was because I simply didn't have the nerve to go back and wait in the horrible darkness of the mine — maybe for many hours — listening to whispering noises in the distance. No, I didn't have the courage for that. I was never any desperado. There was never a time in my life when I would go hunting for trouble. This was infinitely worse than anything I had ever dreamed of being mixed up with.

I sat in the middle of the kitchen, staring blankly out the window where the clouds were chasing themselves across the sky — all except one little silver bit of cloud — no, that was the moon, just a half moon hanging very dimly in the pallor of that sun-flooded western sky. Then I remembered that this would be a moonlit night. That gave me an idea that was just the second cousin to the thought of staying in the mine and waiting for the Mexican. I won't tell you how the idea first came to me, after I noticed that bit of a moon in the sunlit sky. I won't tell you what hours I spent during the rest of the day, sitting there shuddering, telling myself one moment that I would do it, and then telling myself again that it would be too grisly a job.

When the dusk began to grow, I swore that it was better to face the danger, if I could, than to go on living here under the very nose of it. Time and suspense were like a knife-edge, and me standing on the sharpest part of the edge.

In the first dimness after sunset, I built up the kitchen fire, putting in a good load of wood, mostly new-cut, unseasoned, half-green wood that would take a long time in burning. When that firebox was jammed to the top with fuel and the dampers turned down in a certain way, that fire would burn for hours. Then, on the back of the stove, where just enough heat would come to make the pot simmer, I put on a great iron kettle filled with beans, and I dropped in a chunk of salt pork to make the fragrance of that pot seem more natural and home-like.

I put on the teakettle, too, in a place where it would steam, and yet not burn out dry. Then I laid the table with an iron plate, a knife and fork, set out a chunk of bread and a pitcher of cream that I had skimmed on purpose out in the cooling house. I set out a cup and saucer, and I put out a slab of butter. There was a can of jam and a lot of other things, like bottled ketchup, that would make a mountain man, used to pone and bacon and not much else, almost die of joy at the thought of eating them. After that, I pushed the coffee pot onto the back of the stove, where it would steam just enough to keep that house smelling like a restaurant.

When these things were finished off, I went around and closed up the shack good and tight. Except that in the bedroom I left the shutters a little bit open, so that a man could squint in and survey the whole room. In the kitchen I left the western window just a bit open so that the western wind, which was blowing pretty steady after sunset time, would wag the curtain back and forth and give a man a chance to look things over inside.

There was the shack looking as though it were all prepared for the night with an enemy to take thought of on the outside. The two loopholes were arranged so that, if a man glimpsed in through those places, he would see that two of the rooms were empty — everything all set out and a meal steaming hot on the stove. It would look as though I had just stepped into the living room and might be back any minute. A man might wait right there at the kitchen window — or at the bedroom shutter — with his rifle ready.

When these things were all ready, I opened the trap and went down into the cellar with the dog and the lantern. With that hooded lantern, after I had opened the mouth of the tunnel, I started off down it.

It was a damp, miserable job. For one thing, I had a pretty good chance of getting lost in that mine. Because I didn't want to starve to death, I had put some dry bread in my pockets. But I had no water — and if the oil burned out in the lantern before I had found my way out. . . . Well, it made me feel like the first day of school when I thought of that — sick and empty in the pit of the stomach, I mean. But I was too desperate to stop. That murdering face of the Mexican was worse than a living nightmare, and I wanted to get him bad.

I plugged ahead. When I came to the big cross drifts, I stopped for a while, pretty much tempted to turn back. At last I was able to force my way on through it. I took the right-hand drift and plugged away. For a long time we kept going down. Then I came to a place where the timbers had broken — from rotting away in that underground dampness, I suppose. The passage was completely jammed before me. I went back and took the left-hand turn. Now I walked for more than an hour, winding up and down, back and forth, crawling more than I walked. When I did walk I had to bend over. I made up my mind that night that the life of a miner must be worse than any other life a man can lead.

Only by chance I came out right in the end. I took a right-hand instead of a left-hand turn. In another five minutes I saw the broad, white face of the moon hanging before me in the black of the tunnel. When I came out from the mouth of the cave and into the sweet, open air of the night, Barney was glad of it, too. He did a sort of war dance. But he was a pretty silent dog — except when he was left alone — and I was never gladder of his silence than I was on this night.

After that, I cut away through the trees, determined to keep to cover all the way to the shack, if I could, because that moon shining through the thin mountain air was almost as bright as the sun. I put out the lantern and went along pretty slowly, because I did not want to make any great noise.

I hadn't gone a quarter of a mile from the mine when I saw a little red eye watching me from the ground a short distance away. Then I got the smell of wood smoke — just a thin drift of it. That gave me a new idea — to sneak up and find the Mexican, perhaps at his own campfire.

I slipped along, therefore, as quiet as you please. It must have taken me half an hour to cover the distance between the spot where I had seen that campfire for the first time, and the place itself. It was under a great tree that I could see clearly from the top of the cabin. I can remember that big tree perfectly because of its queer, lopsided outline. I had paced it off twice. It was just six hundred and twenty yards from the cabin — what you might call a good healthy long-range shot from *any* man's rifle.

When I came closer to the little red eye of the fire, I saw that it was a final ember of a fire that had been put out — or all out except this spark of life. About the time that I discovered this, something jumped up and went scuttering and scampering away through the brush — something no bigger than a weasel. Its presence there told me that the man who had built that fire couldn't be anywhere near. I lighted

362

the lantern and looked over the spot. It was easy to see why an enemy of mine would select this spot. I have said that I could see the top of this tree from the roof of the cabin. A man who climbed to the very top of this monster could see the cabin almost to the ground.

Whoever my friend was, he had probably cooked a meal here as soon as the light of the day was dim enough to keep the fire smoke from showing where he was. This one spark had escaped, and I put my heel on it.

By the spot I found the heads and skins of two little squirrels. One thing interested me a lot more than anything else about that spot — both of those squirrels had been shot very neatly, and right through the head. I have done my share of good shooting, as I have said before, and I have seen others do their share. Men who bag tree squirrels with bullets placed as accurately as that are not grown on every bush. It made me turn cold and then boiling hot — to think of this cool devil squatting out here under his look-out tree and cooking his squirrels, as he made ready to go in and do to me what he had already done to the squirrels.

XII

"TREASON"

I headed back for the cabin at a faster rate of speed, for I felt strangely sure that I had bagged my bird, at last. I would almost have sworn that I would find the broad-faced Mexican waiting outside the cabin. So I was fairly reckless and paid no attention to danger on any hand. Going straight on until I saw a light from the lantern in my kitchen shining through the western window, I stepped into clear view of the house, my rifle in my hand. I was fairly sick, because I had no lurking silhouette of a man there before me. Instantly I suspected that my elaborate trap had failed completely.

I turned Barney loose ahead of me, and, when I waved him along, he cantered up to the back door and stood there, wagging his tail and sniffing. I didn't need any more complicated message to assure me that the cabin was empty. If there had been the scent of a stranger in the place, Barney would have scooted back to me with his tail between his legs.

Hardly caring what happened, I tramped on, while a dozen shots could have been taken at me from any of the neighboring trees. I got to the cabin and threw the door open. There I found the place was empty, indeed — a good deal emptier than I had guessed. On the table there was only a scrap left of my loaf of bread; the bean pot had been heavily called upon; the can of jam was entirely empty!

Oh, I had had a visitor, well enough. The trouble was that I had stayed away too long. If I had been half an hour — or even ten minutes earlier — I might have nabbed him. Now all that I had of him was a scrap of paper, one edge of which was secured by the weight of a plate. On the paper there was scrawled in large letters only two words:

Gracias.
Mañana.

Or, translating them: Thank you. To-morrow. Well, I could translate them a little more freely than that and get out of them a meaning with a great deal more vigor in it. "Thank you for the meal. To-morrow I will call again, or shortly after to-morrow, and then I'll finish you off."

Now that I had a relic of this enemy of mine to study, I sat down and pored over it — after I had closed the shutters and made the house impervious to the eye of a spy. I decided that the hand that had scrawled out those letters so swiftly and flu-ently must be the hand of a fairly well-edu-cated man. Most Mexicans do not waste their time on good writing and reading. If they can scratch a signature, that is culture enough for one short life. This fellow wrote easily. What was still more important — he wrote with a pen. Now, since there was no ink in the cabin, he must have carried his ink with him. I knew that a fountain pen among Mexicans was about as much to be expected as an aureole on the head of a Wall Street banker. Here was an educated Mexican, then, who shot squirrels through the head when he went about to collect his supper, and who was now bent on putting a slug of lead through my head so that he could enjoy the profit of that little vein of gold ore without any hampering from my hands.

It increased my worry a great deal. You expect that a fellow without any foolishness may be clever and cunning, but you don't expect him to have the patience of a thinking man, and you don't expect him to work out matters so carefully. He makes more mistakes in big things, but fewer in little ones. I felt that I was up against a stronger man than myself, to say nothing of whatever danger there might be from Jerry and Bill in the background of this affair.

Altogether, that was a miserable night that I spent in the cabin. I was glad when the dawn came. It didn't make me get up. It simply gave me enough feeling of safety to make me fall into a short, deep sleep.

I was up, however, not more than an hour after the sun had showed his face. I started my fire for breakfast, and then it occurred to me that I would like to have a look at that tall tree at the foot of which the stranger had eaten his supper. I took my rifle out and around the house, therefore. When I was on the farther side — away from the big tree — I climbed up the wall, which the bigness of the curve of the logs made an easy thing. I managed from the roof to see that tree very distinctly, just as you see a tall man standing head and shoulders above a crowd.

When I squinted down the barrel of my rifle, the first thing of importance that I saw there was the dimly silhouetted figure of a man in the branches. It gave me a shock. There was my quarry — and I knew that tree stood 620 yards from the house — too far for him to expect trouble from me, surely. You have no idea how small the body of a man appears when it is 600 yards away. I got my bead automatically at 600 yards. Just as I was raising the gun a hairbreadth to make an allowance for the extra twenty yards — aye, or half a hairbreadth — the bad luck of the man in the tree made him start to climb down. In doing that, he came out from the partial screening of the branches, and, as he stood on a branch, the morning sun shone full against him.

Having lived by day and dreamed by night of marksmanship, it did not take me long to get my bead and touch that trigger. The next instant, the spot where he had stood on the branch was empty.

He might have jumped down from that place, or he might have been knocked down, but there is a queer instinct that always tells a hunter whether or not he has hit the target. That instinct told me that I had made a bull's-eye, and no mistake.

I was off the roof of that house as though the ground were water, or else as though I had wings. Then I streaked it through that forest with Barney running at my heels — as though he understood perfectly that this time *I* would show the way while he followed. A mighty sensible dog he was.

In a minute I came out near the tree. There I remembered that I would have to use some caution in approaching what might be a wounded man, and what was sure to be a man with a gun in his hands. So I came around in a quick semicircle and came upon the big tree from behind. Very lucky for me that I had done that, because, crouched in some brush ahead of me, not twenty yards from the tree itself, a man with a rifle at the ready was waiting for me.

I was so excited in the hunt that my own gun came to my shoulder automatically. There would certainly have been a dead man in the brush in another instant if I had not luckily chanced to notice that the back of this crouched fellow's neck was not olive brown at all, but red tan.

Instead of shooting, I kept my head, and said: "Look behind you, stranger!"

He gave a sort of groan and said: "Don't shoot, Lang!"

I knew that voice, and, when I saw the face that he jerked around at me, I knew the man that owned the voice. It was no other than Ridgeway himself!

That was a fair staggerer for me. It went sickly through my mind that I was not only fighting open enemies but that there was treason in my own side of the camp, which made it no even fight. He dropped his rifle and stuck his hands up above his head.

So I put my own gun at the ready and said: "Get up and come out of that, Ridgeway. And mind what you do with your hands. I trust you just the way that I would trust a snake!"

He said: "I'd come and willing, Lang. But I can't very well move. Your bullet drilled straight through my leg. I'm about gone. Who would have dreamed that even *you* could shoot like that?"

There was no need to disillusion him. There was no need to tell him that I had twice paced off the distance to that tree so that I had a good deal of a bulge on it in the matter of target shooting. I let Ridgeway think what he pleased. Now I saw that what he said was no doubt true — about the wound, I mean. His face was white, and it was turning whiter all the time. It gave me a queer feeling, I can tell you — to think of a man sitting there and bleeding to death while he waited for an enemy to come along. I took out my hunting knife and kneeled down. It was not pleasant work. The minute that I got close to him, I saw his wicked eyes working at me, while he computed his chances. So I stopped those unhappy thoughts by taking his revolver and his knife away from him.

He started to say: "Look here, Lang, you don't think that I'm really any enemy of yours?"

I broke in: "I'm busy, and just now I don't want to waste any time in thinking. All that I want to do is to get this fixed."

"That's pretty fine of you, Lang," he said. "I want to explain that the reason I was sitting here in the brush with my rifle was that I didn't know what. . . ."

"Shut up!" I said. "I can't work and listen all at the same time. Sit tight and keep still, can't you?"

I cut away the leg of his trouser, and, when the wound was open to the air, I made a tourniquet. Then I made an outside bandage out of his shirt. With that finished, I took his guns and even his knife and started away. The way that he began to carry on was a shock.

He cried: "Don't leave me here without

a gun, old-timer! Don't leave me here. He'll get me sure!"

"Who'll get you?" I snapped at him.

"The greaser!" he said.

"You know about him?" I asked him.

"How could I help it? And. . . ."

I turned my back on him. "If you know that," I told him, "you're a rat for not having given me warning." I walked away and left him, although he stayed there yelling after me until it occurred to him that his noise might tell a third party, if there were one nearby.

I heard his voice drop to a moan.

XIII

" 'IT'S MANUEL!' "

That fellow thought I had gone away with no
intention of coming back to him. Sometimes
I think that you can judge a man's heart by
the suspicions he's capable of having of another man. I can't help thinking that
Ridgeway was the sort of a man who would
have been capable of just that sort of a thing.
Back in Maine they wouldn't leave a
wounded man to die — even if he were
poison. I got one of Ridgeway's horses and
fixed a packsaddle on its back. Then I came
back to the brush, and I found that poor
Ridgeway had burrowed farther back into
shelter.

He was so glad to see me that the tears
came into his eyes. *That* helped me to see
how mean he was, and how ornery. I made
no remarks, because, no matter what he

said or did, I had my duty by him that I had to perform.

I got him into the saddle with a good deal of trouble, because he was turning weak now, and getting faint and limp. Just as I would heave him onto the saddle, he would roll halfway off and come heavily into my arms. What with his weight and a dancing horse that didn't like the proceedings a bit, I was pretty well worn out with about ten minutes of this foolishness. At last I managed to get him fixed and started back for the cabin.

When he found that I had stayed with the job, he opened his eyes a little and smiled at me — a sort of a "God bless you" look. I felt more kindly toward him not because I figured that he was any less a rat, but because I had been doing something for him. You invest a little trouble in another fellow and it is always sure to make you like him — and usually sure to make him dislike you. That's one of the queer things in this world of ours.

I got Ridgeway back to the cabin and unloaded him from the horse. Just as I got him dragged off the saddle a waspish noise hummed past my ear. Something flicked right across my face. What had struck me in the face fell down at my feet — a thin slice of leather that had been clearly ripped away by a flying rifle bullet. I didn't have to ask the horse to go for shelter. He gave a jump and a kick and was gone as I yanked Ridgeway back through the doorway into the kitchen. As I slammed the door, another bullet came combing through, just exactly breast high. On top of that bullet there was a yell of rage out of the woods — a devilish screech of disappointment.

Being shot at was no joke or pleasant party, but hearing a human being let out a screech like that — not a bit human, you understand, but like the squeal of a mad ape — well, that was worse. You could not imagine that man being afraid of the dark. You could almost imagine him seeing better by night than by day. Altogether, I never heard a daylight noise that gave me more the horrors.

It brought Ridgeway back to his senses for a minute. He gasped out: "It's Manuel!" Then he fainted again, but not from the loss of strength, you can bet.

I worked for a good hour after that, cleaning the wound and soaking iodine on it until Ridgeway yelled for mercy. Then I loosed the tourniquet a little, put on a fresh bandage, and got him fixed up in a bunk. He was so thoroughly scared, after hearing that devilish voice out of the morning and the woods, that he begged me not to leave him for a while. I had to go hungry for a whole hour and sit there and hold his hand. He was like a sick child, weak and shaking.

After that I was allowed to go back and fix breakfast. I gave him a little, and, after he had eaten, he fell into a sleep. I sat at the door of the bedroom and ate my own breakfast, none too comfortable. Little use as a sick man was — nothing but an encumbrance, of course, and much as I had reason to doubt and despise this Ridgeway, still with a devil like Manuel hanging around on the outside, it was a comfort and sort of fortification of the soul to have another man in the house there with me.

He babbled and talked away a good deal in his sleep. Then he dropped into a quieter rest, remaining sound asleep that way until long after noon. It was wonderful to watch him change as he lay there. You could tell for yourself that sleep is the finest thing in the world to build a man up. I could see his color get clearer; his cheeks no longer sagged; the straight set came out of his mouth very fast.

When he opened his eyes about one o'clock, he was looking, clear and straight, at me. His head was so level that he re-membered everything that had passed, and he started to say something about it. I headed him off and told him that he could wait until he was a lot stronger before he did any talking. Not that I wasn't anxious for him to begin, but I was still itching with anger, feeling that, if I waited a little longer, I might cool off a bit and be more my real self.

He ate a pretty good lunch, and, when evening came, his appetite was fine for supper. It was simply beyond believing how quickly that man was recuperating. He had one of the best constitutions ever made and the strength of a pair of devils.

By the time his supper was put away, he begged for a pipe of tobacco, and I didn't really see how a good smoke could be harmful to any man, so I let him have it. He puffed away very heartily, enjoying himself fine.

After all of that, and, when I had cleaned up the dishes, he called to me, and, when I came in, he said: "Will you listen to me now, old-timer?"

I said that I wasn't ready to listen to any explanations.

He said: "Well, let me have a Colt, at least, will you?"

That was rather a facer for me. While I rested an elbow against the jamb of the door and looked back at him, he said: "I tell you, Lang, that fellow will find a way to get in here. The minute that he knows that I'm in this cabin, he'll simply go mad until he gets at me. Believe me when I say it, because I know him for sure."

He said it with the sort of emotion that convinces you more than the words do.

I said: "How was it that he didn't get at you when there was not even the wall of a cabin between you and him?"

"He didn't know where I was, then. But he knows now, and he'll be sure to come at me. Look here, Lang, I can guess what you have in your mind. The way I've acted seems queer. Almost as though I had had it in for you. But now you hear me talk. I raise my hand and I swear to God that I never had the least idea of lifting a hand against you. It never came into my head to shoot you down . . . the way you shot me down."

"I didn't know it was you," I told him. "At that distance, the face of one man is a good deal like the face of another. You know that I didn't intend that shot for you."

"That doesn't keep me from lying here

on the flat of my back," he said.

"It didn't keep you from trying to murder me from the brush when I came up with you," I said.

Then he yelled at me: "You fool, how could I guess that it was you who fired? I thought it was Manuel, and that I'd have him snaking around through the trees after me. It didn't occur to me that anybody in the world would be able to shoot like that . . . except Manuel!"

He flared this out at me in a sort of a rage, but that rage wasn't very convincing, somehow. Deep down in my heart I knew that he was lying, and that he was putting on that pretended anger just as a bluff. That didn't make me like him any better, when I hated him already. So I told him that it wouldn't do. I was pretty simple, but I was not a fool.

I said: "There is something crooked about the way in which you've treated me. You know it. I'm not idiot enough to trust a gun in your hands!"

It was astonishing to see how white he got when I said that.

"Look here . . . Lang . . . old partner," pleaded Ridgeway, "do you think that even if I had anything up my sleeve against you, that I'd be mad enough to lift a hand against you so long as I lie here helpless, on the flat of my back . . . not able to help myself against that devil, out yonder?"

That was fairly convincing, you'll have to admit. I went back into the kitchen and smoked a pipe over the idea — the pipe being a grand way to help you when you have to think. When the pipe was down toward the dregs, I decided that after all there was a good deal of truth in the last things that Ridgeway had been saying. I went back to his room and gave him a Colt. As his hand closed over it, he grinned like a starving man who sees food and drink just before him.

"Now sit down, old-timer," he said, "and listen to me yap, will you?"

I only said: "I can't do it just yet. I wouldn't open my mind and listen to you in the right way. It wouldn't be the least use for you to talk to me."

"We've got to come to an understanding and work together, if we're to stand him off," said Ridgeway.

"How bad is he?" I asked.

"I'll tell you just this much . . . he's so bad that I left this cabin because I was afraid that I might have some sort of trouble with him. . . ."

I shouted in a fine rage: "You mean to

say that you knew he was here before you got me to . . . !"

"Wait a minute, man," Ridgeway said. "All that I mean to say is that I was afraid he might show up. But I figured that all of his spite would be directed at me. How could I know that he would hand this grudge on to another man?"

There was a real feeling of truth behind a part of this, at least. I listened and couldn't help believing.

"All right," I said, "and now tell me what good you can do for me, while you lie there on your back?"

"I can watch this window and this side of the house," he answered as quick as a wink. "And that's something. That's a good deal when you have a fellow like Manuel against you."

"Yes," I admitted, "but. . . ." Here I broke off, listening sharp. I could hear a faint groaning out in the kitchen. At first my hair stood on end, because the sound was *inside* the house — not from the outside. "What is it?" I whispered.

"It's Manuel," Ridgeway whispered, whiter than ever. "No matter what it turns out to be, his hand is in it."

XIV

"THE PLAN"

When I started for the kitchen, I was walking slowly. You can depend on it that my mind was working, when I heard that same subdued, bubbling sort of a groan again. I knew that old Barney was stretched out on the floor of that same kitchen, and, if there were any harm to the windward, it was strange that he did not give me some signal of it.

When I got to the kitchen door, I found Barney standing with his head turned toward the big water boiler that was the chief comfort in the house. He had his head cocked to one side, watching, and, when he saw me, he didn't move his eyes toward me — just acknowledged me with a little lowering of his ears and a waggle of his tail.

Then I heard the groan again, deep and

strong, and with the humming sound of pain in it. This time I spotted it, too. It came out of the hot water boiler. I turned on the tap at the bottom of the boiler, and held a bucket under. About three quarts of boiling water and a hundredweight of steam came ripping out.

Then I saw how that devil Manuel had struck at us in our little fort, the cabin. He had simply shut off the water supply. When I thought of what a fool I was for not having considered this possibility before, I wanted to laugh. I didn't. It was a good deal too serious.

I thought of the stove next. If I didn't want the heating pipes to melt, it would be a fair idea to put the fire out, and that was what I did. I put that fire out and had a fine demonstration of how much a fire can smoke when the doors and windows are shut. That kitchen was white with smoke before I finished. But it was better to have smoke in it than bullets. So I kept the windows down.

Then I went in to Ridgeway and started to tell him the news, but he didn't give me a chance.

"There's one thing plain," he said, "we can't go on living in this house without water. And, along with that idea, there is another . . . we can't carry water into the house while Manuel is out there with his rifle, waiting for us to appear."

I looked at him, amazed. He hadn't had a word from me about what had happened, and he had had to figure out everything just by the sound of the escaping steam and by the smoke that he had smelled. I called that brains. Right then and there I decided that if Manuel were as bad as he was brainy, he would have a hard time beating this same Luke Ridgeway of mine. I determined that any suggestions he could make would be the ones that I would want to follow.

I didn't say anything, then, just nodded at him. I sat down and lighted a smoke, and he smiled and nodded back at me as much as to say: "Now you're showing a lot of good sense. I can do the thinking for the pair of us." He appreciated himself, right enough.

While he closed his eyes and began to think, I waited. Every now and then he would open his eyes with a start and stare at the ceiling, and then he would close them again and shake his head, dismissing something that had suggested itself to him. That seemed very queer to me. The only idea that I had was to leave the cabin by way of the tunnel through the mine. But although that way might serve for me, it would never serve for Ridgeway himself. But there was more in the wits of that fellow than I could ever dream of. He went on thinking matters over and shaking his head from time to time. At last he said: "If Manuel were a fool, we could work this matter out. But Manuel *isn't* a fool. And there's the trouble. I've got to get hold of a thing that will pull the wool over the wisest rascal in the world."

"Will you tell me what he's done to you, or you to him?" I asked Ridgeway.

"It's too long to tell," said Ridgeway.

It was plain to me that it wasn't the hardness of the telling that stopped that rascal, but because there was at least as much on the side of Manuel as there was on his own side. However, I couldn't waste time on such ideas as this. I had a pretty good idea that Ridgeway had brought me up here to a trap of which he hadn't warned me, and which he was pretty sure might be the death of me. How that would serve his ends, I didn't know. But I *did* know that Manuel had shot at me from hiding twice, and, although I was no hero and no man-fighter — although I had shot at a man for the first time in my life that same day — still I was in a heat to get at that infernal Mexican.

So I said: "I'd like to have just half a minute alone with Manuel to settle things, but the coward would never give me a chance."

Ridgeway gave me that ugly side glance of his. It was so plain wicked that it scared me worse than a leveled gun.

"Don't you worry about Manuel," he said. "He'll murder you from behind a tree, but he'll also shoot you in a fair fight, because he's that kind of a Mexican. Now if you mean what you say, about wanting to meet Manuel face to face, I'll arrange it for you."

What a rat that Ridgeway was. I couldn't help putting in: "Look here, Ridgeway, as far as I can make out, you and this Manuel, the man-eater, ain't the best friends in the world. How does it come that you want me to take the chance of getting my head blown off? After that happens to me, won't Manuel come in here and just cut you into small pieces, and you there on the flat of your back, unable to help yourself?"

That suggestion made him close his eyes and turn white, he was so sick. But there was something else in his mind that didn't make him sick at all — something that pleased him a lot, because it sent the color back into his cheeks and made a sort of an evil, laughing light show in his eyes.

"Why, Lang," he said, "you don't understand what faith I have in you. I've heard a great deal about this Manuel and the way that he can shoot. But I've seen you shoot and I've *felt* you shoot!" He laughed, but there was an ugly ring in his laugh. It was easy enough for me to see that he wasn't telling his whole mind to me. What the other half of his thoughts were I couldn't guess.

Suddenly I said: "Ridgeway, what makes you want to get me killed?"

He tried to brazen it out and appear hurt and shocked by a suggestion like that, but he couldn't manage the trick. Because although he talked loud enough, yet at first he blanched and winced as that shot of mine went home.

Then he began to say: "Why, old-timer, what sort of a skunk d'you think that I am, to get a man to . . . ?"

I shut him up, then. I couldn't stand to listen to him lie and try to pull the wool over my eyes. I had to show him that I knew he was *partly* a dog. I said: "Look here, Luke, is it because you understand that I've found the real vein in the mine?"

Well, sir, that fetched the man. He gasped and propped himself straight up in the bed on his elbows.

"*You* found it!" he cried. "How could *you* find it?" Which was a sort of polite way of saying: "How could a fool like you find such a thing?"

I only grinned at him. "The dog took me to it," I said. That, in a manner of speaking, was the truth, although, of course, it was the least important half of the truth. I enjoyed that moment a lot, sitting there and seeing Ridgeway eating his heart out with doubt and curiosity and suspicion. Such thoughts and feelings make a man's face a pretty fair copy of the devil's, and that was just Ridgeway's look.

Then he lay back in the bed and closed his eyes, for fear that I would see *too* much in his face. However, there was no point in torturing a wounded man, particularly because I knew that I could never squeeze more than simple lies out of him, and that I would get no nearer to the truth of this matter by telling him what I knew.

"You know it, too?" muttered Ridgeway at last. I can tell you that there was iron in his voice.

"Aye, and Manuel knows it," said I, "and

when three people know the same secret, you may as well say that the world knows it."

"As for Manuel . . . yes, that's bad," said Ridgeway. "But you *should* know I took a liking to you right from the first. But I wanted to have you up here for a while and try you out before I told you the secret. . . ."

"The secret of your six-months' trip," I suggested to him pretty dryly. He gave me one of his quick, side-ripping glances. But I put right in. "Let's not talk like a pair of fools. There's one important thing that I want to do. You've acted in a queer way, Ridgeway . . . just what harm you've tried to do me, I don't know. But I've heard the bullets of Manuel whistle around me on two occasions, and that's all that I want of that. I want to get at him, and you say that you know a way for that. So tell me what the way is, and I'll be done with you for today."

He gave me a grin that put the devil in his eyes again, like a shadow. Then he said: "All right . . . here's my scheme. It's not very complicated, but it might work. My idea is that all that keeps Manuel from closing in on you is that he doesn't know how badly wounded I may be. He doesn't know whether I'm lying pretty near to death or whether I'm up and around now. He doesn't know how I got hurt, most of all. If he had been near enough to see that, he would have had *both* our scalps when you ran out to take a look at your bag. Which was a pretty foolish move, between you and me, partner. For what Manuel saw was you taking care of me, real brotherly. And there you are. Now, son, what I propose is to have you drag me out to the kitchen. Out there, I'll make a noise . . . I'll sing . . . and start up a fire. That will make him think that *you're* there, of course. So, he will focus all of his attention on the back of the house. But while I'm doing that, you sneak out the *front* of the house and begin hunting for him. Or, if you want him to hunt *you*, just loose off a gun and he will quick enough realize that it's the wounded man who is hobbling around in the kitchen . . . y'understand? He'll go gunning for you!"

"Meaning that he would prefer getting me to tackling you?"

"Meaning that he would rather attack a man in the woods than a wounded man in a house with strong walls like these. Besides, he don't know how badly I'm wounded."

Well, I studied this over for a while. I didn't like it, in a way, but I couldn't put any finger upon the exact thing that was wrong.

Finally I said: "Just let me know, will you, how you are going to manage to move around, with a leg such as you have to handle?"

He only laughed in my face. "This is for my life," he said. "And for my life I could manage to go a mile . . . dead easy." He said the last of it through his set teeth, and I believed him. He had enough willpower to serve for a whole army.

I didn't wait to understand any more whys and wherefores. I just got ready for what was to come. I looked to my Colt, and I looked to my rifle. That was just a matter of form, because I always kept those guns in tip-top shape.

"Ridgeway," I said, "I'm going out to try to kill a man, or to *get* killed. All I have to say is that I understand, if I get my share of the lead that flies, where I meet you again will not be in heaven. You're a bad man, Ridgeway, and I know it. I just got to tell you that before I leave, because I don't want you to think that you've pulled the wool across my eyes!"

He didn't answer. He just closed his

eyes, because he didn't want me to see what was in them. Then I helped him out into the kitchen, and he sat down by the stove, where the two windows didn't look in on him. Right away he began to make the noise he spoke of. He began to sing in a voice that was not very musical, but that was louder than the braying of a donkey.

Me, I started for the front of the house, right then. I was almost glad when I had my head outside of that cabin and under the honest sun again, even if I were to get a bullet along with the clean air.

XV

"SOLUTION"

That part of the scheme of Ridgeway worked fine. I managed to get to the edge of the pine woods. There I leaned back against a tree, not mindful of the pitch that I could feel soaking into my shirt between the shoulder blades. Then I decided that the best way was just as Ridgeway had said — to let the Mexican know that I was there and let him come after me, if he had a mind to. I fired the rifle, and, as I reloaded it, I knew that I had begun a duel that would last until either the Mexican or I was dead.

Not a very pleasant feeling, of course. I knew that fellow was poison, partly from what I had seen of him, and partly from what Ridgeway had said about him. Still, I was glad to be out there where we could fight the battle, fair and square.

I had a good place, with a thick hedge of trees around me, and I waited there, only stirring enough to peer out between the trunks every now and then. The most tiresome, heart-breaking, nerve-racking work that was ever invented. I could realize for the first time what a deer feels when it lies wounded and hears the hunters coming.

Then Barney, who had remained there wedged up against my heels all the time, began to loosen up. He yawned, stretched, and came around to look me in the face and waggle his tail. It made me mad, at first. Then I told myself maybe Barney was right. Why should I kill myself with nervousness, instead of with bullets? I decided to hunt the hunter.

That hour had played me out so that, when I started walking, I was as weak and giddy as though I had been sitting up all night at a card table and drinking plenty of black coffee to keep going. However, a little still-hunting did me good. That was my own old game from the Maine woods.

The difference between hunting a deer and hunting a man is that one of them is armed with antlers and a sharp pair of ears, and the other is armed with a revolver and a brain. Which, after all, is not such a big difference as you might think.

I circled slowly around that shack, keeping pretty deep in the woods, until right behind the shack where Barney froze onto a trail. I sneaked over and took a look at it, but I couldn't make anything out of it. It was his nose and not his eyes that was talking to Barney. He followed the trail until he came to a damper place and there I saw the print of a great big naked foot. My Mexican, right enough. You couldn't imagine any white man going barefoot over that sort of rocky country, not even if he wanted to be as silent as a snake in his movements.

Barney went ahead, silent. Just wagging his tail when I patted his back and whispered to him that he was a good dog. He worked that trail out of the edge of the woods — and then he followed it right straight at the kitchen door of the shack!

I tried to tell myself that I was mad, or else that this was an old trail showing that Manuel had sneaked up to the house the day before. But instinct told me that Barney was dead right, and that the Mexican was right there in the house that minute — waiting for me. *That* was an ugly minute, if you'll believe me.

What I did was the strangest part of all. Before I knew it, I had blundered out behind Barney into open view of the shack. Once I was in the view of it, I kept right on traveling — not even crouching, but walking upright. That was a sandy soil, muffling the footfall. There was no dead grass; it was short and green and kept close-mowed by the cow, because that fool cow preferred the pasture around the house — she was too lazy to walk any distance for her dinner.

That was why I managed to get up to the house without a sound of me being heard. The reason that I kept on going forward — well, I don't know what it was, unless it was that I was too afraid to turn back, once I had started, and partly, too, that there was a grisly picture in my mind — caused by the silence of the house — of big Ridgeway lying dead on the floor, with his throat cut from ear to ear, and the Mexican kneeling over him and going though his pockets.

I got up to the back of the house — and Barney ran the trail to the kitchen door and began to sniff and to scratch there. My heart stood still. I was close enough to reach the cabin wall in about two steps, and I dropped on my knees there as I heard a voice whisper loudly in the kitchen: "What the devil is that? Ah, the dog."

"Only the dog," said the softened voice of Ridgeway.

Much as I detested him, and much as I was horrified to find that he was in there talking in a friendly way with the Mexican, still I was glad to hear that voice of his and know that my vision of his death had been a lie.

"Not so loud," said the other. "Where the dog is, there will be the master."

"Don't worry," Luke said, "because Ridgeway is sure to be out there in the pines, sitting tight, no matter where his dog may roam around."

"There is still an hour or two before evening," said the Mexican. "But when the shadows begin, then he will think of the cabin, and he will try to come back . . . and then I shall do as poor Waters would like to have me do . . . and as this *Señor* Ridgeway deserves. Does he not deserve it . . . to speak honestly?"

"The dog ought to die under the knife . . . bullets are a pile too good for him," Luke said. "Why, this Ridgeway is a regular wolf!"

"I know," said Manuel. "Waters used to tell me . . . a sneak. And a wolf is a sneak. Making other people take the dangers . . . the way he left you here in this shack . . .

after he dragged you out of your bed . . . oh, I shall handle this Ridgeway. . . ."

When you hear another man's name saddled on your shoulders it's usually a little irritating, but when you have the name of a fellow like Ridgeway, with himself sitting by, calling himself names, and making it hotter for me every instant. . . . Well, I was half wild. I kneeled there, trembling and fingering my Colt's butt. I've often had people gasp and ask me if I were not too much afraid even to stir. No, I can tell you frankly that, although I'm no hero, I got too angry then to have a bad nerve in my body. I'm not proud, but I'm too good ever to be a Ridgeway.

"But how did you have a chance to get acquainted with Waters?" asked Ridgeway.

"They put us together on the same gang, breaking rocks on the road, and then in doing a lot of easier work. While we were doing that, we got to know that we were from the same section of the country. Finally Waters told me how Ridgeway had railroaded him into jail. Waters is a pretty good man, *señor*. Stupid, but pretty good. I liked him, and when he told me how Ridgeway lived on his money and how Ridgeway got from him the secret of the rich vein, and then how Ridgeway. . . ."

I couldn't stand it any longer. I was savage toward both of them — Ridgeway, who had saddled his identity on me, and the Mexican who had tried twice from ambush for my life. I stepped to that door and jerked it open, and, sticking in my head, I yelled: "You greaser dog . . . here I am!"

Oh, he was a cool fellow. But when you're hunting a man, you don't expect him suddenly to open your door and call your name. I didn't think of it at the time, but, as a matter of fact, I suppose that I did the only thing that could have saved my life.

Manuel was simply paralyzed. He whirled around, and I let him have it with the Colt. I missed him, and the bullet hit the stove with a terrible clangor. Before I could shoot again, he had flashed his gun out and taken a crack at me. Because of his shaken nerves, Manuel missed — oh, just by an eighth of an inch. The man who tells you that a miss is as good as a mile lies, because I've dreamed about that eighth of an inch ever since.

I didn't miss with my second shot. Manuel had dropped for the floor — a snaky but a deadly way of revolver fighting, because it gives the other fellow a smaller target to shoot at, and it gives you a steadier hand for the firing. But Manuel needed a fifth of a second more to put in *his* second shot. That fifth of a second was nowhere to be had, because, just as he dropped to the floor, I let him have the second chamber of that good old Colt.

Manuel flattened out and lay still. The bullet had hit him in the back, near the base of the neck. It remained in his body, after it had smashed up most of him. I turned him over on his back, and he opened his eyes at me.

"God did not hear my prayers," Manuel said.

"You fool!" I yelled at him. "*There* is your man . . . *that's* the real Ridgeway. . . ."

He knew that I knew he was dying, and that there was no point in a lie. He writhed up his lips like a dying dog and tried to drag out his second gun to kill Luke, but I held his hand. After that, he lived about ten minutes altogether. He didn't do a great deal of talking, but there was enough said for me to get the story pieced together before he died. Most of it you have gathered yourself.

Ridgeway had been down in Mexico for three years, and, while he was down there, he ran into Waters, a fellow who had been in prison and made an escape from an

Oklahoma penitentiary. Waters told him a yarn about a rich vein in that abandoned Spanish mine in the Southwest. Ridgeway and Waters finally decided to take a try at it.

They were to sneak over the Río and go north. When they got to the mine, Waters was to show the vein to Ridgeway. Then Ridgeway was to buy the tools and so forth, and he would make all the trips to town for provisions, while the fugitive, Waters, remained in the mine and worked there until they had gutted the pocket or fairly opened up a great vein. Then he would take his half, and drift south again, leaving Ridgeway to manage the mine.

That was the way that they started. When Ridgeway found out how rich the vein looked, he lost his head. They took more than $5,000 worth of metal out of that mine in eight days, working it very clumsily. Ridgeway decided that he would take a try at that mine all by himself. That wasn't hard to do. He simply turned stool pigeon and gave word about Waters to the police. They made a night call, scooped in Waters, and Ridgeway was left with a lone hand to play.

In prison, Waters became a friend of this Manuel and made him hot with this story of a betrayal. Finally the end of Manuel's sentence arrived. Before it came, however, word had leaked out in the prison that Manuel intended to put the wrongs of his prison friend right — he had allowed the police to get hold of the talk. The police, in turn, had passed along a friendly hint or two to Ridgeway, because a stool pigeon has to be encouraged for the good of the profession.

That was about all that I got out of Manuel before he died, except that his last words were a prayer that I would send Ridgeway after him.

Of course, the whole point was that in prison Waters had no photograph of Ridgeway. He could give this Manuel a good description of a tall, bony man, over six feet, with heavy bones and weighing around 200 pounds. Every one of those details fitted in with myself as well as it did with Ridgeway.

That scoundrel was clever enough to guess that the Mexican would have to work by a mere description. When he spotted me in the store at Elmira and saw me do the shooting, he got his grand idea. He would hire me to take care of the cabin, and, when he disappeared, he would hang about in the offing.

In the meantime, the Mexican would arrive, find in possession of the cabin a man who looked like the mine stealer. One of two things would happen. Either the Mexican would kill Lang and feel that his mission was executed, or else Lang would kill the Mexican, which would be the best of all. From the shooting which he had seen me do, Ridgeway was willing to bet on me. Most of all after I brought him down out of the tree.

In any case, his own skin would be safe.

And, confound him, his skin *was* safe!

I took care of him until he was able to navigate. Then I drew down the money that he owed to me, and I left the cabin. Ridgeway was the most surprised man in the world because I didn't shoot him while he was helpless, lay the blame on the Mexican, and say that they had fought each other to the death — a story that the police would have been perfectly willing to believe — knowing as they did what was in the mind of the Mexican when he left the prison.

It was the Mexican, evidently, who escaped that night through the trap door, not Bill and Jerry. They were probably intimidated by my ready rifle, for I never saw them again.

You may be sure that Barney never lacked a home as long as he lived. Good old Barney!

I should like to say that Ridgeway died soon, and died unhappily. This being a true story, I have to tell the truth. That rat left the West and went into Missouri, where he bought a good farm and married. When he died five years later, he left his widow and two children mighty well provided for. If I were to let real names leak out, those children would be mighty surprised to learn that their good dad was really a scoundrel.

Why did he leave the West?

That was because that fine vein turned out to be only a very shallow pocket. The Indian miners had missed something — but not much.

Bill and Jerry I never saw again — but Barney is still with me, not over-spry, but loyal.

If it had not been for my talk with Cobden, I would never have gone West. And if I *had* gone West, I should not have carried along that silly passion for range finding. If I had not had that practice, I should never have known the range of that big tree — or shot down Ridgeway — or in so doing untangled the whole problem.

You see how everything pieces in together, pretty neat?

Besides, I would like to draw a little moral out of this story. I would like the youngsters to see that anything that a man learns to do *really* well may prove to be the saving of him. Even if it's no more than the ability to guess distances.

ABOUT THE AUTHOR

Max Brand® is the best-known pen name of Frederick Faust, creator of Dr. Kildare, Destry, and many other fictional characters popular with readers and viewers worldwide. Faust wrote for a variety of audiences in many genres. His enormous output, totaling approximately thirty million words or the equivalent of 530 ordinary books, covered nearly every field: crime, fantasy, historical romance, espionage, Westerns, science fiction, adventure, animal stories, love, war, and fashionable society, big business and big medicine. Eighty motion pictures have been based on his work along with many radio and television programs. For good measure he also published four volumes of poetry. Perhaps no other author has reached more people in more different ways.

Born in Seattle in 1892, orphaned early, Faust grew up in the rural San Joaquin Valley of California. At Berkeley he became a student rebel and one-man literary movement, contributing prodigiously to all campus publications. Denied a degree because of unconventional conduct, he embarked on a series of adventures culminating in New York City where, after a period of near starvation, he received simultaneous recognition as a serious poet and successful author of fiction. Later, he traveled widely, making his home in New York, then in Florence, and finally in Los Angeles.

Once the United States entered the Second World War, Faust abandoned his lucrative writing career and his work as a screenwriter to serve as a war correspondent with the infantry in Italy, despite his fifty-one years and a bad heart. He was killed during a night attack on a hilltop village held by the German army. New books based on magazine serials or unpublished manuscripts or restored versions continue to appear so that, alive or dead, he has averaged a new book every four months for seventy-five years. Beyond this, some work by him is newly reprinted every week of every year in one or another format somewhere in the world.

A

Accomplices of Silence

The Modern Japanese Novel

MASAO MIYOSHI

Accomplices of Silence

The

Modern Japanese Novel

UNIVERSITY OF CALIFORNIA PRESS
BERKELEY · LOS ANGELES · LONDON

University of California Press
Berkeley and Los Angeles, California

University of California Press, Ltd.
London, England

ISBN: 0-520-02540-7
Library of Congress Catalog Card Number: 73-83062
Printed in the United States of America

To Kathy, Owen, Melina,
Their Sister-in-Law C.-C.
And the Mother of Them All

Contents

Preface

The modern Japanese novel or *shōsetsu* is now nearly one hundred years old. From the very start, it was predominantly Western in impulse as writers turned away from the traditional tales and romances and actively sought new narrative forms to fit the new Age of the West. A literary program gradually took shape: the new fiction would attempt to deal with the ordinary experience of ordinary people and would be written in a colloquial language from the average person's moral perspective. An impossible program, as we will see, and yet by now, after almost a century, there is a distinct sense shared by many Japanese writers that the novel, once an imported art, has been successfully naturalized. What is more, Japanese novelists tend now to talk quite comfortably about their work in the context of the great nineteenth- and twentieth-century Western novels, *Crime and Punishment* and *The Trial*, *Ulysses* and *Remembrance of Things Past*. We can say then that there exists a tradition of the Japanese novel which is formally as well as thematically recognizably "universal," at least in intent.

While it is true that Japanese writers would not have conceived the *shōsetsu* without having fairly close acquaintance with Western literature, this is not to say that in developing the *shōsetsu* they totally abandoned their own tradition, with its distinct logic-style and sensibility built right into the images and vocabulary, the setting and the argument. The ancient goals and values of the people could not be reconstructed overnight, nor, obviously, could the long strands of personal and tribal memory woven into the very sound and syntax and semantics of their language be identified, excised, and replaced in the span of a generation or two. In short, somewhere in the substance of each modern piece of Japanese literature lies an element native to the core and as such utterly intransigent and unreconstructible.

Clearly, such cultural and artistic grafting processes involved in generating a new literature give rise to wide discrepancies between program and execution, theory and the pulse of experience, and they must be understood if we are to get hold of some of the difficulties as well as the achievements of the modern Japanese novel.

I would like at this point to summarize the argument of the book since the plan for the following chapters—each devoted to a particular author and his works—does not allow for coherent discussion of such material. There will be a focus on four basic aspects of the art of fiction—the narrative situation, character, plot, and language—but radiating out from these points are a range of other problems which will be explained and elaborated more fully in the book itself.

I see it as impossible to discuss the narrative situation without treating the notion of character. The story must be told by someone, and the author must choose a voice for his storyteller. In so doing, he inevitably conceives of his narrator as a character, too, thus involving his whole understanding of human personality. And yet, in almost every novel—*The Drifting Clouds, Through the Dark Night,* or *No Longer Human*—we notice something decidedly loose, or overcasual, in the narrative plan. Often, the narrator telling the story is the author's undisguised personal pre-literary self. Or, we may find him choosing to speak through a surrogate character whose mask is nonetheless transparently thin. Often, too, the grammatic person shifts around very freely from first to third, and from one first-person speaker to another first-person speaker. More importantly, we see everywhere—even in Sōseki—a free shift in the point of view, and even in the narrative mode, from the third-person novel to the first-person diary, confession, or letter. It used to be easy to regard the unstable point of view as a sign of a naïve or clumsy art, as Percy Lubbock did in his blanket judgment on all pre-Jamesian novelists. But this won't help us much now when the Jamesian "point of view"—premised on the alienation of the individual, the unbridgeable gulf separating each one of us from the other—is recognized as itself an assumption.

Like the author, the Japanese critic, too, usually pays little heed to the narrative situation. With the exception of Nakamura Mitsuo writing on Shiga Naoya or Etō Jun treating Sōseki, the critics ignore the possibility of voice problems, and concentrate instead on the so-called philosophy of the master novelists. This general indifference to the tale-teller's identity points to the still present belief in a communal storytelling persona that can slip into any story and take on the voice of an undifferentiated narrative self. *Who* tells the story doesn't seem to matter much; it's the action that counts.

Any discussion of the narrative situation thus quickly turns into the question of character in the novel. But before I go on to discuss "character," let me emphasize the importance to this study of those extraliterary essays on the Japanese personality by people like Nakane Chie, Ruth Benedict, Edward Norbeck, Inatomi Eijirō, and Herman Kahn, who have stressed, as I do, that the Japanese attitude toward personality (not any particular trait, but "personality" itself) is basically profoundly negative. The self, that cornerstone of European humanism, is of course academically understood, but is nowhere felt as an everyday experience. The Japanese *Bildungsroman* is not so much about the self's discovery of the self as the self's discipline of itself into a production model hierarchically classified and blueprinted in detail by society at large. And this is so whether we are speaking of Ōgai's *Youth*, Sōseki's *Sanshirō*, or Tōson's *Spring*.

Concomitant to this notion of the self as a production unit is the fact that the characters in the Japanese novel are almost always types, and not living individuals. Thus, one may easily recall situations, scenes, or relationships of characters (say, Kan'ichi and Omiya in *The Golden Demon*, or Shinji and Hatsue in *The Sound of Waves*), but seldom oneself experience intimacy with a character, as one does with Emma or Heathcliff or Isabel Archer. However interesting and absorbing Futabatei's Bunzō, Sōseki's *sensei*,

Kawabata's Shimamura, Dazai's Naoji, or Mishima's Mizoguchi, still they are abstracts finally, markers of the plot-logic, and not portraits of real people. As such they are almost literally bound into the context of their books and simply can't be seen clearly in relief apart from the narrative. We are always aware of the author's fascination with them, but almost never get to grapple with them as real people with their own existence.

This quality of character seems to spring from the same source as the narrative problem: the obscure outlining of the self in the Japanese novel. Although the writer is often preoccupied with questions about "the I and the Other" (with a capital O), this is not the same as "the I and many diverse others." That is, the culture's control of individual awareness reinforces belief in a collective, metaphysical entity, The Other. The traditional novel, woven as it is from the relationships of several individuals, does not thrive in such an absolutist milieu, and so the I-novel (*shishōsetsu*) comes to dominate, replacing the pluralist "real world" with a private universe. The "I-novel" is thus not just one genre among many, but the essential pattern of Japanese prose fiction toward which even the most panoramic social novel gravitates. It is somewhat ironic, surely, that the "*I*-novel," the autobiographic retelling of the author's very personal life, should grow out of a myth of the collectivized self, and not of one celebrating individual personality.

The more we look at it, plot, too, begins to relate to character and narrator traits. We might talk first about serializing, the mode of publication which came to prevail in Japanese fiction. Take Futabatei, who published *The Drifting Clouds* at random intervals over a long period, or Kawabata, whose *Snow Country* and *The Sound of the Mountain* came out unpredictably over several years in different journals, as well as many of today's writers who serialize in various journals. With these writers, as with the Victorian novelists—most conspicuously, Dickens— serialization is both cause and effect of their imaginative makeup: their creativity actively seeks out serialization as a preferred mode every bit as much as the mode then determines the curve of the plot. Either way, novelistic coherence is not the writer's main purpose. Flaubert and James, George Eliot and Joyce, each in his own

way carves out a verbal sculpture which goes far toward convert-
ing the novel's temporal art into a visual, spatial structure. The
Japanese writer, on the other hand, stops and starts the narrative
flow, and uses tension between passages and their crucial placement to propel his story, which will often leap from one episode
to another (see, for instance, Kawabata's later works, particularly
those in which the spirit of *renga* is so powerful).

In the traditional Western novel the plot coheres by virtue of
the carefully laid network of causal relationships. We can see an
egalitarian aspect to this causality, since the expected patterns of
action, made reasonably explicit in the fictional context, apply
to everyone universally, regardless of circumstance. And it has a
bourgeois aspect, given that prose fiction, being middle class in
origin, rejects the heroic whereas clearly the romance and the epic
do not. And finally it is commonsensical, redolent of everyday life.
With such features of the novel in mind, we see that the Japanese
novel contrasts rather sharply with its Western counterpart, primarily because it tends to distrust this egalitarian impulse and
disdain a commonsense explanatory system. Thus for every *Light
and Darkness*, there are hundreds of *The Setting Sun*s, which belong more naturally with the romance, the lyric, the confession,
and such. *The Setting Sun*, like other typical Japanese novels, has
very little plot: events occur, but with no explicit moral or causal
interpretations to account for them. And the Japanese novel still
celebrates the hero's victory or glorifies the anti-hero's defeat, as
in so many novels by Mishima Yukio, a writer who in his own
person was a consciously created hero (or anti-hero) in a heroless
age.

Now to language, which is probably the most significant element in any discussion of Japanese fiction. First, there is the
noticeably large divergence between the spoken and the written
language. Of course, this is not uniquely a feature of the Japanese
language; even in American literature, it was only with Mark
Twain that the gap between speech and "book talk" began to
narrow. In Japanese, however, this gap was immense in the early
Meiji years, almost to the extent of there being two distinct stages
of linguistic development—as that, say, between Middle English
and modern English. *Bungo* (the written style) was refined but

remote; *kōgo* (the spoken style) was familiar but vulgar and certainly no proper medium for art. Gradually a compromise—a sort of dignified colloquialism—was worked out. But even at that, the characters in these "compromised" works did not talk like real people, and the narrative passages came out stiff and quaint. Perhaps the problem is bigger than just that of colloquialism, or "how to write as you speak": it may have something to do with the visual nature of Chinese ideograms as a writing system, or with the stylized speech patterns of ordinary life. Whatever the main reason for it, the remoteness of the *shōsetsu* language seems to place prose fiction at a distance from real life even now.

The next feature of the novelistic language, the system of honorifics (*keigo*), is more important than is usually recognized. In actual conversation *keigo* operates so as to establish immediately the relative social standings of speaker, listener, and referent. This carries an advantage for the novel, providing as it does a calculus of social class that even Jane Austen might have envied for its precision and freedom from ambiguity. And yet there are difficulties. For instance, the narrator must choose a level for himself in relation to the reader. In the early Meiji years, when the social role of the writer was still unfixed, the choice of the *-desu* suffix system over the *-da*, or vice versa, presented him with an agonizing problem in composition. Here too a compromise was negotiated; in this case a neutral level, neither deferential nor condescending, was invented which solved some problems but of course introduced others. For the "neutral" level has no real counterpart in conversational usage; it is strictly an artificial language, for use in fiction alone and thus ultimately itself a fiction also.

There are also both advantages and disadvantages in the floating tense, loose syntactic form, and the like. The vague tense system, for instance, allows for subtlety and ambiguity: in Sōseki's *Pillow of Grass,* the intricate shifting between present tense and past creates an impressive play of its own. However, when the narrative requires expository clarity, it resorts to the stiff "translation style" invented for handling the Western literatures. This style sounds artificial, and it is, imposing a distance between fiction's world and the actual world. Mishima's works, for instance, often have to suffer from this appearance of affectation only because the author is trying to establish a plain discursive narration and there seems no other way to get it than "translation style."

Perhaps more important than any other factor in this whole problem of language and style is the typical Japanese dislike of the verbal. It might be said that the culture is primarily visual, not verbal, in orientation, and social decorum provides that reticence, not eloquence, is rewarded. Similarly, in art it is not articulation but the subtle art of silence that is valued. *Haiku* is the most perfect embodiment of this spirit but it is visible elsewhere as well. Thus the novel, that loquacious art, needs some trimming to fit the Japanese verbal dimensions. By and large, the Japanese novel is very short and only rarely approaches the average Victorian three-decker. In fact, the term *shōsetsu* is applied to both the full-length "novel" and the short story as though no difference existed. But aside from length, this passion for silence is in evidence in the narrator's attitude toward the story. Often, the scene of the Japanese novel is set by suggestion and evocation rather than description. At its best—as in Kawabata's *The Sound of the Mountain*—this silence fairly resonates with meaning. At its worst (Mushakōji Saneatsu's proverbs and platitudes or Dazai's babytalk), the writer is clearly embarrassed by his articulation. On the other hand, when the writer who is well aware of this power of silence still defies it outright, as does Haniya Yutaka in much of his work, the result is often a torrent of intellectualisms without reference to experience, and thus a nearly unreadable work.

I do not believe it an overstatement to say that writing in Japanese is always something of an act of defiance. Silence not only invites and seduces all would-be speakers and writers, but is in fact a powerful compulsion throughout the whole society. To bring forth a written work to break this silence is thus often tantamount to the writer's sacrifice of himself, via defeat and exhaustion. If A. Alvarez is right in seeing an essential relationship between modern literature and suicide, the modern Japanese novel and its authors are surely the most representative case: all three writers discussed in Part Two took their own lives. In the course of the book, I will consider some of the probable causes of this situation, which seem to me inherent in the whole Japanese attitude toward both art and language, and as such, they are closely related to, if not wholly identifiable with, Alvarez's explanations. The discussion of the formal features of art and language will lead out intrinsically to such "life" problems.

The Japanese novel, then, does not conform to the specifications of the Western novel on which it is modeled. But that in itself should not bother us. We are aware that during this century of *shōsetsu* development, lots of things have been happening to the Western novel, too. Robbe-Grillet, Nabokov, and Norman Mailer belong to a different tradition from that of George Eliot. And indeed, the demise of the novel of Fielding and Tolstoy, James and Hawthorne, that has been whispered for some decades is now past history. The new antinovels are distinguished by plotlessness, the disintegration of character, and a deliberate dislocation in the narrative situation. Thus, if the Japanese novel finds no place near the traditional Western novel, one can comfortably think of *Pillow of Grass* or Kawabata's more "Japanese" works in the company of these new Western antinovels. Natsume Sōseki sensed this quite early, in 1905, when he called his *Pillow of Grass* a plotless and eventless *"haiku shōsetsu"* and pointed out how entirely new the work was in the context of the Western novel. Looked at this way, the novel, an imported art to begin with, has at last naturalized itself to Japanese.

Of the six writers discussed in the book, three are old masters of the Meiji and early Taishō era (around the turn of the century), which saw the first flowering of modern Japan. The other three all belong to the reign of Hirohito (from 1926), who presided over the rise and catastrophic fall of his Empire and is now witnessing the rise of an economic empire not inappropriately referred to in some quarters as "Japan, Inc." The six are at the forefront of those who have charted the course of Japanese prose fiction: Futabatei wrote what is considered the first modern Japanese novel, whereas Mishima marks a very special climax in recent literature. Certainly there are others: Izumi Kyōka, Shimazaki Tōson, Shiga Naoya, Nagai Kafū, Tanizaki Junichirō, Yokomitsu Riichi, Abe Kōbō, and Ōe Kenzaburo. And yet these six in many ways better represent the landmark achievements as well as the difficulties and failures of Japanese fiction.

For each of the six there is an intensive discussion of one or two works, all available in English. As for the choice of these novels, I have no rationale other than my prejudice, with the qualification that this is always endorsed by the existence of a good-to-excellent English translation. Apparently, at least in these instances, my preferences and the translators' seem to coincide.

The book is meant principally for the general reader of novels. Twenty years ago it most probably would not have been thought of: with the exception of Arthur Waley's classic translation of *The Tale of Genji* and occasional translations of *haiku* and *noh* plays, on the encouragement of Yeats or Pound, Japanese literature was almost totally unknown outside Japan. Since then, however, a number of Japanologists—Howard Hibbett, Donald Keene, Edwin McClellan, Earl Miner, Ivan Morris, Edward Seidensticker, and several others—have made the Japanese novel so accessible to the English-speaking reader that knowledge of at least a few Japanese works can now be expected from just about everyone who likes to read and think about modern literature.

Although I assume no knowledge of the language in the reader and have made my references in English wherever possible, there are, to be sure, an increasing number of students of Japanese who no doubt prefer to check certain details for themselves against original versions of the novels and the native scholarship. For such scholar-students I have devised and placed at the back of the book a second set of notes referring to bibliographical matters, secondary materials, or the details of Japanese words and phrases requiring *Nippon-go no chishiki*. Apart from these notes, the only section of the book that might conceivably task the English-only reader is the first half of the first chapter where I discuss the problems the prose fiction writers faced in dealing with the Japanese language a century or so ago.

I am grateful for the fellowship I received from the John Simon Guggenheim Memorial Foundation and for the Humanities Research Professorship from the University of California, grants which enabled me to complete this manuscript in a relatively short time. My thanks are also due to Mark Schorer and Nathan Glazer for nudging me forth from my habitat of Victorian literature.

Many friends and colleagues have read the manuscript at various stages, giving me innumerable helpful comments, and I am especially in debt to John Anson, Earl Miner, Carolyn Porter, Edward Seidensticker, Wayne Shumaker, and Henry Nash Smith.

It must have started a long time ago, well before I began seriously to read Japanese literature myself, that I began to encounter American readers of Kawabata and Mishima, Tanizaki and Sōseki who seemed to know exactly what they wanted to read and who read it astonishingly well. I was continually struck by their ways of looking at this "exotic" literature, but I was also necessarily reminded of the translators who had made the novels accessible to such readers over the last few decades. Without the work of this skilled and dedicated cadre offering a glimpse of a "world elsewhere," these readers would never have emerged, and there would scarcely exist any reason for this book. Knowing how difficult it is for foreigners to learn the language, I am indeed indebted to their splendid work.

Berkeley   MASAO MIYOSHI

Acknowledgments

Thanks are due the following for their permission to use passages from the works indicated:

Poems by Wallace Stevens, edited by Samuel French Morse. Copyright © 1959 by Wallace Stevens. Reprinted by permission of Alfred A. Knopf, Inc.

Kawabata Yasunari's *The Sound of the Mountain,* translated by Edward G. Seidensticker. Copyright © 1970 by Alfred A. Knopf, Inc. Reprinted by permission of Alfred A. Knopf, Inc.

Arthur Waley's *The No Plays of Japan.* Copyright © 1957 by George Allen & Unwin Ltd. Reprinted by permission of George Allen & Unwin Ltd.

Harold G. Henderson's *An Introduction to Haiku.* Copyright © 1958 by Harold G. Henderson. Reprinted by permission of Doubleday & Company, Inc.

Sylvia Plath's *Ariel.* Copyright © 1965 by Ted Hughes. Reprinted by permission of Harper & Row and Olwyn Hughes.

The Penguin Book of Japanese Verse, edited and translated by Geoffrey Bownas and Anthony Thwaite. Copyright © 1964 by Geoffrey Bownas and Anthony Thwaite. Reprinted by permission of Penguin Books Ltd.

Note on Japanese Names

Japanese names throughout the book (except my own) are written in Japanese order—surname first—the style Japanologists have adopted in their studies in English. In Kawabata Yasunari, for example, Kawabata is his family name, and Yasunari his given (or "first") name. Even when the writer adopts a sobriquet (such as Futabatei Shimei), this order is followed. To complicate things, however, writers are known in Japan sometimes by their surname and sometimes by their "given" name. Natsume Sōseki (Natsume Kinnosuke) and Mori Ōgai (Mori Rintarō), for instance, are usually known as Sōseki and Ōgai, not as Natsume and Mori, whereas more recent writers like Dazai Osamu (Tsushima Shūji) and Mishima Yukio (Hiraoka Kimitake or Kōi) are known as Dazai and Mishima. It seems that as a writer comes to be accepted into the "great tradition" (usually a while after his death), he comes to be known more by his given name than his surname. This book follows the current usage in this regard.

Part One

So still:
　　into rocks it pierces—
　　　　the locust shrill.
　　　　　　—BASHŌ

Only shape thou thy silence to my wit.
　　　　　　—*Twelfth Night*

To the music of the reaper's flute
No song is sung
But the sighing of wind in the fields.
　　　　　　—SEAMI, *Atsumori*

　　　　Denn das Schöne ist nichts
als des Schrecklichen Anfang, den wir noch grade ertragen,
und wir bewundern es so, weil es gelassen verschmäht,
uns zu zerstören. Ein jeder Engel ist schrecklich.
　　　　　　—RILKE, *Die Erste Elegie, Duino 1912*

Has the Garden of Silence been already lost? Then
　　birds must arm themselves.
　　　　　　—HARAGUCHI TŌZŌ, *Etudes I*

I

THE NEW LANGUAGE

THE GEMBUN'ITCHI MOVEMENT

—*Ban Japanese, and speak English.*

In Tokyo in 1886, several writers decided to circulate their manuscripts among themselves in order to exchange ideas and develop some sense of audience. Their "journal" was a very modest venture; it was not even printed at first but copied in a very neat hand. Calling themselves the Friends of the Ink-Pot (*Ken'yūsha*), most were not more than twenty years old, their birth just about coinciding with the accession of the Emperor Meiji, who was then engaged in his vast program of restructuring the nation. The journal, humorously called the *Rubbish Library* (*Garakuta Bunko*), has a historical significance far greater than most publications of its kind.[1] As with other movement papers (for example, the *Germ* of the Pre-Raphaelites around 1850), its artistic execution fell somewhat short of its intention. The work published in the *Rubbish Library* did not elevate Japanese fiction to a very serious level, nor did it do much to purify the language. Despite this, it claims our attention.

One of the key members of the club was a precocious seventeen-year-old, Yamada Bimyō, whose literary program, published in the third issue of the *Rubbish Library*, condemns the whole development of the Meiji novel, scoffing at its practitioners as mere popular entertainers. In another (unpublished) essay he even

attacks Edo (or, interchangeably, Tokugawa) masters like Kyokutei Bakin, Ryūtei Tanehiko, Tamenaga Shunsui, and Juppensha Ikku, contrasting the low and vulgar state of the Japanese
novel with the situation in Western countries where the form is
taken seriously by writers as well as by the vast novel audience.
His examples of Western "novelists" do indeed constitute a mixed
bag: Voltaire, Rousseau, Spenser, Shakespeare, Milton, and Cer-
vantes. Had he named instead the late-Victorian popular writers,
his argument would of course not have held. At any rate, he did
set up a program for himself that called for no less than the "improvement of literature," and, in fact, of the language itself. If
the manifesto sounds to us today somewhat sophomoric, Bimyō's
diagnosis of the novels of the time was nonetheless cogent. Those
of the earlier Meiji years—from 1870 on—were basically no more
than rehashings of the Edo conventions. And although the younger
writers were beginning, along with Bimyō, to bring in some new
thematic elements via adaptations of Jules Verne or Disraeli, they
also definitely felt the need for a language that could express the
new ideas and new life style they were seeking.

In the Preface to his novel *A Note on the Organ (Fūkin Shirabe
no Hitofushi)*, which was serialized in a feminist magazine in
1887, Bimyō is quite specific in his analysis:

> Ever since someone argued that the correspondence be-
> tween spoken and written languages was a good proof of
> civilization, people have begun to worry about the style of
> our language. But we still have a great enemy in habit and
> inertia. Any new and unfamiliar style provokes people
> preoccupied only with the surface of things and invites
> their negative comments like "vulgar" and "inelegant."
> In the face of these charges, no one dares to try the col-
> loquial style exclusively. Especially as regards the novel
> of manners, the dialogue is barely "vernacular" enough,
> and yet the narrative portions retain the "elegant style"
> characterized by the *-nari, -keri,* and *-beshi* suffixes. This
> inconsistency between dialogue and narrative within the
> same novel is really unsightly. We must remove it no mat-
> ter how difficult the task may be. Some people seem to be

giving up the idea of matching spoken and written styles as hopeless in present-day Japan. But they are too impatient. Of course, the elegant style may have something that colloquialism does not; but in the hands of a skilled writer, colloquialism can offer an indescribable gracefulness with a discipline all its own, which is in no sense inferior to the elegant written style. It is from this perspective that this novel was written: in short, in the style, somewhat modified, of the love stories as recited by the *yose* storyteller Enchō.[2]

What Bimyō is talking about is generally known by the term *gembun'itchi* (the correspondence between spoken and written languages), which he coined around that time with other writers including Mozume Takami, a professor of literature at the University of Tokyo. In fact, Bimyō was only one of a growing number of writers at the time who expressed great concern over the state of the Japanese language. Not only critics and novelists, but editorial writers and even the government demanded some method whereby legal documents and commercial and personal correspondence could be brought linguistically closer to the vernacular. The barrage of earnest responses included one advocating adoption of the Roman alphabet, and another urging total abolition of Japanese and substitution of English.* It is no accident, therefore, that a month before *A Note on the Organ* began to appear, one of Bimyō's childhood friends, Hasegawa Tatsunosuke, was writing the first part of his novel, *The Drifting Clouds* (*Ukigumo*), one of the central concerns of which was the discovery of a new language for the novel.

Before introducing Futabatei Shimei (as Hasegawa was to call himself), we must examine the formidable *gembun'itchi* program, since it is fundamental to our understanding of the new novel of the time and, in some important respects, to our understanding of the modern Japanese novel right up to the present.

---

* This innovative proposal was made in 1872 not by a lunatic but by Mori Yūrei, who later became minister of education for the central government. Yamamoto Masahide, *Kindai Buntai Hassei no Shiteki Kenkyu* (Tokyo: Iwanami Shoten, 1965), p. 117.

Readers who do not understand Japanese may point out here that the adoption of colloquialisms into the novel is a relatively recent event even in English, not to mention other Western languages. Certainly it is true that in the great majority of nineteenth-century novels the characters still do not speak like "real people." Take Thackeray or Meredith, Hawthorne or Melville, George Eliot or even Henry James: their characters, however "vivid," observe a certain decorum in their speech as well as in their behavior, as stipulated by the conventions of the novel. With Twain's *Huckleberry Finn,* and, in a more general sense, with Gertrude Stein and Hemingway, the dialogue and even the narrative voice for the first time attempt to reproduce authentic speech.[3] But the experience of the Japanese novel is entirely different in this matter, not at all comparable to the too formal syntax of a Jane Austen, the overly abstract exposition of a George Eliot, or the too "poetic" stylization of a Dickens. The discrepancy at that time between spoken Japanese and the language of the novel resembled the difference between two historical stages of a given language, say, Old or Middle English and modern English.

This of course raises the question as to how far back one should go in tracing this divergence between spoken and written speech. The usual explanation starts with the contrast between the Edo and the Meiji novel, but this seems to me to suggest more questions than it answers.[4] It makes more sense to go back all the way to the time around the fourth century when Chinese ideograms were first being introduced as a medium of writing into the largely unlettered Japanese language.[5] The Japanese manner of importing the written characters was ingenious. Once having appropriated the ideograms of a language linguistically totally unrelated to their own, the Japanese gave them native pronunciations. An ideogram expressing *mountain,* for instance, was pronounced "yama," the Japanese sound signifying *mountain.** Yet while this "naturalization" of ideograms was being carried out rapidly and on a very large scale, the Japanese was also borrowing directly from the

---

* The nearest analogy to this method of borrowing is the use of Arabic numerals by various languages. The figure "1," for instance, is pronounced as "one," "Ein," "un," "ichi," and so on, although the sign itself does not change.

Chinese sounds. Thus, an ideogram ordinarily had—and still has —at least two different pronunciations, Japanese and Chinese, with little difference in the meaning, although the borrowed Chinese sound itself was of course naturalized by adjusting its phonetic components.* For example, the ideograms expressing *Japan* were—and still are—pronounced as "Nippon" and "Nihon" (Chinese) and "Hinomoto" (Japanese); even the name of the novelist Kawabata Yasunari is very often pronounced "Kawabata Kōzei" (or "Kōsei"), despite his preference for "Yasunari." Some confusion was inevitable, and is still in evidence in the process by which the Japanese child learns the language, not to mention the adult foreigner.

But the matter is still more complicated. Since Chinese and Japanese are not linguistically related, the Chinese written medium could not fully meet the needs of the Japanese language. Hence, the Japanese of those early centuries soon began to use ideograms as phonetic symbols. Because Chinese ideograms number in the tens of thousands, sound notation by such means was extremely cumbersome. By the eighth century the Japanese were somehow managing to write out traditional lore and poetry by this method in the *Kojiki* and *Nippon Shoki* chronicles and in the great *Man'yōshū* anthology of poems. To ease the matter somewhat, a more rational phonetic use of ideograms was also invented by this time: instead of applying more than one ideogram for each sound, only one was chosen to represent any one sound, and the writing of that ideogram itself was simplified by reducing the number of strokes. Thus came into being the *kana* system of syllabic writing with 47 characters for the principal 47 syllables of the language.†

* Actually, the situation is more complex. The Chinese sound for a given ideogram did not remain constant throughout history. At different stages, different sounds (for the same ideogram) were imported, being each time adjusted to the Japanese phonetic properties. To make the situation worse, dialectal variants were also transmitted. Thus, many "Chinese" sounds can exist for one ideogram.

† Actually, two systems of *kana* were developed, *katakana* and *hiragana*. The distinction between the two is not easy to put, but the former is used more limitedly in the *kambun* notation—or, more recently, for the expression of Western words —while the latter is for more general use. This statement requires one more qualification: the sound structure of ancient Japanese was far more complex (as has been

The literature of the Heian period (794–1185) was written either in Chinese ideograms alone or in *kana* interspersed with ideograms. The ideographic text, called *kambun* (strictly, "writing of Han"), looks like Chinese but is not pronounced like it. A *kambun* text, as read by a Japanese, sounds Japanese and is Japanese, although it could also be read by a Chinese and pronounced in Chinese.* Compared with *kana,* the *kambun* style was felt to be more learned and dignified, and, reflecting the Japanese aspiration for Chinese culture, the male courtiers and scholars appropriated it for government documents and for, by and large, a banal poetry highly imitative of the Chinese sources. The *kana* style, considered less learned, was delegated for the use of the sex of weaker mind. Interestingly, quite apart from any feminist persuasion I might have in this matter, it is the *kana* writings of this time, represented by Lady Murasaki and Sei Shōnagon, that make it one of the greatest periods in the history of Japanese literature. The *kambun* style, written exclusively in ideograms, has survived in the way a dead language survives, to torment high school students who must pass the *kambun* requirement in their curriculum.

The *kana* style thus overcame the *kambun,* at least where literary expression was concerned. Yet the mixture of *kana* and ideograms does not necessarily guarantee a more Japanese style than the use of ideograms alone. And this peculiarity of Japanese typically using a compound writing system—foreign ideograms and native syllabary—is important to the understanding of *gembun'-*

---

shown by Hashimoto Shinkichi) than that of modern Japanese, and had many more *kana* letters expressing these now extinct vowels and consonants.

* To give an illustration, suppose that English now, instead of Chinese centuries ago, were introduced to an unlettered Japan. (Keep in mind that English and Chinese have a roughly similar word-order.) It would operate like this: The native sentence, *Konya wa umi ga shizuka desu,* would be written down as "[The] sea is calm tonight," but would be pronounced in Japanese as "Tonight sea calm is," by transposing the written characters. To ease the reader's adjustment, a system of notations must be devised, looking somewhat like this: Sea[2] is[4] calm[3] tonight.[1] With Chinese ideograms being largely non-phonetic, the job was slightly easier than this example might suggest. (I am not quite sure that I have made the matter clearer by this example, but hopefully something of the complicated process is conveyed.) Incidentally, for centuries Japanese learned to read Chinese literature itself by this method of Japanizing via notation, and the same method was used by the earlier teachers of English.

itchi. For one thing, until very recent times, the *kambun* style has always formed the core of academic and bureaucratic orthodoxy. This does not mean that government documents, for instance, were always written exclusively in ideograms; they usually employed both ideograms and *kana*. And yet, the tone, diction, and even syntax of *kambun* were so dominant that they constituted an identifiable literary style, *kambun-tai* (or *-chō*), even where the text was written out in the *kana*-ideogram mixture. So stereotyped was this style that for centuries it effectively worked against any significant integration of the changing patterns of speech with the writing. Second, this process has meant the absorption into Japanese of a very large portion of the classic Chinese vocabulary. It is practically impossible to write Japanese without using Chinese "loan" words in quantity—no more possible indeed than to write today's English exclusively in old Saxon. The borrowed words are clearly much more deeply entrenched in the written vocabulary than in the spoken, and the less familiar (and less "naturalized") ones are those found mostly in the written vocabulary.* Thus, the more lofty and elegant the writing (the more "Chinese"), the more alien it is to everyday Japanese. Third, there is the problem of intelligibility. Japanese is phonetically very limited, and there are innumerable homophones indistinguishable one from another unless identified by appropriate ideograms. The sound "shi," for example, can mean "teacher," "samurai," "city," "history," "Mister," "capital," "four," "stop," "death," "poetry," and many other things. Use of only the *kana* for this sound, without the help of an ideogram, creates a hopeless

---

* It is quite possible for the speaker of Japanese to recognize the rough meaning of a given ideogram without knowing for certain how to pronounce it, which is another way of saying how visual the Japanese language is, compared with, say, Germanic or Romance languages. In this connection, it may be of some interest to observe that the Japanese writer is very conscious about the appearance of the printed page. Japanese are almost always trained in the art of calligraphy, and what an ideogram looks like as a design, or how the mixture of *kana* and ideograms on a page strikes the eye, is in fact a serious matter. There is hardly any counterpart to this in the West—except perhaps in Mallarmé, certain seventeenth-century writers of shaped poetry, and, lately, Robert Creely (who is heavily influenced by Japanese poetry). Mishima Yukio, among others, talks about this phenomenon in his *Manual of Style* (*Bunshō Tokuhon*) (Tokyo: Chūōkōronsha, 1970), pp. 23–26. See my discussion of Sōseki's *Pillow of Grass* below.

confusion in communication, even where the context might provide some direction. The fact of phonetic poverty has thus further
deepened the gulf between spoken and written language. Written
documents, meant primarily to be read silently, not read aloud,
or heard, carry a reduced risk of ambiguity. But a speech or other
text intended to be read aloud requires a vocabulary and style
quite different, since immediate intelligibility is of the essence.
Last, all these factors together have contributed toward the establishment of a powerful expectation that stylization (decorum, convention, stereotype) will be observed in written documents of all
kinds from personal letters to fiction to government publications
—even today in the last third of the twentieth century.*

By the time the young Meiji writers began searching for an
appropriate style, Japanese literature had fifteen hundreds years'
experience of using ideograms and *kana* together. Thus the question was not how best to blend the two, but how to forge a new
writing style out of the various styles already in use, each associated with a different proportion of ideograms and *kana:
kambun-tai,* which depends heavily on ideograms; *gabun-tai*
(elegant style), which also uses them heavily, although its syntax
is looser and its vocabulary more native; *zokubun-tai* (vernacular
style), which, in its attempt to capture true speech patterns, relies
very much on *kana;* and *gazoku-setchū-tai* (elegant-vernacular
mixed style), which tries to combine the last two.

Historically, such a variety of styles indicates the fascinating
sociology of the language. Traditionally, the *kambun-tai* and
gabun-tai both have belonged to the aristocracy and have reflected
the learned and graceful culture of the few who cling to the
ancient manners on which their social distinction so largely de-

---

* This may be one of the reasons skills in public speaking are so underdeveloped
in Japan. Most speeches on ceremonial or public occasions, for example, are no
more than readings of prepared texts (written often in a quaint style) with little
consideration for the audience. (Emperor Hirohito's broadcast announcement of
the surrender in 1945, for instance, was practically unintelligible to most listeners.
They were not certain until they read the text later whether the Emperor ordered a
cease-fire or an out-and-out battle to the end.) Similarly, deficiencies in elocution
are often a serious problem for all who speak in public, even actors. One tentative
solution is the increased stylization of speech, which Westerners may recognize in
Japanese films and in *kabuki* plays.

pends. But during the three-centuries-long Tokugawa period (1603–1867), when Japan was virtually sealed off from the rest of the world and was under the control of the Shogunate, the merchant class was steadily accumulating wealth and political power. And with the gradual rise of this new "middle" (that is, non-samurai) class,* came its own cultural expression. The *kabuki* play, the *haiku* verse form, the *jōruri* recitations, and the novel were the arts of this new class, just as the *noh* play, the *waka* verse form, and *kambun* typified the samurai class. Given the fact that the Japanese language is highly diversified as to class dialects (even now any Japanese can tell one's class background with dead accuracy just from certain vocabulary and suffix-style habits), the literature, too, of the middle classes began to reflect their speech habits with increasing confidence. Especially in the novel, a form which thrives in a democratic milieu, they very boldly recorded the accents and manners of their own speech.[6] Ihara Saikaku (1641–1693) and then Juppensha Ikku (1765–1831), Shikitei Samba (1776–1822), and Tamenaga Shunsui (1789–1843), instead of merely copying the elegant language of the imperial courtiers and samurais, made full use of the more casual, informal speech of the Edo and Osaka burghers, which soon developed into the so-called vernacular style.[7]

Even so, these early novelists were not entirely free of the stereotyped learned language. At its core, the Edo novel, like any other novel tradition, shows time after time the characteristic middle-class hankering after the grace and charm of the aristocracy. Thus did Kyokutei Bakin (1767–1848), for example, use *kambun-tai* almost exclusively to write about those fantastic super-heroes of his whose appeal was not primarily to the samurai class but to the growing number of tradespeople and their families. And other writers, too, chose for the most part to reconcile their impulse toward accurate representation of what they know with the dictates of decorum by writing elegant-formal narrative parts

---

* This is a most inexact term. The increase in capital during the Tokugawa period accelerated steadily, and some merchants in Osaka, Kyoto, and Edo were as wealthy as many of the great lords (*daimyō*). Thus, I am referring here simply to the consciousness of social caste that remained very much intact despite the redistribution of wealth.

interspersed with vernacular-mimetic dialogue. In short, the narrator in these novels assumes an elegant voice for himself, while providing his characters with the everyday speech of the ordinary people the writer himself has no doubt come from.[8] The compromise worked to a degree because the typical reader, accustomed to plays and *yose*-stories (quasi-epic *kōdan* and comic *rakugo* recitations, for example), condescendingly responded to the dialogue as if watching a vulgar performance, while trusting the narrator to describe and interpret it from the loftier moral and artistic position presumably shared by his audience.

The early Meiji writers, Futabatei, Tsubouchi Shōyō, and the Friends of the Ink-Pot, such as Bimyō and Ozaki Kōyō, learned the technique of vernacular dialogue from reading Samba, Shunsui, and other Edo writers, but they could no longer accept the stylized narrative alongside it, as the quotation from Bimyō shows. Verisimilitude was important in narrative too and they were determined to find a style that would suit the whole novel, not just the dialogue.

Another important problem for the *gembun'itchi* movement was the use of the "honorific" (*keigo*), which is basic to any consideration of the narrator's language. For the foreigner, the honorific system, with its "levels of reverence," is probably the most baffling grammatic feature of Japanese. Actually, *keigo* has little or nothing to do with politeness in the Western sense. Sometimes also called "status expression" (*taigū hyōgen*),[9] it can be defined as the expression of degrees of reverence, or irreverence, depending on the relative positions of speaker, listener, and referent. A speaker adopts a reverential level if his listener (or his referent) is superior to him in class, employment, age, and so forth; an irreverent level, if inferior; or any of a number of levels in between, according to the class relationships. Of course, there is something similar to this even in English ("Get the hell out!" as against "Would you mind leaving, sir?" for instance), but nothing in the Western languages comes near the prominence and pervasiveness of the honorific system operating in Japanese. The suffix (and sometimes prefix) of almost every verb and the prefixes of most nouns must be adjusted to signify the relative positions of the three poles involved in speech utterance, and the vocabulary requires sensitive selection, particularly among the personal pronouns. The scrupulous but automatic choice of level operates continuously in speech—even, it should be noted, where the statement concerns neither speaker nor listener (such as "Socrates is mortal" or "It's a holiday today"). The native speaker of Japanese almost reflexively sizes up any new acquaintance within seconds of their first social interaction. Of course, even in a society so steeped in the arts of defining relative "altitude," an occasional pair of near-equals will appear, their honorific level being largely determined by their common social role. By and large, between young male equals, each speaks as though the listener were his inferior (less polite); between female equals, each speaks as though the listener were her superior (more polite); between male and female equals, she speaks with reverence, he without it, as can be expected of a society confirmed in its centuries-old male chauvinism.

In the traditional *kambun-tai* and *gabun-tai* writing styles the honorific system has been somewhat neutralized over its long history (perhaps as a result of high stylization), whereas in the spoken style, reflecting the rigid social stratification established during the Tokugawa period, it is still extremely elaborate. If a novel is to be in the vernacular, therefore, it not only must reproduce the honorific system in the relationship of characters, but also must choose a proper level between narrator and reader. Here, however, there is no tradition, no history, no ready convention to guide the choice. Should the narrator speak respectfully to the reader, as if the reader were patronizing the *yose* hall? Or should he adopt the tone of a lofty teacher to his lowly pupil? Or should he after all assume a more democratic level? Obviously, the precise ground of the narrator-reader relationship can be determined only if the novelist, his art, and his readers are all defined in social and cultural terms. If the writer would be an intellectual, a modern bard and prophet presenting a more or less comprehensive picture of reality, he will take a lofty tone, and he may be revered as a master. If on the other hand he is a mere entertainer trifling in inanities, he had better speak humbly. But whether prophet or entertainer, the question is, who is his audience? * During the early years of the novel, writers were very hesitant about their social-linguistic position vis-à-vis their readers, and there was a great deal of experimentation. For instance, Bimyō and Futabatei tried the reverential *-desu, -dearimasu* suffix system as well as the more casual *-da, -dearu.* But most writers around this time, whenever they felt strain, tended to retreat into the formalized territory of the archaic *kambun-tai* and *gabun-tai.*

The characters' speeches presented a further problem to the *gembun'itchi* program. Here, I must discuss things more generally to include the thematic aspect of the Edo novel. Very much like eighteenth-century European fiction, the novel of the Edo period falls into categories: picaresque (Asa Ryōi, *Ukiyo Monogatari,* 1650s; Ihara Saikaku, *Kōshoku Ichidai Otoko,* 1682); gothic (Ueda Akinari, *Ugetsu Monogatari,* 1776); semi-pornographic, describing the pleasure quarters ("Yellow Books" by Santō Kyōden and others; Shunsui, *Shunshoku Umegoyomi,* 1832; Saikaku's works); the epic romance (Bakin, *Nansō Satomi Hakkenden,* 1814–41); and humor (Shikitei Samba, *Ukiyo Buro,* 1809–12; Juppensha Ikku, *Tōkaido Hizakurige,* 1802–9).[10] They gloried in the exploits of quasi-mythical figures, or chuckled patronizingly at goings-on in the world of geishas and prostitutes and their clients. They were in turn didactic, sentimental, or farcical, but they seldom explored behind the external behavior of men and women. Above all, none were noticeably concerned with the ordinary moral and psychological processes of ordinary men and women that are always the main territory of the novel.

Indeed it would have been noticeable to have been concerned at all. The Edo period is psychologically almost medieval. Japanese society had been so tightly bound all those centuries by a hierarchic structure in which feudal and religious values domi-

---

* A somewhat similar uncertainty is discernible among English writers of the nineteenth century. See, especially, Wordsworth's Preface to the *Lyrical Ballads.* In the novel, though, one can easily think of various relationships between writers and their reading public (which was becoming identifiable and "respectable" in England for the first time in the last half of the nineteenth century) in the period between, say, Austen through Dickens to Henry James.

nated that an unquestioned code of behavior—chivalry (*bushidō*) for samurai, face and obligation (*memboku* and *giri*) for the tradesmen, and decorum for all—was the only guide for conduct. Life's ongoing activities were undisturbed by any rapid infusion of new cultural values, and such an infusion, as in the Meiji period, with its resulting moral and psychological dislocations, was still undreamt of. On the rare occasion when some strange shock of self-recognition brought a darker view of life, a writer could still be consoled by other attitudes such as *wabi, sabi,* and *iki*—the kind of aesthetic nirvana afforded by Buddhism and the development of exquisite taste in the theater and other arts.[11] It was not until the Meiji Restoration—no radical revolution certainly, and yet an undoubted transformation of samurai and merchant classes alike into the efficient managerial bureaucracy which is the basis for today's Japan, Inc.—that the sine qua non of the novel, the looser society that individualizes and introverts man, began to take form in Japan. Modern bourgeois life, for all its ills, at least allows man to look at himself for a time while he interacts with others outside his immediate family and community. Modern man drifts along his own path in a cool and expanding universe, but such sparse worlds alone seem to generate the novel. Take Sōseki's *Light and Darkness (Meian)*—it would have been as unthinkable in pre-Meiji Japan as a *Vanity Fair* by a twelfth-century Englishman.

Thematic changes might ordinarily be thought to have little to do with aspects of language and style. At this stage of the Japanese novel, however, there were several reasons why the two must be looked at together. For one thing, the Meiji period had come up with many new ways of mixing people traditionally separated by geography and social position. (As was noted earlier, the Japanese language is highly diversified vertically as well as geographically.) The Edo novelists, involved in their samurai exploits or with their geishas in the pleasure quarters, saw only part of the problem, as in Juppensha Ikku's comic travelogue where two dudes travel down the Tōkaidō highway and run into some bumpkins. The Meiji novelists faced a new kind of relationship with the multiplicity of social subgroups, the students, the housemaids, the civil servants, the "downtown" merchants, the day laborers, all of whom had their own more or less distinct speech patterns. Could they include all this diversity in their writing, thereby breaking the decorum expected of their "elevated" art? Or would they instead idealize the distinct speech styles in various ways, thereby muting the radical differences?

Even more important was the new outlook on life and society that came with the introduction of Western culture. It is hard to keep in mind that a mere hundred years ago so many words crucial to the conduct of life in present-day Japan were simply not in coin: almost all political terms, Western philosophical concepts, names of Western imported objects; all the Japanese equivalents for, say, democracy, train, equality, idealism, and trousers. The words had to be coined as the concepts or objects were introduced. And the neologisms had to be negotiated into literature with all the uncertainties of intelligibility, connotation, and propriety that this implied. Especially when English and other European words were directly incorporated, the uncertainties were bound to increase, causing writers to worry a great deal about accuracy in the process of Japanizing the sound and sense—as once, centuries before, they must have worried when borrowing massively from Chinese. Insofar as a novelist was concerned with depicting contemporary scenes, he could not evade the job of somehow, either by approximation or new coinage, finding words for Western ideas and things. Even now the difficulty is very acute, neology being one of several serious problems for the Japanese novelist; at the beginning of the novel tradition it must have been immense.

The discovery of the Western novel was both the cause and the effect of the powerful impulse toward verisimilitude in the language of Japanese fiction. Since most modern Japanese writers could read some English, and occasionally French, German, and Russian, the translation of European novels began to flourish with a vigor unknown anywhere outside Japan. Futabatei and Mori Ōgai were both translators, and Natsume Sōseki was a professor of English. Clearly the consideration of which style to use for the translation of a Bulwer novel or a Shakespeare play was bound to yield new stylistic suggestions for the direction of the Japanese novel itself, leading directly to the challenge proposed in the name of *gembun'itchi*.

The issues involved in the *gembun'itchi* program faced every writer during those early years of the novel, whether he articulated a position on them or not, and are far from settled even for writers of the present day. Futabatei, the first modern Japanese novelist, took the first important steps toward confronting them.

"DROP DEAD": THE WRITER'S IMPERATIVE FUTABATEI SHIMEI: *THE DRIFTING CLOUDS*
—*Futabatte shimei.*

There are two facts about Futabatei Shimei (1864–1909) that are important in connection with *The Drifting Clouds* (*Ukigumo*), certain circumstances of his education, and his friendship with Tsubouchi Shōyō.[12] Futabatei was born in Tokyo, still called Edo, in 1864, four years before the Meiji Restoration of the emperor's rule. His father was a low-ranking samurai, a fact that would be insignificant except that his status was both low enough to allow absorption of much of the old burgher culture and high enough to ensure his son's enrollment in a traditional samurai school. Futabatei grew to love *kiyomoto, shinnai, tokiwazu,* and *jōruri*—various types of recitation accompanied by the guitar-like *samisen.* These musical narratives—which are, incidentally, extremely difficult to read, not to say listen to—were vital transmitters of Edo culture, and Futabatei learned from them all the pathos and irony of the Edo people while familiarizing himself with a language very similar to that of the older novels. In the schools he first attended in the home town of his clan, the curriculum was largely Chinese classics (in *kambun*), and he was steeped in the Confucianism that for centuries had been the basis of samurai education. But the clan's official school, like many others at the time, also offered French and English instruction, and Futabatei learned enough French to understand what it means to know a foreign language, while tasting for the first time literary tidbits from the exotic West. By the age of seven, Futabatei had some real experience of a different culture.

His Western studies were accelerated in 1881 when he entered the Tokyo Foreign Language School, an extraordinary institution in its time and even by today's standards. In the Russian Department where he was enrolled, the entire curriculum from physics and chemistry to literature was conducted in the language to be learned, many courses being taught by Russian émigrés who knew very little Japanese. The writers Futabatei read while still a schoolboy made up an impressive list, including Pushkin, Lermontov, Turgenev, Gogol, Goncharov, Tolstoi, and Dostoevsky. It was a far cry indeed from the teaching of languages in present-day Japan, where students learn how to translate a foreign language into Japanese, but seldom the reverse, and almost never how to speak it—which is exactly the old *kambun* method of Japanizing a foreign language.

Futabatei kept up a lifelong relationship with Russian literature. First, his translations from Turgenev, Gogol, Goncharov, and others, published from 1888 on, are far more accurate and sensitive than any other translations of those days when Shakespeare's plays and *Tales from Shakespeare* were virtually interchangeable.[13] His renderings reproduce the original sentence unit, carefully preserving the verbal texture, rhythm, and tone together with the accurate meaning of each word.[14] The style he adopts, furthermore, is remarkably colloquial. "The Tryst" (*Aibiki*) from Turgenev's *A Sportsman's Sketches,* which he published in July–August 1888, between the second and the third installments of *The Drifting Clouds,* is simple in syntax, fresh and graceful in expression, and largely native in vocabulary. Above all, the narrator's tone is surprisingly neutral despite its *-da, -dearu* suffix system, which in the hands of a lesser craftsman would have fallen crude and coarse on Meiji ears. In his translation of a Gorky story, on the other hand, the rough speech of a laborer is matched in Tokyo workers' vernacular. Futabatei learned from his Russian translations whatever can be learned from the style of a modern European text: consistency in the narrative tone, a brief and clear syntactic structure, the craft of *le mot juste,* the true rendition of actual speech. The application of such techniques to his own writing is clearly in evidence in the later parts of *The Drifting Clouds*.

Second, Futabatei wrote many essays throughout his career on various literary subjects—the art of fiction, style, *gembun'itchi*, translation, and Russian literature. Most are newspaper or magazine pieces, quite brief (only a few pages), and often conversational, and none amount to a developed treatment of any single subject. But scattered among these are his astute observations and impressions concerning literary practice, and especially his preoccupations with *le mot juste,* which he learned from Turgenev's well-chiseled art. As for his broad and deep knowledge of the Russian novelists, it was far ahead of anyone else's in those days. In "The Standards of My Translation" (*Yo ga Honyaku no Suijun,* 1906), he confides that all the praise or blame he received for his translations was pointless and irrelevant, and that all along his critical struggle was largely with himself.

Finally, Futabatei's knowledge of Russian literature opened new thematic horizons. In "A Chat on Russian Literature" (*Roshia Bungaku Dan*), for instance, he discusses the lineage of the Oblomov character in Russian novels. He sees the man who would stay in bed all day to avoid an uncomfortable draft in terms of the conflict between the old Russia and the new Western European culture which fragmented and polarized the values and identity of the intellectual. Although Futabatei does not refer in this essay to the analogy between nineteenth-century Russia and Meiji Japan, it is clear to anyone who has read *The Drifting Clouds* what he had in mind in the essay.

Futabatei met Tsubouchi Shōyō (1859–1935) in January 1886, a few days after he withdrew from the Foreign Language School. Shōyō, only five years older than Futabatei, was already a rising figure in the literary world. Fresh out of the prestigious University of Tokyo, he had already published translations of Scott's *The Bride of Lammermoor* and *The Lady of the Lake,* Shakespeare's *Julius Caesar,* Bulwer's *Rienzi,* and had written *The Essence of the Novel (Shōsetsu Shinzui)* and several works of fiction, of which *The Temper of Today's Students (Tōsei Shosei Katagi)* was the most important. Although Futabatei's respect for Shōyō was deserved, their relationship, which lasted until Futabatei's death in 1909, was not one of a teacher-pupil sort. On the subject which brought the two together, fiction and the language of fiction, it was always the younger and lesser known of the two who had the wider knowledge and clearer grasp of the problem. In fact, scholars are unanimous in regarding Shōyō's later turn from creative work to teaching and translation as being largely the consequence of his friendship with Futabatei which made him realize the limitations of his own talent.

The Temper of Today's Students (1885–86) was a new novel in its own way. Presenting the student scene of the early Meiji years, it documents some interesting aspects of middle-class student life: money worries, experience in the red-light district, and slang largely made up of English, German, and French words (as it still is today). But aside from the novelty of the setting, the work is as vapid as most of its contemporaries. The plot follows a series of impossible machinations that would shame even a Bulwer: Shōyō claimed it was modeled on Thomas Hughes's *Tom Brown at Oxford* and Thackeray's *Pendennis,* but it does not merit even those rather modest comparisons. The work is actually a rehash of the Edo pleasure-quarter novels, substituting students for tradesmen. Its language is even more disappointing: the intrusive and extravagant narrator depends heavily on stereotypical epithets, puns, and formulas that by this time had become purely extrinsic ornaments, and in moments of excitement falls into a 5–7 meter (roughly comparable to Dickens' blank verse). Perhaps its main contribution to the novel was the prestige that Shōyō, a respectable university man, lent the craft of novel writing, at that time still considered a rather low and vulgar occupation.

The Essence of the Novel (1885–86) is quite another matter. Here Shōyō is determined to formulate a systematic overview of the art of fiction. Since no native criticism of any significance was available to him to organize his ideas,[15] he had to borrow from English and American journals (the *Nineteenth Century* and *Forum,* for instance), the *Encyclopaedia Britannica,* several textbooks of rhetoric, and lectures by visiting professors such as Ernest Fenollosa.[16] "The Novel as Art," "The History of the

Novel," "The Subjects of the Novel," "The Kinds of the Novel," "The Benefits of the Novel"—such are the headings of the first half of the 200-page volume. The main thesis in this section is the independence of the novel from overly didactic concerns. Verisimilitude, not *kanzen chōaku* (reward virtue, punish vice), is its primary function, according to Shōyō. In the course of his discussion, he blames Bakin and all the Edo novelists and praises Richardson, Fielding, Scott, Bulwer, Thackeray, and George Eliot, about whom, however, he has very little to say in support of his praise. And despite his anti-didactic position, Shōyō quietly reintroduces the notion of morality by pointing out that the effect of reading a novel is elevating by definition. Unfortunately, he does not argue this rather intriguing point thoroughly enough.

The second half of the treatise is devoted to discussions of style, plot, and character in the novel, the historical novel, and other such specific subjects. The chapter on style is fairly significant. Here Shōyō talks about the elegant style (*gabun-tai*), the vernacular style (*zokubun-tai*), and the elegant-vernacular mixed style (*gazoku-setchū-tai*), saying very much the same things as Bimyō was to say soon afterward except that he is more tentative in his recommendation of colloquialism. The elegant style is too effeminate and remote to be the language of the novel; the vernacular style, on the other hand, too local and familiar. His choice falls on a compromise, the mixed style, at least for the present. What is most interesting is his expression here of an urgent hope for the emergence of "some talented man who could find a way of removing all these shortcomings of colloquialism." [17] Little did he know—this Shōyō, already one of the brightest men of his time and soon to become the greatest Japanese translator of Shakespeare—that the talent he called for in this book already existed in his new friend Futabatei Shimei. This circumstance, together with the fact of his own disappointing performance in *The Temper of Today's Students* (which he apparently believed exemplified his ideas of the novel), suggests a great deal about the still inchoate condition of the novel, as well as Shōyō's limitations as a theorist of literature.*

* Despite its vagueness, however, Shōyō's essay is impressive enough for its time: after all, even in England the general discussion of the novel was just about to

Futabatei gave Shōyō a draft of *The Drifting Clouds* in the latter part of 1886 and asked him for suggestions on improving it. The master liked it pretty much as it was, but at the same time —as he later came to regret—advised the young writer to elevate the tone by increasing the Chinese vocabulary in certain passages.[18] Futabatei apparently accepted this wrong-headed advice and made repeated revisions of the work. Shōyō then handled the arrangements for publication even to the extent of lending his name as co-author.

It is at this point that the young author's pen name, "Futabatei Shimei," was adopted. A name such as this—a slightly modified form of "futabatte shimei," the equivalent of "drop dead," *—was fairly unusual at a time when most writers, following the custom of the old Chinese and Japanese men of letters, chose elegant names like "Shōyō" (Wanderer), "Kōyō" (Red Maple Leaf), and "Bimyō" (Beauty and Mystery). Futabatei later confided in his friend that the name was his father's reaction to his decision to make a career of writing. Elsewhere he recorded his shame at having leaned on his teacher's name to get his work published, a self-hatred also expressed very exactly in the pen name.[19] Clearly, the name tells something about this brilliant young man, who was always honest and ironic about himself, to the point of serious self-doubt. It also suggests, in a broader context, the alienation expressed by other writers who felt themselves cut off from the mainstream of the society by contemptuous or embarrassed family members or friends.

The Drifting Clouds, Part One, was published in June 1887; Part Two, completed some time toward the end of the year, was published in February 1888; Part Three, the last, was serialized in July and August 1889 in a biweekly magazine. The exact date of the completion of the last part is not clear, but it was probably

---

begin around this time with James, Robert Louis Stevenson, Walter Besant, and others. And with the exception of George Henry Lewes, there is no one earlier who set forth a coherent treatment of the novel

* I mean the *sound* of the name, the ideograms chosen to fit the sound being elegant and self-ironic: the ideograms for "Futabatei" mean "cottages of two leaves" (the first two leaves of a seedling) and those for "Shimei," "four perplexities" (*mei* means "to be lost," "to go astray"). Marleigh Ryan's inaccurate translation of the name as "go to hell" denies its significance.

around July 1889 (after the beginning of the serialization). As was the case with many Victorian novels, serialization was not then unusual in Japan, nor is it now. It should be stressed, though, that the degree of reader accommodation is often minimal in this sporadic kind of serialization, quite unlike that in a Dickens serialization. Also it should be kept in mind that Futabatei's novel was written and published over a fairly long period of time with the consequence of considerable change in its verbal features.

The title, *Ukigumo*, is evidently intended to suggest the hero's uncertain position relative to both his love and his position in society. Besides "drifting," *uki* can be read as either "sad" or "gay," depending on which ideogram is used. When spoken, *uki* at once sets off the paradox inherent in the pun. Also, *ukiyo* (floating world) is a key term in Edo literature, and the most representative arts of the period are called *ukiyo-e* (pictures of the floating world, chiefly woodcut prints), and *ukiyo-zōshi* (stories of the floating world, or the novel).[20] Futabatei's choice of this title, then, at once signifies the tradition he has inherited, while also pointing to the essential ambivalence of sadness and gaiety, tragedy and comedy (or the *carpe diem* of Edo decadence and Buddhist resignation) quite evident in the work itself.

The novel is brief (less than 150 pages in the standard text), which is often the case in Japanese fiction, and the plot, unlike that of Shōyō's novel, is extremely simple. The young man in the story, Bunzō, is laid off from his government job. His aunt Omasa, in whose house he lives, is annoyed and begins to show her contempt for him. Bunzō is in love with his cousin Osei, but the beautiful girl's reaction to this news is rather indefinite. Bunzō has a worldly and aggressive colleague, Noboru, who presents a threat to his marital prospects. What fills the story is the day-to-day family conversations, Bunzō's unending self-analysis, and a few episodes such as Bunzō's efforts to find another job, and Noboru's visit, in the company of Omasa and Osei, to a chrysanthemum show. The chronology of the narrated events is also very short: less than two weeks (October 28 to November 8) in the first sixteen chapters and a few subsequent weeks in the remaining three.

A simple story with a very brief chronology can indicate either trivialization—which is not the case here—or the internalizing of events. And for the author to have worked hard at it for nearly three years suggests the possibility at least of his continual assessment and reassessment of his material. The work is thus doubly psychological in the sense that, while exploring the inner experience of the main characters, it also reveals the author's fluctuating feelings about this experience. And the temporal structure of the novel, reflecting this psychological complexity, is far from simple.

The story opens with a conversation between two men just after one of them has been given notice of dismissal. As yet unnamed, they are singled out from the rush-hour crowd of office workers and government bureaucrats hurrying home. The next two chapters flash back to fill in the background of the man who was fired: his now deceased father, formerly a samurai, his impoverished and helpless mother, his energetic aunt, his beautiful cousin with whom he is in love, and so on. After that, the narrative progression more or less straightforwardly covers the rest of the short duration. Yet a clear outline of the passing time is not what the reader perceives. For one thing, the "events" of the novel are to such a degree internal that, despite numerous temporal references, it is impossible to mark the calendar. Then, too, the portrayal of the vacillating and pusillanimous young introspective is necessarily a little tedious. One reflection leads to another, still to another, then turns back to the original point, such circularity defeating the projection of any clear sense of passing time and in any case retarding the novel's tempo by lengthening the felt time. There is also the matter of grammatical tense. Japanese has no clearly established tense, and forms for past and present are often interchanged without creating any confusion for the reader. *The Drifting Clouds* is for the most part written in such a past-present mixture, and this, though it might on occasion intensify reader involvement in the manner of the "historical present," usually tends to obscure the linear time development. (The author himself is apparently halfhearted in tracing the passage of time, since the very first sentence contains an error: "at 3 p.m., the twenty-eighth of October, leaving only two days to the end of the month." And there are other discrepancies: in chapter 9, for example, "fifth day [since October 28]," ought to read "seventh day."

As for the repetitiousness, it, too, is deliberate. Take the four successive descriptions of Osei in the first four chapters. The first time the reader hears about her, in chapter 1, she is merely referred to as "your sweetheart" by Noboru. In the same chapter, the housemaid reports to Bunzō how Osei looked earlier that day when she went out with her mother. The description is largely of her clothes and not of her total appearance and expression. In the second chapter, the reader is given a brief account of her schooling and Bunzō's growing love for her, but no direct portrayal. In the next chapter, the reader comes a little closer; she is now reported as Bunzō sees her—as it happens, under the moonlight. A full daylight account of her appearance must await chapter 4, where the narrator attempts to provide a more objective view, though in no less admiring terms. The effect of this is twofold. First, the process by which the reader is introduced to Osei parallels the way one often comes to know another person in real life. Second, the narrative sequence at the same time disrupts the chronology of the events. Chapters 1 and 4 belong to the same day, while chapters 2 and 3 deal with the past. All of this means, simply, that our progress in coming to know Osei does not accord with ordinary temporality, and thus our grasp of the plot is somewhat obscured.

Such temporal obfuscation, however, is not necessarily a disadvantage: in this novel, especially, whose chief movement is "drifting," the absence of a clear linear progression is almost a formal requirement. Even the author's abandonment of definite time references in the last three chapters helps create a sense of temporal dislocation which is the expected consequence of drifting.

This discussion of the novel's narrative sequence leads naturally, I believe, to the question of the language in which the narrative is set forth. The most important feature is the archaism that dominates a fair proportion of this "new" novel. Here is a passage from chapter 2 as Marleigh Ryan* translates it:

> Bunzō was so happy he could have danced for joy. He had been terribly overworked by his aunt since coming to her house and had, in addition, very much disliked his role

---

* Unless otherwise indicated, the quoted passages are from the translation in Marleigh Grayer Ryan, *Japan's First Modern Novel: "Ukigumo" of Futabatei Shimei* (New York and London: Columbia University Press, 1967).

as a dependent nephew. Now that he was back in school, he was able to devote his full time and energy to his studies without any distractions.

But even at school he was continually reminded of his poverty and loneliness. He had no one to spoil and pamper him as the other boys had, no one to give him an allowance. He channeled all his youthful energies into his studies. He was inspired by an overwhelming desire to bring joy to his destitute mother and to repay his great debt to his uncle by being successful at school. And he was. He took either first or second place—but never lower —in every examination. He was the pride of his teachers. His rich and lazy fellow students were very jealous of him. (Pp. 206–7)

A perfectly ordinary style, as any translation probably ought to be, but the original is hardly so plain and clean. In fact, the whole of these two paragraphs is originally only one sentence which runs—at the risk of incoherence—like this:

Till yesterday, in the misery of being but a hanger-on at [his] uncle's home, being slave-driven and anxious, even frightened, to please; today, no longer ordered around by anyone, now able to devote his entire time and energy to study, well, wasn't [he] pleased, so pleased, that [he] jumped up and down in pleasure; but a student though [he] is now, it too being also a life of troubles; of course unlike the spoilt rich sons, having no fancy treats like help from parents, [he] cannot waste even a penny, but then doesn't want to; only being determined that [he] must relieve his helpless, lonely mother, must pay back his uncle for the debt; [his] study—undertaken in struggle and hard work with no wasted time—advancing remarkably; always being ranked the best, not even the second, at every examination; teachers being impressed [by him] as an extraordinary student.*

It may be remarked here that since systematic punctuation in

* My rendering is from the Iwanami Shoten edition of the *Complete Works,* I, 11–12 (see note 19).

Japanese was, in a sense, a new concept developed only a short while earlier, and Futabatei may not yet have learned its full use or significance, it may be a mistake to take his commas and periods too seriously. At the same time Futabatei did learn the concept of syntax from his foreign-language study, as his sentence-by-sentence translation of "The Tryst" will bear out. Besides, archaism can be an advantage. The loose sentence, which he inherited from the *yose* storytellers and the Edo *gabun-tai* writers, while clearly unsuited to precise statements requiring definite syntactic relationship of subject and predicate, is remarkably effective here where the hero cogitates seemingly endlessly and without explicit logical development. At times the style almost achieves the effect of the interior monologue and stream of consciousness—and this a few decades ahead of Joyce.

Unfortunately, this use of the old style is not generally a happy choice for Futabatei. The very first phrase of the novel, for instance, "Chihayafuru kannazuki," means simply "October," for which the ordinary word is *jūgatsu* (tenth month). The epithet *Chihayafuru* is a vestigial formula-term (*makura kotoba;* "pillow word") from the ancient formulaic tradition; it means "who shakes the world with a thousand rocks (thunder and earthquakes)" and hence "powerful, strong"; it is always applied to deity. *Kannazuki* is an old term from the lunar calendar meaning "the *god*less month" (hence the epithet). This type of formulaic expression, together with puns, might of course intensify poetic ambiguity and irony, and William Empson probably would have approved of it. But after centuries of overuse such verbal techniques began to lose their appeal for the reader, and Meiji writers were by this time actively boycotting a convention they felt was functioning now as mere superficial ornamentation. For instance, Futabatei's readers would hardly pause at "earth-shaking godless-month" to consider a possible religious comment by the author on his "ant-like" crowd of modern bureaucrats; they would quickly gloss over the phrase as a quaint name for October.

Then there is the summer evening scene where Bunzō tries to talk to his flippant cousin, and a description of the moon is given:

The cool moon rose, outlining the leaves of ten slim bamboo trees which stood in the corner of the garden. There was not a single cloud and its powerful, radiant, white light lit up the face of the sky. Glistening drops of light poured down to the earth below. At first the bamboo fence between the houses held back the moonbeams and they extended only halfway across the garden. As the moon rose in the sky, the moonbeams crept up to the verandah and poured into the room. The water in the miniature garden there shimmered in the light; the windbell glittered and tinkled. Then the moonlight silhouetted the two young people and stole the brightness of the single lamp in the room. Finally it climbed up the wall. (P. 217)

An exquisite film fadeout. But the highly stylized and heavily Chinese texture is not related at all to the real movement of the characters' feelings. It appears that the elegant and archaic passage with its verse-like rhythm (5–7 meter) provides Futabatei with an escape from his job of scrutinizing the actual situation of that moment as it abruptly leaves the level of reality the novel has thus far been negotiating. The "beauty" and "elegance" of the passage do almost nothing to further the psychological drama between the young lovers. It is too easy a way out.

Another passage of this sort is the description of Ueno Park:

Fall in Ueno Park. Ancient pine trees stood row upon row, their branches interlaced, their needles thick and luxuriant, of a green so deep as to saturate the heart of an onlooker. The fruit trees were desolate in contrast; old and young alike covered with withered leaves. The lonely camellia bushes, their branches laden with flowers, seemed to yearn for companionship. Several of the delicate maple trees had turned a blazing red. The cries of the few remaining birds mirrored the sadness of the season. All at once, the wind blew sharply. The branches of the cherry trees shivered and trembled, shaking free their dead leaves. Fallen leaves strewn on the ground rose as if moved by a spirit and danced about in happy pursuit of one another. Then as if by unanimous accord they lay down again. This bleak and dreary autumn scene cannot compare with a bright and hopeful spring day, but still it had a special magic of its own. (P. 267)

"Branches interlaced," "a green so deep as to saturate the heart of an onlooker," "the lonely camellia bushes," "yearn for companionship"—phrases as cliché as the dance of dead leaves. Futabatei's painterliness is heavy-handed, even in the English. It is a set picture, almost that of a traditional scroll. Compare this with a passage from Turgenev's "The Tryst," which Futabatei translated about this time:

A slight breeze was faintly humming in the tree-tops. Wet with the rain, the copse in its inmost recesses was for ever changing as the sun shone or hid behind a cloud; at one moment it was all a radiance, as though suddenly everything were smiling in it; the slender stems of the thinly-growing birch-trees took all at once the soft lustre of white silk, the tiny leaves lying on the earth were on a sudden flecked and flaring with purplish gold, and the graceful stalks of the high, curly bracken, decked already in their autumn colour, the hue of an over-ripe grape, seemed interlacing in endless tangling crisscross before one's eyes; then suddenly again everything around was faintly bluish; the glaring tints died away instantaneously, the birch-trees stood all white and lustreless, white as fresh-fallen snow, before the cold rays of the winter sun have caressed it; and slily, stealthily there began drizzling and whispering through the wood the finest rain.[21]

For Turgenev, a tree is a tree, the actual physical existence of which is conveyed through the word. If meaning emerges from his words, it is grounded in the life of the trees. For Futabatei, in contrast, meaning is imposed by his verbal trees—words, or pictures, exist, but not trees. (Partly, this is due to Futabatei's lack of ease with outdoor scenes. His genius being in the dramatic presentation of men and women, whenever he has to describe a scene larger than a room, he escapes into the elegant style which offers the security of a stereotyped convention.)

The Drifting Clouds puts the conventions to occasional good use in its imagery, particularly animal imagery for expressing Bunzō's sexual frustration:

> Since Osei had come home to live, worms had been breeding inside poor, unsuspecting Bunzō's heart. At first they were very small and did not occupy enough space to give him trouble. But once they started actively crawling around, he felt as though he were peacefully departing from this world and entering a blissful paradise. . . . But all too soon the worms grew fat and powerful. By the time Bunzō had begun to suspect that he was infatuated with Osei, they were enormous and were crawling about, anxious to be mated. (P. 212)

The translator is surely in error regarding the plural "worms." Although Japanese nouns can be grammatically either singular or plural, the word here definitely means "the worm"—that is, the snake, the phallic being of Bunzō. In fact, there is a boldly explicit pun, *soitai no ja,* in the passage. The phase literally means "anxious to sleep together," but *-ja,* a nonsignifying verbal suffix, being a homophone with another *ja* that means "snake," the phrase can also mean "the snake that wants to sleep (with someone)." Similarly, there are many feminine symbols—*hamaguri* (clam) and *shijimi* (top shell), for instance—and, all told, a surprising number of fairly explicit sexual and scatological expressions.

Clouds of course are a major part of the book's imagery: the clouds in the sky and "to cloud" in the sense of "to obscure" both appear throughout the novel, reiterating its leitmotif. The reader will recall that Bunzō spends most of his time "upstairs," close to the clouds, and in any case quite cut off from the ground floor where most of the daily activities of life are conducted. The upstairs room, suggesting the paradox of claustrophobic one-room confinement and spatial and psychological indefiniteness, is a fit location for him. And the same sort of symbolic notation system operates in the names of the main characters, which all suggest representative qualities. The Oblomov-like hero is named Uchimi Bunzō, meaning "Inland Sea" and "third son of *Bun* (writing)."

The name can also indicate "introspectiveness" and "three letters" (or "three cultures"—Japanese, Chinese, and Western?). Honda Noboru, "main rice field" and "to rise," is a suitable name for an energetic upward mobile in modern Japan. The name of Bunzō's domineering aunt, Omasa, "to govern," is no surprise, while that of Osei, her charming, light-hearted daughter, means the "course of things," though it can also mean "force" and "vigor," which may suggest some untapped strength she inherited from her mother. Given all this, to read a point-by-point allegory of proper names may be overdoing it. We have to keep in mind that Futabatei knew his Dickens and Thackeray well, and must have learned from their not-so-subtle use of names as a prop to reinforce the orientation of a work.

But beyond this, the most important stylistic feature of the work is, of course, *gembun'itchi*, the kind of colloquialism that both Bimyō and Shōyō wished, but could not themselves begin to write. The quaint elegant style appears quite often in Part One, less frequently in Part Two, and hardly ever in Part Three. The time Futabatei spent working on the novel no doubt explains the change, but his own understanding is that the three parts, written at different periods, were modeled after different writers: Edo novelists for the the first part, Dostoevsky for the second, and Goncharov for the third.[22] But whatever the generic circumstances of the gradual disappearance of archaism in *The Drifting Clouds*, it should be noted that the later parts are much more serious in confronting the psychological movement of the characters. Anything that can be called an event in this "novel of no events" occurs in the earlier parts, and toward the end all the action takes place in the minds of Bunzō and Osei. Since the elegant style is linguistically alien to psychological drama, a totally new kind of colloquialism is called for. To twist it around, Dostoevsky and Goncharov—whom Futabatei discovered for Japan—taught him a style that called for a new subject matter. Serious study of an ordinary person's thought and behavior ultimately requires a language rooted in his ordinary life, and a novel written in such a language will of necessity have to deal with the daily life of the ordinary person. Despite Futabatei's occasional successful use of the quaint and unpunctuated style, his real achievement was in forging a plain, ordinary language to be used in the novel of plain, ordinary people.

With regard to the characters in *The Drifting Clouds*, Futabatei's best work is in dialogue and the main characters' self-analysis. He is also, however, adept at the swift presentation of minor characters. Both the old teacher and the department head who fires Bunzō are successful caricatures of the kind of "Westernized" men who have been crowding the Japanese literary scene ever since. Though self-convinced connoisseurs of the West, they in truth know very little of it, or of Japan either for that matter. While drawn with broad satiric strokes, these two characters also amplify certain traits shared to some degree by the younger characters—Bunzō, Osei, and Noboru. And they gloss a noticeable contradiction within Bunzō himself, who, though generally a sympathetic figure, self-righteously refuses to "apple-polish" his boss, at the same time doing exactly that to his old teacher. Using minor characters to gloss or amplify the traits of the major figures is a common enough technique in fiction but Futabatei's skillful use of it here gives us impressive and tangible evidence of his knowledge of such novelistic resources.

Omasa is a type character, and what a sardonic portrayal of powerful maternity she is. Utterly unself-conscious and seemingly indefatigable, she snorts and belches along, secreting her venom for her unfavorite people and then letting them have it. Similarly, Noboru, the vulgar but quite self-assured social climber, is very much alive. The verbal exchange between these two big-mouths is a comic masterpiece.

Where Bunzō is concerned, his extreme shyness and taciturnity make the author's good dialogue technique irrelevant. His thoughts must somehow be conveyed, but there is the problem of how to proceed. Since he vacillates so interminably, a third-person narrator's presentation and interpretation would be awkward and boring: how could any other person, particularly the narrator, be interested in his endless does-she-or-doesn't-she and should-I-or-shouldn't-I debate with himself? Bunzō had better speak for himself. He had better, but he doesn't. The novel is not told from the well-focused point of view of its chief character. In fact, the narrator maintains an ironic and rather condescending distance from the character, especially in the earlier parts. Here is his earliest description of Bunzō, for instance: "His complexion was quite poor, pasty and sallow, but his thick eyebrows lent distinction to his face, and the bridge of his nose was straight. His mouth was not very shapely but it was firm and restrained. He had a pointed chin and prominent cheekbones. He was rather drawn and seemed nervous and not particularly appealing." (P. 198.)* Even at the end of the novel, where Bunzō at long last reaches some sort of resolution, the narrator presents him ironically:

> Restlessly he wandered [back and forth in the corridor]. Eventually he reached a decision. He would try to talk to her when she came back. He would gamble everything on her response. If she would not listen, he would leave that house once and for all. He went back upstairs to wait. (P. 356)

Note his restless movement "back and forth" † in the house; also his final move in the novel, which is a return to his upstairs room, an ivory tower of sorts, protected from the context of life. If a novel can be said to judge events and characters, it must certainly be said of *The Drifting Clouds*.

Now, if the narrator seems ironic at both ends of the novel, it is logical to ask what the perspective of this irony might be. And how about other passages, especially in the later parts, where he seems so intensely involved in the hero? In Browning's dramatic monologue, the authorial stance is unambiguous in its irony and the character is made to reveal himself in spite of himself. It is the same in the omniscient-narrator novel: the narrator's comments add up to a definable commitment on the part of the author himself. But what is the narrator's judgment in *The Drifting Clouds*? What does his irony mean? Is this young man—painfully honest and credulous and finally quite ineffectual—an object of pity to the narrator? Or is he somehow praiseworthy as a kind of

---

* Do we see in this portrait a version of the entire Hamlet-Gothic villain-Byronic hero-Oblomov lineage? A very much tamed version, but it does betray something of Cain's mark.

† Ryan's phrase "wandered about" is imprecise. "To and fro" or "back and forth" would be more appropriate.

modern moralist? Or, still another possibility, is the narrator saying that he *is* modern man? And finally, is life "sad" or "gay" in
Futabatei's eyes? Is Bunzō tragic or comic? Or a little of each?

I do not believe we shall find a clear answer to these questions.
The Drifting Clouds, for all the hero's propensity to moral judgment, affords no perspective in which his broodings might take on
some significance. Melville's Bartleby, Goncharov's Oblomov,
Dickens's Eugene Wrayburne, for instance, all exist in a moral
and psychological context in which their paralysis is precisely defined; in Uchimi Bunzō we have a fragmented modern man portrayed without a clue to his broader significance. The narrator is
as unsure about Bunzō as Bunzō is about himself. It must be then
that the irony in the narrative voice originates in the author's
own feeling of fragmentation, his awareness of his inability to
organize a coherent judgment vis-à-vis his character.

Osei, pretty and faddish—a flapper, if such an anachronism
might be allowed—is similarly ambiguous. Often dismissed by
critics as a superficial "new" girl, she is actually extraordinarily
charming. She has a shallow sort of crudeness, true, but it is nevertheless balanced by her refreshing temperament and free energy.
Osei also undergoes certain changes in the course of the novel.
From chapter 12 through chapter 16, she is no longer such a flirt,
but rather subdued toward Noboru and her cousin and attentive
to her mother. In a rare passage that directly squares with her
inner thoughts, there is even a moment of self-realization. But
what does it mean? What are we supposed to think of her now?
And how does Bunzō see her now? There is no direction coming
from the narrator here. To our frustration, he provides no clue to
such questions. Just as he was uncertain about his modern young
man's predicament in the loss of being, so is he now unsure of the
girl in the picture—this time, simply because he does not seem to
understand what a girl is. Potentially there is a full-bodied young
woman—lively, good-looking, affectionate, shallow, callous, sexy,
pretentious—but the narrator does not gather these features into
a sharp focus so we can see her clearly. We don't know what to
think of her any more than Bunzō does.

The novel is formed by one person's consciousness of another.
Each character's understanding of himself is modified by the

other's notion of him. And this interlocking of consciousnesses creates the world of the novel, the community of men and women as the novelist perceives it. What is curious about *The Drifting Clouds* is how little the characters seem to understand each other despite the fact that they are living in the same house, having their meals together, and sitting down in the evening together. Their physical world is one small house, and yet the residents are worlds apart, each one isolated with no promise whatever of better understanding in the future. Omasa and Noboru, vulgar-minded as they are, dismiss Bunzō too casually, and that ends the matter right there. Between Osei and Bunzō, there is little promise of any greater insight.

What we begin to suspect after a while is that Bunzō does not know Osei at all. Her sexual energy is obviously attractive to him, but Bunzō, Confucian puritan that he is, is afraid to think very well of sex, which is finally "wantonness," even "obscenity," as he unhesitatingly defines it in relation to his rival Noboru. The moral-psychological terms available to him are neither extensive nor sophisticated enough to apply to a modern young woman who owns her own mind, and, alas, her own body. Bunzō does not see Osei herself but his own restricted image of her, which is mere fantasy and illusion, and he knows it:

> Bunzō was certain that her new attitude toward him contained a significance that he was not yet able to grasp, and he was determined to find out what it was. With an enormous effort he concentrated all his energy on analyzing her behavior to isolate this evasive element. He had little success. He became irritated. And then those devilish worms inside him started their tantalizing dance again, teasing him with one hint after another, and finally tricking him into accepting some absolutely absurd solution. Half realizing how ridiculous it was, he accepted it for the moment anyhow and worked on the idea until he had constructed a whole situation from it. He experienced exactly the same hurt and pain from this artificial hypothesis as he would have if it had been a fact. At last he made himself see it for what it was: a ridiculous fantasy. He was

simply looking for trouble. In a rage of self-disgust, he mentally smashed the illusion into a million pieces. He sighed with relief. (P. 274)

And, finally, we suspect that the narrator—indeed the author—shares with his character much the same ambivalence, the same fogginess and irresoluteness. The astonishing lack of mutual understanding among the characters of *The Drifting Clouds* cannot be explained solely in terms of Osei's superficiality or Bunzō's obtuseness. Nor can the surprisingly complete separation of the characters be interpreted as a result of the paradoxical privacy prevailing in the apparently communal Japanese home. There is doubtless something here of Futabatei's personal isolation, which was nearly absolute in a real sense for many periods of his life.

One might connect this moral ambiguity with the technique of temporal obfuscation discussed earlier. *The Drifting Clouds* is a moral and psychological novel in the sense that the hero is possessed of a compelling moral sensibility, and the narrator obviously tries to deal with it. The hero's action must then be anchored in the chain of events arranged from a temporal-causal viewpoint. The novel is, however, quite vague in its temporality, and as a result the hero's action is suspended in its clouds of anxiety without being rooted in the context of everyday temporal sequence. The novel, in short, tries to judge the hero from a point of view, while it has no point of view. The narrative sequence, disrupting the temporal sequence, is both a symptom and a strategy of this frustrated judgmental effort.

The Drifting Clouds neither defines the nature of its own irony nor demonstrates much conviction that irony might turn out a saving grace in a world of grotesque absurdities. And yet it is an important modern work for the way it disdains the crowded panoramas that tease fiction into episodic surveys, and for the way it manages to transform behavior into motivation and action. Similarly, its language, while using the conventions to its advantage, pushes the frontier of the craft of fiction to the border of colloquialism.

Futabatei wrote two more novels after an interval of twenty years. *The Visage* (*Sono Omokage*, 1906) describes a married man's love for his wife's sister. The consummation of their love produces an awful guilt in the girl, and the man, a university lecturer, abandons family and career and disappears on the Continent to become eventually a skid-row alcoholic. Here again, the novel suspends judgment on the tormented man. Though the language is plainer, more in tune with other novels being written at the time (which had caught up with *gembun'itchi* by then), this novel lacks the attractive concentration of *The Drifting Clouds*. Futabatei's last work, *Mediocrity* (*Heibon*, 1908: translated into English in 1927), is quite boldly autobiographical. At the beginning of the *shi-shōsetsu* (I-novel), the orthodox tradition in the modern Japanese novel, *Mediocrity,* is interesting to a historian. But from the point of view of art it does not come up to *The Drifting Clouds*. For one thing, it peters out unpleasantly at the end, confirming a tendency already evident in the author's earliest work, [23] but not so damaging there.

Futabatei is one of the few really attractive men of Japan's modern literature. Honest to a fault, he refused to join the Tokyo literati, with their jealousies, petty backbiting, and continually compromised positions. He hated to think of himself as a writer, preferring the man of action as a self-image. In fact, to be true to himself he abandoned his writing career soon after *The Drifting Clouds,* and during the rest of his short life was in turn a journalist, a colonial administrator, and a teacher. Even in these capacities he refused to sell out, and no doubt as a consequence he never really succeeded in his ventures. Now, of course, his genius is recognized, and despite his meager production he is considered a giant among Japanese novelists.

II

THE IMPORTED LIFE

MORI ŌGAI: *The Wild Goose*
—*Japan is not a land of art.*

Mori Ōgai published his first fiction in 1890. To think of
"The Dancing Girl" (*Maihime*) as anything but juvenilia is hard
for most of us now, but Meiji readers found it otherwise: with the
exception of a very few critics, it was a perfect modern masterpiece for them.[1]

The language of "The Dancing Girl" is in a decorous elegant
style (*gabun-tai*), although contemporary readers took it as a
"mixed style of Japanese, Chinese, and Western" (*wa-kan-yō-
setchū-tai*), feeling that the scattering of German words and names
through the story was the most important stylistic feature. The
elegant style of "The Dancing Girl" reads well even today, being
neither too difficult to understand nor too familiar as the colloquial
style might be. The nostalgia created by the old-fashioned language matches the exotic setting and experience described by the
story, which was at least part of the reason for its instant acclaim.
But at this particular juncture what mainly interests us is the
hero's experience, which provides one of the earliest examples of
an attitude toward the West that has since grown into something
like a version of pastoral in modern Japanese fiction.

The story runs like this. A young career government worker,
assigned to a few years' study in Germany, meets a struggling

young ballerina in Berlin and saves her from a threatened seduction. He falls in love with her, and they live together, but this highly irregular behavior invites his superior's censure, and he is dismissed from his position. Down and out in a strange land, he struggles to survive on a few free-lance writing assignments for Tokyo newspapers. Then an old friend of his who happens to be in Berlin as secretary to a visiting official offers to help him on condition that he give up the girl and return to Japan. He accepts the offer. The girl, now pregnant, discovers his plan and suffers a breakdown. He goes home anyway, but on his return voyage he writes of his feelings of guilt and regret, and this first-person record constitutes the story.

In the earlier part, the young man thinks about the meaning of all the hard work that has put him through the highly competitive university system. Even his sojourn in Europe is part of this life-long program "to become a name, to raise his family's name." [2] Once in Germany, however, he begins to feel profoundly disturbed by his "passive and mechanical" personality. The freedom and independence that he breathes in the European air threatens to float him loose from the tight structure of his native society. Work now appears to him as a deception, of others as well as himself, the motive for work being only greed and the fear of ostracism. What he used to believe was great moral dedication to learning is no more than selfish and bureaucratic careerism.

At this point in his critique of self and society he meets his German dancer, with her "pale golden hair," "pure blue inquisitive eyes bedewed with tears," "long eyelashes," and, of course, "white skin." Clearly, she stands for the "freedom and independence" that are unattainable at home. The interracial aspect of the encounter—the relationship of the darker-skinned young man and the white girl, such as black writers have analyzed recently—is also unattainable except abroad and is a large element in the freedom he is experiencing.* But there is still something else in-

---

* One of the most interesting studies in this connection is an article by Hirakawa Sukehiro, "Fushinchū no Kuni Nippon: Mori Ōgai no Tampen to Lengyel no Jinshugeki *Taifū* o Megutte" ("Japan 'Under Construction': Mori Ōgai's Short Story and Lengyel's Race Drama *Typhoon*"), reprinted in the Nippon Bungaku Kenkyū Shiryō Kankō Kyōkai's collection of essays. According to Hirakawa,

volved. Although the German girl no doubt differs in appearance, in practically every other aspect she is conceived by Ōgai in the familiar terms of a Japanese girl. She is penniless and helpless, so the young man can take her in and be protective; she is "pure," "virginal," and, above all, faithful and devoted in taking care of her new lord and lover; in sum, she is not so much the pure Fräulein as the idealized Japanese wife and mother.†

There is nothing extraordinary about a writer's projecting his own ideal upon the people his hero encounters in a foreign setting. Indeed one could cite a long list of works including Melville's *Typee*, Charlotte Brontë's *Villette*, or, more contemporary to Ōgai, Henry James's European novels. But there are some specific features that should be mentioned in the case of the Japanese traveler-writer. And here we might look directly at the significance of foreign travel for the Meiji era Japanese.

Going abroad, or *yōkō*, was, at least until very recently, a glamorous affair in which the excitement of the event itself was combined with the promise of an élite career to follow. A young man's departure for such a grand tour constitutes a tribal occasion, with a great number of people properly seeing him off and wishing him well. The traveler carries the honor of the celebration with him sometimes, it is true, unduly burdened with a resolve not to let "expectations" down too much. He must test his foreign-language ability; he must know how to handle interracial encounters; he must try and prove his resilience of mind and person.

Melchior Lengyel's play *Typhoon* (1909), which treats a liaison between a Japanese student and a French woman in Paris, was so fascinating to Ōgai that he then translated one of the obscure Hungarian playwright's short stories. A racist work, *Typhoon* shrewdly exploits the European fear of the repressed and enigmatic Japanese. (Incidentally, many Japanese liked the play, which was produced at the Imperial Theatre in Tokyo in 1915.) Ōgai wrote two tracts on the subject of the Yellow Peril, very much in the air at that time, both of which dispassionately introduce the theories of white supremacy, refuting obvious distortions and contradictions. It is to his credit that there is no trace of the counteradvocacy of Japanese supremacy in either of these papers. ("Jinshu Tetsugaku Kōgai" and "Oka Ron Kōgai," *Complete Works*, XIX, 377–420, 421–66.)

† This impression is undoubtedly reinforced by the use of honorifics (*keigo*) necessitated by the Japanese. While he most probably could not have avoided it entirely, he might have done something to soften the tone of male dominance in the work, which even manifests itself in the pronouns.

Traveling, so seen, is a final test in the long apprenticeship to a secure position in the élite corps of the Empire. Still, the temporary release from the constraints of Japanese society is in itself a profound enough experience, more often a positive one than a negative. Instead of being held to a definite slot in a tightly meshed hierarchy, the traveler is cut loose to float free for a while in the unfamiliar medium. Even where he tends to cling to other Japanese tourists, compared to being at home he can move around almost unrestrictedly. If he is young and as yet unestablished, as is typically the case, he is likely to enjoy the freedom that goes with anonymity in a foreign city.

Then, there are of course the differences between his former Japanese life and that in which he now finds himself. Undoubtedly, comparison of cultures is a hazardous business, and the supposed vast differences between the East and West may or may not be bridgeable, or may indeed not even exist. But we are more concerned here with the felt contrast, not any absolute or objective difference, and the Japanese traveler is likely to see the West as the diametric opposite of the East, just as the antonyms imply. By him, the unfamiliar paradigms of Western life—respect for the assertion of individuality, the analytic habit of thought, the general tenets of democratic government—are felt to be the opposite of his native ones. Probably more important are certain matters closer to everyday living: fewer restrictions on the relations between men and women, more self-expressive manners and behavior, the colorful and luxurious appearance of European urban centers—so unlike what the young man had known at home. The tourist may at times react to these experiences with loneliness and alienation, but more often he will show relief and pleasure, even intoxication—until the time for starting home wakes him from his euphoria (as it did the young man of Ōgai's story).*

The re-entry shock upon coming home can cause long-term ad-

---

* The sociologist Nakane Chie presents the opposite view—the typical Japanese traveler as reluctant, homesick, and generally miserable—in her study of today's Japan, *Japanese Society* (Berkeley and Los Angeles: University of California Press, 1970), pp. 134–37. But Nakane is mostly interested in the businessman, for whom the encounter with the West is merely an inconvenient experience incidental to his main preoccupation with careerism.

justment problems. The same century lies there, but the traveler, now so accustomed to his role of observing as an outsider, a voyeur, is unable to reintegrate himself into the familiar become suddenly unfamiliar. He can't get his bearings quickly enough, and in any case he often finds the old scene unaccountably drab and stifling. Writers and intellectuals, even if their time abroad was miserable, as was Natsume Sōseki's, often suffer a particularly severe letdown.* The West has been inescapably internalized for these men in a way that can deprive their resumed life of the simplest pleasures.

To generalize boldly, modern Japan exhibits its contradictions most clearly to its returning émigrés: the country can no longer sustain the feudal fabric of community, but its corporate institutions insist on the bureaucratic loyalty of their vassals. The vertical relationship of parents and children is weakening rapidly, but more democratic family forms are yet to come. While the Empire expects its "subjects" to give homage to the Emperor, the wider world in various ways undermines nationalism as a source of intellectual and emotional satisfaction. Paternalism persists throughout society, cheek by jowl with rising "democratic" expectations. In short, while the old Japan is fast being secularized, the new myths tend to be stillborn.

"The Dancing Girl" is a convenient early index to this new East-West encounter which involves the fact and metaphor of traveling. But the story takes too easy a way out. When the young man finds "freedom" in Berlin, he is not really free. And when he really is free, alone with the girl, he is already crushed by the loneliness that freedom always brings in its train. Unlike

---

* See Ōgai's "Hidemaro stories," for instance. In "Fantasy" (*Mōsō*, 1911), Ōgai describes a certain fear he experienced before his return to Japan: "There is not the proper atmosphere to nurture the seed in the home to which I am now returning. At least not at present. I am afraid that the seed might die, having lived in vain. And I was assaulted by a fatalistic, dull, gloomy feeling." *Complete Works,* IV, 116.

Feelings of letdown are described by many other writers. One of the most typical examples is Yokomitsu Riichi's sprawling novel *Ryoshū*. The young men and women in the novel are continually haunted while in Paris by the idea of the return home, or, more specifically, frightened by the thought they might find themselves changed on their return.

Melville or Dickens or James, who use foreign experience for the projection of their personal vision, Ōgai is inescapably bonded to the vision he shares with the rest of his society. There is nothing "personal" about his Japanizing of the German dancer; it is as though the character—and the author—had not known the independence of the self at all. It never occurs to the young hero, for example, that it might be a real alternative for him to adopt Germany as his new home. Instead, he never doubts for a moment that his "foreign" experience will end sooner or later, and that what is possible in Germany cannot be in Japan. There is something fundamentally circular in his pilgrimage: he will stand at the end exactly where he stood when he started. His sojourn is a glorious moment of suspense to be treasured in memory perhaps, but finally irrelevant to his necessary being. Thus the hero's blaming his friend at the end of the story is an absurd self-deception. "The Dancing Girl," once hailed as Japan's earliest "romantic" tale,[3] unromantically insists throughout on maintaining safe ties to the work-oriented Japanese society, and thus stops far short of a serious examination of the choice between both work and freedom and social bondage and personal fulfillment.*

Ōgai wrote two more elegant-style stories, which, with "The Dancing Girl," form a European trilogy. Both highly successful at the time, they are very much the sort that had great vogue all over Europe in the early nineteenth century. Ōgai, it appears, made use of the exotic "gothic" setting, with its aristocrats and castles and mysterious deaths, to lure the Japanese reader to a land of enchantment far away.

---

*Ōgai wrote "The Dancing Girl," surprisingly enough, as an explanation of his own travel experience. A graduate of the Tokyo University Medical School, he joined the Imperial Army Medical Corps at twenty, and the army sent him to Germany two years later. We do not know what adventures he had in Berlin, but we do know that a German girl called "Elis" (also the ballerina's name in the story) followed him to Japan two weeks after his return. Ōgai refused to meet her, and through his family persuaded "Elis" to go back to Germany at once. "The Dancing Girl," written less than a year and a half later, is thus autobiographical and belongs in a way to the *shi-shōsetsu* tradition. This explanation, incidentally, was intended for his superiors in the army. Nothing is known, of course, about the story's effect in pacifying the misgivings of his inquisitive superior officers.

There are many stories, written much later, that fit better thematically with "The Dancing Girl." For instance, "Under Reconstruction" (*Fushinchū*, 1910). A career civil servant reserves a room in a restaurant undergoing noisy remodeling. While he awaits the arrival of his guest, he notes the depressing mess the room is in: "Japan," he reflects, "is not a land of art." * The woman of the rendezvous finally arrives—a German soprano, now on a world tour, with whom he was once involved during his stay in Germany. As they fill in the gaps since the old days, she asks him to kiss her. His answer, "We are in Japan," carries the crude illogic that the kiss enjoyed in Dresden is not possible in Japan. Reasserting the solution of "The Dancing Girl," though more bluntly, the story reveals a slight tinge of sadness only in the title ("Under Reconstruction"—everything held in abeyance until Japan itself is reconstructed) and the generally depressing scene. The story is taut, with few details, but Ōgai's facile sentimentality manages to break through nonetheless. For instance: "It was still only half past eight when a solitary, black car drove slowly along the Ginza through an ocean of flickering lights. In the back sat a woman, her face hidden by a veil." [4] The loneliness would have been more convincingly *his* than hers. Besides, the temporary wait implied by "under reconstruction" seems to hide the depth and seriousness of East-West differences which Ōgai obviously felt.

While "The Dancing Girl" and "Under Reconstruction" have a measure of fictional autonomy, many other stories are very nearly essays with little care taken for plot or character. For instance, the series built around an aristocratic repatriate (called Hidemaro)—"As If" (*Kano yōni*, 1912), "Hiccup" (*Shakkuri*, 1912), "The Wisteria Arbor" (*Fujidana*, 1912), and "Hammering" (*Tsuchi Ikka*, 1913)—endlessly and rather shapelessly argue the cultural and philosophical issues of the day as they strike the character's (the author's?) fancy. Dozens and dozens of recondite names are dropped, such as von Hartmann, Lange, Schleiermacher, Strindberg, and Eucken, fairly choking the stories. I am

* In *Complete Works*, Volume III (see n. 2). The translation used here is Ivan Morris's in his *Modern Japanese Stories* (Rutland, Vt., and Tokyo: Charles E. Tuttle, 1962), pp. 35–44.

not at all sure these names meant anything much to anyone else at that time except the author, but those who admire Ōgai seem to take them at face value even now, as if the "stories" were important philosophical tracts. The most I can say for them is that they do reveal Ōgai's awareness of Japan's position vis-à-vis the West: Japan must "reconstruct" itself so that, presumably, it will ultimately "catch up with" the West (which, in this view, has already successfully solved most of the problems of modern life). "As If," for instance, questions the origin of the empire myth— precisely in the way that the nineteenth-century European Biblical criticism (say, Strauss and Feuerbach) questioned Christianity—and concludes tentatively that the myth should be treated *as if* it were history, all in order that Japan might eventually secularize the myth with the least pain as the West has done. Tentative accommodation seems to be Ōgai's strategy for most of life's predicaments.*

What *is* interesting throughout this is that Ōgai is no longer able —either in fiction or outside it—to talk about the problems of modern Japan without directly putting them in a Western frame of reference. Somehow an adequate explanation of one's experience requires a context provided by the West; or, more drastically, Japanese experience is somehow incomplete in itself. In order to become satisfying and significant, it asks for placement in a Western context where it can be viewed from a Western perspective. As the writer-hero of Ogai's thinly fictional novelette *The Youth* (*Seinen,* 1913) asks in his darker moments:

> Does a Japanese know at all how to live? As soon as he
> enters grade-school, he tries to dash through the entire
> period of schooling, believing there will be a life beyond
> school. Once he gets a job after graduation, he works year

* A brief look at Ōgai's later life is in order here. Concurrently with the spread of his fame as a writer, he steadily climbed the ladder of the Army medical services hierarchy, holding such positions as president of the Army School of Medicine, superintendent of army medicine, and surgeon-general of the Imperial Army—all at the highest military rank. Honored with doctorates both in medicine and letters, and with many medals and decorations, he is one of the very few Japanese writers to combine literary activities with a very successful establishment career. Yet his favorite motto in life was "Resignation," and as he was dying, in 1922, he is said to have mumbled, "Absurd."

> after year until retirement, always thinking there will be
> a life beyond work. But there is no life beyond. (*Complete
> Works,* Vol. V, chap. 10.)

The young man never seems to find the proper subject matter for
his art: Japan is not interesting to him.

The importation of themes from the West is, then, a provisional
solution to the identity crisis in Japanese literature. Futabatei's
borrowing from Russian and Ōgai's from German are only two
cases out of a whole cultural process which for lack of a better
term must be called the "Westernization" of both art and life. To
clarify, we can force the argument a little. The "Westernization"
of a young man begins with his reading a European or American
novel. The pattern of behavior he finds there begins to loom in the
background of his own conduct. As he puts on jacket and trousers,
he feels "European." He kisses his girl friend, and he looks for a
Tolstoi heroine in her. He trims the Christmas tree (just one more
New Year's decoration), and begins to aspire to "Christian"
ethics. His external conduct affects his consciousness; but the
consciousness also modifies the conduct. At this point he can with
some legitimacy be depicted by a writer as living a "Westernized"
life in Japan, and the reader, too, can visualize himself as doing
the same. Nature indeed imitates art in Japan, and to a degree far
greater than Oscar Wilde could possibly have imagined. Along
with the methods and the products of Western industry and en-
gineering, many post-Meiji Japanese were eager to import not
just the West's literature and literary themes, but a new life-sub-
stance itself. And if all this looks like an insignificant ripple on the
surface of one's being, we must see that in a man's life no surface
change leaves the depths untroubled.

Ōgai's European studies continued, as can be seen in his trans-
lations from his characteristically wide range of authors—from
Rousseau, Goethe, Lermontov, Hoffmann, Andersen, Turgenev,
Daudet, Flaubert, D'Annunzio, Tolstoi, Gorky, Ibsen, Andreyev,
Strindberg, and Schnitzler to Shaw, Maeterlinck, and Rilke.* Dur-

---

* His translations are contained in 18 of the 53 volumes of the standard *Complete Works.* Although they are mostly from German and English, his range of
authors is indeed remarkable.

ing this time, he was also deeply absorbed in rediscovering the roots of his native culture. When, for instance, General Nogi, national hero and Ōgai's personal friend, followed the Emperor Meiji in death by taking his own life in 1912, in accordance with samural tradition, Ōgai's grief expressed itself in a series of semi-historical fictions treating the samurai code of *junshi* (joining the departed lord by suicide). His return to the past becomes even more dominant in the barely fictional and nonfictional historical studies written after *The Wild Goose* up until his death in 1922. And yet, it is as a reaction to the imported West, even as part of the Westernization program itself, that such a resurgence of Japanese themes ought to be considered, as I will try to show.

The Wild Goose (Gan, 1911–15)* was written precisely at the point in his work where Ōgai turned from Western to Japanese themes. Its subject matter is no longer the East-West encounter, and instead of civil servant and aristocratic repatriates its main characters are a coarse-grained moneylender and his naïve mistress. There is a handsome young medical student, but he is not particularly well versed in the lore of the West, and only at the end does he decide to go to Germany, thus joining the host of Ōgai émigrés. The novel then largely focuses on a style of petty-bourgeois life everywhere observable in Tokyo. Even the references the narrator makes to Tokyo stores, streets, and bridges and to the Edo entertainers are familiar ones for the reader and sketch a setting far from the usual Ōgai territory. For once, Ōgai seems to be writing fiction, as he digs out the life of ordinary Japanese in Japan. But is he really weaned from the West?

Suezō, once an errand boy, now runs a prosperous loan operation. He comes across a beautiful girl, Otama, just separated from a bigamous policeman, and wants her for his mistress. Suezō invites Otama and her father to discuss the proposal, and all agree to an arrangement: he buys a home for the girl and rents another for her father. Days go by, but Otama is too timid to go and see

* I use the English translation by Ochiai Kingo and Sanford Goldstein, *The Wild Geese* (Rutland, Vt., and Tokyo: Charles E. Tuttle, 1959). The plural form "geese" in the title is an error, since the title refers to the particular bird Okada kills toward the end of the story.

her father, fearing Suezō's possible disapproval. Soon everything works out, and around Suezō's daily visits to Otama and her occasional visits to her father a semblance of peace prevails. Suezō's jealous wife, however, hears about the liaison, and begins to nag her husband. In the meantime Otama, who had been made to believe that her master was a respectable businessman, finds out that he is actually a loan shark. To avoid worrying her aging father she keeps the news to herself, which only increases her sense of isolation. Just about this time, she begins to notice one of the students who pass her house on their regular evening walks. She learns his name, Okada, and his address. One day Okada hears a commotion in front of Otama's house: a snake is swallowing one of the linnets Suezō bought for her. Being the only man around, Okada kills the snake and rescues the small bird. Otama gratefully helps him wash his hands, but even then she is too shy to speak to him. She knows by now that she is falling in love with Okada, but sees no way to deepen their relationship. One day when Suezō tells her that he will be away overnight, Otama finally sees her chance and, giving her maid the day off, prepares to invite Okada in when he passes by. This particular evening, however, Okada is joined by his friend, who is the narrator of the tale. Otama has no courage to speak to Okada in front of another man, and they pass by. Okada tells his friend that he has been offered a research job at the University of Leipzig and is leaving Tokyo the next day. As they approach Shinobazu Pond, they are joined by another friend, who suggests that Okada kill one of the wild geese so he can cook it that evening. Half hoping that he will just frighten the birds away, Okada pitches a stone and hits a big one. As the three walk back with the dead bird, Otama stands frozen in her doorway. "Her eyes, opened beautifully wide, seemed to contain an infinite wistfulness and regret" (p. 118).[4] The next day Okada leaves for Germany.

The narrative structure of *The Wild Goose* is a bit awkward, a frequent problem with Japanese novels. The narrator, Okada's friend, begins by reminiscing on past events, but soon disappears from the tale, almost making it a third-person story. He returns in chapter 18 when it becomes increasingly clumsy to present events which the narrator cannot have been in a position to know.

His explanation of his knowledge is offered at the end—"I learned half the story during my close association with Okada [and] I learned the other half from Otama, with whom I accidentally became acquainted after Okada had left the country" (p. 119)— and is unpersuasive. (How could he, even with Otama's help, ever come to know the minds of Suezō and his wife?) Although the narrator resumes his role as a participating character toward the end, the occasional comments throughout the work are more authorial than first-person. In a way, the typical Japanese sentence form which allows omission of the subject (the verb having no inflection to indicate person or number) serves to reinforce this ambiguity around the narrator.

What might usually flaw a novel, however, is not altogether a weakness in this case. In the opening, the narrator's "I" is very prominent ("That date comes back to me so precisely because at the time I lodged in the Kamijō . . . and because my room was right next to that of the hero"). This implies that his relationship with Okada is more than just thematic. The "I" meets Okada as a self meets the other and becomes an observer of the other. Interestingly, the hero is himself a passive observer rather than an actor. Thus, as the voice shifts, confusing the hero's with the narrator's, the effect is to distance the events from the reader altogether. Similarly, the returning narrator's disavowal of involvement with the heroine at the end of the story—"It is unnecessary to say that I lack the requisites that would qualify me to be Otama's lover; still, let me warn my readers that it is best not to indulge in fruitless speculation" (p. 119)—further increases the irony, putting the reader outside the story to look at the goings-on from the perspective of an aloof observer.*

* In chap. 22, comparing himself with the hero, the narrator makes a curious remark about his own feelings for Otama (p. 109). The self-contradiction detectable in the statement ("I would have been happy if, like Okada, I had been loved by such a beauty" and "I would have gone so far as to stop at her house [and] love her as one loves a sister") is not an instance of authorial irony but poor artistic judgment on Ōgai's part. There are two circumstances one should be aware of in this connection. First, Ōgai knew only a certain kind of relationship with the women in his life. He used to call his second wife (having divorced his first) his "objet d'art." He seems to have been unable to engage himself at a close emotional level with women, and his relationships were all carried on as though from a dis-

The work explores several possible man-woman relationships in Tokyo life. To begin with Suezō, such an ambitious and energetic man cannot possibly be satisfied with an ugly woman like his wife, Otsune, who "press[es] on his stomach her heavy breasts, like pocket-warmers, which had supplied ample nourishment for each of their children" (p. 59).[5] As his store of wealth increases, his vitality seeks fresher outlets, although not to the extent of breaking up his marriage. With Otama, however, his sexuality does not seem as fully engaged as it ought to be under the circumstances. When he buys linnets for her, feeling "How charming [it is] to see her with them" (p. 83), he is utterly un-ironic. He really is in love with his bird-girl in a cage. No doubt he is happy in gently tutoring her, but the book clearly indicates their relationship will be short-lived. Sooner or later, Otama will have to fly from her cage. Thus does *The Wild Goose* coolly write off the shrewd moneylender's claim to fulfillment.

The narrator-author is plainly sympathetic toward Otama's growth from a gullible child "bride," to a beautiful young girl willing to sell herself for her father's comfort, and thence to a woman aware of her own need for happiness. This process of maturation is marked by several image notations along the way (of which the bird imagery is of course the most conspicuous). Here Ōgai avoids sentimentality rather well. Where necessary, Otama is portrayed as capable of shrewd scheming almost matching Suezō's. Not the "pure" nothing that wafts through so many Meiji novels (or their Victorian counterparts), she perfectly understands her sensual needs: "[Warm in bed after waking up] Otama would let her imagination go unbridled. Her eyes would glow, and the flush would spread from her eyelids to her cheeks as though she had drunk too much sake" (p. 101).[6] She must find the right man.

Her restlessness shows itself, just after she moves into her new

---

tance. Second, Otama was evidently modeled after a girl Ōgai himself saw occasionally, but only as Okada and the narrator saw Otama. In a more explicitly autobiographical, if rather parodic, story, "Vita Sexualis" (1909), the narrator-author presents a girl just like Otama. In the same way, *The Wild Goose* distances the author's personal experience by several removes through its narrative structure.

house, when she discovers Suezō's true status. A seemingly un-related incident occurs when a self-announced ex-convict invites himself into the house and forces money from Otama at *knife point*. Thus the intrusion of male sexuality into Otama's con-sciousness commences, and it is about this time that she begins to notice Okada. When the linnets are attacked, it is Okada who runs to the rescue, cutting the snake's head off—castrating him-self, and Suezō, too, at the same time. Thus this St. George, though reputedly a fine athlete and a connoisseur of Chinese erotic liter-ature, is neither a very virile lover, nor any substantial succor to anyone, linnet or girl.

Ōgai's almost too explicit handling of symbols culminates in Okada's killing of the wild goose. Otama's possibility of freedom is annihilated by this one, partly unintentional, act. Okada, the linnet's defender, has become the slayer of a goose, undergoing this change just as his involvement with Otama becomes a possi-bility. Clearly, she is left here with little but the prospect of frus-tration.

Accident plays too conspicuous a role toward the end. By acci-dent, Okada is not available for Otama's carefully arranged meet-ing; by accident, he hits the bird; and by unhappy coincidence, he is to leave for Germany next day. And yet, there is something much more stunning about the story in the way it—not Okada—kills off this "jewel of a girl" (a literal translation of her name). Despite the sympathetic treatment of her growth, the book thor-oughly extinguishes any hope she may have for the future when it quenches the possibility of Okada's becoming her lover. It is the same with all the other failed relationships—Suezō and his wife, Otama and her policeman "husband," Suezō and Otama, even Otama and her father—and by the end it is as though her story itself had been stoned to death like the wild goose. Of course, there are the two survivors, Okada and the narrator. But they, too, seem headed toward a dead end. As for Okada, whether he meets another ballerina in Germany or not, he will almost certainly have to come home again eventually, and then what? As to the narrator, he makes it plain to us that his life is a purely vicarious one. And so, with both appearing all too ready to join the other Ōgai

émigrés, we see that the Japanese setting has not after all engaged Ōgai as fully as he might have wished. There is no hope
at present for personal happiness in Japan.

But not having a happy life to live is not the same as having
no life to write about. In the very culture that Matthew Arnold
called "not interesting," Hawthorne and Melville were writing
their great novels.* And Otama's life, despite its desolate outlook,
does provide Ōgai with a subject matter to hang a story on. Yet
even here one recalls—as Ōgai's contemporaries must have—that
The Wild Goose was to some extent inspired by *The Wild Duck*
(1884), by Henrik Ibsen, whom Ōgai had been translating off and
on since 1903.† (Ōgai, by the way, is not responsible for the absurd
effect of the English title, "the wild goose"; the Japanese equivalents for the two titles, *nogamo* [duck] and *gan* [wild goose],
bear no such similarity.) It is not that the novel was modeled
on Ibsen's play, for the plot similarity is really very thin: the
friendship of Gregers and Hialmar; Hedvig's innocence and her
love for her father; Old Ekdal as a dependent father; Werle's
illegal business deals; Gina as Werle's mistress; such roughly
parallel circumstances do not add up to recognizable "sources"
for the Japanese tale. Besides, Ibsen's drama shows the master's
sure command of the form and his symbols weave thick layers of
meaning, whereas Ōgai's control of narrative form is often shaky
and his symbolism all too thin. Ibsen engages in the current pro-
lems of the culture in a way Ōgai does not. Still, despite all the
real differences between the two, the killing of the wild goose at
the end of Ōgai's work cannot be considered without reference to
the killing of the wild duck, which in fact turns into the murder
of the innocent girl Hedvig. The landscape of Shinobazu Pond

---

* *Civilization in the United States: First and Last Impressions of America*
(Boston, 1888), pp. 172–73. Of course, Arnold was not thinking particularly of the
novel but of the whole situation of American culture and there are vast differences
in circumstance between the two situations. Still there is some resemblance between
the cultural unsettledness of Meiji Japan and young America's lack of "culture" in
the nineteenth century. Also, one recalls that Hawthorne and Melville both wrote
"romances," which enabled them to transcend the restrictions of the culture with
a greater freedom than the strict "novel" would ever allow.

† He published translations of *Brand* in 1903, *Hedda Gabler* and *John Gabriel
Borkman* in 1909, *Ghosts* in 1911, and *A Doll's House* in 1913.

may have little in common with the Scandinavian parlor scenes of Ibsen's play, but the climactic emphases given the episodes in both works are remarkably similar in their effect.

A large inference is tempting here. Ōgai requires for his fiction a mode of experience that belongs to a foreign context of life. When he treats ordinary Japanese life, his creativity is not engaged: he either adheres too closely to actual life (as in his émigré cycle or his historical studies), or loses control and turns preposterous (as in the hero's relationship with an older woman in *The Youth*). In *The Wild Goose* the Suezō-wife-Otama relationship is stalemated, and Ōgai clearly had difficulty resolving it, as we can infer from the publication chronology. Chapters 1 through 21 were serialized between September 1911 and May 1913, but the intervals between installments gradually widened toward the end of this period. Then he was unable to continue at all for two years, until in May 1915 he added chapters 22 through 24 and published the whole work in book form. It is of course in these last three chapters that the killing of the wild goose takes place. In short, his worry over the ending of *The Wild Goose* did not abate until he developed the notion of the bird-killing and the exile of the hero.

The hero's departure for Germany is not just another plot detail. Only by taking him out of Japan and Japanese experience could Ōgai bring the story to its conclusion. Okada's further stay in Japan would surely have had to mean his involvement with Otama, and that would have required embedding the relationship in the Japanese context, thus reducing its significance and interest for Ōgai. Terminating the relationship by any other course of action on his part, such as going to another part of Japan, would have made him more active in deciding his role toward Otama, thus contradicting his essentially passive character, whereas the offer of the overseas job takes it out of his hands. Like the church bell in Victorian fiction, "going abroad" says something final and inevitable in the Meiji novel.

Ōgai was not alone with his problem. It may be that Japanese life was not yet amenable to the form of the novel as it is understood in Western literature. Possibly, the novel could not readily be born there at that time, as it could not in, say, seventeenth-century England. The novel needs a particular kind of life—a certain expectation or assumption—which Japanese culture, even today, does not easily make available. This necessary life withheld to greater or less degree, the modern Japanese writer seems to have two choices. He can fall back on his own personal life, which, having been lived, is factual and hence presumably plausible. The consequence of this choice is the tradition of the *shishōsetsu* (beginning around the time of *The Wild Goose*) which uses details of the writer's daily life, often at the expense of the work's form or even of his life's form, as we will see later on. Or he can invent, even fabricate if he will, a life outside the context of ordinary Japanese experience. Characters can be free and events extraordinary in any situation beyond everyday experience. Ōgai sends his characters abroad so that they may behave like the sojourners and outsiders they are for the moment. Of course, the foreign style can be found at times in Japan itself— among the aristocrats, for instance, about whom the bourgeoisie know very little. But then, the aristocratic class is itself a sort of Western colony, since its members are almost always expected to be more "Westernized" than the Japanese middle class, as we know from Ogai's "Hidemaro" stories and from Dazai and Mishima. Either way, abroad or at home, the introduction of Western life offers a solution for the problems that have arisen in the Japanese novel, itself an imported form. And it will continue to do so, until the imported life itself has truly taken root in Japan, making ordinary life a suitable substance for the novel.

III

THROUGH THE GLASS DARKLY

NATSUME SŌSEKI: *Pillow of Grass*
and *Light and Darkness*
—*What right have we to hope?*

When Lafcadio Hearn resigned from the University of
Tokyo in 1903, his replacement, Natsume Sōseki, found it difficult to inherit even a small part of his great popularity. The literature students had especially loved to hear Hearn (known in
Japan as Koizumi Yakumo) talk about Tennyson's poetry in his
elegant yet informal style. Unlike Hearn, Sōseki was a Japanese,
an obscure provincial college teacher no one had ever heard of,
and his lectures were much too theoretical. Still worse, for students at the all-male university, he taught *Silas Marner*, a "high-
school textbook by a woman writer." [1] Clearly, the new lecturer
would never make it with the students. Fortunately, he was no
longer convinced he had much of a vocation anyway, and after
the great success of two novels he retired completely from teaching
in 1907 and decided to live as a writer. Since he was quite famous
by then, Sōseki's resignation was a newsworthy event, as was his
refusal later to accept the doctorate conferred on him by the Ministry of Education, no other public figure having ever taken such
an audacious action in those years.

Natsume Sōseki (1867–1916) had been a very serious teacher-scholar in English. Having first taught in Tokyo and in the provinces, he was sent to England by the Ministry of Education in 1900. With no more to spend than £15 (150 yen) a month, he lived an extremely frugal life—even by the foreign-student standards of recent years. He took the assignment altogether seriously. Not having luck like Ōgai's, he seldom ventured away from London, and spent his time shopping for books when he could spare the money, reading them, taking notes, and writing. He first attended W. P. Ker's lectures at the University of London; then, feeling the course was too elementary, he arranged for personal tutoring with W. J. Craig, the noted editor of the Arden Shakespeare. Having no way of meeting English scholars and writers, he found his intercourse with the English limited to nodding acquaintance with the lower-middle-class residents of his boarding-house plus the few missionaries he had met on board ship. He never could sit down and talk to an Englishman who knew anything about literature or who could begin to guess some of the problems a Japanese scholar of English had to face. Craig, whose half-hearted tutorials cost Sōseki a precious seven shillings each, took him exactly as that, an extra source of shillings. Though pleasant enough, Craig was too much taken up with his own studies to take serious interest in the diminutive Oriental gentleman who came so punctually for his "lessons." [2] Thus Sōseki, it is safe to say, was considerably more miserable and less comfortable than most Japanese scholars who have come, apparently in very similar circumstances, in recent decades to the United States or England to study. His diary entries and letters of this time point less to his homesickness than to his bitterness toward England, a bitterness that he immediately directed back at himself for being a Japanese in the first place, especially a Japanese scholar of English literature.

> The two years I spent in London were the most unpleasant two years of my life. Among English gentlemen, I lived miserably like a lost dog in a pack of wolves. (Preface to *Theory of Literature,* in *Complete Works,* IX, 14; see note 2.)

> Everyone I see on the street is tall and good-looking. That,

first of all, intimidates me, embarrasses me. Sometimes I
see an unusually short man, but he is still two inches taller
than I am, as I compare his height with mine when we pass
each other. Then I see a dwarf coming, a man with an unpleasant complexion—and he happens to be my own reflection in the shop window. I don't know how many times
I have laughed at my own ugly appearance right in front
of myself. Sometimes, I even watched my reflection that
laughed as I laughed. And every time that happened, I was
impressed by the appropriateness of the term "yellow
race."

I was looking in a shop-window the other day when a
couple of women passed by, commenting on the "least
poor Chinese" [Sōseki's phrase]. I was more amused than
angered by these expressions. . . . A few days ago I went
out in a frock coat with top-hat, and a couple of working
men sneered at me, saying "a handsome Jap." ("A Letter
from London," ibid., XII, 36–37.)

If you want to be a scholar, you should choose a universal
subject. English literature will be a thankless task: in Japan or in England, you'll never be able to hold up your
head. It's a good lesson for a presumptuous man like me.
Study physics. (Letter, September 12, 1901, ibid., XIV,
188.)

Talked with Brett. He said that the Japanese race needs
improvement, and that intermarriage with Westerners
should be encouraged for that purpose. (Diary, February 24, 1901, ibid., XIII, 43.)

We are country bumpkins, nincompoop monkeys, good-
for-nothing ashen-colored impenetrable people. So it's natural the Westerners should despise us. Besides, they don't
know Japan, nor are they interested in Japan. So even if
we deserved their knowledge and respect, there would be
no respect or love, as long as they have no time to know us
and no eyes to see us. (Diary, about April 1901, ibid.,
XIII, 87.)

As time went on Sōseki became more and more isolated and depressed. But as though to fight off the despair, he was determined to read voluminously and continue working on a general theoretical ground for all literary studies. As we see from the theoretical studies—*Theory of Form in English Literature* (*Eibungaku Keishiki Ron,* 1903), *Theory of Literature* (*Bungaku Ron,* 1907), and *Literary Criticism* (*Bungaku Hyōron,* 1909)— for which the basis was laid during his stay in London, his orientation was of necessity toward justifying *his* English studies as compared with those of native scholars.

The *Theory of Form,* the first and shortest, discusses systematically what Sōseki proposes as the three areas of literary form. Here is the paradigm as he wrote it in English:

Form
{
   I. Arrangement of words as conveying the meaning.
      (A) Form pleasant as satisfying intellectual demands.
      (B) Form pleasant from various associations in a general way, outside of mere intellectual demands—Miscellaneous.
      (C) Form chosen by our taste cultivated in historical development.
  II. Arrangement of words as conveying combinations of sounds.
 III. Arrangement of words as conveying combinations of shapes of words.[3]
}

Unfortunately, neither the principle of such a classification nor the contents of the categories can be easily understood, and the formula does not seem, finally, worth decoding. But what is clear and interesting to us is Sōseki's effort to classify, as for a taxonomy, all the "components" of literature, in order to know what territory he could appropriate as legitimately his in English without inviting the charge of intellectual deception. Like many such ambitious conceptions, his efforts at system building were bound to fail. We see how he necessarily falls short of an adequate definition of "universal literary form," which becomes a mysterious something that "appeals to our intellectual understanding in literature." One imagines he knew his shortcomings: the essay peters out to a shapeless conclusion despite the grand goal he sets for it. I am impressed nonetheless by the wide range of his references—from the classic figures to the major and many minor Romantic and Victorian writers. Moreover, Sōseki's analysis of a number of passages reveals an acute rhetorical sensitivity as well as his excellent historical command of the subject matter.

The second work, *Theory of Literature,* is the most ambitious of the three, with its objective of formulating the entire "content" of literary composition and response. According to some Japanese scholars, Théodule Armand Ribot provided the basic terms for this project, but Sōseki's framework, one suspects, being too singular to be anybody else's, is very much his own. Apparently believing that he has disposed of the problem of literary "form" in his first book, he now turns to the "content," which he divides broadly into two categories: "F" and "f." Large "F" stands for the intellectual focus of any content, and small "f" for its emotional overtones. I am, again, not at all sure how such a grand dualism can be expected adequately to explain complex literary processes, nor indeed am I clear as to what he means by literary "content." The titles of the sections seem to point vaguely to a general direction of argument: "Classification of Literary Content," "Quantitative Change in Literary Content," "Characteristics of Literary Content," "Mutual Relationships of Literary Content," "Collective F." Unhappily, by throwing every aspect of literature—from its materials, to rhetoric, to genres, to history, to grammar—into the "content" bag, he fails to make even the underlying assumptions of his system intelligible to the reader. And yet what impressed one about his first theoretical book is impressive here, too: his need to assess objectively the foreigner's claim to English literature, his continuous efforts to expand his own knowledge of English literary history, and, finally and very conspicuously, his sensitivity in actual analysis of passages and works.

The third work, *Literary Criticism,* is really a survey of eighteenth-century English literature. A belletristic history pure and simple, it yet again shows Sōseki's skill in close reading as well as his vast scholarship, his treatment of Pope and Swift being notably brilliant. That this book, the most historical and least theoretical of the three, achieves the most suggests that Sōseki's real gifts as a scholar lay in practical criticism where his sharp insights were backed up by his wide knowledge. At the same time, we should remember, Sōseki's theoretical objective was to prove that his studies were genuine and useful scholarly contributions. The sad part was that while his quasi-scientific theorizing failed to establish the possibility of a universal response—which, in transcending cultural and linguistic differences, might justify Sōseki's claim to scholarship in English literature, neither was there any good English critic around who could read his work in Japanese and tell him just how good—very good indeed—his practical criticism was. Thus in the Preface to *Literary Criticism* he seems to be conceding that a Japanese response to English literature cannot be significant to the English critic and reader, except in the way that the English historian's view of Japan is to the Japanese (naïve, interesting, exotic). While this is a kind of solution to his problem, his concession here thoroughly undermines the premise of his elaborate system: universality in literature.

Worries about the nature of literary scholarship were beginning to take form about this time. Within a decade or so, I. A. Richards and Kenneth Burke were publishing their attempts at rationalizing the discipline. And, a couple of generations later, academic critics the world over are again having their doubts about literary pursuits and the raison d'être of it all. Reflecting the unrest and discontent of their students, professors of literature are being forced to examine radically the ground of their work, if not their lives: a process leading them almost inevitably to the meanings of "relevance" on the one hand and "objectivity" on the other. For the Japanese professor of any European literature, however, such doubts are even more intense. He has the same fundamental uncertainty about his discipline, but on top of that is the nagging doubt about his personal authority as a professor of a literature completely foreign to his own. He may think he understands English, but what does "understanding" mean? How does he know whether he understands or not? Until recently at least, Japanese scholars have somehow managed to survive by repressing the basic problem and resignedly limiting their work to translating and annotating European works as "accurately" as possible. For the conscientious Sōseki, however, such worries could never be ignored while he continued to teach. Since he was never to gain much confidence in this work, he became increasingly depressed, until he found it almost unbearable to have to prepare his lectures and face his students. He disliked his colleagues, too, who at that time were beginning to emerge—there as elsewhere—as efficient and pretentious bureaucrats of learning. Thus, as his creative energy began to assert itself, he resigned from the university and became a staff novelist for the *Asahi* daily newspaper in 1907. He was to devote the rest of his short life— he died in 1916—to fiction writing.

It is perhaps significant that evidence for the theoretical basis of Sōseki's understanding of English literature should be so prominent in his own "Japanese" fiction. It is not merely that his works are full of the ironic spirit of Jane Austen, George Meredith, and Henry James, all of whom he loved. Rather, I am certain, the very form and substance of his fiction would not have materialized had he not been possessed of that rich and deep feeling for English fiction. The technique of the English novel which he knew and taught palpably shapes his own fiction and, furthermore, his knowledge of the English language works at crucial points in helping him forge a new language for the Japanese novel at this still early stage in its development.*

Before his university resignation, Sōseki published two novels, *I Am a Cat* (*Wagahai wa Neko dearu,* 1905–6) and *Little Master* (*Botchan,* 1906), and several short pieces, including essays on his visits to the Tower of London and the Carlyle museum and an adaptation of Tennyson's *Idylls of the King. I Am a Cat,* serialized very much like Dickens's *Pickwick Papers,* is a loose, open-

---

* I am of course not arguing that Sōseki's knowledge of English literature was his only inspiration here. As one can immediately discover, he read extensively in Chinese and Japanese literature as well. His friendship with Masaoka Shiki, one of the most important Meiji *haiku* poets, is also highly significant in his literary career.

ended satire which is surprisingly dark in places. The narrator
is a stray cat adopted by a schoolteacher. Although this novel is
at times too broad and transparent a caricature, its social milieu
—that of ineffectual intellectuals and dilettantes surrounded by
unsympathetic money-oriented bourgeoises—constitutes one of Sōseki's lifelong preoccupations. His next work, *Little Master,* is
a first-person record of an innocent young mathematics teacher
encountering older and more experienced professionals in a provincial high school. The comedy here is even broader than in
I Am a Cat, and while it reads with a refreshing pace and vigor,
I miss the customary subtlety of Sōseki's satire.

Pillow of Grass (*Kusamakura,* 1906)[4] was written in a great
spurt of energy and completed in just a week. It is by no means a
"novel" in the usual sense, since Sōseki is boldly experimental
here, as he will be for the next few years, producing a Bulwer-like
melodrama, *Wild Poppy* (*Gubijinsō,* 1907), and the Kafkaesque
Miner (*Kōfu,* 1908) before stabilizing his novelistic style, beginning with the trilogy of *Sanshiro, And Then,* and *The Gate*
between 1908 and 1910.

The narrator of *Pillow of Grass* is a Tokyo poet-painter, well
versed in both Oriental and Western arts and literature, who
escapes the bustle of big-city life by visiting a remote hot-spring
resort. Paralleling this movement, the work, which Sōseki calls
his "*haiku* novel," [5] itself provides a tour out of "real life." There
is little in the way of a story line: the "I" arrives at Nakoi, meets
Nami, the eccentric and beautiful divorcée, and also gets to know
her family, the Shiodas, and their friend, a Zen priest. At one
point he witnesses the encounter of Nami and her former husband, and at the end he sees off Nami's cousin bound for military
service in Manchuria. With so slight a plot, most of the significant
"events" of the story take place in the narrator's mind, making
Pillow of Grass a semi-diary account of an artist's moods and
reflections.

Going up a mountain track, I fell to thinking.
Approach everything rationally, and you become harsh.
Pole along in the stream of emotions, and you will be

swept away by the current. Give free rein to your desires, and you become uncomfortably confined. It is not a very agreeable place to live, this world of ours.

When the unpleasantness increases, you want to draw yourself up to some place where life is easier. It is just at the point when you first realise that life will be no more agreeable no matter what heights you may attain, that a poem may be given birth, or a picture created.

The creation of this world is the work of neither god nor devil, but of the ordinary people around us; those who live opposite, and those next door, drifting here and there about their daily business. You may think this world created by ordinary people a horrible place in which to live, but where else is there? Even if there is somewhere else to go, it can only be a "non-human" realm, and who knows but that such a world may not be even more hateful than this? (P. 12)*

The reader of the Japanese text is struck, first, by the wide use of the present tense and the prose cadence sustained by the extremely ornate diction, and after that, by a certain paradoxical feature in almost every statement. Although both of the English translations render the greater part of the book in the conventional narrative past, the original, like the quoted passage, is in the present tense throughout. Thus, while most novels move along a flow of time defined by the temporal sequences and consequences, *Pillow of Grass* progresses along a line of accumulated present moments. It remembers the past, of course, and it imagines the future.† And yet it constructs no novelistic perspec-

---

* All quotations are from the translation by Turney (see note 4).

† The most interesting way Sōseki indicates time in the novel is by his liberal use of the notions of East and West. Throughout *Pillow of Grass,* both Eastern and Western poets and artists are mentioned frequently, and generalizations drawn from the instances. According to the narrator, the East seems to represent an attitude that somehow transcends everyday matters—the "non-human" aspect of life—while the West suggests a down-to-earth involvement. (See his numerous comments on Shelley, Faust, and Hamlet versus Wang Wei, Tao Yuan-ming, and so on, as against his viewing the Western novel as "emotional," "intellectual," "social," "moral," "rational," "analytical.") Clearly, the correctness of his generalizations does not matter, for what Sōseki is trying to do is, first, locate the "non-human"

tive that can look back at a past incident or experience and place it in the plot. Things happen, and the narrator reflects on them as they are happening, but he does not know, as the novelistic (that is, past-tense) narrator usually does, where things will turn next. In such a story line the reader, of course, gets no ready-made interpretation and must puzzle and grope—as the narrator, too, appears to have to do—for a perspective that will make a "meaning" out of the story. There is an immediacy, even a certain excitement, in this for the reader, who is forced to pay attention to things as they happen or lose the thread.

The ornate diction is lost in the translation to English. But the Japanese version, too, has problems for its readers in its considerable number of Chinese ideograms that are both quaint and obscure. Although most Japanese can manage to approximate their meaning when they see them printed (on the basis of the components and, of course, the context of the ideograms), very few recognize them on hearing them. It follows that very few speakers of Japanese would know how to pronounce these obsure ideograms without the aid of *kana* notations,[6] even when they can guess the meaning. Such ideograms have effectively dropped out of the spoken language and may never in fact have been part of it. What this comes to is that Sōseki's writing in *Pillow of Grass* is, quite literally, far more visual than auditory; certain passages must be *seen,* not *heard,* to be understood. It is not accidental that the narrator is a painter. The very shape of an ideogram can suggest powerfully the shape and form of both a highly developed abstract concept and the vaguest sort of precognition.[7] This is not to deny the pleasant sonority of this passage in particular and the book as a whole—quite the contrary. But it appears to serve a purpose other than the pure euphony of the prose. The sound, in this view, is a useful propellant of the narrative line. Without it, we would pause too often in our reading and be tempted to parcel out the narrative time into a series of timeless scapes. In other

---

tour in the context of the world, and, second, to identify the roots of his imagination in the Eastern tradition. To treat the East as though it were exemplified by the spirit of Nakoi village is to look at the city, say Tokyo, as Western. The East is tradition and the past, the West the future. His sojourn in Latmos is then also a return to the past.

words, the cadence carries the reader along and occasionally makes him forget the untemporal, or spatial, features of *Pillow of Grass* that would otherwise distract and hold up his progress.

Paradox is the narrator's modus operandi in argument. At the outset, he divides man's faculties into intellect, emotion, and will, all of which he at once finds to be closed options. Life is disagreeable no matter what. Escape is necessary, except that there is no other life to turn to. Poetry and art, he argues, are born from this realization of having no choice. Quite early the narrator locates art (loosely including all the arts—literature, music, sculpture, and so on) outside the pale of the day-to-day human intercourse that leads only to the inescapable bog of paradox. Art is then what survives and transcends our disagreeable life.

The second cycle of this dialectic, reversing the order, begins on the next page. The narrator tells us that at twenty he thought life worth living; at twenty-five he found it paradoxical; and now at thirty, he seems to say, he finds ambivalence in everything— both joy and sorrow, health and pain, money and financial worries, love and fatigue. And how to resolve such an on-the-one-hand, on-the-other dilemma? The rock he slips on at this point, like Dr. Johnson's, stems his stream of thought and opens new possibilities. For a time, at least, the poet-painter stops worrying life into ever extending paradox and just sits and looks.

But the mode of progress throughout the work stays essentially the same: acceptance of life, its analysis into paradox, a new experience shifting the perspective of argument. When Sōseki called it a *"haiku* novel," he was thinking of a narrative movement determined by the juxtaposition and reversal of short scenes or thought sequences.

The movement of the argument is reinforced by the narrator's actual and metaphorical journey—from Tokyo and his "real-life" involvement with noise and paradox to an obscure mountain village and an aesthetic experience of uninvolvement. The poet-painter is determined to see the life he encounters in Nakoi as if it were "part of the action of a *noh* play" or, variously, to think of people as "moving about in a picture" (p. 23). He will keep his distance and irony in relation to life there: the "non-human tour" will be an exercise in disengagement.

Thematically, it is a familiar story. The English Romantics and post-Romantic writers Sōseki quotes in *Pillow of Grass*—from Shelley to Wilde—have argued time and time again: art needs distance from life, and at times almost supplants life to become a truer reality. Like Latmos in Keats's *Endymion,* Nakoi will give the protagonist a glimpse of Ideal Beauty. (The ideograms for "Nami" mean "that beauty.") To grasp it, however, the artist must first forego life. Although this position is almost always reversed at the end—as it is in *Pillow of Grass,* too—with the disinterested artist turning back into the thick of paradox, at the beginning at least, distancing to the point of alienation is the sine qua non of modern art. So much for the bare thematic restatement of what is clearly a very intricate narrative form designed to bring the reader along into the same perspective that the narrator takes for himself. His assumed aloofness toward Nakoi, the place and its people, is reflected remarkably in his verbal stance, as he proceeds to present Nakoi in almost purely visual terms, and the reader, too, begins to *see* the place as if it were a painting. Take, for instance, the scene of the tea-house in the spring rain; or the painter's dreamlike encounter with the Nagara maiden. There are also Nami's two histrionic performances—one in the bridal gown, the other with a dagger; the misty bathroom scene; Nami's rendezvous with her former husband; the Mirror Pond with the bloody red camellias; the final train-station scene. And every one of them a nineteenth-century topical painting—very "realistic," Pre-Raphaelite—translated into language, it is true, but altogether visual in effect. In fact, the scenes do not even refer so much to actual people and places as to certain already ordered visual forms. What is more, these self-contained stills are often extended into further metaphors and similes that are also visual and painterly. The pack-horse driver melts away in the fog "like some figure on a flickering magic lantern screen" (p. 25); the tea-house woman looks like a figure out of *Takasago,* a *noh* play, which in turn is said to look like a "tableau vivant" (p. 28).[8]

That a painter should see the world though a painter's eyes appears quite natural. But Sōseki's maneuver here is not for achieving an ever closer mimetic representation, but for creating a literary form that will more fully and more immediately involve his reader, who will thus be enabled to *see* the painting that Nakoi is for the painter. An essentially temporal art, the novel, is being maximally spatialized here. (One might recall here my earlier remarks about the visual feature of Chinese ideograms.) Instead of following a temporal evolution as the drama of the work unfolds, we are shown a series of discontinuous frames, with the effect of an ever changing perspective and the promise of a fresh, surprising perception with each new frame.

Take, as a good example of this, the way Sōseki introduces us to the heroine. The narrator hears about her from a conversation between the tea-house woman and the pack-horse driver in which they refer to her wedding. The painter pictures to himself the bridal procession and expresses it in a *haiku,* which then turns into an image of Millais's drowned Ophelia. (The Pre-Raphaelite Ophelia floating down the stream is a central image in the work, "floating" and "drowning" being its two important leitmotifs.) Meanwhile, the tea-house woman proceeds to compare the Shioda girl to the legendary maiden of the ancient *Man'yōshū* anthology who centuries before drowned herself, being unable to choose between suitors. Here is, then, the ever expanding (living) series of images—some gossip, a *haiku* image, an oil painting, a *Man'yōshū* poem; each one is taken up at a different angle and from a different context, a different tradition. And the metamorphosis in imagery continues after the poet-painter arrives at the inn: he dreams of the legendary maiden in a bridal gown, looking like Millais's Ophelia. The mixture of old Japanese poetry and art with Shakespearean drama and Pre-Raphaelite art almost crowds out the appearance of the actual girl we are about to meet. But there is even further amplification. Wakeful into the night, he keeps seeing a shadowy figure flitting about in the moonlit garden, and he tries again to arrest the vision in a series of *haiku*. He has a brief, very casual contact with the girl next morning, but the real meeting with this peculiarly elusive yet ever present girl comes much later, and that meeting *is* the whole extension of *Pillow of Grass*.

As the artist comes to know her better, Nami continues to appear from all sorts of unexpected angles: as a dancer-performer, a sharp wit, an eccentric. Her montage, too, becomes more com-

plex: besides the Shakespearean Ophelia, the Pre-Raphaelite
Ophelia, and the legendary maiden, we now have her own ancestor
who drowned herself, and the generations of crazy women in her
family. As each adds her own peculiarities to the composite, Nami
takes on more and more the aspects of a generalized woman figure
without at all losing her vitality and unpredictability.

The bathroom scene provides in a way the synecdoche of this
process of knowing her.

> Leaning my head back against the side of the tank, I let
> my weightless body rise up through the hot water to the
> point of least resistance. As I did so I felt my soul to be
> floating like a jelly-fish. The world is an easy place to live
> in when you feel like this. You throw off the shackles of
> common sense, and break through the bars of desire and
> physical attachment. Lying in the hot water, you allow it
> to do with you as it likes, and become absorbed into it.
> The more freely you are able to float, the easier life be-
> comes, until if your very soul floats, you will be in a state
> more blessed than had you become a disciple of Christ.
> Following this train of thought, even the idea of drowning
> is not without a certain refinement and elegance. I believe
> it was Swinburne who, in one or other of his poems, de-
> scribed a drowned woman's feeling of joy at having at-
> tained eternal peace. Looked at in this light, Millais'
> 'Ophelia,' which has always had a disturbing effect on me,
> becomes a thing of considerable beauty. (P. 102)

The sensation of floating recalls to him again the painting of
Ophelia, which he now realizes attracts him because it epitomizes
the notion of detachment, a loosening of the self and an abandonment to the flow of the water. It is as though he also has in the
back of his mind some recall of the Edo *ukiyo* (floating world)
tradition, for he now remembers his childhood experience of
listening to a neighborhood girl practicing *nagauta*, the traditional
Edo period *samisen* music.

Deep into memory though he is, he becomes aware of someone's
approach. He account moves very slowly:

The dark shape descended to the next step without a sound, making it seem that the stone underfoot was as soft as velvet. Indeed, anyone judging from the sound would have been excused for thinking that there had been no movement at all. The shimmering outline had now become a little more clearly discernible. Being an artist, I have an unusually good sense of perception concerning the structure of the human body, and no sooner had this unknown person moved down a step than I realized that I was alone in the bathroom with a woman.

I was still floating there, trying to decide whether or not to give any indication of having seen her, when quite suddenly and without any reserve she appeared directly before me. She stood there surrounded by swirling eddies of mist into which the gentle light suffused a rose-tinted warmth, and the sight of her lithe and upright figure, crowned with billowing clouds of jet-black hair, drove all thoughts of good manners, civility and propriety out of my head. My whole being was filled with the realisation that I had discovered a beautiful artistic subject. (Pp. 105–6)

From disinvolvement to an instant of half-embarrassed interest to recovery, almost reflexively, of his customary aesthetic response to life. Continually emphasizing the need for distance between body and viewer, he recapitulates in the manner of an art historian the whole development of nude representation from Greek sculpture to modern French painting. Although the woman is at first only dimly visible through the thick steam, her shape becomes clearer moment by moment, until—the ornate diction almost suspending narrative movement—we are viewing an opalescent painting of Nami's body. Do we see her clearly? It is a case of now-we-see-her, now-we-don't, for just as he, and we, are about to close the distance and see her face to face,

Just then, however, her thick blue-black hair streamed around her with a swish like the tail of some gigantic legendary turtle cleaving through the waves. Next moment her white figure was flying up the steps tearing through the veils of mist. A clear peal of feminine laughter rang out in the corridor and gradually echoed away into the distance, leaving the bathroom quiet again. The water washed over my face, so I stood up. As I did so, startled waves lapped against my chest, and splashed noisily over the sides of the tank. (Pp. 108–9)

The narrative movement is as unexpected as a *haiku* reversal. Electrically, still art is transformed into swift drama. Also, only for an instant. For, just as his distance from the picture shrinks and the possibility for dramatic involvement emerges, the actress flies away, leaving the by now partly aroused narrator without any participant. Irony, it seems, is built into the narrative movement itself.

The discontinuous story-line of *Pillow of Grass*—call it *noh*-like, or *haiku*-like—is made fun of in one passage where Nami and the artist talk about a Western novel (Meredith's *Beauchamp's Career*, although not identified in the book):

> "And because I am an artist I find any passage of a novel interesting even when it is out of context. I find it interesting talking to you—so much so in fact that I'd like to talk to you every day while I'm here. I'll even fall in love with you if you like; that would be particularly interesting. But however deeply I were to fall in love with you it would not mean that we had to get married. If you think that marriage is the logical conclusion to falling in love, then it becomes necessary to read novels through from beginning to end."
>
> "What an inhuman way of falling in love you artists have."
>
> "Not '*in*human'; *non*-human. It is because we read novels with this same non-human approach that we don't care about the plot. For us it is interesting to flip open the book as impartially as if we were drawing a sacred lot, and to read aimlessly at wherever it falls open." (P. 124)

If you think love leads to marriage, you must read novels from beginning to end. The logic of *Pillow of Grass* is its converse:

love does not lead to marriage, and therefore novels do not need to be read sequentially. Only breaking the chain of causality will make life agreeable. And the thrust of this argument is reinforced by the way the intricate relationship of theme and form is woven. While the characters talk about making random dips into the novelistic reading sequence, *Pillow of Grass* is itself discontinuous, dip-into-able. Like two mirrors facing each other, the material of the novel reflects and amplifies the ironic dimension of the telling.

Perhaps the most fundamental irony of *Pillow of Grass* depends on the notion of detached art, or, to use its own term, "nonhuman" art. Nami, the Ideal Beauty, who like *Endymion's* Phoebe continually appears in a new phase, lacks something in her expression, despite the painter's repeated attempts to arrest her image in a picture. For the poet-painter, the best understanding of her comes, naturally enough, from seeing her as a remarkable pictorial subject. He is forever searching for that something required to complete *the* picture of the attractive girl. His final meeting comes about when he discovers for the first time an expression, never shown before, of what she may have been all along. He knows Nami's aloofness to her former husband, now impoverished and ready to leave the country; he also knows her bitter indifference to the fate of her cousin, who may die anytime on the battlefield. But in the last scene, where time and life reassert themselves in a crescendo through the symbols of river and train (very much as in Dickens' *Dombey and Son*), Nami betrays an emotion that is all too human. The painter at once realizes that the missing element all along was this "compassion." The picture of his Ideal Beauty is finished at last through his meeting with the real Nami. The Latmos of *Pillow of Grass* is not all that far from the call of life; the ideal picture a "non-human" art can produce must finally be utterly human. We see now that his notion of art— detached and uninvolved, "non-human"—must be radically modified. Art does not remain self-contained outside human intercourse. Beauty requires compassion; art needs humanity.

Just as it is about to close, *Pillow of Grass* thus opens up a new perspective. I see it as quite fitting that the novel should be so open-ended instead of completing itself as a self-enclosed art-form. A work that can begin anyplace can begin at the end. Sōseki is right: *Pillow of Grass* is indeed very much like a *haiku*.

There are ten years between *Pillow of Grass* and *Light and Darkness,* a decade in which European novels were being translated and published in great numbers along with much new Japanese fiction written in more traditional styles. Ideologies, too, ranging from nationalism to Marxism, were sprouting vigorously. The Japanese literary scene then, as now, strongly resembled the national political scene, with factions and schools centered around favored leaders, and with a kind of loyalty developing between master and disciples much like the feudal relationship of lord and retainers. In such an atmosphere literary theories tend to be less substantial than the vehemence of the adherents' convictions might suggest. The dominant literary school, for instance, was that of the "Naturalists," having as their spokesmen writers like Tayama Katai (1871–1930), Shimazaki Tōson (1872–1934), Kunikida Doppo (1871–1908), Tokuda Shūsei (1871–1943), and Masamune Hakuchō (1879–1962). But their actual works are far from "naturalistic" as we understand the term. Although they professed a debt to Zola and Maupassant, the influence is apparent only in their subject matter, which is usually restricted to the shady side of life. Otherwise, their techniques and assumptions are about as conventional and moralistic as those of any other group of writers at the time. Tayama Katai's *The Quilt* (*Futon,* 1907), commonly considered the best example of Naturalism, is the story of a middle-aged writer's suppressed love for his beautiful disciple. The most famous scene, almost embarrassing to read nowadays, occurs at the end where the hero buries his face in the girl's bedding after she leaves him for a younger man. But the story was shocking enough to Meiji readers, and it was at once ranked with *Germinal* and *Une Vie.*

The "Naturalism" of these writers consists then of little more than their misuse of the imported term, and before long in fact their manifestos pretty much disappear from the literary scene. There is one feature of their works that stands out, and that is their markedly personal and confessional quality. Soon to develop into a genre called *shi-shōsetsu* (I-novel), these works require that literature be "truthful." To simplify a bit, telling the truth here means: one, accuracy in recording; two, honesty in disclosure; and three, sincerity in confession. According to this recipe, the writer, in recording his own life, must present it in the worst light possible, but to do this, he must first have a "disreputable" life to write about—something of a problem, given the typical puritanic restrictions of Japanese life. Thus the adventures of these "bohemians" are pretty tame stuff, confined for the most part to the purchase of a willing lady for an evening. The rebels' politics, too, are disappointingly sedate, being largely apolitical and tacitly accepting the established social hierarchy of the Empire. Except for the few truly proletarian novelists who were able to survive the repression by the militarist regime around the 1930s, very few radicals were ever heard from throughout this whole period. In sum, the rebels' outrage is not outrageous, and their "accurate" recounting of aseptic political mischief and sexual misdemeanors (daily budgets and wife-beatings recorded as though of monumental importance) rapidly approaches the tedious.

The I-novel, nurtured in this stern tradition of absolute sincerity, however picayune it may become, banishes fiction as outright deception. Unfortunately, in the process it foregoes art as well. And Apollo is a vengeful god all over the world. For the primary task of the artist becomes, then, not exploration of good and evil in the framework of fiction, but the raw experiencing of them. The writer must now live the very substance of his work. The I-novel, in short, is essentially less a discipline in verbal craft than a "discipline" in lifemanship, an effort toward the achievement of a poetic life style.

Despite the early demise of "Naturalism" per se, the credo of confessionalism dies hard. In fact, it is the one most conspicuous characteristic of modern Japanese fiction as a whole, whether we are talking about Shiga Naoya or Dazai Osamu or Akutagawa Ryūnosuke or Nagai Kafū. And this abandonment of art and fictionality, the sine qua non of the novel, is one of the reasons so many of these same Japanese writers are almost unreadable to Western readers.

Mori Ōgai and Natsume Sōseki were the "anti-Naturalists" of

their time, both being strongly against fiction's abandonment of fictionality. While it is true that "accuracy" was important to Ōgai in his historical semi-fictions, he thoroughly parodied sexual confessionalism in *Vita Sexualis* (1909). And Sōseki, too, gave in somewhat to the naturalistic pressures in providing most of his novels with settings close to everyday life, and, in *Grass on the Wayside*, by following his own personal life in outward detail. Still, throughout Sōseki's works, there is much evidence of a critical awareness carefully sifting personal experience, so that even in *Grass on the Wayside*, his most autobiographical novel, the self is *material* for fiction and not the unadorned art object itself.

The three novels immediately following *Pillow of Grass*—*Sanshirō* (1908), *And Then* (*Sorekara*, 1909), and *The Gate* (*Mon*, 1910)—are usually called a trilogy, though not for any discernible reason, and are all third-person novels, less venturesome in technique than the earlier works. *Sanshirō*, the most explicitly social of the three, deals with the choice faced by an academically disillusioned student of English literature. There are three possibilities for his future endeavors: the world of Japan's past that existed until the early 1880s—tranquil but unexciting to him; the Western humanistic tradition; and third, the world of commerce, characterized by an enormous sexual vitality —obviously attractive, but very frightening. The novel traces Sanshirō's gradual awareness of his inability to choose a career and his bowing to the authority of a wise but unsuccessful teacher nicknamed "Great Darkness." The gloom that hangs over *Sanshirō* becomes heavier in the later novels, most noticeably in *The Gate*, whose quiet hero grumbles at the end, in response to his wife's pleasant notice of the coming of spring: "Yes, but it will soon be winter again." [9]

Sōseki is more experimental in his next three novels, *Until the Equinox* (*Higansugi made*, 1912), *The Wanderer* (*Kōjin*, 1913), and *The Heart* (*Kokoro*, 1914), which show him in his brilliant maturity. *Until the Equinox* is a series of episodes starting with a third-person narrative describing the detective work of a young student. It then moves on to the student's friend Sunaga and his family, whom the student spied on earlier. This is followed by Sunaga's first-person account of his relationship with his mother and his cousin. The series ends with another first-person story, this by Sunaga's uncle, which however contains letters from the nephew. Despite the shift in the narrative voice from one episode to the next, continuity is maintained by the use of a single listener, the student of the first story. Thus, in the course of the building tension among the voices, the central theme of love and loneliness in Sunaga's life becomes an aspect of the first student's mind as he takes it all in. The success of this novel comes largely from the haunting ambiguity of the multiple narrators amounting at times to a suggestive and elusive feeling of the double.

But Sōseki's multiple narrative arrangement is perhaps best utilized in *The Heart,* one of his finest novels. Here the "I," a student, tells the story of his friendship with the *sensei.** From the beginning there is the suggestion of the double, one the actualized and the other the potential of the same man—a motif often visible in Sōseki's works, as in many modern novels. The relationship has aspects of both the homosexual and the parental-filial, although at the same time the student is very curious about the older man, again like a detective.[10] He sees in the teacher what he wants to become; the teacher sees in the youth what he once was. The protagonist's search for a father, however, fails in various ways. First, his actual father becomes ill, and he has to leave the *sensei.* While he is in the country taking care of his father, he hears the news of the Emperor's death, in the context of the novel the Emperor Meiji being the universal father figure. There follows the loss of another father, General Nogi, hero of the Russo-Japanese War, who took his life to be with the Emperor in death. With all these father-figures leaving him all at once, the student is pushed to finish his growing up and get settled in life, and he writes asking his *sensei* for help in finding a job. The answer is a suicide note (albeit a rather lengthy one). He catches the first train back to Tokyo, leaving his father on his deathbed. The last part of the novel consists of the long letter of the sensei—an

---

* *Sensei* means literally "earlier born"; hence, master, teacher, guru. The term is applied to almost anybody nowadays. A *sensei* is not only a professor or spiritual guide, but anyone higher in seniority in almost any occupation. Thus politicians, writers, attorneys, and even entertainers are often called *sensei* by their younger associates.

autobiography really, telling of his loneliness, guilt, and love for his wife. He writes how he has always blamed himself for the suicide of his friend "K" (the initial of *Kokoro,* "The Heart"), who was in love with the girl who is now his wife. As K was then, the *sensei,* too, is now utterly lonely, and death is the only possible choice.

The book is remarkable for Sōseki's careful authorial withdrawal. Although the *sensei* is obviously a sympathetic character, there are moments where his egotism comes under the author's censure. So with the student. Both speak from a limited point of view, which only intensifies our need to apprehend a truth closer to the center of the novel but not disclosed.

What is most fascinating about the book, however, is Sōseki's near despair about the limits of communication, a feeling explicitly stated by the *sensei* at several points (for instance, Part III, chap. 39). And yet *The Heart* achieves its final effect in the language of silence. One memorable passage occurs (Part One, chap. 26) when the young man, having just finished his graduation thesis, takes the older man out for a walk on a beautiful spring afternoon. The two are of course fond of each other, but they are not really close; there is an invisible wall somehow separating them.

> There were also peonies covering an area of about ten *tsubo.* It was too early in the summer for them to be in bloom. At the edge of this field of peonies was an old bench. Sensei stretched himself out on it. I sat down on the end and began to smoke. Sensei gazed at the sky, which was so blue that it seemed transparent. I was fascinated by the young leaves that surrounded me. When I looked at them carefully, I found that no two trees had leaves of exactly the same color. The leaves of each maple tree, for instance, had their own distinctive coloring. Sensei's hat, which he had hung on top of a slender cedar sapling, was blown off by the breeze.[11]

The clear imagery of the scene surely contains "meaning," but without naming it. Its beauty is verbal, of course; symbolic, too. But all these named objects—transparent sky, young maple leaves, the fallen hat—bespeak their meaning as though requiring no words to mediate. It is not painterly, it is hardly literary. As in life itself, things address themselves directly to the reader. The force of the passage comes from its uttermost condensation of language to the thingness of the named, from the powerfully resonating *haiku* brevity and plainness.

Sōseki's steadily darkening vision of life is expressed in *Grass on the Wayside* (*Michikusa*, 1915), his last complete novel and his only I-novel in the sense that all the narrative events come from the actual history of his own life. This is not to say, however, that it banishes fiction entirely. In narrative selection as well as in the narrator's careful maintenance of distance from the characters, the work is imaginative in the most fundamental sense. Many Japanese claim it as their favorite of all Sōseki's works, and it also has supporters among American readers.[12] To me, however, it is the only tedious work he wrote. The main character, the author's surrogate, is an unpleasant egotist, petulant yet depressed, and overly preoccupied with money. Although the narrator makes clear that he is just as critical of the hero as the reader is, this does not relieve the dismal impression he creates. If a certain sincerity strikes the reader occasionally, it derives from the pitiful situation being presented, and not from the full persuasion of the Sōseki art. For me, *Grass on the Wayside* is interesting mostly because it differs so vastly from *Light and Darkness*, Sōseki's final effort, but also because this very difference suggests the discoveries he must have made during its writing, preparing him for the next undertaking.

Light and Darkness (*Meian*), like most of Sōseki's works, was serialized daily in the *Asahi* newspaper—in 188 sections from May 26, 1916, to December 14 of the same year, five days after his death. Daily serialization obviously differs from the monthly or even weekly installment form of the Dickensian novel, not to mention its differences from the publication of a whole work in book form. While a typical weekly installment—of, for instance, *Hard Times* or *Great Expectations*—runs to about a dozen modern-edition pages, each daily unit is of necessity extremely short, amounting in English translation to less than two pages.

With each unit, however abbreviated, requiring some autonomy, the whole work takes on the aspect of a mosaic pattern, the work comprising many uniform-sized tiny sections. Thus, there is a tendency toward sparseness in descriptive detail, even though one episode may range over several installments. Short installments affect the suspense element, too, which often appears like the couplet at the end of a sonnet. This is necessarily different from Dickens' use of suspense in his longer installments. Sōseki's work, in fact, with its regular occurrence of subtle surprise elements between units, gives an impression much like that of a grand sonnet sequence.

This is not to say, however, that, given its sonnet-sequence structure, *Light and Darkness* should be identified with the indigenous *haiku* or *waka* sequence (*renku* or *renga*). For this work, of all the Sōseki novels, perhaps of all the modern Japanese novels, comes closest to the orthodox Western novel.

Light and Darkness, the longest of Sōseki's novels even though incomplete, tells a story of only a few weeks' duration. The thirty-year-old hero, a corporation employee, finds he must have an operation for a fistula. There is a money problem arising from this unexpected medical expense, but this is only a symptom of the general budgetary pattern in his household, relating to his wife's taste for luxury and his vanity that encourages it. After the operation, the hero goes to a hot spring to recuperate, where he arranges to meet the woman he was in love with before his marriage. Soon after their encounter, the book breaks off, leaving scarcely a clue as to subsequent development.[13] The story being so uneventful, the drama of the novel is intensely psychological. And what makes it unique in modern Japanese literature is that its characters have discernible personalities, which most novelistic characters, especially those of the I-novel, very rarely achieve.

The notion of personality is quite different to a Japanese from what it is to a Westerner. Whether he will become an electronics worker, a teacher of English in a high school, or a fish-processing worker on a whaler, the young Japanese studies his assigned role till he perfects it. His worth will be measured by his approximation to the ideal of his type (*the* teacher, *the* electronics worker, *the* fisherman)—"Sensei wa sensei rashiku shiro" (Be like the teacher you are). Personality is thus not a valued seed to be nurtured into flower, but a bud that must be "withered" (*kareta*) as soon as it shows itself. At maturity, having been tamed in this way from early childhood, the Japanese "personality," like an age-old redwood *bonsai,* ought to be a truly balanced and pleasing form.

Since the Meiji era, with Western philosophies of individualism and egalitarianism being increasingly propagated in Japanese society, strict role-definition has loosened to an extent. Probably the greatest difference takes the form of today's much increased inter-generational mobility (a tenant farmer's second son becoming a cabinet minister), which does not touch the reorganization of the vertical structure itself. As Nakane Chie so persuasively argues in *Japanese Society,* the old vertical organization has survived almost intact in today's highly corporate and industrialized Japan.

Such a society still fosters a high degree of ritualism in everyday activities, whether economic, social, or cultural, as can be seen in the disciplined style and movement of the *noh* play as well as in the high development of the honorific system in the Japanese language. It also encourages the deep and wide establishment of whatever common myth is circulating, as recent Japanese history shows very clearly: the disastrous national dream of military glory has been followed by the concerted passion for industrial preeminence. If such national programs do not invariably capture the imagination of writers and intellectuals, this does not mean the latter have any real alternatives to offer. Even the traditional religions manage to do little more than affirm collective enterprise and discourage individualism.

Japanese society does not, in short, promote the necessary condition for growth of the novelistic imagination: the egalitarian sensibility that sees a unique human personality in powerful statesman and day-laborer alike. Instead, people are regarded according to their assigned social slots. One is a noodle-truck driver or a university professor before one is Yamada Tarō or Kimura Hanako, and is, accordingly, comical or dignified, disreputable or respectable, on a subtly shaded scale of social connotation. The novel, on the other hand, in order to explore the inverted universe that an individual consciousness is, always pulls toward freeing people from their role characteristics, and it is against such energy that Japanese society works so relentlessly with its tribalism and ceremonialism.

Novelists need people—men and women with their own motivations, their own mannerisms, their own style of intelligence, their own unique expression and appearance. The problem for the Japanese novelist is that there is no general acknowledgement in his culture that noticeable personalities should be allowed to exist. A carpenter who sounds like Adam Bede or a governess who behaves like Jane Eyre—not to say a gamekeeper who acts out like Oliver Mellors—will not only be disapproved of morally but disbelieved artistically as well. (The situation is not unlike that prevailing at an early stage in the development of the European novel.) From this impasse, the writer frequently falls back on his own kind for his character types, déclassé writers and intellectuals, who offer several advantages. First, they are a new category of people, unknown before the Meiji importations from the West, and thus there is greater freedom in defining them in the social hierarchy. Second, and in part because they are a new class, writers and intellectuals really are freer in attitude and behavior than conventional middle-class people. Third, using the life style and character types of his own kind allows the writer to deal with what he supposedly knows best.

But even this more liberated and liberally regarded class presents some problems upon adoption into the world of fiction. One concerns their usual sense of alienation from the society at large; the other, the interior of the writer's "personality."

We recall that "Futabatei Shimei" meant "drop dead" in no uncertain terms. But the writer has been a social outcast, "dead" to the world, from the beginning of modern literature in Japan. No doubt, even in Victorian society (which bears better comparison in many ways with modern Japan than present-day America or England does) writers felt a degree of disenchantment. And yet a Mill or an Arnold still felt himself an active member of the society he chastised. He was still an established insider. Contrastingly, the alienated Japanese writers, having dropped out more completely and visibly, were given up on by the society and were thus more bitterly isolated. Rare is the man like Mori Ogai or even Sōseki, who kept a successful career going within the establishment all the while he was writing. More usual are the writers who associated themselves almost exclusively with other writers and artists, and who suffered from— or enjoyed—the three common conditions of an artist's fate— poverty, loneliness, and a certain degree of sexual freedom. Not bothering to acquaint themselves with most people's ordinary activities of life, they lived lives which were narrow in perspective and extremely limited in variety. And when they wrote their counterparts into their fiction as rebels and outcasts, they tended to repeat these same patterns monotonously.

The notion of the inner self, whether that of author or his character, throws a more serious impediment in the way of the novel's development in Japan. Japanese writers are essentially lonely souls who in their inward search for the core of existence often identify themselves with a Dostoevsky or a Rilke. And yet, in finally facing themselves, they discover a strange emptiness. Long accustomed to viewing the self as a blemish on Nature, their Buddhist tradition inclines them not to define and assert the borders of the self, but to long for the obliteration of such outlines in a fusion with the All. And Nature, through ceremony, can offer a substitute in which the ancient collective experience of the people can be relived. Ironically, such ceremony is the genius of modern Japan. There is another irony, and a bitter one, that the alienated writers should be found to be even more loyal to this ceremony, little else by now but the ghost of the collective memory, than the establishment men and women who would promote the myth.

Writers often refuse to see such irony, however, by obfuscating the fact that their "self" is much more the heritage of Confucius and Buddha than the modern self of Descartes and Nietzsche. Similarly, they often mistakenly identify the seductive Buddhist nothingness with a post-Christian stoicism. Unfortunately, such misidentifications have had fairly serious personal consequences. The imported view of the self distorts the meaning of moral action as of art—as we will see in the discussion of Dazai Osamu and Mishima Yukio. It is a high price these writers have paid for an imported product, and to some extent the value received has not been commensurate with the cost. The modern Japanese novel, not yet succeeding in penetrating the inner life of its national identity, has likewise been unable to develop consistently authentic novelistic characters with an identifiable personal core.

Up until his very last work, characterization in Sōseki's novels follows pretty much the same pattern as that of his fellow novelists. In *Pillow of Grass* both the poet-painter and the elusive heroine are presented as facets of a single attitude rather than as full and distinct personalities. Even in *The Heart,* the young man and the *sensei* are more functions of the mind than two real people, and as such they are conducive, as in a romance, to rich symbolic interpretations, but not to dramatic development. In *Light and Darkness,* however, Sōseki for the first time creates a world in which novelistic characters breathe and feel and talk just like people one might know. Where does their authenticity come from?

In *Grass on the Wayside* Sōseki began to experiment with full characterization. Kenzō, the author's surrogate, is scrutinized in detail psychologically as well as morally, as is his wife, the author's wife's surrogate, who is one of the very few complete characterizations, female or male, in the whole Sōseki canon. It is as though for the sake of the analytical novel that the author proceeds systematically to dissect himself. Here he seems especially to be perfecting his skill in voice modulation, all the while keeping himself clearly apart from the characters. In *Light and Darkness* he goes further, abandoning the stance of the omniscient narrator and adopting instead the dramatic mode of individuals speaking with their own voices.* Each character thinks and feels, and wonders about the others, and the narrator conveys with remarkable sensitivity each one's uncertainties about himself and others. The characters are islands of self-consciousness in the novel, rising up from the deep that separates them, and connects them.

---

* The novel has been translated by V. H. Viglielmo (see note 14).

The book opens on the scene of the doctor palpating Tsuda's fistula. We are not told what Tsuda's physical sensations are during this examination; only his response to the doctor's prognosis is given. Going home, Tsuda recalls what the pain is like, but the people on the streetcar do not even know he exists. The opening thus establishes the basic scheme of existence in *Light and Darkness*: a man's most private sensation (which he often conceals even from himself), posed against his awareness of others, posed in turn against his recognition of others' unawareness of himself. Superimposed on this is a question which will be raised repeatedly: "Why did she [Tsuda's former sweetheart] marry him [another man]? She must have wanted to. But she wasn't supposed to. And why did I marry her [Onobu, his own wife]? The marriage must have come about because I wanted it. But I hadn't wanted to marry her." (Chap. 4.)[14] We can never know what another person is to himself, and when we fully understand that fact, our certainty about our own self-understanding, too, is threatened.

Tsuda and Onobu's marriage, the central relationship of the novel, is very intricately understood by Sōseki, as the next incident, apparently of small significance, shows. Tsuda arrives home from the medical examination to see his wife in front of their house in expectation of his return. The minute she sees him, however, she turns away from him slightly, facing straight ahead and appearing to be looking at something. It seems to him she feigns surprise when he asks her what she is looking at: "Oh, you frightened me," she says, "Welcome home." (My translation.) She then tells him she was watching some sparrows, and Tsuda can see no evidence of these. Tsuda possibly interprets her behavior as a form of "coquetry" not unusual in a new bride, although this possibility is only vaguely suggested by the mention of "his wife's coquetry" as applied to the whole situation. Onobu's response in turn is not given either, except that she proceeds at once to the next items on her agenda of wifely ministrations: relieving her husband of his walking stick, opening the door for him, helping him change clothes. Maybe she takes it for granted that her flirtatiousness is natural in the situation and that he will take it at that. But we cannot be sure.

Light and Darkness is almost clinically precise in measuring degrees of taciturnity corresponding to the uncertainties in human relationships. The reader is never given an easy summary of complex interactions between people. The interaction of Tsuda and Onobu, for instance, could be analyzed as: Tsuda's sensation/ feeling/ understanding; Tsuda's feeling for Onobu; Tsuda's understanding of Onobu and his attitude toward it; Tsuda's understanding of her understanding of him and her attitude toward it, as well as his feeling for it; Tsuda's understanding of Onobu's understanding of his understanding of her and his attitude toward it, and his attitude toward this whole understanding. Then, the whole process must be repeated on Onobu's side: Onobu's sensation/ feeling/ understanding; Onobu's feeling for Tsuda, and so on. We are given clues to these levels and gradations of self-consciousness at every stage of the novel, the first 44 chapters being from Tsuda's perspective, the next 47 from Onobu's, and the remainder alternating between the two. Tsuda thus conjectures about Onobu, as Onobu conjectures about him, and yet the narrator never lapses into any facile guarantee about the rightness or wrongness of either one's conjecture about the other. He seldom even compares the two versions, since that would imply his omniscience. Thus the irony does not principally operate on the discrepancies between the two sets of conjectures, but elsewhere. It is almost as if to say that the more intelligent and self-conscious one is, the more completely one is cut off from others; the more luminous one's self-awareness, the darker the world around. We are of course not told this explicitly, but the novel effects this dark separation through a specific narrative technique, that of indirection and silence.

Of the major characters, Tsuda is the most unpleasant. He is a role-player, being many different things to different people. With a habitat well below the level of interpersonal relating, he prefers always to understand his understanding of Onobu's understanding of his understanding of her, and so on. The heavy-knotted fabric of his self-consciousness incapacitates him for the experience of any direct emotion. Nonetheless, he thinks he can read other people. When he discloses to his wife, for instance, his plan to go to a resort without her, he believes he is able to manipulate her by controlling the amount and type of information she gets. Meanwhile, he is totally unable to feel her craving for his love and her loneliness for lack of it. She is mostly for him an object of observation, not someone to feel with or feel for. Ironically, it is his own performance, not hers, that becomes increasingly transparent to more and more people as the novel progresses. The overbearing Mrs. Yoshikawa sees through his mask (chap. 141), as does his humorless sister (chap. 102) and his sardonic friend Kobayashi (chap. 166). And with each successive uncovering of his motives, Tsuda appears progressively more vulnerable.

Although Tsuda is not explicitly interpreted for us, his gradual physical recovery suggests the possibility of a parallel spiritual recovery. It is notable, for instance, that his meeting with Kiyoko, the girl he was in love with before his marriage to Onobu, is preceded by an unexpected self-encounter. Returning from the bath, he loses his way in the maze of hallways, and he is suddenly confronted by a "ghost":

> He soon turned away from the water. Then, since with the same glance he suddenly encountered a man's form, he gave a start, and stared at it. But it was only the image of himself reflected in the large mirror hung by the side of the wash basins. The mirror was almost as tall as an average man. And, like one in a barber's shop, it was hung upright. Consequently, not only the reflection of his face but that of his shoulders, waist, and hips as well, were on the same plane as he was, and faced him directly. Even after he realized that it was himself he was looking at, he still did not remove his eyes from the mirror. He noticed that he was rather pale, even though he had just come from the bath, but he was at a loss to know why. Since he had neglected to have a haircut for some time, his hair was bushy and unkempt. It shone like lacquer because it was freshly wet from the bath, and for some reason he thought it looked like a garden after it has been devastated by a windstorm. (P. 345)

Having been so "lost," Tsuda does not really know the "mean-

ing" of this experience, nor do we for sure. But he does seem
to be perceiving just a small crack on the smooth surface of his
mask as he begins to "retrace his steps." Precisely at this moment he sees Kiyoko at the top of the staircase, like Beatrice
in the *Vita Nuova*. There is the suggestion, then, that he might
begin to accept the isolating darkness and thus be himself more
fully. Only the merest suggestion, though, just as in life we are
never allowed any clearer foresight than the ghost of a hint.

This careful matching of narrative concealment and disclosure
to people's knowledge of one another in actual life is certainly
the most important feature in the characterization of *Light and
Darkness*. It is a precision which gives life to its characters and
a mystery of being to their existence that extends well beyond
the pages of the novel spatially and temporally. Judgment is
urged but not imposed on us, while all the provided bases for
judgment contain the uncertainty always present in the act of
human judgment.

As for Onobu, she is one of the most attractive women in the
Japanese novel, being unusually intelligent for a female character in that tradition. Although her explanation to herself of her
sole motivation—to win her husband's love—is subjected to some
further scrutiny, it is evident that she is genuinely concerned
with him. She is shrewd and calculating to a degree, and she too
performs, but she is aware of these traits in herself and is vulnerable because of that knowledge. And then she knows her
vulnerability also, which is probably what makes her so much
more attractive a personality than her husband.

There is a scene in which her usually well-guarded defenses
nearly break down, and she pleads with Tsuda to give her complete confidence in him:

> She suddenly cried out:
> "I *want* to trust you. I *want* to put my mind at ease. I
> want to trust you more than you can imagine."
> "Are you saying I can't imagine?"
> "No, you can't possibly. Because if you could, you'd
> have to change. Since you can't imagine, you're as un-
> concerned as you are."

"I'm not unconcerned!"

"Well, you certainly aren't sorry for me and you don't have any pity on me."

"What do you mean by feeling sorry for you or having pity on you?"

After he had in effect rejected her criticism, he was quiet for a while. He then faltered a bit as he attempted to evade the issue.

"You say I'm not concerned about you—no matter how much I actually am. Because you can be sure that if there's reason to be I will be. But if there isn't, what am I supposed to do?"

Her voice trembled with tension.

"Oh, Yoshio, listen to me!"

He said nothing.

"Please tell me I don't have to worry, I beg of you. Put my mind at ease and rescue me, because I have no one else to turn to but you. I'm helpless, and I'll die if you turn me aside. So please say I can put my mind at ease. Just one word will do, but please say I don't have to worry."

"Everything's all right. Don't worry, I tell you." (Pp. 286–87)

Significantly, the energy and intelligence of this passage derives less from Onobu's character—vital as that is—than from our knowledge of her uncertainty about her husband. We see her craving his total reassurance, and when he rations out something very partial—"Everything's all right. Don't worry . . ." —she cannot be satisfied and fights for more. Tsuda, of course, who doesn't know how much she knows about his past and how much she doesn't, somehow manages to protect his façade by shortweighting her demand for reassurance every time. Sōseki knows precisely the quality and amount of each one's ignorance of the other. And although he puts us close to that privileged position, he leaves ample space for uncertainties and ambiguities.

Ohide, Tsuda's self-centered sister, is a forceful but also subtle person, able to ferret out the childish elements in her brother's and his wife's behavior. She bullies them singlehandedly, all the while unaware of her own deep commitment to the confrontation.

The hospital scene (chaps. 104–110) where Tsuda and Onobu defend their financial judgment against Ohide's criticism is interesting in several ways. First, Tsuda's antiseptic recovery-room, charged with intense emotion (there are two more visitors later on, Kobayashi and Mrs. Yoshikawa), is a perfect reflection of the hero's personality, which passively registers and reacts to things rather than actively taking the initiative. Second, the scene sensitively presents the separate thoughts and feelings of three very different people. Third, at any given moment, we are able to see the one person alert to the other two while not quite knowing, however, exactly what their thoughts and feelings are about himself.

The individual as basically alone—this, as I have mentioned earlier, is the general outlook of *Light and Darkness* on human relationship. Chapter 106, for instance, turns the narrative into a drama script in which there is hardly any narrative comment on the inner responses of the three main characters. As in a drama, their relationship is formed and defined in the intervals between the speeches and the space behind the speeches rather than in narrated passages providing such information and an attitude on it. The result is—somewhat more subtly here than in the typical example of this terseness, a Hemingway novel— both an increased objectivity and an intensified sense of their isolation one from another. Even more significant is the reader's realization of *his* distance from the characters, owing directly to this increased need to conjecture their every reaction.

My meaning will perhaps be clearer if the scene in the recovery room is compared with one from a novel in a different tradition:

> Maggie gave the tips of her fingers, and said, "Quite well, thank you," in a tone of proud indifference. Philip's eyes were watching them keenly; but Lucy was used to seeing variations in their manner to each other, and only thought with regret that there was some natural antipathy which every now and then surmounted their mutual goodwill. "Maggie is not the sort of woman Stephen admires, and she is irritated by something in him which she inter-

prets as conceit," was the silent observation that accounted for everything to guileless Lucy. Stephen and
Maggie had no sooner completed this studied greeting
than each felt hurt by the other's coldness. And Stephen,
while rattling on in questions to Philip about his recent
sketching expedition, was thinking all the more about
Maggie because he was not drawing her into the conversation as he had invariably done before. "Maggie and
Philip are not looking happy," thought Lucy: "this first
interview has been saddening to them." (George Eliot,
The Mill on the Floss)[15]

Here we have a scene involving several people all desperately trying to guess each other's thoughts. But in this work there is a
strong voice letting us know that she at least knows her characters' minds. The omniscient narrator can in this way serve as a
sort of communal voice linking the separate members into a single
understanding which is then confidently offered the reader, who is
in turn reassured. Like belief in the omniscience of God, there is
operating in this tradition an implicit faith in the author's presentation which is assumed by both reader and author. What separates Henry James from George Eliot is the withering away of
this assumption that the narrator is voicing shared concerns and
interests dealing with everybody's business. And Sōseki, in this
novel at least, takes his place on our side of the breakdown.

It is for this reason that the similarities often found between
Sōseki and Jane Austen are not quite accurate.[16] There is no doubt
that he experimented with what she had done novelistically a
century earlier: her stern moral stand relentlessly exploding her
characters' self-illusion, her abstract diction, her nonphysical, non-
visual description, precise syntax, and deceptively simple dialogue
—all these techniques are used in *Light and Darkness*. Even that
subversive irony directed at the unwary reader as well as the characters is also in evidence. And yet the important distinction between *Light and Darkness* and *Emma* or *Pride and Prejudice* is
its loss, through rejection of narrative authority, of the community
of the novel which draws the characters into a world shared with
each other and with the reader.

There are two other characters—Mrs. Yoshikawa, the wife of

Tsuda's employer, and Tsuda's friend Kobayashi—who deserve some comment. Mrs. Yoshikawa is a thoroughly alive, enjoyable person, confident, overbearing, and shrewd. She overwhelms the passive Tsuda, and punctures his self-illusion, I believe to our pleasure. Up to the point where she visits Tsuda in the hospital, her quasi-maternal domination, her busybody curiosity and cavils are all put into a perfectly understandable context. But her scenario-writing for Tsuda's reunion with his old love is quite something else. Her motives for this are much too unclear: can she be that much interested in Tsuda's simply clarifying the circumstances of the end of his affair? Or is she simply trying to help him recover his spiritual buoyancy? Maybe. But at the risk of his losing Onobu? Does she hate Onobu that much? And if so, why? Sōseki does not let us in on her secrets.

We do notice, however, that as Mrs. Yoshikawa plots the reunion, she becomes the plot-maker of the novel itself. Tsuda, at her suggestion (order?), is lifted out of the Onobu-Ohide-himself stalemate to face a new situation in a new setting. Mrs. Yoshikawa in a sense rescues the book at this point by bullying Tsuda into a new experience. As a character, she is no longer a likable self-indulgent woman, but a rich and powerful and exploitative one. And by this change she becomes a novelistic device, a dea ex machina who in coercing Tsuda coerces the novel.

Mrs. Yoshikawa's transformation has some bearing on another character of a type new in Sōseki's novels. A down-at-the-heel, rather unattractive journalist, Kobayashi appears to have emigrated right out of Dostoevsky's underground. Sōseki's fiction has almost always dealt with middle-class life style, which is generally a comfortable one, if occasionally hard up for money. Kobayashi's background is different: though he is well enough educated to be a professional, his origins are lower class. He also happens to be a rude, jealous, angry, brazen, irritable, cynical, and, with all this, admittedly lonely fellow. He has no steady job, feels his disorganized poverty acutely, and is so dependent on his friends that even his scheme of going to Korea to look for work depends on his getting their help. In return, he despises them. He attacks Tsuda's snobbery every way he knows how and almost resorts to blackmailing him to get what he wants.

Etō Jun is no doubt right in seeing the social victim in Kobayashi, the outcast writer type who attracted Sōseki's interest and
sympathy more and more toward the end of his life. According to
Etō, the author of *Light and Darkness* is in transition from being
a writer concerned with the self in the universe to one interested
in the self in society. Etō's thesis is right insofar as he disputes
several critics and biographers, such as Komiya Hōryū, Karaki
Junzō, and Takizawa Katsumi, who interpret the later Sōseki in
the light of his favorite dictum, *sokuten kyoshi* (accord to the
heavens, depart from the self), as if the slogan described what was
in fact the case with him and his work.[17] It does not. Sōseki is
neither saintly nor selfless, and to identify an author's aspirations
with the reality of the man is clearly absurd. At the same time,
Etō's interpretation of Kobayashi as the champion of Sōseki's
newly awakened social conscience is a bit overdrawn. The down-
and-out journalist's alienation and loneliness never develop significantly beyond that into full political consciousness. Etō talks
about Kobayashi's feeling for working-class people, citing the bar-
room scene (chap. 34). But I wonder if Kobayashi genuinely has
love for the workers or is merely using his firsthand acquaintance
with their life style to intimidate a middle-class snob like Tsuda.
Isn't Etō's great socialist hero in fact rather condescending to the
"lower orders," the same working-class people for whom he claims
to "have a great deal of sympathy" and whom he likes to meet in
such "wonderfully plebeian" places? Kobayashi the victim invites
the author's—and the reader's—sympathy for his misfortunes,
but he cannot carry the burden of Sōseki's mature social or political philosophy. Maybe he is fundamentally one of those shadowy characters who, operating on the symbolic level, haunt the
heroes of novels everywhere, like their darker self-images, their
doubles.

Earlier I mentioned Mrs. Yoshikawa's manipulation of Tsuda
and its effect on the plot. I think it notable that in their relationship Tsuda is the victim, whereas between him and Kobayashi we
find Tsuda is the exploiter, who can afford to be aloof, contemptuous, manipulative. Of course, he does not succeed in brandishing
his power nearly so well as Mrs. Yoshikawa does. (Actually, Kobayashi's uncanny insight sometimes almost frightens Tsuda, but

theirs is one of those relationships of master and servant, as Hegel saw it, where the servant is able at several points to overturn the master psychologically.) Nonetheless, the chain of exploitation runs through the whole society of this novel. And with Mrs. Yoshikawa as the bully of the whole book we cannot help but feel that Sōseki's dark irony is directed on the capitalism of Taishō Japan, which, as we are seeing, encroaches on the development of the novel itself.

Sōseki's near despair for human relationship permeates this last, unfinished novel, and yet we sense also the compassion of the man who can see, if darkly, the painfully clear boundaries of the modern self. It is in this sense that the Japanese novel has developed a mind not in the least impenetrable to the West—an unusual achievement, since most other novelists have worked within the familiar native consciousness. It is important that we not attribute Sōseki's performance solely to his knowledge of English literature; clearly at its root is his extraordinary personality, his very mind and heart. But in the light of those lifelong painful doubts of his about his claim to English, it may not be such an irrelevant tribute to suggest that Sōseki had indeed learned well the literature of England.

Part Two

Words dry and riderless,
The indefatigable hoof-taps.
While
From the bottom of the pool, fixed stars
Govern a life.

—SYLVIA PLATH, "Words"

Making no sound
  Yet smouldering with passion
    The firefly is still sadder
      Than the moaning insect.

—MINAMOTO SHIGEYUKI

        It was her voice that made
The sky acutest at its vanishing.
She measured to the hour its solitude.
She was the single artificer of the world
In which she sang. And when she sang, the sea,
Whatever self it had, became the self
That was her song, for she was the maker.

—WALLACE STEVENS,
"The Idea of Order at Key West"

Did it yell
    till it became all voice?
   Cicada-shell.

—BASHŌ

IV

THE MARGINS OF LIFE

KAWABATA YASUNARI: *Snow Country*
and *The Sound of the Mountain*
—*I am a citizen of a lost country.*

Mr. Kawabata, as everyone knows, is a great stylist,
but I believe he is finally a novelist without a style. Because style for the novelist means the will to interpret the
world and discover the key to it. To arrange the world,
separate it, and bring it out of chaos and angst into the
narrow framework of form, the novelist has no other tool
than style. . . . What is . . . a work of art, like Kawabata's masterpiece, which is a perfection in itself, but has
abandoned the will to interpret the world so entirely? It
fears no chaos, no angst. But its fearlessness is like the
fearlessness of a silk string suspended before the void. It
is the extreme opposite of the plastic will of the Greek
sculptors who committed themselves to the permanence
of marble; it is in sharp contrast to the fear that the har-
monic Greek sculpture fights with its whole body.

Thus Mishima Yukio on Kawabata Yasunari, in 1958.[1] Like so
much of Mishima's work, the comment shows a remarkable critical acuity. Yet I am bound finally to disagree. While it is true that
Kawabata's poise is unshakable and that, unlike most Japanese

novelists of the last fifty years, he does not feel compelled to scream his *Weltanschauung* at us, nor sermonize, nor organize, it does not follow that he has no "will to interpret the world." My crucial difference with Mishima, then, lies in how we see this "style," which is at once powerfully idiosyncratic and subtly suffused with a rich sense of life.

Early in his career Kawabata Yasunari (1899–1972) was a member of the Neo-Perceptionist school (Shin Kankaku Ha). The existence of this group, as a part of Japanese literary history, is not so interesting or important in itself: its creed, like those of the Naturalists, the Anti-Naturalists, and other groups, derives from imported avant-garde European manifestoes, and, like most, suffers from poor digestion of same. Thrown into their modernist mélanges are bits and dollops of Paul Morand, Andreyev, Croce, Bergson, futurism, cubism, expressionism, dada-ism, symbolism, structuralism, realism, Strindberg, Swinburne, Hauptmann, Romain Rolland, Schnitzler, Lord Dunsany, Wilde, Lady Gregory, and a lot else*—all assembled, presumably, to spice the domestic literary staples, but in fact to preserve a conservative aesthetic against the encroaching Marxists. Most of its members are now forgotten (with the exception of Yokomitsu Riichi, who, however, became a very different sort of writer later on), and Kawabata's position in the group was not a dominant one. Nonetheless, when looked at as a serious attempt at enlarging the novelistic possibilities of the Japanese language, the modernist practices of the group must be recognized as vital in the formation of Kawabata's style.

Kawabata's main contribution to the group's platform, "The New Tendency of the Avant-Garde Writers" (*Shinshin Sakka no Shinkeikō Kaisetsu*), published in 1925, makes a plea for the new

---

* Conspicuously absent from this list are names such as Cocteau, Breton, Eliot, Joyce, Gide, Valéry, Rilke, all of whom were introduced and translated within the next few years. The list is garnered from references in the collection of articles by members of the group such as Chiba Kameo, Kataoka Teppei, Kawabata Yasunari, Akaki Kensuke, Inagaki Sokuho, Yokomitsu Riichi, and Nii Kaku in vol. 67 of the Nippon Gendai Bungaku Zenshū series, *Shin Kankaku Ha Bungaku Shū* (Tokyo: Kōdansha, 1968), which is also my text for the discussion of Neo-Perceptionism.

—new perception, new expression, and new style—and strongly emphasizes the importance of sense perception for the novelist. While not being very precise in his "epistemology of expressionism," and dodging most of the hard problems of his theme, Kawabata does spell out the need for a new language to replace the existing "lifeless, objective narrative language." "Dadaist," "Freudian," "free associative," "subjective, intuitive, and sensuous" expression—all such terms are left undefined, but in the context of his discussion they do suggest a coherent feeling for a certain style. He would have a language for the novel that would reflect immediately the inchoate state of a man's thoughts, feelings, and sensory experience. Instead of syntactically complete sentences, the characters (or the narrator) ought to be allowed to speak sometimes in fragments, which will not only suggest more accurately the author's view of the particular situation but will give the reader a fuller picture of the characters and their surroundings. In such a language, the seer is not yet separated from the seen, the speaker from the spoken. To illustrate his point, Kawabata provides a sample sentence or two ("My eyes were red roses" as preferable to "My eyes saw red roses"), but unfortunately this tends to muddle the discussion more than clarify it.[2]

Another member of the school was a little more articulate on this same point. According to Kataoka Teppei, "The small stations along the line were ignored like pebbles" effectively expresses the train's speed, whereas an ordinary statement like "The express rushed along without stopping at any station," though referring to the same observation, is merely reportorial. In the latter sentence, there is no relationship "between the express train, the small stations, and the author's own feeling," whereas the Neo-Perceptionist version allows the author's immediate perception, and the reader's, to flow with the movement of the train. It also provides, Kataoka says, a way for the writer to recover his own individuality from the "general, commonsensical, and public" language ordinarily so resistant to the individual's imprint.

I am not sure that even this argument is really persuasive—perhaps because the example of "The small stations along the line . . ." is undistinguished, Neo-Perceptionist or not.* Besides, the singularity of a particular expression, its oddness, does not guarantee its liveliness or perceptual precision, or even its individuality. We are aware of course that these arguments flourished around 1920, about the time the imagists and vorticists and a variety of dadaists were urging basic changes in literary language. Thus, the apparent vagueness and confusion on the part of the Neo-Perceptionists are, without being unduly sympathetic, quite understandable. If their arguments seem to us now of rather modest significance, the efforts of these writers in behalf of a responsive novelistic language was nonetheless beneficial to its development.

What is really curious about the whole movement is that its exponents regarded the whole rationale of their movement as Western in origin, and felt that the recommended changes were only a further step in the inevitable westernization of the novel —a Western art—and the language of the novel. Besides Kawabata and Kataoka, other Neo-Perceptionists read and rehashed the arguments they found in European and American literary journals, while ignoring the lessons of their own tradition to be found in the *haiku* and *waka*—those arts of suggestion and evocation, reversal and juxtaposition, so deeply rooted in the alogical, intuitive, and "irrational" sensibility of the East itself. By expedition into their own tradition they might have realized a sufficient freeing of the "reportorial narrative" prose without moving all the way to a distortion of idiomatic Japanese. Or if they had read Ezra Pound—or indeed Ernest Fenollosa, who lived in Japan for fifteen years toward the end of the century—they would have learned that what the European surrealists were searching for existed in their very own indigenous poetic method consisting of the *haiku* and *waka* and the ideogrammic form. But the young Kawabata and his friends were much too bent on "modernizing"

---

* Aside from the eccentricity of the expression, the sentence is taken out of context. Kataoka's model sentence, in the original written by a young writer, is preceded by "It is high noon. The packed special express train was running at full speed." As Kataoka presents it, the sentence is supposed to contain all the information which is in fact given by the very ordinary antecedent sentence. Although this model has been frequently quoted by scholars, no one seems to have noticed the Neo-Perceptionist's error.

their art to notice what lay so close at hand.* In their view, the course of Japanese literature was to run more or less straight from the "conventional" narrative entertainment to naturalism, to proletarian literature, and to surrealism, just as the Japanese theorists had read was the course for the European literatures.[3]

The imprint of Neo-Perceptionism on Kawabata continues strong in those works written over the ten years following this "modernist" manifesto. Stories and longer works like "The Ghost of the Rose" (*Bara no Yūrei,* 1927), *The Red Gang of Asakusa* (*Asakusa Kurenai-Dan,* 1929–30), "Needle and Glass and Fog" (*Hari to Garasu to Kiri,* 1930), and "The Crystal Fantasy" (*Suishō Gensō,* 1931), to mention only a few, are all marked by boldly experimental features. The deformation of idioms, such as in the sentence "an illness entered the core of the body"[4] in "Needle and Glass and Fog"; a long interior monologue, very much after Molly Bloom's, in "The Crystal Fantasy"; the predominantly nominal and asyntactic construction of *The Red Gang of Asakusa;* the hundred miniature "novels" later collected into one volume as *The Palm-Sized Stories* (*Tanagokoro no Shōsetsu,* 1922–50)—these are the most conspicuous examples. Determinedly "modern" too are their themes and settings. The characters are typically urban "new types," whose life style is self-consciously "Western." The wife in "The Crystal Fantasy," for example, living in a "Western" room with "Western" furniture, sits at her dressing table polishing her nails and looking out on her greenhouse. Her stream of consciousness could be that of a European woman, since, with the exception of one mention each of Tokyo, a Japanese writer, and a Japanese swimmer in the strange catalogue of items several pages long, the story is quite cosmopolitan in its references.

I do not mean, of course, that in these experiments Kawabata succeeds in creating anything like the cosmopolitan as a type of

---

* The relationship between imagism and Japanese literature (and Chinese ideograms) has been discussed by many critics. The best book on the subject remains Ernest Fenollosa's *The Chinese Written Character as a Medium for Poetry,* ed. Ezra Pound, collected in Pound's *Instigations* (New York: Boni and Liveright, 1920), pp. 357–88. See Pound's numerous comments on the ideogrammic method in his earlier books and Hugh Kenner's *The Poetry of Ezra Pound* (Norfolk, Conn.: New Directions, 1951).

person recognizable across all linguistic and cultural borders. The notion of a cosmopolitan is itself quite specific to modern Western culture. The fact is, in the complexion of their feelings and emotions his characters are unmistakably Japanese. "The Crystal Fantasy," for instance, puts the cosmopolitan wife in the context of a tension between her medical and scientific interests and her sexual fantasies—in itself an unlikely situation for a Japanese woman of the time—and yet her relationship to her husband at once defines her as Japanese. There is a very uncomfortable gap in the work between its intellectual intention and its actualization by a sensibility formed out of the traditional expectation and response. Whatever stylistic feat Neo-Perceptionism may have achieved here, one realizes, it is not so much surrealistic in effect as *haiku*-like, still imbued as it is with the age-old associations and conventions despite its being set in a modern frame of reference. Natsume Sōseki undoubtedly knew this a generation before, and Kawabata, too, came to know it as he matured. For all its youthful wrongheaded theorizing, Neo-Perceptionism taught Kawabata a great deal about the possibilities of Japanese for prose fiction, as we will see in our discussion of *Snow Country* and *The Sound of the Mountain*.

One of Kawabata's earliest and least experimental stories, "The Izu Dancer" (*Izu no Odoriko*, 1926), stands up better than his modernist attempts. Like *Pillow of Grass*, "The Izu Dancer" is a first-person story of a trip to the country. Unlike the Sōseki story, however, the voice here is lyrical throughout, and not mediated either by irony or by manipulation of time between the events and the telling. The student-narrator's experience is set in the fresh provincial scene by means of an evocative, slightly nostalgic language which is neither elaborate nor learned. While *Pillow of Grass* is a complex experiment in the narrative sequence, "The Izu Dancer" has the forthright appearance of a single unadorned episode. There is more quiet understatement and less surprise. And, finally, as against Sōseki's hero who moves from uninvolvement toward greater involvement, Kawabata's moves in the other direction, toward less involvement.

The student is attracted to a girl in a traveling family of dancer-entertainers whom he meets while on vacation, but he does not exactly know what he wants from the encounter. Right away, he realizes he is tormented with the thought of her "entertaining" her clients. Next morning, however, as a fierce storm clears, he sees her nude in the outdoor bath:

> One small figure ran out into the sunlight and stood for a moment at the edge of the platform calling something to us, arms raised as though for a plunge into the river. It was the little dancer. I looked at her, at the young legs, at the sculptured white body, and suddenly a draught of fresh water seemed to wash over my heart. I laughed happily. She was a child, a mere child, a child who could run out naked into the sun and stand there on her tiptoes in her delight at seeing a friend. I laughed on, a soft, happy laugh. It was as though a layer of dust had been cleared from my head. And I laughed on and on. It was because of her too-rich hair that she had seemed older, and because she was dressed like a girl of fifteen or sixteen. I had made an extraordinary mistake indeed.[5]

No longer threatened by the need to discover and test his sexuality, the "I" really comes to love the girl as they roam from one mountain village to another in the company of her family. She responds to his affection, and they discover very gentle and tender feelings for each other. The story ends as they part and the young man returns to school.

There are several episodes which are seemingly unrelated to the main line of the story. One is toward the end where another boy, bound for Tokyo to take his high school entrance exams, consoles the narrator for his loss. The hero's initiation is effectively postponed and in a sense universalized as he goes to sleep "warmed by the boy beside [him]" (p. 114), who of course faces his own initiation into school life away from his family.

The avoidance of direct total involvement in heterosexual love is not unique to this story, since most of Kawabata's central man-woman relationships do not build upon the mutual full engagement of two people. Frequently, his women are remote and virginal—"pure" as he sometimes calls them—and, whatever the author's psychological determinants for this may be,* there is a kind of aching persistent eroticism permeating his later novels which is inseparable from the wistful and often intense longing that typically marks Kawabata's male characters.

The atmosphere of freshness and innocence enveloping "The Izu Dancer" comes, I think, from Kawabata's utterly simple language which sets the experience down among the trees and clean air and wet grass of a country resort. In contrast to the urban environments of his Neo-Perceptionist works, the setting of this story recalls the province of the traditional *haiku*. There is also the circumstance that Kawabata, instead of explaining the characters' thoughts and feelings, merely suggests them by mentioning objects which, in a country setting, are certain to reverberate with tangible, if not identifiable, emotions.

> It was after midnight when I left their inn. The girls saw
> me to the door, and the little dancer turned my sandals so
> that I could step into them without twisting. She leaned
> out and gazed up at the clear sky. "Ah, the moon is up."
> (P. 112)

Here Kawabata, as he chisels this plain, clear prose reaching back to the old tradition, appears determined to find some alternative to the eccentric internationalism of his "modernist" stories.

Snow Country (*Yukiguni*) combines elements of Kawabata's Neo-Perceptionism with his *haiku* style of juxtaposition and understatement. The first thing that must be mentioned in this connection is the curious evolution of the work. In January 1935 Kawabata wrote two related short stories for different journals, "The Mirror of an Evening Scene" (*Yūgeshiki no Kagami*) and "The Mirror of a White Morning" (*Shiroi Asa no Kagami*).[6] Roughly corresponding to the first two sections of the final version

---

* Those with a psychological bent might consider his very early loss of both parents and grandparents as significant. Kawabata continually thought of himself as an "orphan." Also, in several works he quite candidly admits his adolescent homosexual experience.

of *Snow Country,* they were merely the start of that work, for in November and December 1935 two further related stories appeared, then two more in August and October 1936, and one more story in 1937, each in turn adding some development to the last published. All were then collected into a full-length work called *Snow Country* in 1937. But that is not all. In 1940 and 1941 he added still two more stories. The whole was revised some six years later, and it was actually not until December 1948 that Kawabata felt he was finally done with it.

What is extraordinary in this is of course Kawabata's free attitude about the wholeness and unity of a piece of literature. First, it took fourteen years for the story as a whole to be completed; second, the sections were published in different periodicals with little expectation that readers would have access to any section previously published; third, the final addition and revision, coming years after the earlier tentative completion, brought considerable changes in the text. All this seems to indicate that Kawabata had a sense of the novel as a temporally changeable entity built on the autonomy of each part. Clearly, the impact of such a fragmentary mode of publication on the form of the work as a whole is greater than, and different from, that of regular serialization. For instance, Kawabata most probably had no scheme at all at the beginning for any larger context. Each addition came as though it were the conclusion, implying no further future. And only much later, when he saw the possibility of a larger whole including what was already published did he begin to fit the new sections into this later conception. Such loose serialization allows also for adding to a work almost anytime if a larger scheme suggests itself. With a work of this sort, the search for "structural unity" is likely to end in one's grappling with the author's mere schematization, a ghost of the story, rather than with the energy and movement of the artist's spirit-quickening words. It is good to keep in mind here that while the imposed mode of publication may be prior to and thus determine the form of a work, the reverse could just as well be the case. That is, it is possible that Kawabata's particular temperament and artistic need actively sought out and chose this unusual mode of publication. Since he wrote so many other works, including *The Sound of the Mountain,* in this fashion, I am convinced that he knew what he wanted from serialization.*

Another way of getting at the situation is to stress the essentially temporal nature of Kawabata's art. Instead of spatially schematizing the continuity, planning a unique shape like a sculpture, Kawabata just lets his language flow in time, lets it weave its own strands, almost come what may. The "shape" of the novel is thus not architectural or sculptural, with a totality subsuming the parts, but musical in the sense of a continual movement generated by surprise and juxtaposition, intensification and relaxation, and the use of various rhythms and tempos. The *renga* form is often mentioned in connection with Kawabata and for good reason: it too is characterized by frequent surprises along the way and only the retrospective arrangement of the parts into a totality as they approach a possible end.

Snow Country recounts the love affair of a writer, Shimamura, with a resort geisha as it develops over a period of some twenty months during which he is intermittently a guest at a mountain spa. The story opens in the winter with Shimamura about to begin his second stay, but the sequence is interrupted shortly after his reunion with the geisha by a long flashback describing their first encounter the previous spring. After that, the story progresses in chronological order to the end, telling of the rest of his current stay and of a third visit the following fall. The seasonal order is thus from winter to spring, back to winter, then to fall which is

---

* Kawabata's explanation for publishing the first two sections in two different magazines in the same month is as follows: he couldn't finish the "Mirror of an Evening Scene" part before the deadline of one of the monthlies, so he decided to write the unfinished part for another with a later deadline. As he spent more time on it, his ideas about it changed.

Kawabata once called *Snow Country* a "work that could have been completed at any point." He said elsewhere, however, that he had wanted to include the fire scene "even while [he was] writing the earlier sections." As if to make the provisional nature of his structure still plainer, he also said that *Snow Country* might better have ended without the last sections—that is, those corresponding to the last 25 pages in Edward Seidensticker's translation (New York: Knopf, 1956), the edition used throughout my discussion. Kawabata's remarks are in Terada Tōru's article "Yukiguni nitsuite," reprinted in Mishima Yukio's collection of essays on the author (note 1).

passing slowly into winter. Not a complicated sequence, certainly, and yet the long flashback, together with numerous brief references to earlier events throughout the rest of the book, effectively disrupts the single sequentiality and thus creates a subtle sense of passing time. In fact, the persistent back-and-forth time motion is just confusing enough to lead the author himself into a miscalculation of the total time (three visits in "three years")[7] but the "error," not at all seriously misleading the reader, has the salutary effect of reinforcing the novel's diffuse sense of time's passage.

The flow of time which defines the shape of *Snow Country* is also an important thematic element, established at the very beginning by the celebrated mirror image. Shimamura struggles to remember the appearance of the girl he will soon see again. Only his tactile recall is strangely vivid: the forefinger of his left hand suddenly feels "damp from her touch." * In this frustrating state of sexual immediacy yet final remoteness of the loved one, he sees a woman's eye "float up before him." It is the reflection in the coach window of a girl sitting opposite him.

> In the depths of the mirror the evening landscape moved by, the mirror and the reflected figures like motion pictures superimposed one on the other. The figures and the background were unrelated, and yet the figures, transparent and intangible, and the background, dim in the gathering darkness, melted together into a sort of symbolic world not of this world. Particularly when a light out in the mountains shone in the center of the girl's face, Shimamura felt his chest rise at the inexpressible beauty of it. (P. 9)

---

* In the first printed version of this section, the word for "finger" was suppressed by the government, or by the publisher in fear of censorship. Though such deletion is irrelevant to the critical problem at hand, it does suggest an aspect of the modern Japanese novel which I have not touched on. The prewar and wartime censorship policy was codified into a dozen or more ruthless criminal laws ensuring the silencing of any "subversive" or "depraved" expression. Although the release from such repressive and puritanical censorship was celebrated briefly after August 1945, it was soon replaced by a number of regulations decreed by the American Occupation Forces which were almost as stringent in some respects.

The montage of the girl's face transparent over the continually moving landscape provides a good visualization of the book's main motif—the passage of time and man's continual struggle to slow it or pin it down to something substantial, or at least an image of something substantial. Shimamura, like anyone else, is continually compelled from the past to the present, and from here into the future, but he lives the present as though it were a somehow lasting extended stasis, the experience of beauty occasionally shocking the moving darkness into a radiant stillness.

Kawabata's handling of the mirror image is characteristically delicate. The reader is not let in on the full "symbolic" import of the superimposed image on the train window, and only after spending a considerable time with Shimamura is he allowed to discover—retrospectively as it were—that Yōko, the girl in the train window, is enmeshed in various relationships with Komako, Shimamura's geisha. The two girls complement each other to create the fullness of womanhood—one static, more timeless, less individualized (the name *Yōko* meaning "girl of leaves"); the other, dynamic and more fully alive in time (*Komako*, "girl like a colt"). Shimamura, as the reader discovers later, is attracted to both, but transient that he is, is capable only of observing them through the train window. Essentially a traveler, a passerby, he can only pass them by without becoming fully engaged with either of them.

Komako is one of very few life-sized and full-bodied female characters in Kawabata's novels. Uninhibitedly passionate, but she knows the futility of it all. She really loves Shimamura, but does not expect their relationship to proceed beyond a casual once-a-year arrangement. Time and again, she is described as "clean" or "pure" (*seiketsu*), as though she somehow embodied the crystal purity of the mountain snow. But at the same time, red is the color most often associated with her. Her character resonates on the poles of this oxymoron of purity and fire, carefully underlined by the mirror image at the beginning and the fire scene at the end. I find it remarkable that Kawabata is able to flesh out the logic of such a character into a real person, yet he does so, keeping her fire and ice somehow in balance. The other characters, principally Yōko and Shimamura, tend to be fainter embodiments. Against the boldly tactile realization of Komako, the intense and ethereal Yōko is hardly tangible. We are frequently told about her beautiful eyes, and her voice which seems to "come echoing back across the snowy nights" (pp. 5, 83). Yōko, thus disembodied, is the other half of a woman, the spirit or soul of a woman, always eluding men's reaching hands, always fragile and more than a little mysterious. Just as her voice seems an echo, her whole person appears not to belong to this world either. She is a fairy-tale figure, a symbolic marker, living not by her own will and desire but at the beck and call of the heroine—that is, to fulfill the logic of the drama.

Yōko's characterization deficits are thus fairly well justified by the central time-stasis paradox in the novel, but Shimamura's insubstantiality as a character is not so easily explained. Although the story is in the third person, it is told almost entirely from Shimamura's point of view. So much so, for instance, that the narrator does not even identify Komako by name until their reunion is fully told and a quarter of the story is well over (p. 51 of 175 pages). Thus, despite its third-person form, *Snow Country* is essentially a first-person novel. Similarly, if there is little distinction between character and narrator, neither is there much room between character and author. With "The Izu Dancer," a lyric inviting no ironic examination of the narrator's experience, this problem never arises. *Snow Country,* not being a lyric, calls for some critical investigation of Shimamura's point of view. Had this been provided, as in a dramatic monologue, we would have had clues to the author's stance toward the hero. As it is, the story remains disturbingly inconclusive in its judgment on its principal character.

Shimamura is an art critic. He is also the translator, supposedly, of "Valéry and Alain, and French treatises on the dance from the golden age of the Russian ballet" (p. 131). He writes articles and collects documents on Western dancers and productions although he has never seen a ballet, nor does he attend Japanese dance performances.

> Nothing could be more comfortable than writing about the ballet from books. A ballet he had never seen was an art

in another world. It was an unrivaled armchair reverie, a lyric from some paradise. He called his work research, but it was actually free, uncontrolled fantasy. He preferred not to savor the ballet in the flesh; rather he savored the phantasms of his own dancing imagination, called up by Western books and pictures. It was like being in love with someone he had never seen. But it was also true that Shimamura, with no real occupation, took some satisfaction from the fact that his occasional introductions to the occidental dance put him on the edge of the literary world —even while he was laughing at himself and his work. (P. 25)

This portrait of a self-ironic dilettante, a westernized intellectual who knows no ballet at first hand, no real West, indeed no real Japan, but who acknowledges his ignorance, even flaunts it. Such a portrait is uncomfortably close to one version at least of the self-image of the younger Kawabata himself. Note especially Shimamura's irony directed at both himself and his work, but more important, the total absence of irony operating on the portrait of Shimamura as a whole.*

Shimamura's behavior toward Komako, too, is left suspended finally in the novel's attitudinal limbo. Take the celebrated passage (pp. 146–47) where he tells her that she is a "good girl." Komako asks for some elaboration, and he repeats his remark, but with a variation: "you're a good woman." Many critics in discussing this change argue that Shimamura *inadvertently* reveals in his second remark his real attitude toward Komako as a mere sexual object. But there is no evidence for this. Besides being genuinely attracted to the girl, Shimamura is fully sensitive to the moral implications of his relationship. He knows he will never

* There are several literal-minded "scholarly" studies about the "real" setting and people that supposedly served as models. Kawabata himself has this to say about Shimamura: "I have remarked—in the Afterword to the Sōgensha edition of *Snow Country*—that 'Shimamura is of course not myself. . . . I am more Komako than Shimamura.' Probably that is correct, but it seems to me now that this is the kind of thing one cannot say decisively. Shimamura bothers me as the author of *Snow Country*. I would like to say that Shimamura is not really there, but even that is dubious." (Quoted by Terada Tōru, in Mishima's collection, p. 245.)

marry her and he feels some guilt about this, even if he never acts on it. There is overall a kind of neutrality in the book regarding Shimamura's character which a "moral" interpretation is bound to misrepresent.[8]

Despite the fact that *Snow Country* gives great prominence to the Tanabata legend, the scene of the starry heavens that concludes the novel is not clear enough in its significance to serve as a gloss on the work. According to the legend, Kengyū and Shokujo loved each other so much that God turned them into stars placed on either side of the Milky Way (conceived of in the myth as a river, Ama no Kawa). They are allowed to meet only once a year, on Tanabata, the evening of July 7, a holiday still widely observed by Japanese children. In the last scene of *Snow Country,* Shimamura, hurrying with Komako to watch a burning building, feels the "naked" Milky Way "wrap[ping] the night earth in its naked embrace" (p. 165);* the next moment it seems to flow "through his body to stand at the edges of the earth" (p. 168); and finally "the Milky Way flow[s] down inside him with a roar" (p. 175). The overwhelming galactic image here is very much like the rainbow in D. H. Lawrence's novel which operates as a symbol of promise of sexual fulfillment. The double message comes with the Kengyū-Shokujo reference which appears to emphasize the anguished separation of the lovers.

What I have come to believe is that Kawabata is ultimately indifferent to moral considerations in art. He will always, for instance, shift the narrative line so that the human action or situation is implicitly compared with a natural object or event which has in itself no single definite meaning at all, though it may be powerfully evocative of certain emotions. Take the passage describing the dying moth (pp. 89–90) or the one concerning the *kaya* grass (p. 92): they are there not so much to interpret and comment on the hero's action as to break the line of the story, or drop a hint that no matter what the characters may be up to, the

---

*It is unfortunate that the English equivalent of Ama no Kawa (literally, "River of Heaven") should be the "Milky Way" with its connotation of the breast and fecundity. Also, another name for it, Ginga ("Silver River"), has an association of coldness and clarity which most Japanese would automatically feel even in the name Ama no Kawa.

world around them is always present but uninvolved, insensible, and not really attended to often enough. He reminds us to stop and look. The kind of resigned sadness or loneliness one always feels in Kawabata's novels comes, it seems to me, from his acceptance of man's helplessness before such a comprehensive flow of things in time. It is not all sadness, of course, because Kawabata finds quiet pleasure in this acceptance.

Mishima's grasp of what Kawabata is about is correct in the sense that he does not interpret the world as novelists are supposed to do. Yet he does interpret it. Time flows through the process of his work, and he, having abandoned the effort to make particular judgments all the time, sees men and women on a larger canvas than human actions and their consequences can provide. Kawabata sings the tune he picks up from the changing world just as he hears it. In this way the acceptance of things as they are becomes, in Kawabata's hands, a vital act of interpretation.

As we have seen from the discussion of the window-mirror and the fire, *Snow Country* employs Neo-Perceptionist techniques consciously distilled in the spirit of *haiku*. But there are numerous other image-markers in the novel which act to animate and intensify the narrative movement. Such images at times approach the gratuitous—Shimamura's visit to the town known for *chijimi* linen (pp. 150–59), for instance, is not easy to justify without forcing one's argument. Yet we can't help but see that the use of the near irrelevancy is the strong new feature in Kawabata's art.

> The windows were still screened from the summer. A moth so still that it might have been glued there clung to one of the screens. Its feelers stood out like delicate wool, the color of cedar bark, and its wings, the length of a woman's finger, were a pale, almost diaphanous green. The ranges of mountains beyond were already autumn-red in the evening sun. That one spot of pale green struck him as oddly like the color of death. The fore and after wings overlapped to make a deeper green, and the wings fluttered like thin pieces of paper in the autumn wind.
> Wondering if the moth was alive, Shimamura went over to the window and rubbed his finger over the inside of the

screen. The moth did not move. He struck at it with his fist, and it fell like a leaf from a tree, floating lightly up midway to the ground.

In front of the cedar grove opposite, dragonflies were bobbing about in countless swarms, like dandelion floss in the wind.

The river seemed to flow from the tips of the cedar branches.

He thought he would never tire of looking at the autumn flowers that spread a blanket of silver up the side of the mountain.

A White-Russian woman, a peddler, was sitting in the hallway when he came out of the bath. So you find them even in these mountains— He went for a closer look. (Pp. 89–90)

The kaleidoscopic succession of images—a dead moth, a cedar grove, dragonflies, dandelions, the river, silver flowers, a White Russian woman—effectively suspends the narrative progress and forces us to pay attention to those large margins in the canvas of life. Here, as in several other passages in *Snow Country,* Kawabata's use of one-sentence paragraphs strongly suggests the *haiku,* or the *renga,* a technique which will become a dominant feature of *The Sound of the Mountain.*

Overall, as compared with his earlier works, the verbal surface is more sedate in *Snow Country,* yet there are several residual experimentalist expressions. The opening sentences offer an example. In a literal translation, Ivan Morris puts it thus:

When [the train] emerged from the long tunnel at the provincial border, it was snow country. The bottom (or depth) of the night became white.[9]

Seidensticker gives this rendering:

The train came out of the long tunnel into the snow country. The earth lay white under the night sky. (P. 3)

There is another passage that is often talked about:

He leaned against the brazier, provided against the com-

ing of the snow season, and thought how unlikely it was
that he would come again once he had left. The innkeeper
had lent him an old Kyoto teakettle, skillfully inlaid in
silver with flowers and birds, and from it came the sound
of wind in the pines. He could make out two pine breezes,
as a matter of fact, a near one and a far one. Just beyond
the far breeze he heard faintly the tinkling of a bell. He
put his ear to the kettle and listened. Far away, where the
bell tinkled on, he suddenly saw Komako's feet, tripping
in time with bell. He drew back. The time had come to
leave. (P. 155)

For the bilingual, Seidensticker's excellent translation may seem
a little too clear, but the point is made very well for the English-
only reader. The metaphor of the wind in the pines is so intricately developed, changing to the sound of a bell, and then to
Komako's steps, that we can almost see Komako herself dancing
among the pines. The real and the fantasied are so closely woven
that we realize with a start that Komako's appearance is only in
Shimamura's consciousness. "The time had come to leave" is remarkably convincing as the reader is awakened from the reverie
he has been allowed to share. In the syntactically looser Japanese
version, the tenor and vehicle are even more subtly fused with the
effect of maximally blending the human movement into the occasions of Nature.

Snow Country essentially belongs to the prewar years, despite
the date of its final revision. (Other works written before and
during the war are: *The Flower Waltz* [*Hanna no Warutsu*, 1936],
The Master of Go [*Meijin*, 1942–54; translated into English in
1972], and a number of short stories.) During the time between
publication of the larger part of *Snow Country* and that of *The
Sound of the Mountain* falls, of course, the war, the single most
important event in modern Japanese history, and Kawabata is not
the kind of writer who could work comfortably under the increasing tension of those days. Unable to sift out his thoughts enough
to act politically, he was at the same time and for the same reason even less able to write. He spent this time reading deeply in

the Japanese classics—*The Tale of Genji, The Pillow Book, Hōjōki, Tsurezure Gusa,* Saikaku, Chikamatsu, and many *haiku* poets—and only gradually as his depression over the lost war and the lost national purpose slowly lifted did his pent-up creative energy begin to flow again. His postwar novels and novellas—*Thousand Cranes (Senba Zuru,* 1949–51), *The Sound of the Mountain (Yama no Oto,* 1949–54), *How Many Times, The Rainbow (Niji Ikutabi,* 1950–51), *The Dancer (Maihime,* 1950–51), *Days and Months (Hi mo Tsuki mo,* 1952–53), *The Lake (Mizuumi,* 1954–55), *To Be a Woman (Onna de Aru koto,* 1956–57), *House of the Sleeping Beauties (Nemureru Bijo,* 1960–61), and *Kyoto (Koto,* 1961–62)—were all published in the characteristic separate installments in different periodicals.[10]

What I have said about *Snow Country* also applies, in various ways, to many of these postwar novels. *The Sound of the Mountain* was published in seventeen sections in eight different periodicals over four and a half years (September 1949 to April 1954).[11] And again, each section is, to a large extent, autonomous, carrying a peculiar sense of completeness, yet open-endedness: for instance, had he decided in, say, April 1969 or July 1970 to add another section to *The Sound of the Mountain,* it need not have changed the novel materially. This non-Aristotelian aspect of his work must always be taken into account in any talk about Kawabata.

Once again, the flow of time that propels *The Sound of the Mountain* is inseparable from the substance of the novel. Written almost entirely from the point of view of Shingo, a man past sixty, it establishes at once that his memory of recent events is fast declining, while the people and events he recalls from the remoter past are becoming more and more vivid. As he shuttles back and forth between Tokyo and the suburbs, he remembers his home village, the girl he secretly loved there in his youth (his wife's older sister, long dead), and particularly the flaming maple tree she used to take care of. Against the general background of present dissolution, the remembered past offers him rest, solace, and solidity. But his life does have its present, too. More and more he sees the beautiful girl of the past in his daughter-in-law, Kikuko. If there is anything like a plot in the novel, then, it can be found commuting between these well-matched poles of the past and the present, death and life, with no perceptible advantage on either side.

Dissolution and death are everywhere around Shingo. His own marriage has for long lacked real warmth; his son, Shinichi, has a liaison with a war widow; Kikuko has an abortion in protest; his daughter leaves her husband, who soon thereafter attempts suicide with another woman; and his old friends die one by one of old age and the exhaustion of their struggle for survival in the difficult time after the war. Yet life rallies somehow. Shinichi and Kikuko begin to piece their marriage together again after he puts an end to his affair. Kinuko, Shinichi's woman, refuses to terminate her illegitimate pregnancy and fights to raise the child. Shingo's daughter Fusako, embittered and coarsened by her experience with her addict spouse and now probably a widow, nonetheless clings tenaciously to life.

If the balance of life and death has something to do with what *The Sound of the Mountain* is all about, the movement of the novel, its ever passing present, is also, paradoxically, a stasis, since it is all largely within Shingo's consciousness. The three locales—Kamakura (where the family resides), Tokyo (where Shingo and Shinichi work), and Shinshū (their country home) —function less as distinct settings than as spatial correlatives of Shingo's present and his past. More, even Shingo's workaday motions around Tokyo and Kamakura serve as occasions for reminiscence which set off at a moment's notice his reveries on long-lost things. Even the lesser characters are used at crucial moments mainly as prods to Shingo's memory: for instance, the novel begins with his asking his son to help him remember the housemaid's name.

Always at the center of Shingo's time-crossed consciousness is his daughter-in-law, Kikuko. She is his "window looking out of a gloomy house," * and he connects with the past and the present only through his love for her. His attachment is quite a different experience from an old man's purely erotic entanglement with a

---

* *The Sound of the Mountain,* trans. Edward G. Seidensticker (New York: Knopf, 1970), p. 37. This text is used throughout my discussion.

young woman, the kind Tanizaki Junichirō, for instance, so fondly describes.* Thus Shingo's many dreams all involve a degree of sexuality, but none of them unmistakably identifies the partner of his dream, nor do any of the dreams approximate real sexual union.[12] His erotic longing for his son's young wife appears to be powerfully restrained even on the unconscious level. Shingo fights against himself, continually "paternalizing" his attitude toward Kikuko. For union with Kikuko would be taboo in more than one sense: through Kikuko, Shingo reaches out not only to his wife's dead sister, but also to his own lost past. Kikuko is, in other words, much more Shingo's living memory standing before him than a living person. To abandon himself to his love for this young girl would be to surrender to the past, to a dead memory. His past must remain just out of touch, so he can live on in the shambles that the present is for him.

Kikuko is Kawabata's eternal untouchable woman, his Izu Dancer, his Yōko, exquisite and elusive. Once again we see that an approach to Kawabata's work in the expectation of meeting a fully realized female character is bound to be disappointed. Nor is Shingo, for that matter, a fully developed character. As is true of *Snow Country* and most other Kawabata novels, *The Sound of the Mountain* does not operate on ordinary novelistic logic. Rather, the play and performance of the images of things and their settings—whether related or unrelated to the characters— animate and move the novel. In the usual novel—here I have, say, Sōseki's *Light and Darkness* in mind rather than *Emma* or *The Ambassadors*—imagery serves mainly to reinforce the logic of the plot as it comments on the human drama. In *Light and Darkness* the night that envelops the hero toward the end—his dark night of the soul, as it were—suggests a crisis that might lead him to the "light" of self-knowledge. The image is there to amplify, intensify, and elaborate on the character's experience, not as it would be in *The Sound of the Mountain*, to dilute or deemphasize action. Of course, elsewhere in Kawabata's work, too, one

---

* In a sense, *House of the Sleeping Beauties* comes closest to Tanizaki territory. But Kawabata's eroticism is much more tenuous than Tanizaki's, the old man's contact with the sleeping girls merely setting off reveries in which he reminisces on his lost youth.

can find imagery that functions in this fashion. But *The Sound of the Mountain,* which is written for the most part in very brief paragraphs, moves at crucial points from image to image by a series of leaps. And these leaps are the novel's movement, the batteries that energize it.

The moon was bright.

One of his daughter-in-law's dresses was hanging outside, unpleasantly gray. Perhaps she had forgotten to take in her laundry, or perhaps she had left a sweat-soaked garment to take the dew of night.

A screeching of insects came from the garden. There were locusts on the trunk of the cherry tree to the left. He had not known that locusts could make such a rasping sound; but locusts indeed they were.

He wondered if locusts might sometimes be troubled with nightmares.

A locust flew in and lit on the skirt of the mosquito net. It made no sound as he picked it up.

"A mute." It would not be one of the locusts he had heard at the tree.

Lest it fly back in, attracted by the light, he threw it with all his strength toward the top of the tree. He felt nothing against his hand as he released it.

Gripping the shutter, he looked toward the tree. He could not tell whether the locust had lodged there or flown on. There was a vast depth to the moonlit night, stretching far on either side.

Though August had only begun, autumn insects were already singing.

He thought he could detect a dripping of dew from leaf to leaf.

Then he heard the sound of the mountain.

It was a windless night. The moon was near full, but in the moist, sultry air the fringe of trees that outlined the mountain was blurred. They were motionless, however.

Not a leaf on the fern by the veranda was stirring.

In these mountain recesses of Kamakura the sea could

sometimes be heard at night. Shingo wondered if he might have heard the sound of the sea. But no—it was the mountain.

It was like wind, far away, but with a depth like a rumbling of the earth. Thinking that it might be in himself, a ringing in his ears, Shingo shook his head.

The sound stopped, and he was suddenly afraid. A chill passed over him, as if he had been notified that death was approaching. He wanted to question himself, calmly and deliberately, to ask whether it had been the sound of the wind, the sound of the sea, or a sound in his ears. But he had heard no such sound, he was sure. He had heard the mountain.

It was as if a demon had passed, making the mountain sound out.

The steep slope, wrapped in the damp shades of night, was like a dark wall. So small a mound of a mountain, that it was all in Shingo's garden; it was like an egg cut in half.

There were other mountains behind it and around it, but the sound did seem to have come from that particular mountain to the rear of Shingo's house.

Stars were shining through the trees at its crest. (Pp. 7–8)

Obviously, Shingo's experience is being described by the narrator from Shingo's point of view. But it is not at all clear what this litany of objects—the moon, Kikuko's dress, the locusts, the sound of the mountain—and the precision with which they are observed really amount to. Only free association of an aging man's night thoughts? For that, the bright moon, the dress hanging on the line, the screeching locusts and, of course, the sound of the mountain have something too ominous about them. A direction is being felt out, but where? The transitions between the very autonomous paragraphs are disjointed (hardly any conjunctions are used) and it seems that the sequences could stop at any time. In fact, with each new paragraph, we feel a surprise, however delicate, at still a new turn in the train of thought. It is not the suddenness of a new percept that surprises, although the sound of the mountain is indeed unexpected. "The moon was bright," "Though August had only begun," "Not a leaf on the fern," "Stars were shining"—the paragraphs, highlighting the objects of his consciousness, nonetheless gradually move away from the interior of his existence toward the container of all the drama—the world around, the wide margins of the novel.

As for Shingo's hearing the sound of the mountain, there is a mimetic aspect to it, certainly. First, the fact of his hearing the sound is stated unqualifiedly. Next, his causal inventory is given—windless night, nearly full moon, motionless trees, and the rustling leaves of the fern. Then, his more generalized question "If it is not the sound of the waves?" is answered, followed by a description of the sound as like "wind, far away." The next paragraph brings the question back to himself: isn't the sound coming from his own body? With his denial of every such possibility, the sound suddenly stops. Shingo is frightened. In this longest paragraph in the passage, he is said to "want to" ask the same questions again; that is to say, he can no longer ask since he already knows the answers. The fearfulness of the experience is underlined by the reference to the "demon." [13] Thus, Shingo's psychological reality is available to us here: an aging man's fear of death by some inexplicable and possibly diabolical natural event. And yet the attractiveness of the passage does not depend entirely on the mere representation of the old man's state of mind. The man and his presence approach transparency as we begin almost to hear *through* Shingo the ominous sound of the mountain. Shingo himself is not really very substantial in this moonlit reality; rather it is his instrumental role in making accessible the wide world that spreads around him. For Shingo, as for Kawabata, the awareness of the large margins of the world around human beings and their actions, the large area of silence that stays intact despite human speech and the words of the novel—that is what powerfully informs his mind.

Shingo is no Leopold Bloom, whose stature and massive weight can carry the burden of everyman everywhere, in the whole city of Dublin and beyond. Mrs. Dalloway—or Mrs. Moore, for that matter—might be a closer analogy, with her delicacy and apparent fragility. But as a character Mrs. Dalloway has a rich and substantial interior life; she has angst and terror and tenderness, frivolity and sensuality, and an overall self-awareness embracing both her past and her present. Shingo as a character shies away from such definition, and it is only his remarkable sensitivity that identifies the context of his personality within the novel.

Kawabata's achievement, it seems to me, lies in just this, his keen awareness of the objects around men that exist in themselves as solidly as people do. Objects, in the world and in the world of the novel, are somehow or other related to people, but Kawabata seldom makes the connection between them explicit for us. With each of his brief paragraphs self-contained in this way (and, I should perhaps add, with each of the brief installments also self-enclosed), these objects tend to stand autonomous. Although he continually invites us to make our own efforts to connect, he stops short of giving us the keys to the house.

> Far distant flow of time. White chalk. The picture of a flower on the blackboard at a girls' high school. A brief life, a girl. A white sail on the horizon. The crystal in the eyes of a fried fish served at a hotel. Near-sighted fish; oh, poor fish. A gynecologist's instrument looking like a fork. ("The Crystal Fantasy," *Complete Works*, II, 195)

What I would call Kawabata's nominal imagination is apparent even in his earliest work. The objects here are not organized syntactically. He does not relate them, with verbs and conjunctions, into a sentence, a proposition, but just leaves them as he finds them. Exactly in the same way, *The Sound of the Mountain* reaches out and gathers objects into a narrative, but refuses to hook them into a chain of cause and effect, a plot.* They are

---

* Kawabata wrote a book on the theory of the novel, *Studies of the Novel* (*Shōsetsu no Kenkyū*) (Tokyo: Kaname Shobō, 1953), which is not on the whole very interesting to those who already know James, Lubbock, Forster, etc., whom Kawabata considerably simplifies in his discussion. However, his brief discussion of plot is of note, largely because he complains here about the lack of a well-constructed plot in Japanese novels. He argues that the Japanese writer regards fiction as somewhat against the "laws of nature," and even in writing a novel he wants to follow nature as it is: like the *haiku* and the *waka*, the novel rejects falsification and, together with it, the carefully constructed plot (pp. 44–50). Kawabata also published a collection of essays on prose style, *Bunshō* (Tokyo: Tōhō Shobō,

assembled but unconnected. What emerges, then, is not an argument—which any construction of plot (the whole cause-effect complex) implies—but a perception of the world and an acceptance of it as perceived, one thing at a time. It is a world parceled and scattered in a way more ruthlessly than even the broken family and society in *The Sound of the Mountain* can justly reflect. Yet even while referring to the myriad objects in the margins of human existence, Kawabata manages to be happy in the radiant beauty he finds there.

Kawabata's art is always immediately recognizable. As Ivan Morris and others have pointed out, it is finally traceable to the traditional sensibility of sadness (*aware*) over the transience of men and things, as exemplified by Lady Murasaki, Sei Shōnagon, and countless other writers and poets. As such, it is not easy to talk about in modern critical terms, as Mishima's incomplete statement seems to imply it is. What is so convincing to me about Kawabata's art is the vibrant silence about it; the delicate strength in the leap of images, and finally, in his refusal to connect things into an easy meaning, his embrace of the shambled world. The lack of "structure," often mentioned as though it were a blight on his work, is Kawabata's way of adjusting the novel to the flow of time so that art can survive and teach men and women to survive.

Kawabata's suicide in the spring of 1972 surprised people. There were many speculations: his shock at his friend Mishima's *harakiri,* his overexposure since winning the Nobel prize in 1968, his general exhaustion and sense of decline, and—correlative no doubt to all these—his dependence on barbiturates. Now, a little later, with the gossip quieted, if not stilled, the self-administered death begins to look more accidental than essential. Because with Kawabata, there is no evidence in his art of any compulsion toward this end. His writing did not derive from his personal life in the way Dazai's or Mishima's did and thus reach a dead end following a life-decline. He had a way too of always clearly know-

1942), certain of which are fascinating in their discussion of children's writings in comparison with "literary" works.

ing the risks of the artist's life, and knowing the measures to take to avoid them. All his life he managed to keep up a working détente between his art and his life and the terrible demands of both by always closely attending to what I have chosen to call the margins of life. His suicide terminated his life no less abruptly than Dazai's or Mishima's, but the feeling is inescapable that it was something almost natural in Kawabata's case, an easier and gentler crossing than theirs had been. And all the more difficult, then, to resist the seductiveness of death. For Kawabata, the margins of life blend imperceptibly into that yawning voiceless world and are finally commensurate with it.

V

TILL DEATH DO US PART

DAZAI OSAMU: *The Setting Sun*
—*Forgive me that I was born.*

People loved Dazai. Friends and hangers-on were always around him, recording his slightest gesture and memorizing his utterances as if they were prematurely preparing hagiographies on the master. For all his liberal handouts of cash and drinks, it really was him they seemed to require. This sardonic clown, generous and compassionate to a fault, was at the same time selfish and perverse to a greater fault. For many adorers, he was a decadent saint, tireless in his search for the grounds of belief. For other acquaintances, he was a fool and a loser, whose embarrassing self-consciousness disabled him from forming any decent product out of the bathos of his life. Japanese critics writing on Dazai are unanimous in seeing real talent in his rare sensitivity for language. His friends and disciples, however, seldom write about his works; instead, notes, personal memoirs, books like *Dazai Osamu: His Life, Dazai Osamu the Man, Dazai Osamu's Charms,* and *Seven Years with Dazai Osamu* pour out every year, and now there is even a periodical called *Dazai Osamu Studies*.[1] Young people modeled themselves after him, to the extent of committing suicide with a copy of a Dazai clutched close. He was an institution of postwar Japan—until the catapulting prosperity of the sixties skipped over the traces of those wretched years.

Dazai lovers look for the man in his works, and there is good reason: he is less open to consideration apart from his work than any other writer discussed in this book. There is a monomaniacal "first-person" quality about everything he wrote. No matter what mask he assumed, it is always his own, very personal self who is speaking. He wrote everything furthermore with the expectation that his reader would recognize and enjoy *his* words, *his* thoughts, *his* feelings. For him a novel was a personal record, and its fiction-ality consisted in its tonal manipulations, the various ways he looked at himself. The seer was Dazai, and the landscape Dazai, and despite the high degree of tonal variation, Dazai always be-lieved he was being absolutely honest. Fiction was the "truth" for him, that is, non-fiction—a paradox that shows itself whenever a Dazai is read.

First, then, to the "truth"—those facts of his life which he felt compelled to review and report time and again throughout his career. Dazai Osamu (1909–1948) was born Tsushima Shūji, the tenth of eleven children of a rich, locally powerful landlord in a small town in the north. In that part of Japan at that time, to be one of the younger sons in such a home meant relative neglect by the parents. Worse still, his father, a member of the House of Peers, died when Dazai was only fourteen. Dazai was sent away to school in a nearby town, and it was there he made his first suicide attempt. Around this time he came to know a young geisha, Koyama Hatsuyo, whom he eventually invited to live with him when he entered the French Department of the University of Tokyo in 1930. His eldest brother, now head of the family, inter-vened and Dazai was forced to send the girl home. A few months later, he tried to drown himself with a cafe waitress, whom he had known only two weeks. The girl died, Dazai survived. Charges of abetting a suicide were brought against him but were quietly dropped. A few months later he finally managed to get together again with Hatsuyo, though at the cost of formal sever-ance from his family. Active for a while in support of communist causes, he gave up his underground activities upon learning that Hatsuyo was not a virgin at the time of their marriage. I am not quite sure what the connection might be between one's politics and one's wife's premarital experience, but that is Dazai's explanation for his "conversion" (*tenkō*) and surrender to the police in 1932.[2] In the meantime he had dropped out of school as well, unable to master the first lessons in French.

Only gradually, as he began to publish some short stories in magazines, did he become serious about his writing. Chaos persisted in his life. In 1935 he tried to hang himself after failing to get a newspaper job. By now addicted to morphine, he was sent away several times for withdrawal and treatment. Returning from one such cure, he was told by Hatsuyo about her adultery during his absence. He attempted suicide again—this time with Hatsuyo —but neither died. They separated, however, and the next year he married a quiet high-school teacher. Legally, at least, the marriage lasted till his death.

Dazai remained prolific throughout his *Sturm und Drang,* and by the time he was in his late twenties his work began to attract wider attention. Japan was on the eve of the Pacific War, and writers were censored by the war policy-makers on grounds of subversion, depravity, or irrelevance. Then when the American air raids intensified, both his home in Tokyo and his wife's in the country (to which he had moved) were bombed out. Toward the end of the war and into the postwar period, he wrote for Tokyo newspapers and magazines from his parents' home in the north.

He returned to Tokyo in late 1946 appearing frantic to burn out whatever was still uncharred in his life—talent, energy, life itself. He earned money only to throw it away on alcohol and women. By this time seriously ill with tuberculosis, he nonetheless wrote, drank heavily, and got involved with women, all in utter indifference to his health. One woman, a young war widow, sent him her manuscripts for advice. Later she asked him to father a child for her. He complied. The affair went on for a while and then he came to know another war widow, a former hairdresser, whose apartment he began to use occasionally for writing. And so it went, until it was all over on the day—it was his thirty-ninth birthday—they found his body tied by a cord to that of the devoted former hairdresser in a rain-swollen stream near his home. The novel he was currently serializing was called "Good-Bye" (*Gutto Bai*).[3]

So much for the "facts" of his life. Take any segment of the chronology, and you will find it amplified and "fictionalized" in at least one of his works, often in several. The central events are repeated in slightly different form in many stories: there is, for instance, his tragic-comic "marriage" to Hasuyo which is told in several versions, ranging from the fairly factual "Eight Scenes of Tokyo" (*Tokyo Hakkei*, 1941), using real names, to the more imaginary *No Longer Human* (*Ningen Shikkaku*, 1948). Not that this "truth" should be compared to a more "objective" version of it based on external evidence. Simply, one should recognize the habit of Dazai's imagination to fold back continually on his own life and feed on it.

The earliest collection of his stories, published in 1936, was called *The Declining Years* (*Bannen*). Dazai apparently meant by the title that his end was already present at the beginning, which is true: the book's most conspicuous features precisely forecast those of his later works. First, there is the absence of a coherent unity. Even as short stories, the items in the volume are fragmentary. There are a few meant to be collections in turn of shorter units, these having, however, no evident common denominator among them. For instance, the very first item, called "Leaves" (*Ha*), is no more than a few dozen aphorisms and paragraphs which at times string out to something of a story. Second, the "first-person" quality of Dazai's work is fully present in his first book. I do not necessarily mean here the use of the pronoun "I" specifically, although it is indeed prominent. Rather, the first person is implicit even in stories employing dramatic personae.* "The Monkey-Masked Clown" (*Sarumen Kanja*), for

---

* "Autobiographical" is the word I am deliberately avoiding here. *David Copperfield, The Mill on the Floss, Sons and Lovers,* and *A Portrait of the Artist* are all usually called "autobiographical," but the difference is that in these books the authors have managed to provide their surrogate characters with emotions and thoughts to some extent independent of the authors' own by taking a more or less clearly discernible stance vis-à-vis the characters. The fact that "events" in their works often derive from their own experience is, finally, not very important when considered in the context of the works themselves. Dazai's "first person" is in a sense *meta*-autobiographical: the "I" is insufficiently filled out to constitute a truly independent character in the book, and thus so much is left to the reader's assumed knowledge of the writer himself. This is true even of a work written and

one, maintains an ostensible third-person framework, insisting on the presence of a would-be writer distinct from Dazai Osamu. But the mask is admittedly transparent. In the first paragraph, "this man" is said to have a "habit of thinking of himself as a 'he' "— as though the "he-ness" had no "reality." Dazai soon seems uneasy with even this thinnest of masks, and before long he abandons it by turning the story of "this man" into a series of letters which are not only first person, but no longer pretend to be "in character." The requisites for a complex narrative manipulation are all there. With Dazai, however, his apparent preference for vocal complexity derives less from his overall artistic plan than from his serious unease in the discipline of maintaining an even fictional distance from his work.

Concomitant with this is the author's preoccupation with the "truth" of his life which is boldly evident in "Recollections" (*Omoide*) describing the childhood of an "I" identical with Dazai. But the almost compulsive confessionalism is prominent even in supposedly fictional pieces like "The Paper Crane" (*Kami no Tsuru*), which describes the "I's" extortion from his wife of a confession about her premarital experiences, and his reaction to the revelation. The whole story enclosed in quotation marks, "The Paper Crane" is to be taken as a letter addressed to a "you" who is a fellow writer. More concerned with the speaker's own reaction than with either the wife's act of confession or her premarital life itself, the story quickly becomes the speaker's confession, and it is *his* urge to confess and show himself that energizes the work. Clearly, the confessor's presence is vital, but the story also maintains the structure of a double listener: the "I" who receives his wife's "truth" and the "you" (or reader) to whom his own confession is addressed. The final effect of the story thus very much depends on the reader's willingness to accept the intimate role of a "you" who is a kind of father-confessor for the speaker. If he is inclined to feel friendly toward the "I," he will like the story; if not, he will be bored by it.

---

read during his relative obscurity. Although many Japanese writers and critics tend to identify this type of first-person work or I-novel (*shi-shōsetsu*) with the post-Renaissance individualism of the West, the two traditions are really quite different.

Dazai's movement in "The Paper Crane" from the relatively simple form of a confession to that of a confession about a confession is part of the larger pattern of involution in his writing. The "I" in "The Paper Crane" is a writer who writes about himself as a writer. He also writes to a writer. Such an imaginative realm is bound to be self-enclosed. Where unable to penetrate the boundary of the self even a little, Dazai's imagination must forever turn back on itself. His self-consciousness is a series of Chinese boxes, endlessly reduplicating themselves. His work talks about his work, which talks about his work, which . . . Formally, we can see how this is related both to confessionalism and to the tendency toward division and subdivision in his work. The involutionary substance of his work is also inseparable from his habit of authorial intrusion. Dazai is not interested in sustaining a certain level of fictionality in his work, which would mean wrenching himself away from the self and constructing a separate world. That would be a lie. Fiction is a lie, and he must be honest at all costs. So he breaks in at points with a new intimate revelation, disrupting whatever fictional order exists. He is a cannibal, his compulsion to nullify the distance from his work—and from his reader—amounting to eating them up and eating himself up. Fiction is after all a trivial matter, while his hold on himself is of vital importance to him. But if his self-digestion must stop somewhere, it should be at the innermost core of the self, where there is possibly some resistive substance that will stand revealed in art, in spite of art.

If Dazai's art were no more than a cloak of rags to be torn away to disclose the truth, his work would prove quite tedious at the end, being merely the redundant self-analysis of a seedy self-indulgent individual. Such, fortunately, is not the case. Unlike the run of the mill "I-novelists," Dazai is remarkably versatile in varying his tones. The subject may be the self-same "I," but he is looked at variously from a wide range of angles including a self-ironic braggadocio, a sly mischievousness, and an immovable depression. In "Leaves," for instance, there is a quote from Verlaine attached to the title: "The ecstasy and the agony of being select, I have them both." From such Romantic stridency, he moves on to the insouciance of the first aphorism:

> I thought of suicide. Last January I was given a present,
> a piece of fabric for a kimono. The material was linen,
> woven in narrow grey stripes. It is for a summer kimono.
> I thought I would live until summer.

The funny second one breaks the mood nicely:

> It occurred to Nora [of *A Doll's House*], too. It occurred
> to her when she got out to the hallway and slammed the
> door. Shall I go back?

Thus we are invited to join the author on bright days and dark
nights along the wayward progress of the work. And since the
characters in his work, being essentially inseparable from the
author himself, grow up and age along with the author, over the
years we get to know him as though he were an old friend whose
whole past is continually open before us. Rather than being confined to any specific work, Dazai's art transpires over the long
period of time and the numerous works shared by author and
reader.*

Dazai wrote a great deal, filling the twelve volumes of his *Complete Works*[4] during a mere dozen years after 1935, the most interesting "Dazaistic" works appearing in the postwar period, his last
three years. Most of his works are characteristically brief; some,
medium length ("The Flower of Clowning," 1935; "Das Gemeine" [his title], 1935; "The Spring of Fiction," 1936; "Human Lost" [his title], 1937; "Eight Tokyo Scenes," 1941; "The
Sound of the Hammer," 1947; "Villon's Wife," 1947), and several, book-size (*The New Hamlet*, 1941; *Justice and Smile*, 1942;
Lord Sanetomo, 1943; *Pandora's Box*, 1946; *The Setting Sun*,
1947; and *No Longer Human*, 1948).

---

*I agree to a large extent here with Howard Hibbett's articles, "The Portrait
of the Artist in Japanese Fiction," *Far Eastern Quarterly*, XIV (May, 1955), 347–
54, and "Tradition and Trauma in the Contemporary Japanese Novel," *Daedalus*,
XCV (Fall, 1966), 925–41. Hibbett's tracing of the *shi-shōsetsu* back to the old
"wayward essay" (*zuihitsu*) is, I think, the correct one. Only, I would like to add
that the sensibility (*fūryū, aware,* and so forth) energizing the *zuihitsu* imagination
is no longer available to modern writers. Although some residual attitudes are
certainly to be found in their work, the old sensibility is hardly ever of much help
in a real spiritual crisis.

The "first-person" quality is relentless in these works. Its simplest manifestation is Dazai's occasional use of his own name in the middle of a "story" (as in "Das Gemeine"), ever threatening to transform it into a kind of familiar essay. There are also frequent references to his earlier works (to *The Wandering in Fiction* in "A Small Album," and to "Human Lost" in "The Brazen Face," to name only a couple) and the occasional introduction of an old character (Ōniwa Yōzō of "The Flower of Clowning" in *No Longer Human*), both of which tend to open up a larger context of intimacy with the reader, complemented by Dazai's habit of directly addressing him. Other first-person features are the predominance of diary and letter forms in his work and the use of the dramatic monologue.

The diary form comes to Dazai almost effortlessly. "Human Lost," written in November 1936, covers the "I's" life in October and November of that year, referring at one point to his stay at a mental hospital very much like the one Dazai himself retired to at this time for treatment of his drug dependency, and, at another, to his relationship with his wife, identical to Dazai's and Hatsuyo's. As with all diaries, this one begins and ends with the start and finish of the duration of time covered, and there is little organizing impulse arising out of the work itself. Its "fictionality" depends almost entirely on the degree of one's ignorance about the author: a reader who knows nothing about the author's life might be impressed by the "inventiveness" of the situation and the "imaginative" arrangement of the characters, and respond positively to its various verbal and stylistic features such as the recurring waves of pathos, the *haiku*-like disjunction, the rhythm of involvement and detachment, and indeed the aura of confidentiality inherent in the form itself. Of course the better-informed reader will tend to consider first the generic aspect of the diary form and make some comparisons between the real or imagined private "truth" of the author and the public "fiction" of his work. Such a reader will be prepared to admire—or not—the author's insight into a situation in which he, the author, was in fact involved. A human being's life experience and his response to it are what constitute the work, not some severed self-enclosed imaginary experience. Among Dazai's diary-form works, even the more fictional ones like *Justice and Smile* (*Seigi to Bishō*) arouse similar reactions, depending on the reader's information.

The letter form occasionally poses similar problems, when as in *Pandora's Box* (*Pandora no Hako*) at least some of the letters composing the work are slightly altered versions of the author's actual correspondence. When these personal letters are addressed to the generic "you," as they often are, the reader's role as confessor is quite explicitly set. Of course, there are letter stories with distinct personae for both writer and addressee, and in these works Dazai can be quite successful in striking a balance between truth and fiction. After all, the epistolary form permits the author to invest his thought and feeling in the letter-writer, while enabling him to stand at the critical distance implied by the identified addressee. "The Sound of the Hammer," for instance, describes the writer's recurrent hearing of a hammer striking, which inexplicably drums down whatever energy and interest he might feel at crucial moments of his life. All the defeated man's gloom and despair is gathered into the dry, hollow sound of the hammer, while Dazai's self-ironic awareness is expressed in the comment on the letter attached at the end.

For this reason, too, the dramatic monologue is Dazai's most natural métier. While it allows him to commit his ideas and emotions to the assumed persona, it also leaves room for critical irony. Unlike Browning, Dazai always treats his speaker gently, never stooping to undercut him with too poisonous an irony (as can be found in "My Last Duchess" or "The Bishop Orders His Tomb"). Humor and mischievousness best fit a sensibility like Dazai's; he can straddle the fence, lampooning and pleading at the same time. "Villon's Wife" (*Viron no Tsuma*), for instance, is a woman's apology for her abusive writer-husband. By creating a speaker who is a sympathetic victim of his surrogate, Dazai can simultaneously plead for understanding from his reader and project a fair degree of ironic judgment on the whole matter. Thus by balancing his distress and his critical intelligence, he can go as far out of the self as he ever can for an outside view.

To be sure, Dazai's works are not all "first person." There are some that try to be "third person." Among the most conspicuous are his renderings of old well-known works. Dazai's fictional imagination, seldom sustained enough to fabricate a whole tale, requires some ready-made lifelike material if his own life is not to be used. So he reinterprets and reevaluates *Hamlet,* the life of a samurai hero, an obscure German play (translated by Mori Ōgai), various pieces from folklore and fairy tales. But even here, the plays and tales he whimsically remodels are fascinating—we see *his* imprint everywhere—while the works he took seriously, like *The New Hamlet* (*Shin Hamuretto*) and *Lord Sanetomo* (*Udaijin Sanetomo*), are almost unreadable. The reason is obvious: works having their own existence forced an examination on their own terms before they would submit to a rewriting. Clearly Dazai was a thoroughly first-person writer.

Dazai's first-person techniques are best utilized in three of his last and best works, "Villon's Wife," *The Setting Sun,* and *No Longer Human* (*Ningen Shikkaku*), which are the climax, and the conclusion, of his writing career. Since Dazai himself, as I read the modern Japanese novel, constitutes both climax and conclusion of the I-novel tradition, a closer examination of the best known of these novels is in order.

The Setting Sun (*Shayō*) was completed in June 1947 and serialized in a monthly magazine from July to October of that year. Dazai thus had no numerous deadlines to fight, and this novel is consequently somewhat more of a piece than his other long works. But fragmentation, of course, is the inescapable shape of his vision, and this work, too, inevitably breaks up into diaries, letters, and confessions, with all that such first-person forms imply.

The story is told by a young divorcée, Kazuko, born to a declining aristocratic family and now living with her old, ailing mother in a small country villa. When Kazuko's younger brother, Naoji, a war veteran and an addict, comes home, he is chaotic and depressed, upsetting his mother and sister by his wild habits. Having once wanted to be a writer, he still hangs around with his old teacher, an alcoholic named Uehara, who earns drinking money by writing. After the mother's death, Kazuko decides to have a baby by Uehara, who once kissed her on an impulse. Thus one day when Naoji comes to the house with a bar-girl in tow, she slips out to visit Uehara and asks him to make love to her. She returns

home to find Naoji has killed himself. The novel ends with Kazuko's letter to Uehara announcing her hoped-for pregnancy.

The characters and many episodes of *The Setting Sun* undoubtedly have their sources in Dazai's personal life. The two
writers, the aspirant Naoji and the fast deteriorating Uehara, are
impersonations of Dazai himself. The central event, Uehara's
fathering a baby for Kazuko, is of course Dazai's experience.
Dazai's family, if not precisely "aristocratic," was old enough
and once rich enough to make many people attribute that status
to it. Narcotics usage played a considerable role in the author's
life, and the depression permeating the novel closely resembles
Dazai's. To the extent that Kazuko makes excuses for both Naoji
and Uehara (as Villon's wife does for her husband), the novel
becomes Dazai's self-apology. Thus, what we have here in *The
Setting Sun* is the *shi-shōsetsu* par excellence—in its imaginative
energy, as well as the events, characters, setting, and tonality.

The one element of the novel which does not entirely succumb
to the prevailing death-wish is the heroine Kazuko herself. But
even at that, she is scarcely brought to life in the novel, being
little more than a half-hearted rekindling of the author's by then
almost smothered life-force. Indeed, her quasi-immaculate conception, like so many Biblical references in Dazai, sits there rather
isolated, without significant integration with the rest of the work.[5]
And there are other elements of the novel deriving from extra-
personal sources that also fail to cohere with the rest. One is the
running reference to *The Cherry Orchard*. Thematically, Chek-
hov's play of course treats the decline of the aristocracy, but beyond this thin resemblance, there is no reasonable basis of comparison between the play and the novel.[6] Another is the snake
imagery that appears at the death of both parents. Regardless of
the reptiles' possible psychogenetic origin, they are not adequately
shaped into a significant artistic role in the book. For instance,
there is Kazuko's disposal of the snake eggs, a snake's appearance
at her father's deathbed, the snakes' "mourning" in the garden
at his death, the "delicate, graceful" mother snake's search for
her lost eggs, and then the by-then expected appearance of a snake
at the mother's deathbed—all these episodes seem to carry some
elaborate symbolic significance, but they fall far short of making

it clear and become merely props for the scenery of impending death.

If there is one "idea" dominating the novel, it is Dazai's notion of "aristocracy." On the first page Kazuko quotes her brother's opinion: "Just because a person has a title doesn't make him an aristocrat. Some people are great aristocrats who have no other title than the one that nature has bestowed on them, and others like us, who have nothing but titles, are closer to being pariahs than aristocrats. . . . Mama is the only one in our family." [7] Later she refers to her mother as "the last [noble] lady in Japan" (p. 135; my restoration). And Naoji's "Testament" ends with the sentence, "I am an aristocrat" (p. 181; I omit "after all"). Aristocracy in this context is not merely the equivalent of a class title or birthright, but is a spiritual achievement. Alas, what constitutes such attainment is nowhere made clear in the book, since the characterization of those persons styled "aristocrats" is not full enough to bear analysis. Kazuko's mother, for instance, possessed of gracious table manners and free-spirited enough to pee in the garden under the full moon, is also stoical enough to keep smiling regardless, never be mean, always be considerate, and always be cheerful. But do such attributes make an "aristocrat"—a noblewoman, an elect? Nowhere in the novel is this titled lady allowed to be a full character, with her own thoughts and feelings, and the reader can see in her only her children's wistful longing for some distinction in their lives, for which no clearer definition or formula is provided than Dazai's global concept of "aristocracy."

As for Naoji's being an "aristocrat" there is even a larger question. The novel twice presents Naoji in his own words, once from his notebook and again from his will. "The Moon Flower Journal" is a series of aphorisms the Dazai reader has long been accustomed to:

Philosophy? Lies. Principles? Lies. Ideals? Lies. Order? Lies. Sincerity? Truth? Purity? All lies. (P. 66)

When I pretended to be precocious, people started the rumor that I was precocious. When I acted like an idler, rumor had it I was an idler. When I pretended I couldn't write a novel, people said I couldn't write. When I acted like a liar, they called me a liar. When I acted like a rich man, they started the rumor I was rich. When I feigned indifference, they classed me as the indifferent type. But when I inadvertently groaned because I was really in pain, they started the rumor that I was faking suffering.

The world is out of joint.

Doesn't that mean in effect that I have no choice but suicide?

In spite of suffering, at the thought that I was sure to end up by killing myself, I cried aloud and burst into tears. (Pp. 70–71)

His last note is more of the same, the fact that it is addressed to Kazuko only slightly differentiating the tone from that of the supposedly readerless diary:

I wanted to become coarse, to be strong—no, brutal. I thought that was the only way I could qualify myself as a "friend of the people." Liquor was not enough. [I had to be perpetually in the whirlpool of dizziness.] That was why I had no choice but to take to drugs. I had to forget my family. I had to oppose my father's blood. I had to reject my mother's gentleness. I had to be cold to my sister. I thought that otherwise I would not be able to secure an admission ticket for the rooms of the people. (P. 166)[8]

Beneath the debauchée's mask, the note asserts, Naoji conceals a noble spirit and some tender feelings. Maybe. But the reader finds in this supposedly final revelation nothing to substantiate his claim. It contains in fact little besides self-pity and an over-acquaintance with exhaustion and defeat: he cannot cope with life, so must choose death. Now, a capacity for stylish suffering may be the sine qua non of the elect, but that alone does not suffice. As Dazai himself recognized in his quotation from Verlaine in his very first publication, what is also needed is the intelligence to understand the despair and the strength to transform it into the joy of life. Naoji's death-wish is perfectly understandable—

his life does seem wretched enough. But the death-wish alone cannot admit one to the aristocracy.

One has to question why Dazai felt he had to revive the notion of aristocracy anyway, especially in those postwar years when so much of the legal and hereditary hierarchy was being dismantled. Of course, "class" might reasonably survive and even flourish in a vertical society such as Japan's, suddenly leveled in the early postwar period by starvation, worthless yen, and the U.S. occupation policy. But even more to the point, perhaps, is the author's own quasi-aristocratic background. That he was an "aristocrat" is usually taken for granted by the largely middle-class Japanese critics,[9] who also believe that his underground politics in the 1930s and his lifelong rebellion against various authority figures (father, eldest brother, the state, teachers, the literary establishment) had a common origin in his guilt for having been high born.[10] But there is something unauthentic about Dazai's so-called high birth. Rich and powerful the Tsushimas may have been, yet they do not belong to the families of feudal lords (*daimyō*) or courtiers (*kuge*). Dazai was brought up like any other small-town middle-class child of the 1920s. For instance, he attended regular public schools (not the Peers' School and College—the Gaku-shūin), and he had no firsthand knowledge whatsoever of the Japanese aristocracy, which was a very exclusive club indeed in prewar days. It is no exaggeration to say that Dazai's upper-class identification was more dream than reality. True, among radicals he may have felt a little sheepish about his landlord father and comfortable upbringing, and yet can't we see this "guilt" as at least in part a sneaky regret for not *really* belonging to the actual aristocracy, which alone could presumably license for him some genuine guilt about his background, in the style of a new Hamlet or a latter-day Lord Sanetomo?

The lie can be accounted for in several ways. During the Meiji era writers, as we saw in chapter 1, had considerable difficulty locating the right level of reverence for the narrator. Should he look up to his reader or talk down to him? Is he primarily teacher or entertainer? Since that time, the Japanese novelist has studied the West and learned about the serious role of the artist in modern society as well as certain things about the Western art of novel writing. But exactly what constitutes the artist and his "voice" has never been satisfactorily decided: he is neither a poet-philosopher who speaks for the whole nation, such as Balzac and George Eliot wished they could be, nor an alienated critic like Proust or Joyce who speaks for a select few. Surely he is a *sensei*, a master. But what does he teach? Except for a few like Kawabata, most Japanese writers had to fall back on the old Confucian notion of the master respected not primarily for his craft but for his knowledge, experience, and wisdom. Dazai too wrote from the assigned position of a wise teacher documenting his learning and experience even while totally rejecting the conventional morality. It is on such insights, well hidden behind the cloak of depravity, that the "aristocratic" label should be pinned. As a decadent rebel, however, Dazai discovered early in the game that his peerage would not be recognized by the philistines at large, whose support he certainly needed, especially in his moments of loneliness. It is at this point that he made the imaginary leap from the fictional (but in a way real) claim to selection by achievement to the literal (but fake) claim to selection by birth. Very much like Oscar Wilde's double-edged paradox of fiction and reality, this complicated manipulation of fact and fabrication must have had enormous appeal for Dazai the "soothsayer."

Still there is a confusion inherent in the notion of "aristocracy" in *The Setting Sun* which I see as inseparable from Dazai's childlike uncertainty about the whole social milieu and how to relate to it. He defied authorities all his life, but he was also invariably in awe of them. There are many stories about his hankering for acceptance, of which his desperate wish for the Akutagawa prize, a kind of Japanese Pulitzer prize, is only one example.* And he was never able to resolve conflicting impulses in relating to others. He fared better with those socially beneath him, but even then he

* When Dazai's "The Flower of Clowning" was nominated for the newly created Akutagawa prize in 1935, he pestered his sponsor Satō Haruo to fight for the prize for him. Satō records his annoyance at Dazai's greed in his "Akutagawa Shō," collected in Koyama Kiyoshi's *Dazai Osamu Kenkyū* (Toyko: Chikuma Shobō, 1956), pp. 397–415. Incidentally, one of the judges voting for one of Dazai's rivals was Kawabata Yasunari.

was no Whitmanesque prophet of the streets. Only with his youthful admirers does he seem to have felt truly at ease.

In a vertical society, a person with no developed sense of his own place, one who cannot "size up" at once his relative position of superiority or inferiority with anyone he comes into contact with, is lost. He will not even be able to conduct a comfortable conversation with anyone except a close friend. If he happens to be a writer, the results might very well be disastrous. For the novel, unlike poetry, must define a character within an actual society; the writer must locate his sympathy or hostility on the social map so that he may set out the novel's scenes, shape its plot, and populate its world. And this is exactly what Dazai was unable to do. Those early radical activities of his notwithstanding, he soon became wholly indifferent to political problems; despite his frequent references to Marxism and the Revolution, his social and political understanding did not go beyond the level of the average high-school student. True, Dazai was an uncomfortable person, and he felt vague sentiments for social justice. But he possessed neither an analytic mind nor adequate knowledge of his society to do anything about it. *The Setting Sun* is not only vague in its notion of aristocracy; it also lacks sufficient scale and the sort of developed attitude toward its society that would provide a powerful and comprehensive vision of postwar Japan.

And yet we recall that the book was wildly popular around 1950, contributing the word *shayō-zoku* (the people of the setting sun) to the nation's vocabulary. Besides, Dazai accomplished something no other writer could do in recent Japan—he brought colloquialism back to the written language.

In the multiple-leveled Japanese language, Dazai's awkwardness in finding the correct social position for himself in the pyramid parallels his inability to find the correct level of reverence in speech. It should be remembered here that the system of honorifics is, as we saw in chapter 1, not a level of politeness, and not "cultured speech." It is a whole involved process of minutely adjusting one's every utterance to conform to tacitly assumed relative positions among speaker, listener, and referent. However distasteful one may find this assumption of hierarchy—although very few Japanese would readily challenge *the* first principle of their society—there is simply no easy way out of the linguistic constriction. A neutral level exists only in the artificially created area of official announcements and technical writing, and nowhere in ordinary speech situations involving speaker, listener, and referent. Even more difficult to learn is the art of silence—the highest decorum in Japanese culture—whereby the socially inferior expresses deference to his superior by the shut mouth, not speaking at all. Expression, even of respect, is often a rude assertion of the self that is rejected by those who hold firm to the tradition of the language and its value. Dazai, however, at once rebel and philistine in language as in life, could neither commit himself fully to the system of honorifics nor abandon it entirely. Use of a formal and correct Japanese employing subtle gradations of hierarchy would place him as a member of the fold, which he is not; a rough and slangy Japanese overriding precise gradations would make him a churlish schoolboy, which he also is not—besides, even the most vulgar speech is never free from implied caste. Thus, as in social intercourse, Dazai is always slightly bewildered, slightly fidgety where Japanese is concerned. And this speech embarrassment, part and parcel of his social awkwardness, is powerfully operative in the making of his style. For instance, no one is more sensitive than Dazai to the possibility that any mode of speech may turn absurd. Whenever his writing turns a bit too ponderous, or affected, or cumbersome, or rigid, or just too formal, he shifts into reverse and writes with humor, or a meticulously measured colloquialism, or vulgarisms, or babyish onomatopoeia, or a sprinkling of learned diction and foreign words, here and there a grotesque word, an archaism or two, or he omits a pronoun or a postposition, or he staccatos a passage with overpunctuation. Occasionally, especially in the aphoristic diary pieces, he can somehow manage to stay neutral, but even there his remarkable awareness of the ever-possible absurdity keeps his style clear of the turgid and the affected alike.

Those who know Japanese sense this at once, although I am aware of how hard it is to convey the sense of it to those who don't know the language. What Edward Seidensticker meant when he called Dazai a "poet" [11] is at least partly this quality, I believe. And I regret that discussion of the precise dynamics of one language is extremely difficult to conduct in another. The translations of the works are of little help sometimes in getting across this "poetic" quality. Donald Keene's version of *The Setting Sun,* for example, though generally excellent, fails at times to transmit the nuances of the rude and the polite in Dazai's writing that makes his style dance with such rare grace. I can only point to the drunken chant at Uehara's party, "Guillotine, Guillotine, shooshooshoo" (p. 147), or the old mother's use of the word *oshikko* (wee-wee) as bringing in just the right touch of absurdity to the respective passages which, by a sort of juxtaposition and reversal, set in motion waves of rich connotation. Probably Dazai's most notable stylistic accomplishment lies in his creation of that pervasive feeling of shyness and embarrassment in his work, reflecting the overwhelming absurdity he so purely perceived all around him. The gap between the spoken and the written language is still a very serious problem for the Japanese writer, and Dazai managed to show at least one direction for a possible coming together of the two.

The "I-novel" reaches a dead end once the author's life is completely exposed. After that, further writing risks a redundancy which is nauseating for the writer himself as well as for his reader.* Then his imagination must get to work inventing new experiences to write about. The rewriting of older works, *Hamlet* for Dazai or *The Tale of Genji* for Tanizaki, may afford temporary relief, but when that has been tried, unless the writer's psychic makeup is extraordinarily vigorous, like Tanizaki's, he will not have much to do except tackle the one experience no one has ever personally reported on—death. Thus the *shi-shōsetsu* writer is never free of the temptation of suicide. Dazai's four fail-

---

* Deliverance from the cursed *shi-shōsetsu* maze is certainly not by way of "polished style," as many Japanese critics seem to believe. Shiga Naoya, for instance, whose scorn of Dazai drove the author to almost hysterical fury (as expressed in "Thus Have I Heard" [*Nyoze Gabun*], 1948), is as much a victim of the whole convention as Dazai himself. Shiga's extraordinary failure of self-criticism is repugnant to any critical reader, and yet, quite surprisingly, his smug self-portrait, *Through the Dark Night* (*An'ya Kōro*) (1921–37), is quite widely hailed as a masterpiece by Japanese readers—with the exception of a few such as Nakamura Mitsuo. See his *Sakka Ron* (Tokyo: Kōdansha, 1957), I, 10–139, esp. 83–89.

ures at death were in a way requirements of his art. His fifth attempt, the successful one, was also required.* The *shi-shōsetsu*, by its own logic, will not close until the writer's life closes. And Dazai himself had to bring it to its conclusion. If Naoji and Kazuko and Uehara are "victims," so is Dazai a victim—of the Japanese novel, of the Japanese language.

* Some biographers believe that Dazai did not really want to take his own life, but was forced into the double suicide by his companion. While this is not impossible, there seems to be little hard evidence for it. Besides, whatever may have been the immediate circumstances of his suicide, Dazai's lifelong will to death is hard to deny.

Shocked at Mishima's death, several critics wrote about suicide and Japanese writers. Yoshida Seiichi, in his article "Bungakusha no Jisatsu to Mishima no Shi," *Gunzō*, XXVI (February, 1971), 205–11, chronicles about thirty suicides by writers just since the Meiji era. His list does not pretend to be all inclusive, of course. In a special issue of *Kokubungaku: Kaishaku to Kanshō* (December, 1971) entitled *The Writer and Suicide (Sakka to Jisatsu)*, Ōhara Kenshirō (editor of the issue) points out that the suicide rate for Japanese writers is "three hundred times higher than that for Japanese men as a whole" (p. 18). Although Ōhara's evidence for his figure is necessarily quite flimsy (who is a "writer," for instance?), there is no question but that the suicide rate for Japanese novelists, poets, intellectuals, free-lancers, pulp writers, and so on is extremely high. For further discussion of this see chapter 6, on Mishima.

VI
MUTE'S RAGE

MISHIMA YUKIO: *Confessions of a Mask* and *The Temple of the Golden Pavilion*
—Nothingness was the very structure of this beauty.

The shocking harakiri was called for by the shooting-star course of his life. This most talented and spirited of the postwar Japanese novelists produced over thirty novels, scores of plays, and numerous essays and pamphlets totaling well over a hundred volumes.[1] Yet he also found time and vitality to practice *kendō* and *karate*, weight-lifting, and other body-building exercises, to sing, model, act in films, organize his own army and design its uniforms, get married, stay married, travel, run with the jet set, and entertain lavishly. There were hints along the way, particularly during the last several of his impatient forty-five years, when there appeared a kind of frenzy in his life, though we know from his well-known bursts of uninhibited laughter that he stayed courteous and full of fun and self-irony. Mishima had also read the world's literature exceptionally well, from Euripides to Witold Gombrowicz, and Japanese works from *Kojiki* to unknown new writers, and in his own life he would allow not the slightest hint of any misidentification of book and life. Indeed, he often expressed unqualified contempt for men like Dazai who had supremely confused the two. Referring to the *shi-shōsetsu* writer, he asked, "Why do some Japanese writers feel the curious impulse to become characters in fiction?" [2] He wanted his characters to speak for themselves, not for their author. Yet, for all that determination, there is a strange still point just beneath the dizzying whirl of words and gestures, the silent decibel of an ever-present horror.

The horror is discernible even in his analytic writing about fiction. Mishima wrote a great deal about the novel, and one of his most serious discussions is a long, incomplete essay, "What Is the Novel?" (*Shōsetsu towa Nanika*), which was being serialized at the time of his death. Here he categorizes fiction (as against the quasi-fiction of the historical novel, the I-novel, the documentary novel) as "having a conclusive finality in language expression" (meaning, no further reference beyond language) and as "belonging to a dimension totally different from that of facts, no matter how much resemblance to facts the objects and events within a work may have." [3]

This direction in Mishima's thoughts about fictional language says something about the complex organization of his imagination. For instance, referring to the need for right naming, he says that, faced with the job of naming, in fiction, any object little known to the general reader, the novelist feels he has three choices. Take the problem of naming something like the obscure type of door known in Japanese architecture as the "Maira door": the writer can explain it without giving it a specific name ("the door, often seen in old homes, that has many horizontal crosspieces"), or he can coin a descriptive phrase ("the horizontal-crosspiece door"), or he can use the right name while sneaking in an explanation ("Maira door, is that the name?, the door with many horizontal crosspieces"). Mishima's method is still another, to name it by its right name, leaving to the uninformed reader the job of finding what exactly the name refers to. Of the three substitute expressions, the first is unsatisfactory because, while the writer is observing the object correctly, he is not at all earnest about locating the right name; the second, coining an expression, is irresponsible because, quite simply, no such expression exists; the third, however, is the worst. Mishima dislikes this the most because the writer, though vaguely aware of the accepted name, is shifting responsibility for confirming its accuracy onto either the character or the reader. The writer is not committed to language, and this attitude of indecision and hanging back is grafted onto the character as well.

There is a good deal to be said in favor of his argument. Somewhat reminiscent of Ezra Pound's principle of "ching ming" (true naming), Mishima's essentially conservative insistence on the use of the right name for a thing is salutary in view of the chaos of neologisms and loan words of the modern Japanese vocabulary. At the same time, there are two notable unclarities, which might reveal something important about his fictional stance but which are never resolved here.

First, Mishima's notion of a "conclusive finality of language expression" ("language is all") is not argued thoroughly enough. Does he mean that "meaning" in fiction is determined solely by the context of the work without further reference to the outside world? If this is so, shouldn't we say that the differences among the four names for "Maira door"—the right name and three spurious "names"—constitute different meanings? Why this puristic attitude that one "right name" alone can assure fictional autonomy, regardless of context?

Second—and this is surprising—Mishima consciously and assertively takes a stand against letting characters choose their own language, regardless of dramatic necessity: "It is an annoying wrongheadedness to make use of a deliberate pretension of ignorance for the purpose of expressing the character's carelessness." That is, every word written in fiction reflects only the author's own judgment, and not the character's. In its final sense, this is of course true of any literary work, but that is not what Mishima means here: when his characters are allowed to speak, their language must always be their author's. All expressions must be "accurate" in the sense of "correct," "right," or "authentic." And, although this statement may explain Mishima's usually orthodox and decorous style, it points at the same time to an essential contradiction between his practice and his often pronounced belief in objectivity.

It seems, then, that what Mishima means to stress by insisting on the autonomy and finality of expression is not so much the ontological independence of a work from both author and subject matter as a sort of finish or hard-polished surface which in actuality may have very little to do with the sought-for "objectivity" in a work of art.

The essay includes an analysis of his last work, *The Sea of Fertility,* the third volume of which had just been completed, and here Mishima returns to the question of the autonomy of fiction. He talks about the uncertain future awaiting both the tetralogy and himself, but goes on to say this does not mean that "the future world of the work itself and the future of the real world will ever merge and mix, just like the parallel lines in a non-Euclidian mathematics. . . . The future of the work is already potentially there in the two thousand sheets so far written, and its future will not be able to avoid the inherent inevitability. It is inconceivable that the end of the future world of the work and the end of the real world will perfectly coincide in time." This insistence on the essential separation of art and life is of course gratuitous: no one questions that the two will never meet. And yet he must emphatically reiterate it. "When Balzac was sick," he remembers, "he had to cry for a doctor out of his own work. Writers often confuse the two realities. For me, though, the most essential methodology in art and life has been never to confuse them. . . . For me, the fundamental impulse for writing is born from the contrast and tension between the two realities." The expression "contrast and tension" is ambiguous enough; with a slight shift in emphasis, the meaning could almost be reversed:

> I cannot think of the world after the end of this work; I hate and fear to imagine that world. When these floating realities finally part, one to be discarded and the other to be sealed into a work, what will happen to my freedom? . . . Unless the reality outside my work forcefully carries me away, I will someday fall into deep despair—though I am fully prepared for it. To come to think of it, I was even in my childhood always waiting for a disaster that might never come. . . . And that childhood habit still continues, turning me into a writer who cannot work without the sense of crisis coming from the contrast and tension between the two realities.[4]

Life and art must be kept separate, but the "contrast and tension" between them intensify to an unbearable pitch as they hopelessly mingle and threaten to merge. In the subtle dialectic of Mishima's imagination, the face and the masks, life's reality and art's, are forcibly separated, and yet they continually move together. The "objectivity" of his fiction is itself but one more mask, and rather a transparent one at that. How absurdly appropriate, then, that the date of completion, November 25, 1970, attached to the end of the last volume of the tetralogy, his final and most ambitious work, should be the day he chose to end his life.

Mishima Yukio, or Hiraoka Kimitake (or Kōi), the oldest son of an upper-echelon civil servant, was born in Tokyo in 1925. Though remotely connected with the last generation of the Tokugawa shogunate family, the Hiraoka family had no claim to a title. Despite this, they had some pretensions to aristocracy: Mishima's given name, for instance, means "princely dignity." And his parents felt their son should be educated at the Peers' School and College (Gakushūin), which until the end of the war was an institution belonging to the Imperial Household and devoted largely to the proper education of the royal scions and the children of the aristocracy. He was a sickly child, but he did well in the school. At his graduation, he was cited by the Emperor for the highest achievement in his class. He began to write while still in his teens and adopted his pen name soon afterward. Although he graduated in law from the University of Tokyo and worked briefly in a promising post in the Ministry of Finance, he resigned from his job in 1948 on the strength of a score of short stories published in various journals. He was just twenty-three years old, but from the beginning of his writing career, he had the knack of making just the right contact at the right time in the closely knit Tokyo literary world, and his rise was dazzling.

The early works are not very good. Mishima's first volume, *The Forest in Full Bloom (Hanazakari no Mori,* 1944), is a collection of precociously decadent and detachedly romantic stories, many of which recollect a colorful but boring upper-class life long gone even then. Also they provide a heavy dose of nationalistic rhetoric glorifying the beauty and elegance of the Imperial past

—a fact interesting in view of their author's later works. The elaborate and archaic vocabulary and general aloofness to the drab and wretched scenes of wartime Japan similarly foreshadow his mature works, whose motifs, images, and themes are already apparent. With *Confessions of a Mask* (*Kamen no Kokuhaku*), published in a single volume in 1949, Mishima entered the forefront of the Tokyo literati.

The book is divided into four chapters of varying length. The account of the protagonist's relationship with Sonoko lasting for some four years occupies the second half, while his development up to the late teens constitutes the first. Overall, the progress of the plot follows the protagonist's growing-up years with no temporal disruption. Structurally, however, there is no clear beginning, middle, and end, nor is the division into four marked by any discernible stages. It is notable, too, that the narrative tempo slackens considerably as the work proceeds.

In the earliest part, the "I's" memory is spotty. At the opening, we are told of a rim of light he remembers from his own birthscene, reflected from the edge of the round basin in which he had his first bath. The story quickly turns to his survival, at the age of five, of a near fatal illness caused, we are told casually between dashes, by autointoxication. Without dwelling on the possible meaning of such spots of time and experience, he hurries on to an account of how as a child he was inexplicably excited by such things as the sight of a nightsoil man, the smell of soldiers' sweat, or a picture of Joan of Arc. The references are all in quick succession in the first ten pages with little analysis from the narrator. As the "I's" self-awareness develops, there is an increase in frequency of more analytic comments which connect the episodes. Also, as he grows older and the distance between experiencing self and narrating self diminishes, the narrator begins to concentrate on his sexual impulses, which focus alternately on Sonoko and his own body. There is now a full analytic commentary on each episode, retarding the passage of time and intensifying self-consciousness. The change in narrative style of course underlines the changes that occur between childhood and youth, in the perception of time and the self, but more importantly it dictates a change in the modality of the work from that of a highly imagistic, "poetic" narration to a more novelistic one. The gain in psychological fullness appears to be at the expense of lyrical intensity.

Since the term "lyrical" presupposes subjectivity and privacy, what is the significance of the title, "confessions of a mask"? How confessional is the work, and what is the mask?

It is undeniable that Mishima makes full use of the material of his personal life. The "I's" family, education, induction, and job experiences, even his life-chronology parallel Mishima's own, even to the extent that the "I's" first name, "Kō-chan," mentioned a few times, is a common diminutive of Mishima's real first name. There seem to be only a few deliberate alterations of details, such as his father's first name. As for the dominant circumstances of the work, the narrator's sexual inversion and his relationship with Sonoko, there is no reason to believe either that they are literally true, or that they fall completely outside the author's experience. Although I am not thoroughly familiar with the biographical details of Mishima's youth, nor am I aware that a good study of his early years as yet even exists, autoeroticism and homosexuality themes do appear continually in his works, some of the scenes from this novel recurring elsewhere in almost identical form. Presumably, too, Mishima's pursuits in later years—his military games and relentless practice of body-building exercises, for instance—also confirm his main sexual orientation. Thus there is little question that the narrated life and Mishima's personal experience do conform at least in outline.

But to locate such a correspondence between life and art need not mean that *Confessions of a Mask* is a personal account. For justifying the paradox, we need only refer to the truism that *any* literary work, even if intentionally "autobiographical," is always fictional, since it is bound to select and arrange, and hence interpret. Mishima's is an even more daring gesture, as though the purpose of his "confession" were solely to mock the Japanese literary preoccupation with the personal I-novel. There is evidence here of a calculated aura of exposure meant to deflate the slightest suspicion of dishonesty; and there also appears to be a determination to "show the worst" so that possible charges against it of fictionality, deception, and hypocrisy may be dismissed once for all. The bull (of the I-novel) is thus taken by the horns (of honesty and truth). And once successfully released in this way from the clutches of confessionalism, he would be free to tell his story, which is a fictive form despite its use of nonfictive facts, circumstances, and truths. Those who want to know the inner and outer reality of Hiraoka Kimitake's personal life will learn very little from the book. The character of the "I" is surprisingly flat and volumeless, as I would like to show later.*

Confessions of a Mask is in the first person. Obviously, the narrated self merges into the narrator at the end where both are a young man in his early twenties. But even at the very beginning the distance between the two is not really noticeable. Unlike the mature Pip recalling the young Pip, the narrator takes no advantage of the great ironic possibilities inherent in age and experience distancing. One reason may be that the narrator himself is still a young man and thus not so "distant" from the scene after all. But there is something more to it than that. Just as the imaging in the earlier parts is of such a striking clarity, the immediacy of the narrator's recall of his earliest days is also remarkable. Thus, instead of an older man interpreting as he presents his younger self, this younger self is essentially one with a still-young narrator. For this effect, the loose tense of the Japanese is highly successful. The narrator's story is often in the present tense, which essentially obscures the distinction between time past and time present.

---

* *Confessions of a Mask* is obviously susceptible to psychoanalytic interpretation. Its bizarre fantasies (especially the Saint Sebastian image, and the dream fantasy of cooking a live friend, stabbing a fork into his heart, and slicing his flesh), together with the narcissism and inversion themes, clearly invite such treatment. There is one psychoanalytic study called *Mishima Yukio niokeru Nanshoku to Tennōsei* by Yamasaki Masao (Tokyo: Guraffiku-sha, 1971), but its argument is both unscrupulous and unintelligent. There is also a publication giving Mishima's Rorschach responses and their analysis by Kataguchi Yasushi, but I have not been able as yet to obtain it. In the "Writer and Suicide" issue of *Kokubungaku: Kaishaku to Kanshō* (December, 1971), Hasegawa Izumi gives a biographical sketch that is as of now the fullest account of Mishima's life. His father, Hiraoka Azusa, has published a memoir, *Segare, Mishima Yukio* (Tokyo: Bungei Shunjū, 1972); it is quite incoherent and contains little information. An American article tracing the bloody images throughout Mishima's works, "Greek Hero and Japanese Samurai: Mishima's New Aesthetic," by Gwenn R. Boardman, *Critique*, XII (1970), 103–113, while not specifically Freudian, is suggestive.

Where this happens, the narrative sequence following the "I's" chronology does not easily yield a thoroughgoing consequentiality which arranges events into a plot, nor does it suggest an over-all connected meaning. The power of the work arises instead from intensity and concentration of feeling. In this sense, *Confessions of a Mask* takes rather the form of a lyric than of a novel.*

What then is this feeling that focuses the narrative? We may consider some possibilities. Is it the narrator's agonized isolation resulting from his knowledge of his sexual inversion? His recognition of the gap between ought and is? His despair over the conflict between homosexual impulses and his determination to be fully heterosexual? Or, the obverse of such awareness, an utter narcissism? Perhaps they are all represented in the book, and yet we sense they are finally a little irrelevant. The "feeling" I am talking about here is not particularly the "I's," but our own feeling aroused as we read. The "I" in fact is amazingly devoid of most normal feelings; it is almost as if he had set out to eliminate from the narrative any trace of an emotion he might once have felt. Take his relations with his family: he never records his emotional responses to them. When his sister dies, at the beginning of chapter 4, he remarks how he "derived a superficial peace of mind from the discovery that even [he] could shed tears." [5] How are we to take this? Should we be impressed by his toughness? Or tacitly grant that he has some tender brotherly feelings under that mask of indifference? Or is it possible that the writer is sitting on the

---

* One might recall here some of Virginia Woolf's works, although her "lyrical novels" like *Mrs. Dalloway* and *To the Lighthouse* are informed by a rigorous time-sense.

In "My Wandering Years" (*Watakushi no Henreki Jidai*, 1961), collected in a book with the same title (Tokyo: Kōdansha, 1964), Mishima, talking about the background of the *Confessions,* maintains that "ignorance as youth's privilege" is an idea "suitable for poetry, but not for the novel," adding that even so he "tried to force it into the novel form" (p. 42). He made several assertions elsewhere regarding the "un-autobiographical" nature of the work. Toward the end of his life, however, in remarks on the *Confessions* during his interview with Akiyama Shun— in *Taidan: Watakushi no Bungaku,* ed. Akiyama Shun (Tokyo: Kōdansha, 1969), p. 88—he seems to have admitted that it reflected his actual feelings during much of his adolescence.

fence, striking a pose for both effects, while not really knowing for sure what sort of sensibility he should give his character? *

Of the more important relationships in the book, take that of the "I" and Ōmi. Clearly, he loves Ōmi as he does nobody else. But to say that is to say that Ōmi arouses him sexually as does no other friend (we leave aside all the soldiers and laborers the very sight and smell of whom has excited him since childhood). Ōmi is beautiful, strong, and rebellious. But his character qualities do not matter much; it is his appearance—his body—that arouses the narrator. It is as if the adored Saint Sebastian had stepped right out of the Guido Reni painting and stood before him. If the "I's" passion here is genuine, it is also exclusively physical. And Ōmi isn't even aware of it, as the Saint Sebastian in the picture would not be either. Actually there is hardly any reciprocal feeling between the two. If there is on the narrator's part a sort of painful groping for Ōmi, it should not be confused with a striving for Ōmi's love or approval, for his expectations exclude all but the hardest sexual pleasures, which he can, after all, indulge all by himself. There is the lovely scene of the early morning after a snowstorm, where the "I" follows a set of fresh footprints with the vague feeling they may be Ōmi's, until they spell Ōmi's name and the "I" and his friend stand face to face. For a moment, there is just a hint that the "I" may be encountering someone as lonely and fearful as himself: "The instant I had seen that enormous OMI drawn in the snow, I had understood, perhaps half-unconsciously, all the nooks and corners of his loneliness—understood also the real motive, probably not clearly understood even by himself, that brought him to school this early in the morning . . ." (p. 60). But that is not the way the "I" meets Ōmi or anybody else. Ōmi, boyishly shy and awkward, thrusts his leather gloves against the cheeks of the "I," whose reaction is "a raw carnal

---

* In a short-story essay, "Chair" (*Isu*, 1951), Mishima describes his relationship with his mother and grandmother in greater detail, although even here the narrative voice stays detached and ironic. *Selected Works* (see note 2), X, 65–80. At the same time, in a short essay called "The Departure from the Feeling of an End" (*Shūmatsukan kara no Shuppatsu*), his actual feelings on his sister's death are described as violent. He writes that he loved his sister almost incomprehensibly, and that he totally broke down when she died. *Collected Essays* (see note k), p. 416.

feeling" that blazes up within him (p. 61). Sympathy and irritability, intimacy and self-defensiveness, affection and hatred —such impure combinations of feelings that muddle and enrich human intercourse are almost totally alien to the "I," who chooses to keep his crystal-clear sexual image of Ōmi and his own specific sexual response free of all such ambiguities. Thus, once Ōmi is expelled from school (only about thirty pages after he first appears in the story), he promptly ceases to exist for the "I." There is, for this young man, no silly missing his friend, no indulgent dwelling on the past.

Sonoko's entry into the *Confessions* is preceded by the sound of her piano practice which the "I" overhears while visiting her brother. (The piano music motif recurs later on in the *Confessions* when the "I" tries to pick up their relationship again after her marriage.) Thus *Sonoko* is of sound, as Ōmi is of images. In this sense, as sound penetrates more deeply than the visual image, Sonoko is ready from the beginning to move more deeply into his consciousness than Ōmi can. Here then there may be more likelihood of some reciprocity. But does it happen really?

The narrator is moved by her innocent beauty. Under the threat of war and all its dangers, they are drawn to each other. But can he love her? He begins to feel that for a fulfilled life he must be close to Sonoko, but can he develop real feelings of pleasure in sexual contact with her? He wonders, and Sonoko thus becomes a test by which he might prove his heterosexuality. Her family leaves Tokyo for the duration, and he visits her in the country. Their courtship now assumed by her family, he feels he must conduct the final test. When he kisses her and feels no pleasure whatever, he at once concludes he can never love her.

They break off but he meets her again after her marriage, and they resume the relationship. On one of their rendezvous he takes her to a dance hall, only to find his attention drawn irresistibly to the nude perspiring torso of a young laborer.

At this sight, above all at the sight of the peony tattooed on his hard chest, I was beset by sexual desire. My fervent gaze was fixed upon that rough and savage, but incomparably beautiful body. Its owner was laughing there under the sun. When he threw back his head I could see his thick, muscular neck. A strange shudder ran through my innermost heart. I could no longer take my eyes off him.

I had forgotten Sonoko's existence. I was thinking of but one thing: Of his going out onto the streets of high summer just as he was, half-naked, and getting into a fight with a rival gang. Of a sharp dagger cutting through that belly-band, piercing that torso. Of that soiled belly-band beautifully dyed with blood. Of his gory corpse being put on an improvised stretcher, made of a window shutter, and brought back here. (P. 252)

Sonoko has to go home at that point, and as the "I" stands up, now fully realizing what he is and what he is not, what he can be and what he cannot be, his eye catches the puddle of a spilt drink "throwing back glittering, threatening reflections" from the table (p. 254). We may recall the bright rim of light he remembers from his birth-scene.

Even from this brief outline of their relationship, one can see how the story is centered on the narrator himself, and how it ignores her side entirely, dismissing even her response to him. Just as Ōmi was no more than a part of his fantasy, Sonoko, too, is merely an aspect of his self-experiment. She will do as he dictates. If she cannot arouse him, she is of no use to him and he must leave her. If there is any discomfort on his part, it is not over the injustice to Sonoko, but related solely to his realization of his "destiny." Throughout the book, there is only the "I" who feels and does not feel, thinking about himself, looking at himself. This "I" fills the whole story, leaving no room for anybody else. Where then does the intense lyricism, the almost moving sadness, come from?

There is nothing about narcissism which is essentially antithetical to lyricism. Some of Wordsworth's poems are just as self-centered as the *Confessions*, if not more so. But even in egotism, Wordsworth knew how to let himself go and move toward otherness, often in doing so lifting the weight of the mere self to the height of sublimity. With Mishima, however, the narrator seldom lets himself go with his powerful emotions. As soon as they are registered, loneliness and despair—or joy and pleasure on a few occasions—are intelligently outlined and effectively dealt with. For instance, when still a further test of his heterosexuality fails —he visits a whore with a friend—he describes this reaction:

> I assumed that my friend had no suspicion of what had happened, and surprisingly enough, during the next few days I surrendered myself to the drab feelings of convalescence. I was like a person who has been suffering an unknown disease in an agony of fear: just learning the name of his disease, even though it is an incurable one, gives him a surprising feeling of temporary relief. He knows well, though, that the relief is only temporary. Moreover, in his heart he foresees a still more inescapable hopelessness, which, by its very nature, will give a more permanent feeling of relief. I too had probably come to expect a blow that it would be even more impossible to parry, or to say it another way, a more inescapable feeling of relief. (Pp. 226–27)

The paradox seems to sustain him for a while. Then, his friend lets him know he knows.

> My cursed visitors finally left at eleven o'clock, and I shut myself up for a sleepless night in my room. I cried sobbingly until at last those visions reeking with blood came to comfort me. And I surrendered myself to them, to those deplorably brutal visions, my most intimate friends. (P. 228)

Where even his visions are part of a rational plan, there would seem to be little room for lyricism.

In this book of confessions in which almost everything is taken note of and accounted for, there is one thing the narrator leaves largely unanalyzed, and this is the gradual change in the attitude of the "I" toward his self-understanding. In the first chapter the story is wholly episodic, and the "I" understands, in his own way, what he is doing. But he is never self-conscious about his mode of self-understanding. His reaction to the nightsoil man and other physical workers; his fascination with the picture of a knight on a white horse (ending abruptly when he is told the knight is a

woman); his excitement at smelling soldiers' sweat; his early
transvestitism; his sadistic rewriting of Andersen's "Nightingale";
his war games with his cousins that inevitably end in his own
death in battle; and his ecstasy over the riotous drunks at the summer festival—these spots of time are arrested in cold clear pictures. And there is little intervention by the narrator as he records
these scenes from his childhood, or what he calls his "preamble to
[his] life" (p. 20).

In chapter 2 the "I" is already an adolescent, but still unbur-
dened by the full knowledge of sexuality. Thus, in the scene of
his first masturbation in front of the Saint Sebastian picture, the
"I" is essentially innocent of the meaning of his act. Rather, it is
an immediate experience of sexuality that allows him the pleasure
without the knowledge of "perversity." Such pleasure, an experience of beauty really and one still unpolluted by knowledge and
guilt, is granted him only a little longer. His erotic vision of the
ocean as he dreams of Ōmi (pp. 86–87) is one of the few really
beautiful passages in the book, because his observation, clear of
worrisome self-consciousness, allows him to respond sensuously
and immediately with a remarkable freedom from the distortions
of analysis and introspection. The scene ends in masturbation
(this time involving, almost incredibly, his own armpits), yet still
glows with innocence.

By the time Sonoko makes her appearance, however, his time
of grace is over: knowledge and doubt have begun to torment him.
All pleasure, all experience of beauty, must now be dissected in
terms of other relationships. His indifference to women is now
"impotence"; his autoeroticism "inversion"; and his male friendship "perversity." Instead of the pure experience of pleasure and
beauty, a gnawing doubt and anxiety seek to name and evaluate
it, with the inevitable consequence that the edges of experience
itself are dulled and obscured. The "I's" innocence is irrevocably
lost.

It is absurd to see *Confessions of a Mask* as simply a record of
a young homosexual, almost as absurd as calling *Lolita* a memoir
of a child molester. There is a certain aspect of loneliness that only
a sexual pathology can accurately shape. Thus homosexuality and
autoeroticism in Mishima's work are not allowed to be the end-

meaning of the story, but are made to serve as metaphors. What is more, the worry over one's perversion can serve as a fit metaphor for a knowledge, only gradually and painfully attained, of the transience of childhood and the passage of time. There is an intense sadness to this loss reverberating far beneath and beyond the author's personal life.

There are two further aspects of the *Confessions* that need at least brief discussion: first, its aristocratic setting, and second, the background of the War.

Upper-class experience is no doubt a fact of Mishima's personal life. But in this work, the life style of privileged families—with their numerous servants and regular summer vacations—is not so obtrusively center stage as it often is in later works. To be sure, the connections and friendships developed at the "I's" school—Gakushūin, obviously, though not identified as such—are an integral part of the work, just as they were very important to Mishima personally in his youth. And yet even in this novel, there is already at work an extraordinary sensibility regarding class distinctions. The boy's sexual response to the nightsoil man, for instance, is not just one example of a rich kid's romantic sympathy for the poor and underprivileged; there is something more psychological here, resembling a masochistic identification. One may note, in this connection, that the youngster's friendships are exclusively with other students of the same school, and yet the narrator is completely silent about the relatively inferior position he must have held within the group itself, a clique known for its morbidly acute sense of social hierarchy and characterized as such in the book itself. More important, the narrator chooses to talk of things and experiences belonging exclusively to this class. The reference inventory of *Confessions of a Mask* gives its territory an aura as artificial and romantic as that of any Camelot. With Mishima—even more so than with Dazai—devotion to the aristocratic life style is pure pastoral wish-fulfillment, but it is also a defensive tactic which would manipulate the unwary into suspending some important critical responses. If it works here, it is because the young hero's behavior is not so different from that of an ordinary middle-class youth. At times, especially in those novels serialized in the women's magazines, Mishima is downright vulgar in the way he hands over the sagas of aristocrats—almost like fan magazine exposés of the semi-scandalous lives of movie stars of whom the reader is assumed to have no intimate knowledge at all. And while we understand that the "aristocratic" setting is in some sense Mishima's way of presenting more and greater possibilties for life than those allowed by middle-class experience—his equivalent of Ōgai's "imported life"—we also get the feeling he may be playing with fire.

Indeed, this snobbishness was more damaging to Mishima's work than he realized. Take the scene in which the narrator has just returned from a visit to Sonoko's brother. He arrived back in Tokyo on March 10, 1945, the morning after the great air raid that destroyed overnight the larger part of downtown Tokyo, a district mainly populated by working-class families. Here is the narrator's observation:

> I was emboldened and strengthened by the parade of misery passing before my eyes. I was experiencing the same excitement that a revolution causes. In the fire these miserable ones had witnessed the total destruction of every evidence that they existed as human beings. Before their eyes they had seen human relationships, loves and hatreds, reason, property, all go up in flame. And at the time it had not been the flames against which they fought, but against human relationships, against loves and hatreds, against reason, against property. At the time, like the crew of a wrecked ship, they had found themselves in a situation where it was permissible to kill one person in order that another might live. A man who died trying to rescue his sweetheart was killed, not by the flames, but by his sweetheart; and it was none other than the child who murdered its own mother when she was trying to save it. The condition they had faced and fought against there—that of a life for a life—had probably been the most universal and elemental that mankind ever encounters. (Pp. 160–61)

The sophistry of the passage is quite poisonous. By this view, the suffering survivors are in fact victors in a war, a war for survival of one against another, the disaster having brought out these "universal and elemental" conditions of man's existence. Is man then more truly himself when warring with his fellow man? The perversity of such a view, presented here almost as an epiphany, is achieved only by practicing a determined aloofness from others. And that distance, we must remember, is the design-specified foreground of Mishima's literary architecture, which is to add one structure after another in the next twenty years.*

The war affects the work in several ways. For one, the relationship of the "I" and Sonoko would not have developed at all had the hero not felt his impending death. Death, after all, condenses more of the future into the present moment. But more important, his feeling for the parts of the past now irrevocably lost is also tied to his sense of imminent death. Sudden violent death is beautiful, too, because it is unknown, but also because it cuts people down while they are still full of possibility. Death can rescue one from ugly decline, and preserve one forever in the garden of innocence.

The narrator escaped his own dying at this point, but not the threat and charm of death. The war ought to have killed him and saved him from his future: such regret is inextricably there in the book's mourning over the passage of time and beauty. Likewise Mishima Yukio who survived the war seems to have lived through the postwar years in mourning for the death denied him. This heightened sense of death only possible during war never leaves Mishima's mind. Viewed this way, his suicide is a revenge on the war that did not provide him his end at that youthful time.

During the seven years between *Confessions of a Mask* and *The Temple of the Golden Pavilion* (1956), Mishima wrote several plays, short stories, essays, and as many as eleven novels. Of the three published in 1950, *Thirst for Love* (*Ai no Kawaki*; translated into English in 1969) is the best, although the Mauriac-like obsession with passion and death is peculiarly qualified by its homosexual sensibility. Several people have commented on the similiarity of the heroine's sexual feeling toward her servant-lover

---

* In the aforementioned interview with Akiyama Shun in January, 1968, for instance, he refers to the same air raid experience and asserts that his literature began to develop out of the feeling of gladness that while others had been killed, he had survived (p. 89).

and the "I's" relationship to men in *Confessions of a Mask*. The *Blue Period* (*Ao no Jidai*), based on an actual event, is in many ways a forerunner of *The Temple of the Golden Pavilion*. Into the persona of a brilliant undergraduate briefly successful as a usurer, Mishima projects his quasi-Nietzschean world-system, thus experimenting with a kind of philosophical novel.

Forbidden Colors (*Kinjiki* and *Higyō*) was published in two parts in 1951 and 1952–53 (translated into English in 1968). Continuing the homosexual preoccupation of the *Confessions,* this novel is one of the gaudiest and emptiest Mishima ever wrote. The relationship between the handsome young man and his aging mentor is straight out of *Dorian Gray* but lacks Wilde's charm and world-weariness. The old man's use of his protégé to retaliate against the women in his past is embarrassingly sentimental. In the second part, one detects Mishima's recent reading of Thomas Mann, especially *Death in Venice,* and throughout there appear passages reading like a Takarazuka libretto simulating Tokyo high society.

Mishima knew its failure,[6] and his next work, *The Sound of Waves* (*Shiosai,* 1954), shows his effort to purge his writing of this artificiality. A deliberately simple love story set in a fishing village, it is in a way his challenge to Kawabata's "The Izu Dancer." In his next book, *The Sunken Waterfall* (*Shizumeru Taki,* 1955), Mishima returns to his more sophisticated interests: a brilliant, rich, and handsome civil engineer, tired of easy women, runs into a genuinely frigid one—to his delight and refreshment. He falls in love, and the woman, too, begins to thaw. But to keep his ecstasy at a fine pitch, he goes away for a six-month winter stay at a remote dam site. Despite their serious attachment to each other, the war of nerves goes on until she is unable to contain herself and leaves her husband for him. But her surrender revolts him and this time he freezes. Just as her husband arrives to take her home, she drowns herself. The place where she dies, the waterfall of the title, is itself submerged as the dam is completed and a deep reservoir is formed. Mishima's plots do not outline well as a rule, and this story is perhaps less absurd in its fullness than the digest might suggest. Yet the thinness of characterization in this work, too, mars its apparent intention to present a type of new hero for the technological age.

The Temple of the Golden Pavilion (*Kinkakuji*) was serialized at the rate of a chapter a month from January to October of 1956. The story was based on an act of arson committed by a mad Zen acolyte in the summer of 1950, but it is important not to make too much of that fact. Mishima borrowed only the barest report of the event, which he then used as a scaffolding for his own characterization and notions of motivation. Much more than *The Blue Period*—or even *After the Banquet* and *Silk and Insight* of later years—*The Temple of the Golden Pavilion* unfolds Mishima's unique vision of the world which has almost nothing to do with the facts of the actual event which instigated it.

The Golden Temple—to shorten the title—is, again, in the first person. Whereas *Confessions of a Mask* somehow maintains the form of a "confession," the narrator confiding his inner events as if in a diary, *The Golden Temple* is a much more indefinite soliloquy. Here the arsonist Mizoguchi is presumably telling his story after having committed the crime. But nothing is said about his present whereabouts (is he in prison?), his listener's identity, or about the circumstances giving rise to his soliloquy. (Compare Nabokov's careful, if tongue-in-cheek, setting of the narrative situation in *Lolita*.) Is his narrative meant to be a written document? If so, who is his intended reader? In one passage, for instance, Mizoguchi directly addresses this reader/listener, asking him to remember the way he (Mizoguchi) felt at his father's funeral.[7] But even here his idea of this audience is quite unclear. Who is it? Such vagueness in Mishima's central conception of the narrative situation says a good deal about the work.

The story is told from the viewpoint of the man who has already burned down the Golden Temple. But is his voice (as he relates scenes from his boyhood, for instance) sufficiently modulated by the later experience? Does the work take account of the temporal distance between the earlier boyhood experience, the narrator's pivotal act of destruction, and the present act of narration itself? What was said as regards the *Confessions* must be repeated here, and even more emphatically: this work, too, evades consequentiality by the most subtle means. What happened earlier is connected with what comes later only thematically, not novelistically—that is, not historically, psychologically, or causally.

For evidence of this, it is notable that the narrator's sophisticated aesthetics has no endorsement in his experience. Nothing thus far in his background would have been likely to develop such a high degree of articulation on the meaning of beauty. (I am not insisting that Mizoguchi's aesthetics is "incredible," given his origins and education, but am arguing that *The Golden Temple* simply disregards the job of making it appear probable or even feasible in the light of his background.) The limits of his knowledge and consciousness are quite arbitrarily drawn according to the situation at hand. On the occasion of his picnic with Kashiwagi and the girls, for instance, the narrator refers to a *noh* play, and there is nothing in the book to support his familiarity with this esoteric art. A more serious matter, the narrator's sanity is temporarily in doubt at one point, the purpose of this ambiguity being far from clear. As he goes to the brothel (in chap. 9), he fantasizes that Uiko, long dead, is "still alive" (p. 222). Is Mizoguchi really under the illusion of her being alive? Or is he merely *imagining?* The narrator's comments are of little help: "While Uiko was still alive, I had felt that she was able to go freely in and out of a double world of this kind. . . . Perhaps for Uiko death had been merely a temporary incident" (p. 225). One recalls no indication whatever of such thoughts about the girl earlier. Are we to understand then that Mizoguchi is too far gone into his schizophrenic withdrawal to keep clear about things like who is alive and who is dead? Doesn't his insanity—be it the case—change the book's reading of the hero as a philosopher of beauty with brilliant insights, though admittedly nihilistic and perverse? Either way, Mizoguchi as a full novelistic character is at best dubious.

It is tempting to generalize here and talk about Mishima's overall failure in characterization. There is no question that he created very few memorable characters. Perhaps he is "too much himself" to feel with other people, to become them, as a character-novelist might do. But to point out what a writer cannot do very well is only a very small part of criticism. He is what he is because of other things which he does uniquely and other writers may not do nearly as well or at all. We must look elsewhere than in characterization for Mishima's accomplishment.

It is surprising that there is hardly any good full treatment of this book, which has attracted so much attention in its English translation. The author of the Introduction to Ivan Morris's translation, for instance, seems to take it as a dramatic novel whose hero is afflicted with a "sick mind" (p. x). Although she reverses this somewhat in saying the work is "free of judgment" (p. xi), she views *The Golden Temple* by and large as a "Dostoevskian" look into a psychopath's act of destruction. Of course this is patently absurd, and, probably sensing the shortcomings of such remarks, she escapes into an all too easy refuge: "[It] could only have been written by a Japanese" (p. xviii). The impenetrable East! Nakamura Mitsuo, in a review published in 1956, is shrewd enough to detect the "ghost of the I-novel tradition" in this work by a self-proclaimed opponent of that tradition. Calling the arsonist's action inevitable only "logically" or "ideologically," he finds the "I" of the novel quite devoid of "internal development," not a young man alive but "the author's idea of youth." Similarly, the critic argues, in omitting all mention of the simple moral question involved in the destruction of the temple, Mishima wipes off all the shabbiness and absurdity from his acolyte and turns an outrageous criminal act into a young aristocrat's intellectual prank.[8]

Another point of view helpful for understanding the book appears in an interview with Mishima in January 1957 conducted by Kobayashi Hideo, known as the dean of Japanese literary criticism. Here Kobayashi suggests that *The Golden Temple* is no novel. Comparing it with *Crime and Punishment,* he observes that Dostoevsky need not be concerned with Raskolnikov's motives, while Mishima must be—since *The Golden Temple* deals with the young man's whole development up to the crime itself— and yet fails to. He goes on to say that, with the book offering no real interpersonal relationship, no real relationship between the hero and society, the hero remains trapped throughout within his own subjective view of his motivation, and that such a book, having no "character," is more a lyrical poem than a novel. Obviously cornered, Mishima switches the topic here, and the two men go on to talk about Dostoevsky, Mozart, talent and genius, and such things for a while. Then, as the conversation drifts back to *The Golden Temple*, Mishima blurts out, as he rarely did in innumerable talks and interviews since, what he sees as the book's intention:

> MISHIMA: I wrote about a man, the symbol of the
>   artist, pursued by the idée fixe of beauty.
>   Some critic has told me that it is an artist
>   novel—with not an artist but a priest as its
>   hero, and that that's what makes it unusual
>   and interesting. My intention was some-
>   thing like that.
> KOBAYASHI: But I still don't consider it a novel.
> MISHIMA: No, no. I understand.[9]

For a true reading of *The Golden Temple*, one must resist the impulse to see it dramatically. Mizoguchi's tale is not a dramatic monologue; nor is it a clinical self-observation of a schizophrenic. But his view of beauty, which recurs in one form or another in all Mishima's works up to the very last, may safely be taken for Mishima's.

The narrator's relationship with the Temple of the Golden Pavilion begins as he builds its image in his mind, solely on the basis of his father's comments. The temple so imagined is as real and complete as is his whole inner world, in which he is shut off from the outside by his stuttering. Between his consciousness and the world in which he lives, there ought to be a bridge of language, but there is not.

> When a stutterer is struggling desperately to utter his
> first sound, he is like a little bird that is trying to extri-
> cate itself from thick lime. When finally he manages to
> free himself, it is too late. To be sure, there are times
> when the reality of the outer world seems to have been
> waiting for me, folding its arms as it were, while I was
> struggling to free myself. But the reality that is waiting

for me is not a fresh reality. When finally I reach the
outer world after all my efforts, all that I find is a reality
that has instantly changed color and gone out of focus—
a reality that has lost the freshness that I had considered
fitting for myself, and that gives off a half-putrid odor.
(Pp. 5–6)

He is congealed inside himself, and his "solitude grow[s] more
and more obese, just like a pig" (p. 9). The "pig" is the temple
of his imagination—his curse—and at the same time his existence
itself.

His love for Uiko proves but another failed bridge, doomed
from the beginning. For as he seemingly runs toward her, he has
"made a desperate dash only inside the interior of himself" (p.
11).[10] The girl sees him only as a stutterer who is continually
about to speak without being able to. And so completely frozen
is he in his speechless internality that he is unable to do anything
else either—a failure he will atone for by a destruction which
is at least in part an assertion of his relationship to the outside
world. If Mizoguchi fails her here, however, so does Uiko fail
someone else. Her lover is a deserter whom she betrays to the
military police. Mizoguchi feels that by this betrayal she now
belongs to him, for they are both outsiders now. But the possibility of such an alliance is illusory. In the violent succeeding scene,
the lover, being gunned down by his pursuers, shoots Uiko and
kills himself. Mizoguchi remains alone after all, condemned by
his stammer to his Temple of the Golden Pavilion.

Yet he is not certain even about the temple now. If the temple
is beautiful there in Kyoto, far away, that means it can exist
without him and his own existence is "a thing estranged from
beauty" (p. 21). How does the temple out there relate to him?
When his father takes him to Kyoto to see it, he is rather disappointed: it is "merely a small, dark, old three-storied building"
(pp. 24–25). Thus it is not until he returns home in the provinces
that the temple comes back to "exist more deeply and more
solidly within [him]" (p. 29) than ever before. As of this point,
the temple stands, it would seem, only in his inner world.

All of this happens in chapter 1. As in the *Confessions,* Mishima

provides most of the major themes and motifs of the work at the very beginning, although he is unwilling to weave them into any discernible pattern at this point. The connections become more evident to the reader—as they do to the narrator himself—as events unfold later on.

Mizoguchi's move to the temple as an acolyte is not in itself the occasion for a closer tie. It is the threat of the American bombs and the possible consequent destruction of the Golden Temple that accomplishes this. Whereas *Confessions of a Mask* mourned over the passage of time that erodes the experience of beauty, here it is the anticipation of the soon-to-come destruction that intensifies it. "[In] this last summer, in these last summer holidays, on the very last day of them" (p. 44), the "real temple" has now "become no less beautiful than that of [his] mental image" (p. 45). What the stutterer cannot resolve by himself is resolved for him, momentarily, by the all-annihilating war. At this moment, his inner temple and the actual temple remarkably correspond.

It is also under the threat of war that Mizoguchi meets Tsurukawa, who ignores his stammering and becomes his only good friend. The two witness the scene of a soldier taking leave of the woman he loves in a tea ceremony. The sense of imminent death makes their parting seem intensely sexual to the watchers: before their eyes, the woman takes out her breast and expresses her milk into her lover's tea. For Mishima, it seems, the erotic is only possible in the shadow of coming death.

But when the war ends with no damage to either the temple or Mizoguchi, the relationship between the two must again change. For one thing, the building's expression of eternity is now majestically restored.

> Never had the temple displayed so hard a beauty—a beauty that transcended my own image, yes, that transcended the entire world of reality, a beauty that bore no relation to any form of evanescence! Never before had its beauty shone like this, rejecting every sort of meaning. (P. 63)

The actual Golden Temple expands and fills not only its space

but beyond with the substance of all time, the past, present, and future, while it crowds Mizoguchi's inner Golden Temple, his whole congealed inner being, to absolute zero. The country's defeat meant for the "I" nothing more than this personal experience of defeat: peace—death momentarily suspended—severs him from beauty completely.

Mizoguchi's strategy for rebuilding his inner world seems to lie in his acceptance of evil. From the hilltop behind the temple, he views the sea of lights now liberated from the wartime blackout:

> At the thought that these countless lights are all [wicked] lights, my heart is comforted. Please let the evil that is in my heart increase and multiply indefinitely, so that it may correspond in every particular with that vast light before my eyes! Let the darkness of my heart, in which that evil is enclosed, equal the darkness of the night, which encloses those countless lights! (P. 71)

He does not analyze the relationship now in effect between the changed meaning for him of the Golden Temple and his new determination to be wicked. The connection must reveal itself as time—and the story—progresses. His first evil act—helping an Occupation soldier stomp on a prostitute to induce abortion and then concealing the deed from his Superior at the temple—begins to glitter in his memory, as if evil were to take the place there of the shining structure. Also about this time, Kashiwagi, the clubfooted evangelist of evil, is introduced, and the stammerer and the cripple become fast friends in their dark knowledge. What clubfootedness is to Kashiwagi, stammering is to Mizoguchi: both are hemmed in from the outside world by their infirmities. (Kashiwagi's twisted metaphysics of love and lust, reality and appearance, is hard to follow, but then it is not really central to the narrator's development, or the novel's. The one is the other's tutor, yet the two are not really very much alike. Kashiwagi's sadism is not Mizoguchi's; nor is his typical accommodation to life similar in any important respect.)

Twice through Kashiwagi's encouragement the narrator comes close to relating to women: once with a girl Kashiwagi has introduced; another time, with a teacher of flower arrangement, the woman whose goodbye to her lover Mizoguchi had witnessed. On both occasions, however, the temple looms up, rousing itself from its indifferent and incomparable eternity to reduce all his efforts, essentially to nullify life. In such moments, it embraces him as though no gulf at all existed between his restricted inner world and beauty's boundlessness. But its embrace is brief. As he awakens from transport, he knows how he is being separated from life by the capricious Golden Temple. The two are incompatible; in fact they are adversaries. As long as the Golden Temple exists, he is essentially incapacitated for existence. In order to live, he must bring it under his sway and even destroy it.

In the meantime, his life at the temple deteriorates. He neglects his schoolwork. His friend Tsurukawa dies, leaving him all alone except for the black patronage of the crippled philosopher. And the Superior, that enigmatic spiritual guide, becomes totally uncommunicative. In his attempt to "find him out," Mizoguchi repeatedly provokes the older priest, but with little effect. His attempt to penetrate the Superior's "hypocrisy" is wholly frustrated. The contest between the "I's" power of evil and whatever evil may lie in the Superior is one-sided from the beginning. His spiritual father is utterly secure in his corruption, against which Mizoguchi's evil, his substitute Golden Temple, seems to amount to little more than a schoolboy's petulant defiance.

At this point, his trip home becomes a pilgrimage to confirm his existence. In the bleak country of western Japan, which for him is the "source of all [his] unhappiness, of all [his] gloomy thoughts, the origin of all [his] ugliness and all [his] strength" (p. 190), he rediscovers a life without a trace of beauty. It is as if he were baptized anew by the desolation of this, his birthplace, and he knows he must dissolve all beauty into this shapeless ugliness, into the elements of the earth. "I must set fire to the Golden Temple" (p. 191).

The succeeding events only further confirm Mizoguchi's belief in death and destruction. First, Kashiwagi tells him the circumstances of Tsurukawa's death (despite his serene appearance, Tsurukawa, too, was afflicted by misfortune; his death was a suicide). Second, when Mizoguchi visits a brothel, he finds that the memory of Uiko no longer interferes, she is "out" (p. 224); nor does the Golden Temple obtrude any more. He does not even stutter as he talks to the whore. And in that unobstructed relationship with the outside, the "I" has sex with her in a completely routine way. There is only one more task still to be done: he must overcome all doubt about the action. "Having so completely dreamed the deed, having so completely lived that dream, is there any need to act it out physically? Wouldn't such action be quite useless at this stage?" (p. 256). What is the reality finally? Knowledge or action? Does doing add anything to what is known? Will the outside confirm the inside? A little over a dozen years later, Mishima must have asked himself the same question, and answered yes. And his Mizoguchi in *The Temple of the Golden Pavilion* said yes, "precisely because it [is] so futile" (p. 258). The Golden Temple burns to ashes in a few moments.

Any synopsis of *The Golden Temple* will necessarily ignore the apparent irrelevancies that deepen and enrich it, and will, unfortunately, impose logic on a work which in many respects resists logic. Clearly, nothing substitutes for reading the novel itself and experiencing its whole texture. Although threading the various strands into a pattern is often a helpful exercise, such a reading still will not yield a clear outline. Several nagging questions need to be heard. What happens to beauty by the burning of the Golden Temple? And how does it affect the future of the "I's" relationship with the outside world? Also important, in what way does the arsonist "symbolize the artist"?

That no beauty exists without constant threat of perishing is a given of this book. As long as the bombing continues, the "I" is at ease with the Golden Temple—in love with it, really—feeling no gap between the mind's image and the actual structure. The moment the danger disappears, beauty loses its evanescence, and it now belongs to a different order. The "I" must restore the danger so that equilibrium can be restored between external beauty and his inner world in all its vulnerability.

There is also the problem of beauty's destructive force over life. Because the Golden Temple is ordered into an exquisite form, it rejects the chaos that life is. And the perceiver, if unable at the same time to bear with the disorder and shapelessness of life, must either reject experience totally or shut his eyes to the form that exists only in lifeless art. To escape the paradox, the "I" finds another way: he will destroy the form in order to be released from its spell; in this way he feels he can at least live, even if his life is consequently disordered and unbeautiful. Action, whatever its particular nature, at least has this faculty of reclaiming life over sterile order.

Let us now look at Mizoguchi as an artist. Pursued by his vision of beauty, the stutterer repeatedly tries to confirm it in the world out there and repeatedly fails. Is his beauty the same as the world's beauty then? The gnawing feeling never leaves him that the two have at least a very tenuous connection. His beauty is, after all, his alone. But even when it adequately sustains his inner world—at the expense of his participation in life—it always fails him crucially in the face of the insistent actual. Unable to taste the ordinary pleasures of life and also frustrated in sustaining a continuous ecstatic relationship with beauty, the "I" is utterly alone in his desolation. Neither the resonant silence of the Golden Temple nor the ordinary stir of human life can be heard in this no man's land where his stammer alone interminably hisses and gasps its non-meaning on the dead air. What's worse, this stammer—the artist's very means of art—is a curse that will never be lifted from him. He stands eternally condemned by his own art.

Burning the Golden Temple may be a mad act even for an artist, since obliteration of the temple does nothing to guarantee the authenticity of his inner vision. But still, coexistence is impossible, and as his logic goes, he imagines his act of destruction may do something to change other people's awareness of beauty. Since the order that makes beauty possible consists in the end of disordered matter, the reduction of the form to its chaotic components ought to make people realize beauty's ultimate nothingness. Indeed, it should make the artist himself realize that his efforts to prove that his vision is more than nothing are also futile. Meanwhile, the Golden Temple is something: an obese pig that grows and grows inside him, feeding on what remains of his isolated self.

Finally, the portrait of the artist emerging from *The Temple of the Golden Pavilion* is almost totally negative, with little in it to justify either the artist's craft or his vision. Only the near-mad act of total devastation generates any meaning for the artist. But then, Mishima's art is seldom a cheerful one. He raises questions, disturbing, destructive ones, for which he is uninterested in finding answers. *The Temple of the Golden Pavilion* is a dangerous, disturbing, and beautiful book mostly because beauty really is dangerous, existing only where life itself is threatened with annihilation.

Mishima was thirty-one when he wrote *The Temple of the Golden Pavilion*. Within three years he had built a new home, a hodgepodge "Victorian Rococo," and married. His home life was highly regulated: he woke up at noon, spent the afternoon working out physically, entertained his friends in the evening, and wrote from midnight to dawn. Undoubtedly such a strict routine contributed to his enormous output of plays, essays, pamphlets, and novels.

Many if not most of the fifteen novels written between *The Temple of the Golden Pavilion* and the tetralogy are remarkably trivial. Some could be soap opera scripts. *Too Long a Spring* (*Nagasugita Haru*, 1956) recounts a young couple's ups and downs during their year-long engagement. In *The Tottering Virtue* (*Bitoku no Yoromeki*, 1957) a bored upper-class housewife has an affair. *The Young Lady* (*Ojōsan*, 1960) is the nondescript tale of a corporation executive's daughter getting married, becoming jealous, and then happily pregnant. *The Scamper of Love* (*Ai no Shissō*, 1962), a feeble experiment in double narrative, tells of a provincial author who writes of the love of a young working-class couple. *The School of Flesh* (*Nikutai no Gakkō*, 1963), a popularized version of *Forbidden Colors*, has a rich divorcée befriending a cool bisexual. *Music* (*Ongaku*, 1964) is a quasi-Freudian account of a frigid girl unable to "hear music." *A Complicated Man* (*Fukuzatsuna Kare*, 1966) tells of an uncomplicated airline steward's love for a rich girl and his sudden change of heart at the end. In *The Evening Dress* (*Yakaifuku*, 1966–67) former aristocrats and royalty brighten up the story of a rich young couple's marriage. Finally, *A Life for Sale* (*Inochi*

Urimasu), published as late as 1968, is the story of a quasi-Mafia organization, complete with a female vampire. They are, every one of them, practically worthless, but probably the worst thing about them is that Mishima seems utterly contemptuous in them of his readers, tossing out what he told himself they wanted. I do not know what commercial success these publications brought him, but critically, at any rate, the less said the better.

Of several more interesting works, *Kyōko's Home* (*Kyōko no Ie*, 1958–59) deserves mention. Kyōko, a rich divorcée, is friends with four different men, who represent four aspects of Mishima's self-image: a businessman who is also an eschatologist, an artist, an actor, and a boxer. "Kyōko" means "mirror girl," and the novel is intended to be a reflection of postwar Japan. Here Mishima is trying for once to look panoramically at the whole society. The book, overly discursive and lacking in full characterization, fails as a novel, but it does show the author's serious intention to confront broad social problems.[11] As he confessed to Ōshima Nagisa, the film director, nearly ten years later, he was shocked by the lack of response to this work. "I am a bit embarrassed to say this, but I wanted the book to be understood by everyone. I was going to throw my baby into the river, as it were. I was waiting for someone to stop me. But no one came. In despair, I threw it. That was the end. Of me. It's all finished. I am not yet arrested. So I'm doing all sorts of things now to get caught. The coldness of the literary world, then! . . . I must have gone mad ever since."[12] It is interesting that Mishima's overtly subversive "politics" dates from the time of *Kyōko's Home*.

After the Banquet (*Utage no Ato*, 1960), translated into English in 1963, is based on an actual Tokyo mayoralty campaign and is one of the most unified of his works. It is also unique in presenting fully drawn characters. The heroine's tenacious optimism and will to live are rare qualities in Mishima's usually bored and frigid population. *The Play of Beasts* (*Kemono no Tawamure*, 1961) and *Beautiful Stars* (*Utsukushii Hoshi*, 1962) are both moderately experimental works: the former, for dealing with complex ideas of death, crime, and love in a compact setting;

the latter, for its use of the conventions of science fiction. *Beautiful Stars* is also especially interesting as an eschatological reading of the fate of the earth.

The Towing in the Afternoon (*Gogo no Eikō,* 1963), translated into English as *The Sailor Who Fell from Grace with the Sea* in 1965, is in my view the best of his work after the *Confessions* and *The Golden Temple.* Its teen-age hero, an accomplished voyeur, spies on his mother as she has an affair with a sailor. In the original title, *Gogo no* means "in the afternoon," and *Eikō,* "towing," while its sound suggests "glory." The sailor, for a time the boy's mythical hero, loses this status ("grace with the sea") when he becomes an ordinary landlocked householder. The story relates the boy's revenge on the sailor for destroying the myth, and his attempt to revive it by means of a ritual murder with the help of his gang of brilliant delinquents. Its language is concise, and its imagery—if unremittingly gory in certain passages—is clear and impressive. Even Mishima's frequent plot-flabbiness is nowhere apparent here. It may be a bit too neat and terse, although it is innocent of many of the more usual weaknesses that often mar his novels.

Silk and Insight (*Kinu to Meisatsu,* 1964), another work based on an actual event, describes a textile factory strike. Although one recognizes in the old-fashioned patriarch Mishima's efforts to open a new path in his art, the character is stereotyped and uninteresting. Where *After the Banquet* succeeds in building solid characters, this novel reverts to his usual schematic abstractions.

His tetralogy, *The Sea of Fertility* (*Hōjō no Umi*), was published over five years between September 1965 and January 1971. The work as a whole traces the observations and experiences of Honda Shigekuni, who is an undergraduate in Part One and an old man in Part Four. The first volume, *Spring Snow* (*Haru no Yuki*), translated into English in 1972, concerns itself mainly with the love affair between Honda's friend, Matsugae Kiyoaki, a marquis' son, and Ayakura Satoko, the daughter of an earl. The romance intensifies after the girl becomes affianced to a prince and, in defiance of the Imperial taboo, the young Matsugae insists on continuing to see her. She becomes pregnant and, having sought refuge with the Imperial Abbess, decides to become a nun herself. Failing in his desperate attempts to see her, Matsugae becomes ill and dies. The romance is told in a dazzlingly rich prose carrying a strong nostalgia for the courtly life of the last years of Emperor Meiji's reign.

The second volume, *Runaway Horses* (*Homba*), translated into English in 1973, jumps ahead twenty years to the early 1930s. Honda, now a judge in the Court of Appeals, comes to know the son of a right-wing agitator who was once a houseboy at the Matsugaes'. The young man, a radical patriot like his father, has three moles under the left armpit, just as the young Matsugae did, and Honda becomes convinced that he is the reincarnation of his dead friend. The youth plans a coup d'état with other extreme nationalists. Their conspiracy is uncovered, and he is arrested. Honda, now convinced of the transmigration, resigns his judgeship to defend him, and wins the case. Within a few days of his release, however, the young man assassinates one of the most prominent financial giants of the empire and escapes to commit harakiri alone. Mishima's by now confirmed aesthetic of bloody suicide and belief in the quasi-mystical ways of the samurai are both evident in this work, which he apparently thought of as the "masculine" counterpart to the "feminine" sensibility prevalent in the romance of volume 1.

In the third volume, *The Temple of Dawn* (*Akatsuki no Tera*), Honda is a successful lawyer. In Thailand on a business trip, he is introduced to the young Princess Ying Chan ("Moonlight"), daughter of a Thai prince he once entertained with Matsugae (in vol. 1). The princess, coincidentally a fanatic Japanophile, appears to him as still another resurrection of the friend of his youth. The war breaks out soon after his return to Japan and when it is over, Honda, who has become a millionaire, builds a sumptuous summer home and invites the now grown-up princess to visit him there. Despite many schemes, he fails to win her affection and is reduced to peeking through a secret hole in his study to see her make love to another woman friend of his. That night, a fire breaks out and reduces the villa to ashes. Years later, as an old man he learns that the princess died back home of cobra venom. This is the weakest part of the four volumes. There are several inconsistencies surrounding the Thai princess; the many incidents rushed through at the end—the lesbian affair, the fire, and the princess's death—appear ill-timed and arbitrary; and in its whole conception the Thai episode is not well articulated with the rest. Perhaps in an effort to fuse the work, Mishima devotes a good many pages to lecturing about theories of metempsychosis as if writing for an encyclopedia.

The last volume, *The Decay of the Angel* (*Tennin Gosui*), is the most ingenious. The Matsugae-terrorist-Ying Chan transmigration enters still another phase, when Honda discovers an orphan in a fishing village with the same three moles and adopts him. This boy, a typical Mishima egoist, turns out to be a false incarnation and, soon recognizing his power over his wealthy adoptive father, proceeds to scheme against him. Told the reason for his adoption, the boy tries suicide but falls short and succeeds only in blinding himself. Old Honda is now alone and, feeling the approach of death, visits the Abbess of Gesshū Temple, who was once Ayakura Satoko, the girl Matsugae was in love with. Though now eighty-three, she is still beautiful. But as Honda recalls the days of their youth, she tells him she has never known a Matsugae Kiyoaki. "If Kiyoaki never existed from the beginning," mumbles Honda, "then Isao too didn't exist, nor Ying Chan. Furthermore, possibly even I myself . . ." The Abbess gazes at him intently and says, "That too depends on the way you think." As she shows him the garden of the temple, Honda hears the sound of absolute silence.

> It is a gracious, bright garden with no special artifice. The place is full of the cries of cicadas that sound as though many worshipers were telling their rosaries. There is not a single sound otherwise in the extreme tranquility. There is nothing in the garden. I have come, Honda thought, to a place where there is no memory, nor anything else.
> The garden is quiet in the full summer sun. . . .[13]

The ending thus reverses and obliterates the myth of metempsychosis so elaborately unfolded in these four volumes. But the final passage is meant also to punctuate Mishima's entire career, his entire life. It is not just the matter that the date given for the completion of the tetralogy was chosen as the day of his suicide. But there is the haunting feeling that the last scene of *The Sea of Fertility,* describing a silence that evacuates even memory, seems to be an epitaph Mishima would choose for himself.

The Sea of Fertility is not finally a satisfying novel. Its passion is not the passion of art, but the passion of life. So many impulses tear at the work, the craving for eternal youth—by metempsychosis, if by no other way—and the knowledge of the sure arrival of age, for instance. But even more fundamentally, its clearly Eastern theme and setting, its Meiji aristocracy and exotic Thai temples and palaces, reveal its maker's plans for export. It is his sales pitch to markets abroad, in which he seems interested mainly in redressing the balance of payments on a once imported product, the novel, and exporting this one to the West. What finally brings the four volumes or parts together is the uncontrollable urge in the work to bring them to a close, the eschatological will to death. So exuberant by now in the foreknowledge of death, Mishima refuses to allow any possible vitality or richness that life might yet bring forth. The stillness that dominates the garden at the end of this long novel is, one realizes, the silence of Mare Fecunditatis, the barren sea on the lifeless surface of the moon.

Mishima was an amazingly consistent person, who never forgot his wartime catechism—the myth of Japan as a ritually ordered state, the samurai way of life characterized by manly courage and feminine grace, and the vision of imminent death as the catalyst of life. Fixated as he was on this early training, Mishima never stopped feeling that he was living a leftover life after the war ended. *Confessions of a Mask* and *The Temple of the Golden Pavilion* each in its own way tells of this longing for the end that ought to have overtaken him. And many of the other works seem attempts at brightening the sickened atmosphere that sooner or later was bound to suffocate the earth.

All his life he despised the passivity of intellectualism and the impotence of democracy. Shortly after writing *Kyōko's Home* he developed a program calling for the revival of the warrior's death-threatened way of life in contrast to the all-too-easy life of peace. His grotesque short story "Patriotism" (*Yūkoku*, 1960), minutely describing the suicides of an officer by harakiri and his wife by cutting her throat, preceded by passionate love-making, is one of the earliest works to militarize what would later be a major preoccupation with sado-masochistic death "beautified" by an aesthetic of blood and sexuality. Soon he would begin, too, to be deeply concerned with the "essence" of Japanese culture, and numerous propaganda pieces appeared in rapid succession— a story-essay, "The Voices of the Spirits of the Lost Heroes" (*Eirei no Koe,* 1966), advocating resurrection of the principle of the Divine Emperor, and pamphlets such as *Spiritual Lectures for the Young Samurai* (*Wakaki Samurai no tameni,* 1968–69), *An Introduction to Action Philosophy* (*Kōdōgaku Nyūmon,* 1969), and *The Theory of Patriotism* (*Yūkoku no Genri,* 1970).

It should be remembered that these were years when Japan was shaken by a great number of social and political crises signaled by a nearly endless series of demonstrations and protests. Compared with those in the United States in the sixties, the Japanese demonstrations were many times larger in force and scale. They were more massively organized and far more efficiently disciplined, and their cry of outrage—against, say, the Japan–United States Mutual Security Pact—was focused and demonstrably effective. Mishima was a frequent participant in university debates and teach-ins, always leaping into the turbulence from the side of the extreme right-wing.* In all his battles, he seems to have been convinced that a revolution was imminent —probably in 1970—and he himself was ready to fight—with,

* His single-handed debate with the assembled students of the University of Tokyo is published in *Mishima Yukio versus the Strike Coalition Committee of the University of Tokyo* (*Mishima Yukio–Tōdai Zenkyōtō*) (Tokyo: Shinchōsha, 1969). Some of his views are similar to those expressed by hostile critics of university affairs during the 1960s in the United States. The tone is suggested by the title of one essay, "Turn the University of Tokyo into a Zoo" (*Tōdai o Dōbutsuen ni Shiro*), collected in *Spiritual Lectures for the Young Samurai* (Tokyo: Nippon Kyōbunsha, 1969). Yet Mishima and the striking radical students seem to have found common ground in their rejection of the "hypocritical," "liberal" administrations of the universities and the nation. He reportedly said at the time that he felt warm toward the students and would join them if only they would accept the principle of the divine Imperial order.

characteristically, his own ancient sword in his hand and his hand-groomed corps of handsome young swordsmen at his side. He dreamed of revolution, because it would have served him in a way as a second chance. And as 1970 passed into its second half without any sign of general insurrection, he had to plan and stage one of his own.

Read as political statements, the books leading up to his last act are fantasies. Over and over again Mishima advocates the way of the samurai, and pleads for a revival of the kamikaze spirit as if the pilots were martyrs for beauty and sanctity. Though full of the images of *Blut und Boden,* the books fail to set out a coherent politics. In fact he carefully avoids identification with any recent fascism. His play *My Friend Hitler (Waga Tomo Hitler,* 1968), for example, is not quite the fanatic endorsement suggested by the title and appearance of the book (the wrapper with Hitler's portrait, and the black binding complete with swastika). The *Führer* of the play is an aesthete trying to survive the game of black politics and still needing lessons from the foxier Herr Gustav Krupp. If this does not exactly mitigate what amounts to a vulgar diabolism on the part of Mishima, the play is at the same time certainly no apology for the demented Nazi. Also, in his supposedly political manifestoes, his thoughts continually dwell on the idea of death. (*The Introduction to Action Philosophy,* for example, devotes more than half its length to a series of brief eschatological essays on the "end" of things, like "The End of the Hero," or "The End of the World.") And even in his proposals for the reconstitution of Japan, he is totally indifferent to the economics either of wealth or of power. Thus, having nothing to offer as a political program except the revival of a defunct Imperial order, his criticism both of capitalism and communism is historically a piece of nonsense.

Mishima was of course the embodiment of the unpolitical. Unless one takes "being unpolitical" as itself a political position (as it is in most contexts where politics is broadly construed), his program was organized by the kind of sensibility that is indifferent if not thoroughly antagonistic to the drives and aspirations of actual politics. His lack of interest in planning for the follow-up stages of his own program testifies to its essentially visionary quality. The "coup d'état" he had so carefully planned—presumably to catalyze certain counterrevolutionary elements in Japan's National Self-Defence Force—amounted politically to no more than a ceremonial dance performed in honor of something quite unrelated to politics. In all Japanese history, in fact, there has been no attempted coup that was more scrupulously staged to produce a null effect. It was as if he had done his best to ensure that this time he would be able to finish what the war disastrously failed to finish for him. Although he no doubt saw through the illusions of those who see modern Japanese culture as essentially "Western," and although he probably intended to present a serious alternative, what he came up with is no less a fantasy than what he would replace. For what he called the "culture, history, and tradition" of Japan became in the end little more than his own personal mythology, and his last "political" act merely demonstrated the essential tautology of his life: what he had always demanded of life was something so valuable one can only pay for it with one's life.

Mishima may have considered suicide quite often since adolescence, but he became really serious about it during his last few years. There were hints of this in a number of interviews he had with other writers, but no one at that time took them for what they were. In one such talk, recorded only a week before he died, he is unusually serene and lucid as he recalls and analyzes his long writing career and explains his present politics. Referring very generally to the action he knows he is about to take in a few days, he remarks how exhausted he is and jokes about how he may be "finished" as a writer, having said all he can think of saying and being unable to make any plans for the future.[14] Then, in a more subdued mood, he recalls how his "self-formation" was completed by the time he was "fifteen or sixteen, at the latest nineteen," and in a moment of rare self-revelation, he calls his recent "Romanticism" a "*Heimkehr* [his word, home-coming] to his teen-age" (p. 167). It is clear he is aware of the circle drawing to a close. He is now where he was once in his youth. He knows too, by this time, that he is in art where he is in life: the two places are identical. And if this means that he—like so many other practitioners of the novel in Japan—could not help confusing life with art, perhaps that problem was of no great concern to him any longer. He was close at last to what he had always wanted. Death was finally something he could pay for with his own life.[15]

Mishima's suicide, like that of Kawabata and Dazai, carries an important social meaning that may help us understand something about the death wish operating throughout modern Japanese literature.*

Earlier, I talked about the poverty of real content in Japanese life, and argued that the novel as a middle-class art form demands more richness and variety in experience than is normally supplied the writer in Japan. I also talked about the underdevelopment of character in Japanese fiction, and how it is rooted in the Japanese hostility toward personality. The Japanese writer must somehow hammer out a personality for himself which he essentially must hide from view since he is not encouraged to express it; and he must fabricate lives in fiction which neither he nor his reader really know at firsthand and which thus lack the authenticity demanded by the novel. Further, as the artist shapes the self and takes it into account, so he must learn ways of ignoring it too at times, if he is to be the kind of artist envisioned by the objectivists. Few are able to. Kawabata managed it by retiring early to the silent margins of life. Mishima craved the absolute, but his own strange god turned out to be the nothingness of death itself.

And there is an even more formidable trial for the Japanese writer, the language itself that discourages formation of tangible individuals and a distinctly personal experience. It does this espe-

---

* Some readers may recall Gore Vidal's article on Mishima and his answer to Ivan Morris's criticism of it (*New York Review of Books,* June 17 and December 16, 1971) in which he poked fun at both Mishima and Professor Morris. Elegantly wrong on several points, Vidal stated, for example, that "Japan's most popular (and deeply admired) writer has been W. Somerset Maugham" (June 17, p. 8), and that Mishima's death was "entirely idiosyncratic, more Western in its romanticism than Japanese" (p. 10). (Did Mr. Vidal, this one time, cruise with the wrong crowd?) Yet I must agree with him that what is finally most fascinating about Mishima is not his work but his life: what he was, what he did, and what he meant in the context of modern Japanese literature.

cially by its tendency to omit the subject, especially the first-person pronominal subject, in its sentences; by its extraordinary development of the honorific system; by its writing medium whose ideograms resist being spoken aloud; and by its loose syntactic form that baffles straightforward statement. Furthermore, as we saw, the language is severely ritualistic and ceremonial, particularly in its dedication to silence. Mishima was one of the best technicians of prose style, and yet his achievements there lay largely in the correctness and orthodoxy of his usage. He never succeeded in matching the language to the strong personal identity he managed to develop. Loose and adaptive as it may appear, Japanese is iron-tight once the speaker violates the rites of community and the sanctity of silence. He must learn to hum along very measuredly as he performs the ceremonial dance, or his speech will become a shriek, or a futile stammer. Kawabata learned this language of silence to perfection—at the expense of his personality; Dazai embarrassed the language with his clowning, until finally it embarrassed him to death; Mishima, who understood the problem better than anyone, had to turn to his body as his "second language." *Sun and Steel* (*Taiyō to Tetsu*, 1968), presents the clearest statement of this option:

> As I pondered the nature of that "I," I was driven to the conclusion that the "I" in question corresponded precisely with the physical space that I occupied. What I was seeking, in short, was a language of the body.[16]

The body can dance, it can kill, and it can die, but it never speaks words. His body disemboweled itself, and through this deed, enacted in his "second language" in homage to his god, he felt he could speak to the people and be heard by them, despite his contempt for them. This, I believe, is what Mishima himself meant when he told Nakamura Mitsuo in 1967 that "suicide activates a writer's entire works." He also remarked later in the same interview, "suicide is art."[17]

Silence powerfully invites the Japanese. But for the writer, accepting the invitation is always fatal. Mishima knew it as soon as he began to write. From *Confessions of a Mask* to *The Sea of*

Fertility, his fiction was a thin mask veiling the ultimate void. His language was only a stammer repeatedly breaking the awesome quiet of that void that persisted as long as he lived.* And, as he knew at the end, his terrible body speech too was finally an utterance in a mute language.

* A. Alvarez discusses a very similar view of suicide which is held by the dadaists. In the chapter "Dada: Suicide as an Art," in *The Strange God: A Study of Suicide* (London: Weidenfeld and Nicolson, 1971), he writes: "When art is against itself, destructive and self-defeating, it follows that suicide is a matter of course" (p. 189). The anti-art context of dadaism is of course totally different from the "anti-art" stance seen in the Japanese novel. But their effects bear striking resemblances and Alvarez's prognosis for Western literature (the "post-Arnold, post-Eliot" writers) is peculiarly applicable to Japanese writers as well: "The existence of the work of art . . . is contingent, provisional; it fixes the energy, appetites, moods and confusions of experience in the most lucid possible terms so as to create a temporary clearing of calm, and then moves on, or back, into autobiography" (pp. 211–12). Certain Japanese writers today, like Abe Kōbō and Ōe Kenzaburō, seem aware of this though in varying degrees.